Rules of Transition
Book Six

The Core Series

By

Maquel A. Jacob

Published by

MAJart Works LLC
2001 NE Aloclek Dr Suite 211
Hillsboro, Oregon
www.majartworks.com

Copyright © 2023

978-1-950438-35-8

Cover illustration by Keith A. Johnston
https://keithdraws.com/

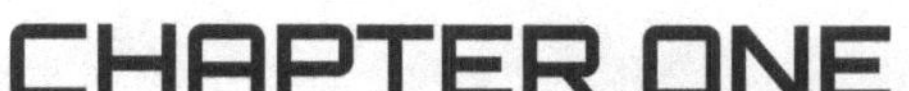

CHAPTER ONE

Away Game

Evening fell on the Dreridian home world, casting it in a soft peach glow. Smokestacks from the industrial plants blew out slow swirls of white and grey that drifted up, only to dissipate in the air. Transport units whizzed along the surface and sky highways. Blue and yellow lights emanated from windows in the residential areas.

A picturesque scene, warm and inviting.

On the palace's top level, Lord Pondur stood at the panoramic wall window looking out over the entire northern region of the planet. His craggy face remained neutral as he took in the workings of trade before him.

Wearing an all-black suit with an almond-toned ascot and matching handkerchief in the left breast pocket, his attire emulated austerity. The holoscreen's reflection on the far wall ruined the view as he glanced at it without moving his head, suppressing a frown.

The alien enemy rose again.

This time to defend their solar system against the Dreridians coming to take over their poorly run trade system. Lord Pondur should have realized their emperor's level of relentless pursuit. The cretin took close to seventy percent of his forces and left their home world under defended. Dreridians occupied the surface while ships sat on guard in space, blocking entry.

Lord Pondur clasped his hands behind his back, exhaled slowly, then turned to face the holoscreen once more.

What imbecile in their right mind would attack and destroy their own manufacturing source?

Charred remains of manufacturing plants scattered across the landscape a minor planet in their system.

Aftershocks rocked its mountains while delayed explosions from chemical reactions erupted with black smoke. The Dreridian forces managed to push the enemy back after days of engagement. As usual, the enemy retreated when the battle turned from their favor.

The damaged planet's major trade manufactured combat fighter ships and artillery. Their primary customer, the enemy who called themselves Boretkz, enforced a contract that barred them from building for others.

A preemptive strike.

Lord Pondur snorted. How ridiculous. Because his Dreridian technicians would scrape every data bank on that planet and use it to restart production. And with an exclusivity clause of their own. The attack on the trade planet constituted grounds to nullify the contract. His admins went to task, getting it cleared by the federation.

The door slid open with a soft swoosh, closing behind his chief science officer, Lord Graggor. His wide girth blocked its frame. He used a hair strand thin picking rail to clean between his teeth. Whatever he had finished eating, Lord Pondur felt he needed to send a rite of the dead. Not that he had ever seen Lord Graggor consume another intelligent species. The claims made it obvious he had.

"Lord Graggor, you are late."

"Ah, my apologies, my lord." He removed the pick. "I couldn't bear to let one morsel of my meal go to waste."

"Understandable."

"You were not at the royal banquet hall."

"I will eat later." Lord Pondur pointed at the holoscreen. "This takes precedence."

"Hmm." Lord Graggor removed a slender velvet pouch the width of a pencil and slid the pick inside. He placed it in his jacket's inner pocket, patting it gently, then stood beside Lord Pondur. "Stubborn, isn't he?"

"I would commend him if it wasn't so comical."

"You laugh, my lord, but he still has close to three hundred thousand ships."

The crags on Lord Pondur's face knitted together.

"Are you not seeing the pattern?"

"Oh, I do, my lord. I merely reject their ability to come out on top. They are heading back towards our main fleet within their home world's system."

"They want another round. I will make sure they taste bitter defeat this time." Lord Pondur raised his arms, resting one elbow on the other arm. "I'm done playing with these creatures."

"Well," Lord Graggor moved towards the window. "At least you have the meeting with Azrom coming up to amuse you."

Yes.

Time to get more information about Azrom technology. Specifically, their planet bombs. Dreridian might went unmatched for centuries until they encountered Azrom. Brutal, blood-thirsty savages who showed no mercy. Dreridians' superior weapons meant nothing in their eyes.

Over time, Lord Pondur's grandfather concluded to leave Azrom to their own devices. No reason to poke a monster. And he agreed.

Now a new threat emerged from the shadows.

Not those incessant beasts running amok.

No. Lassians.

A race of beings forced to evolve into a superpower because of the enemy's invasion long ago. Awakened monsters who have no idea what they truly are.

Lord Pondur's lips pursed.

"Ah." Lord Graggor nodded his head. "I see what disturbs you." He glanced over. "Are you going forward with your plan for the Lassians?"

"Do we have any other choice?" Lord Pondur clasped his hands behind his back. "If I don't, they will surpass us. Best to keep them on a leash."

"I couldn't agree more."

The two watched the giant cranes moving at one of the man-ufacturing plants below. Profit being made in real time. It soothed their souls.

Repairs of the royal houses on Azrom moved at a steady pace. Mine workers converted much of the enemy debris for other uses. The fourth house, hit worse than the others, took more time to bring back its former glory. Smoky grey clouds were now pale, fading away. An acrid stench lingered near the areas of old battles. Blood seeped into the soil gave birth to fat insects that gorged on the spoils.

Dawn lit the sky a dusty yellow hue, almost pastel. Its rays swung across the land, piercing the sliver of opening in Lord Elendar's chamber curtain. Sound asleep, he didn't move until the thin beam hit his eyelids. He suddenly saw orange and red inside his vision. Squinting, he rolled over to where darkness clung.

I'm tired.

His body wouldn't do what he wanted anymore. Already two years since the battle, he seemed to not recover. The royal physicians advised he should be grateful to be alive considering his injuries. They didn't seem that bad at the time. Adrenaline.

He had moved around on fumes for months after receiving only basic triage. The day he collapsed, the entire royal house went into a state of despair, fearing he would die soon after.

And yet, I'm still here. Broken and weak.

He clenched his hands under the bedding, disgusted with his current state. His healing would take another three years. A blip in time. For him, it felt like an eternity.

"You're awake." Dalfir, his guardian and mate, walked to the foot of the bed. "Are you able to rise today? Take a short walk?"

"Why?" Elendar whispered in an anguished tone. "Why do you keep coming here? Taking care of me?"

"I vowed to always be by your side. That is where I belong. No matter what state you are in. I am yours."

He moved to the side of the bed and helped Elendar sit up.

Elendar's hair fell across his shoulders and down his back, a tangled mess from his fretful sleeping during the night.

Boots clacking against the marbled floors outside his chamber made him look over towards the door. Dalfir also appeared puzzled.

"Are you expecting guests in my chamber?" Elendar asked.

"No. I can't imagine who'd come in such early hours."

The already open door went slamming into the wall behind it as two soldiers in full battle gear forced their way in.

"Huh, you're finally awake," the one on the right smirked. Taller than the other by a good four inches with dark blond wavy hair that landed on his shoulders, he moved his over muscular body towards the bed. The armor beneath his robes made him appear larger.

"Well, at least he's not dead," the other quipped. A thick blond mane like Elendar's hung to his waist. His slender build didn't hide his strength when he crossed his arms, revealing well-toned biceps.

"Not yet." The first stepped further in. "Though I really don't want to deal with our father falling into despair if that happens."

"So, you should make an effort to speed your recovery, mother."

Elendar stared at them with irritation. Their offspring graced them with their presence after decades of noncommunication.

"Why have you come here?" Elendar's voice rose. He gritted his teeth at the pain in his chest. "Is this some form of amusement for you?" He leaned forward as he yelled, struggling to get out of Dalfir's grasp. He held fast. "You show yourselves after slandering my name, disrespecting me at every turn, and for what?"

Their sons stood silent; both their brows furrowed. They had nothing to counter his words. The younger one moved closer.

"Are we not allowed to inquire about our mother's wellbeing?"

Elendar's eyes glowed, narrowing into slits.

"You take your pity and give it to someone else," he seethed. Blood dribbled from the corners of his mouth. "I don't want any of it from you!"

"My love," Dalfir squeezed him closer. "Please, calm yourself."

Their sons' expressions turned to fear. The older one moved forward, outstretching a hand. Elendar smacked it away.

"Call for the physician," Dalfir ordered him, gesturing at the commlink on the table against the far wall.

Elendar's eyes fluttered. *No. Not now!* His body felt like it was deflating. All the strength he had left him in one rush. He slumped against Dalfir. Muffled yelling reached his ears before his vision faded into darkness.

Large swaths of colored fabric covered the sections of the main palace, concealing the damage being repaired. They swayed in the wind, their movement restricted by tethers attached to the ground. From a distance, the palace resembled the symbol of regality. The morning sun made the white and grey marble and its fixtures gleam.

Workers milled out into the field to harvest the day's haul for meals. Soldiers patrolled the top center and ground levels to deter prying eyes. The inside of the palace, not matching the outer, the residents move about seething.

Royal scholars, family counselors, along with a handful of house leaders waited patiently in the throne room for Supreme Ruler, Romnus, to arrive. Whispers carried upward through the massive hall. A few first-time attendees stared at the nearly one hundred feet high ceiling, straining their necks to do so. Not ridiculous in size like the Razznian palace, though still impressive.

The side door on the left of the throne opened. An entourage flanked by imperial guards made their way into the room. General Kur led Queen Farin and Lord Romnus. Behind them, Biandra, Romnus' personal guard and Batis, Farin's guard, kept close while General Rass took up the rear. They exuded an air of intimidation, fearlessness…power.

Over the past century, they had proven their status more than once. Beneath Queen Farin's fair skin and playful demeanor lay a ferocious beast. Batis and Biandra, seasoned warriors, given titles as rewards for their service, no longer required to fight.

The generals? Monsters.

Both had their versions of aesthetically pleasing bloodshed.

Romnus and Farin walked up the wide steps to the platform and sat on their thrones. Biandra positioned herself on Romnus' left, settling onto a giant cushion. The generals and Batis stood across the bottom of the throne platform in a row, daring anyone to try them.

General Kur nodded to the court recorder. The man moved to the side of the room near the center and cleared his throat.

"To Supreme Ruler Romnus and the beautiful Queen Farin," he bowed his head, the rest of the audience following his gesture, "may your reign be prosperous and mighty."

Years before, the standard greeting involved the throwing down of one's body to their knees, followed by the beating of the chest with a fist, and loud exclamations of devotion. Pretentious, bordering on insult. Romnus decreed the ritual removed.

The palace became much quieter since then.

"I see royal house members, but not the ones that should be." Romnus propped his elbow on the armrest of his throne to rest his head against his palm. "Where is Lord Elendar?"

A fourth house representative came forward. His old, haggard appearance gave a clue to how the occupants still struggled.

"My apologies, Lord Romnus. Lord Elendar had an episode this morning and is unable to attend meetings for a while."

Romnus gripped the other armrest. That's not what he wanted to hear. He regretted his actions when he first realized fourth house members had formed a coup with the enemy. Lord Elendar barely recovered from the injury he gave him before the battles broke out across the five systems.

"Has a royal physician been sent?"

"Yes, my lord."

The man bowed again before stepping back in line.

Romnus took a deep breath before his next question.

"And what of the second and third houses? Are they so far above me they chose not to send a representative in their steed?

The crowd grew uneasy. He could hear feet shuffling and robes swishing on the floor. Low murmurs of speculation spread. The left side of Romnus' face twitched, a sign of his annoyance.

Biandra reached into her robe sleeves and produced the toxic orange fruit. Romnus glanced over at her, dropping his arm. She held it out, not meeting his gaze. He finally took it, shoving the whole thing into his mouth. Farin gave him a side stare.

Yes, I know.

He had to refrain from rage-fueled outbursts. Which he found difficult when his own family was hell bent on disrespecting his title. Done chewing the fruit, he swallowed, letting the juice take effect. He took a few deep breaths, closing his eyes.

When he opened them, the audience stared back in apprehension.

At least they fear me.

The head counsel clapped his hands to get their attention.

"Our agenda for today is to establish new protocols regarding trade and the fourth house rebels,"

"Why haven't we executed them yet?" A house member cried.

"They shouldn't be allowed to breathe Azrom air," shouted another.

Rumblings of an impending riot filled the air.

"Enough!" Romnus sat all the way back on his throne. "There has been too much bloodshed against our own. I too am guilty of that. Or have you all forgotten?"

The hall fell into a hush. How could they? Romnus slew everyone who stood in his way during the transition after he took reign.

"No one," the counsel said tersely, "is to harm anyone from the fourth house. That is the Supreme Ruler's decree."

A few dissenters voiced their objections under hushed tones before going silent.

With the audience under control, the counsel proceeded to go over the new rules. Romnus tuned it all out. The real meeting would start once the hall cleared after this one. Farin seemed to do the same, focusing on a needlework project she carried with her.

An hour later, the only ones left were the royal counsel and Romnus' entourage. Batis turned around to face him.

"We have two imperial guard battalions to escort the Dreridian party when they arrive. I have made a list of restricted areas. They will not be roaming freely around Azrom."

"Do they think we're stupid?" A royal councilman scoffed. "Their reason for this meeting is transparent as the sky."

"Oh, they know very well." Halfar, Romnus' cousin, and the former Supreme Ruler came out of the side door, followed by Lt. Treshur. He stood to the side next to the council while Lt. Treshur stayed close to the door. "Lord Pondur is gauging how far he can push. Dreridians have never set foot on Azrom. This meeting alone will give him far too much insight."

"Lord Halfar," a councilman began, "I fear you may be right. For all we know, they have retrieved fragments of the planet bomb and Lord Graggor is analyzing as we speak."

"Not possible," General Rass blurted. "Any fragments, if they survived, would disintegrate. We made sure no traces remain."

"And, as clever as Lord Graggor is, he's yet to duplicate our work." Lt. Treshur crossed his arms. "They've known about these bombs for centuries now."

"How is the containment going?" Halfar asked.

"Almost back to one hundred percent," Rass replied.

"I am erecting a sturdier barrier," Treshur said. "It would take ten times the effort than before to crack into this one."

Romnus listened without interruption. What he heard sounded good. He nodded to the servant standing along the far wall on his right. They raised an oval-shaped fob, aiming in the air, and clicked.

"Now." Romnus sat up on his throne. "Let's talk about this."

A holoscreen appeared in midair spanning the width of the room. On display sat a frozen image of the enemy forces ravaging an industrial planet.

"This is one of three they have tried to decimate. It manufactures forty percent of their gear."

"So, if they can't make a profit, no one will?" The council member asked incredulously.

"That seems to be the case," General Kur said. "How selfish."

"The Dreridians are proud of themselves at the moment. Having taken control of another planet under enemy contract."

Romnus stared down at his royal court. His gaze met Halfar's. "What say you, cousin?"

Halfar's mouth twitched into a grin.

"I think there are planets ripe for the taking. It's always a good idea to expand one's empire." His grin widened into a smile.

"Wait!" Batis whirled around and stared at Halfar, then back at Romnus. "While Lord Pondur and his minions are taking a tour of Azrom, we're going to snatch up real estate in enemy territory?"

"Absolutely." Halfar replied.

"I love it," Farin said. Everyone's gaze turned to her. Having been quiet the whole time, she let out a small laugh. "I enjoy conquests just as much as you do. It's in my blood, right?"

Romnus broke his composure and snorted before leaning over laughing, his head almost in his lap.

Batis nodded towards her.

"I know better than anyone how much bloodlust flows in that little demon's veins."

"Forgive me, my Queen," another councilman said. "My lord." He bowed to Romnus out of habit. "But we barely managed to run them off during the battle. We would surely be met with hostility in their own system."

"We fear casualties, is what he's trying to say."

The head counsel added with a snort.

"That's only because we weren't taking them seriously." Halfar frowned. "We still don't'." He glanced over at the royal council.

"This time we won't half-ass it, as the saying goes on Earth," Batis smirked.

"At least half the effort this round," Farin said, her saccharine tone not quite concealing her animosity. "No need to go all out."

The room took on a sinister air as the royal councils' mouths watered as they dreamt of new revenues while taking down rivals.

Time for the enemy to get a taste of true Azrom might.

Sort of.

Ships of gleaming white alloy with silver underbelly emerged from the vortex on the outskirts of Azrom. Four in all, their massive size conveyed Dreridian power. They spread out into a single row holding pattern.

The second ship's forward bay opened and a string of eight smaller vessels flew out towards the surface. One led, with two flanking the middle on each side and two more securing the rear.

Romnus and his entourage stood on the landing platform twenty miles from the palace watching their descent on a holoscreen while they waited for them to land. Used for shipping commodities, Romnus had it all rerouted to accommodate the Dreridians.

"Was coming in those gigantic things necessary?" Farin stared at the convoy breaking the stratosphere. "They'll be an eyesore sitting in the open like this."

"At least we'll be able to see them clearly," Batis said.

As the ships approached, they saw how big the vessels were. They indeed took up the entire landing platform, concealing the dock beneath them. Hot exhaust filtered out, causing a layer of fog around the area.

Not wanting to appear rude, Romnus and his entourage took a larger transport to the dock to greet them. Farin had her assistant stay behind to finish preparing for the visit. They arrived as the middle ship's ramp came down on the platform with a soft thud.

Lord Pondur and Graggor rode the conveyor ramp with a group of eight soldiers as guards. Farin's lips thinned at the heavy grade weapons they carried on their hips.

Batis glanced over at the generals.

Both of their expressions told them they weren't having that.

"Supreme Ruler Romnus," Lord Pondur stopped a few feet away. "Queen Farin. How honored to meet you on your home."

Lord Graggor gave the same greeting while Rass signaled his own guards to surround the group.

"I find it quite bold to bring weapons to our meeting." Romnus cocked his head to one side. "Is this not a friendly endeavor?"

"Oh, of course." Lord Pondur met his gaze. "I'm simply mimicking your protocol."

Can't argue with that!

Azromnians never surrendered its weapons, regardless of the situation. Halfar marched into meetings on other planets with full might, daring anyone to approach him, let alone demand he disarm. He saw Halfar smirk.

"As long as they behave, we have no qualms with it."

Rass had his men step back.

Not wanting to deal with the situation, Farin left ahead of them. Returning to the palace to oversee last minute tasks. After the initial greetings were complete, the entourage made its way towards the transport that would take them to the palace.

Lord Pondur's gaze swept along the terrain, taking in Azrom's aesthetic. He seemed to be amused yet something else lurked behind his expression. Romnus grew alert. Lord Graggor did the same.

Halfar laid a hand on his shoulder. A gesture of reassurance. Whatever the Dreridians were plotting, they won't succeed.

"How do you find our home?" Halfar asked Lord Pondur.

"Intriguing."

"How so?" Halfar tilted his head.

"Hmm. How should I put it?" He rubbed his craggy chin.

"I, myself, expected a more robust horticulture and advanced mining facilities," Lord Graggor interjected.

"Yes. How do you produce enough for trade? I can't see where it comes from."

Halfar snorted. Romnus tried to suppress a grin.

"There's no need for us to upgrade the mining facilities," Romnus replied. "The current process has kept up with demand."

"There's an Earth saying," Halfar said. "If it ain't broke, don't fix it."

"What primitive thinking. There's always room for improvement when it involves trade." Lord Pondur gave them a tight grin.

The insult was not lost on anyone in the transport.

"What an audacious thing to say in such close quarters on a world you have never visited."

Halfar smiled while his eyes narrowed.

"Surely, with your might, Azrom cares not what others think."

The transport stopped at the bottom of the palace steps where Farin stood with her guards. She had changed robes. As the doors opened for Lord Pondur and Graggor, she moved forward.

A communication holoscreen floated at her side.

"And that is why we demand respect." Farin's eyes glinted in the setting sun's rays.

"Queen Farin." Both Dreridians bowed their heads slightly as they greeted her.

"How lovely you look on this day," Lord Pondur said.

"Save your false sentiments for someone less gullible." She smiled sweetly and gestured towards the entrance with a sweep of her arm. "Please follow me. Welcome to Azrom."

Her expression held no warmth for their presence. Even Romnus and Halfar hesitated. My mate can be terrifying. He could see Halfar thinking the same about his child.

Lord Pondur scrutinized everything in his line of sight. What he didn't see, Lord Graggor picked up. Romnus felt a pull of anxiety in his stomach. The last thing he wanted was Dreridian blood spilled on Azrom.

Inside the conference room Farin had prepared, the two groups sat opposite each other around the oval table in the center. Drinks and snacks lined down the middle. Servants filled glasses and small plates, setting them before those in attendance. When they left, Batis cleared his throat, getting everyone's attention.

"Now that we have drinks in hand, let's get to it." He raised his glass and winked. "We know why you're really here."

Lt. Treshur gave a stern glare. Lord Pondur simply nodded.

"Yes. We made it no secret what we want." He raised his glass and took a tiny sip. "Why so paranoid, withholding such technology?"

"Because we know what can be done with it," Treshur replied.

"Oh? As opposed to how it's used now?"

Halfar stiffened, knowing where the question was going.

"Mistakes have been made. It happens with these things."

Lord Graggor gave Halfar a stunned stare.

"One would remedy that scenario beforehand, I think."

"So you think Dreridians can do better?" Farin asked.

"We are more advanced," Lord Pondur answered.

"Yet, here you are." Farin folded her hands under her chin. "Falling over yourself to get any crumb of data about our technology."

"I like to acquire new things."

The way Lord Pondur sipped his drink while glaring over the rim at her made the others in the room tense with foreboding. Romnus clenched his fists, begging inwardly to Farin.

Please! Don't start another war.

Farin didn't look his way. She sent him a telepathic message, not letting her gaze waver from Lord Pondur. Neither refused to submit.

Calm down. I'm only testing him a bit.

"Queen Farin." Lord Pondur set down his glass. "You should know better." His beady eyes turned cold. "Dreridians do not fawn over other worlds. We absorb them."

☼ ☼ ☼

Chastan didn't enjoy taking orders from anyone other than Farin. But he also had his pride as an Azromnian. Romnus assigned him to monitor the Dreridians assembled in the holding area on the North wing. As suspected, six of them split into pairs and went in three directions. Lord Pondur's suspicions after seeing the mostly barren territories spurred their movement.

He let one pair go towards the nearby village where a handful of the giant soldiers guarded the gates. They would not come back from there unscathed. The other pairs went into separate palace entries. Chastan's eyes narrowed as he followed the first. One of them carried a small device that detected underground activity. They headed straight for the hidden doors leading to the labs.

Not on my watch.

Blending into the dark shadows along the stone walls of the tunnel entrance, Chastan crawled the ceiling above them. Both walking oblivious to his presence.

Only the dim light of the device guided them.

"To think, Lord Graggor deducted the reason for Azrom's lack of technology on the surface."

The one holding the device grinned.

"So deceptive. For all we know, they have an entire cluster of cities beneath." The other looked around the dark tunnel, making sure no one else entered. He never looked up. "Kind of disturbing, though. No one knows this planet's true might."

Exactly.

Chastan waited until they cl;ose to the doors' first landing, then scratched the stone with the tip of one of his pincers. It screeched like nails on a chalkboard, causing the two soldiers to halt.

"What was that?" The first yelled.

"What's in here?" The second pulled his blaster from a holster attached to his hip.

"I thought you were watching!"

The second raised his weapon and scanned the dark.

"I saw nothing!" His voice rose in a panic.

While they searched behind them, Chastan dropped from the ceiling. Sensing his presence they turned around, unable to decipher his shape.

The second soldier got off one round that went wild as Chastan knocked the blaster from his hands. His right pincer clamped around the soldier's throat while he punched the other in the chest, knocking him into the wall.

"We really don't like invited guests or otherwise snooping around our home without permission."

The sound of his altered voice slithered, then echoed across the air. He could see the skin of their necks prickle. To deter the one on the ground from moving, he tightened his grip. Tiny drops of blood emerged from where the tibial spines punctured his flesh.

Romnus made it clear not to kill unless absolutely necessary. He dared one of them to make a move and justify such action. A surge of bloodlust filled him. It had been a long time since he felt that.

Pursuit

For eight days, Azrom hosted the Dreridians. Farin kept a close watch on Lord Pondur and Graggor. They acted accordingly. Not prying too much with their questions. Feigning ignorance when the topic of spies arose on two separate occasions. Her lips thinned, thinking about the end result. She caught whiff of Romnus' order to Chastan.

Bloodshed was inevitable.

The royal entourage followed her and Romnus, flanking their guests as they strolled along the paved walkway in the center of a manufacturing town. Identical square buildings with flat roofs lined each side of the streets. Some were shops that stocked necessities. The rest were residential in a range of muted colors.

Everyone worked at the manufacturing plant on the outskirts. Having a town close by eliminated the need for mass transport. The workers could walk, getting exercise and fresh air.

The plant never shut down. Five shifts made sure it stayed that way. People walking around in drab grey jumpsuits and knee-high boots were either going to work or coming from it. Those with the day off wore flowy kaftans and sandals. All said, it was a booming commercial town.

Farin half listened to her father relaying the town's origin. Romnus rarely spoke. She marveled at her father's dominant aura.

He knows how to handle them.

Today, the Dreridians would depart without the information they seek. Farin contacted her own spy network to reach Chastan and learned the total of agents sent around the planet. Can't blame them for trying. She let out a small laugh.

"Does something we said amuse you, my queen?" Her father turned to her with his brow raised. "Please enlighten us."

"My apologies." Farin smiled. "I wasn't paying attention. The weather is lovely, so I'm soaking in the air, lost in my thoughts."

Her father's face twitched, suppressing a frown. Lord Pondur gave a hearty laugh.

"How candid you are, Queen Farin."

"I try not to hide my feelings these days." She tilted her head towards him.

"The lady lacks a filter," Lord Graggor added.

The entourage slowed to a crawl as her and Romnus' guards waited for a response. Farin's mouth twitched upwards at the corner as she wondered if the slight warranted punishment. She felt the tension close in. People roaming the surrounding streets halted their tasks to focus their gazes on the Dreridians.

"You have not spoken truer words, Lord Graggor." She replied while laughing. "It must be a sign of my immaturity."

The entire entourage halted. Lord Pondur stared at her. She couldn't make out what kind of expression he wore. Not shock or concession. Something she didn't like.

"That is not the case I was trying to make." Lord Graggor bowed his head. "My apologies if I offended you."

Farin waved away the sentiment.

"None taken."

Lord Pondur tapped the tip of his cane on the ground.

"Well, I am quite surprised how you managed to produce so many goods with the size of your workforce." He pointed his cane at the plant in the town's epicenter. "Your race is truly efficient."

"We like to do things right the first time," Romnus said.

"Shall we head back, my lord?" Batis asked. "We don't want our guests to miss their window to return home."

"Ah, yes." Lord Pondur sighed. "Our time has ended. I would've liked to explore more of your facilities."

"I bet you would," Batis muttered.

They made a U-turn and headed back to the transport. Climbing back in, Farin saw the townpeople's angry faces watching them leave. A two-sided anger. One for the insult of their queen. The second stemmed from shame at thinking the same. Hearing it come from an outsider brought it glaring to the forefront.

You can't have it both ways. She chided silently.

Imperial guards, along with the royal entourage, escorted the Dreridians to their ship. Farin and Romnus walked together with her father behind them. They kept a wide distance further back. A gust of wind passed through, refreshing Farin. The Dreridians turned around at the bottom of their ship's ramp.

"It was a pleasure to finally speak with you on friendly terms." Lord Pondur placed his right hand on the left side of his chest. "We thank you for entertaining us on your home."

"We were entertained as well. Thank you."

Farin emphasized the you part.

As Lord Pondur and Graggor went to ascend the ramp, Farin let out a loud gasp, causing everyone to pause.

"I almost forgot!" Farin stepped to the side, allowing a large group of soldiers to arrive. "You can't leave without all your belongings."

The soldiers made a pathway, dragging a total of ten Dreridian spies into a pile at Lord Pondur and Graggor's feet.

"I hope you didn't think we wouldn't notice." She grinned.

Halfar and Romnus frowned at the pile. She knew why Romnus seemed miffed. His secret had been found out. Lord Pondur and Graggor appeared unfazed.

Another set of Dreridian soldiers came around and retrieved their bloody, unconscious comrades.

"This was fun. Let's do it again sometime." Farin's high pitch solidified her fury. Her eyes glowered at them.

"Let's not," Halfar replied.

"Yes," Lord Graggor watched the soldiers being lifted off the ground. "I fear it won't be as amusing next time around."

"Have a safe journey home." Romnus' eyes glimmered with ire.

"We shall." The Dreridians went up the automatic ramp, receding as it reached the ship's entrance.

The doors sealed after its passengers boarded.

"Good riddance," Batis scoffed.

The royal entourage watched the ships take off and disappear into the late afternoon sky. A vortex shadow appeared.

"Now that that's over with," Halfar blurted. He turned to Farin. "Want to tell me what happened with those soldiers?"

"Hmm?" Farin smiled sweetly. "You should ask our Supreme Ruler about that."

Romnus' eyes widened.

The others remained silent, not wanting to get involved.

"Farin," Romnus reached a hand towards her.

She turned away and headed back to the transport. Inside, she fumed. Romnus had used Chastan without her permission.

Serves you right.

Farin wanted to get back to her own council to check on Azrom's planet requisitions. She knew the Dreridians, Razzna, and other races in the alliance were already ahead of the game.

The Razznian general watched the procession of enemy ships move closer to the outskirts of their solar system, leaving eleven ruined planets in their wake. His thin, forked tongue slithered out, rattling as he hissed. Energy saving lights dimly lit the bridge of his battleship, giving it a somber ambience. The crew worked in silence at their stations as the main viewscreen played the feed.

His ship was one of ten scattered among the system to keep track of the enemy whenever they popped out of nowhere to raise havoc. The Dreridians handled the dirty work so far. It seemed now it would turn to the Razznians and Azrom forces.

He knew the enemy would eventually try again to bring the five systems down. More specifically, any race deemed part of the alliance. No doubt, they knew the locations of each checkpoint leading into the five systems territory.

"Incoming from the Dreridian post." The comms lead yelled.

"Patch it through."

The face of a Yaos soldier replaced the image on the viewer.

Their uniform's black and silver collar accented their blue skin.

"Greetings, general." The Yaos soldier tilted his head forward.

"Greetings to you, commander." He returned the gesture.

"As you may have seen, the enemy is on the move. I fear they are attempting to leave. And they have one goal."

"Not without first trying to regain their dominance here."

"A last stand?"

"Yes. Regardless if they succeed, they'll then come after us."

The Yaos commander's smooth face creased, narrowing their eyes. One word summed up the enemy: Relentless.

"At least they are consistent. Do you need additional forces at your station?"

"Hmm. Not sure yet. So far, they are coasting across with no signs of engaging."

"Keep us posted. My ships are not far away from you."

"I will indeed." The general bowed as the screen went blank.

The feed ended, and the screen reverted to the view outside the ship. Two planets loomed in the distance amongst a sea of stars. A wondrous sight he could never tire of. As a reptilian race, they understood why other races found it comical.

Until they meet them in battle.

The five systems considered Razznians on par with Azrom as a powerful adversary. They fought with each other numerous times over the centuries, yet the Razznians always knew Azrom held back. The last battle with the enemy under the alliance made that clear.

"Detecting jump sequence." The comms leader called out.

"Intercept. Where are they headed?"

"Here. Third planet over out of our current viewing range."

"Expand."

The viewscreen zoomed out in time for them to see the vortex open directly in line with the medium-sized planet. The enemy's weapons immediately bombarded it as they moved out of it. Their signature move.

This time, return fire came their way from the planet's surface.

"Set coordinates," the general ordered. "We're going in. Relay it to the rest of the fleet and the Yaos commander."

"As you command."

The general nodded to the comm leader's second. Negotiations for a stake in that planet required a diplomat on the scene. It being the Dreridians' goal, the Yaos commander probably had the same idea.

We all want a piece of the pie.

He saw a message blink on the second screen before being sent to Razzna. Lord Pondur should have known he couldn't monopolize another system on the alliance's watch. And they call Azrom and us arrogant?

Pfft!

"Same strategy as before?" The weapons tech asked.

He saw the enemy ships in the rear close to the vortex change formation to protect it. Smart. They learn fast.

"No. We're going to side swipe them this time."

That move could potentially knock them out of range of both the vortex and the planet. A risky maneuver worth a shot. The worst that could happen is his forces needing to fall back into their usual formation for a head on strike.

A short hyper jump and his forces landed along the side of the enemy. Each ship turned to sit perpendicular with the side view of their prey, weapons ready. They fired, hitting the first row before them. The enemy ships rocked sideways away from the onslaught, their shields taking damage.

The general smiled.

That's it.

As expected, enemy ships on the other side of the first row moved out of formation to turn their weapons on his. Now the real fight begins. Coming out of a jump behind them, the Yaos commander's ship hit them as they came up, making their shots go wide, missing the general's fleet.

They had the enemy surrounded from every angle.

On the far side of the enemy system, a Dreridian fleet engaged with a faction of them. Previous reports alerted the alliance of their divide and conquer tactic. Swarms of ugly fighter jets attacked the armada ship, leading an eclectic group of Alliance ships composed of different races at the frontline.

The battle went on for days until the enemy tired of it and fled through a vortex. What they hadn't anticipated was half the alliance ships taking pursuit. It shocked the other commanders left in their wake as well.

"How far behind are we?" The commander asked his navigator.

"About half a light year. We can catch up whenever we want."

"Do we know where they're headed?"

"Looks like another planet used for their own needs. According to the data our surveillance team received, it manufactures chemicals."

"Is that right?"

The commander stroked the bottom of his chin. As a science officer, the prospect screamed at him. So many possibilities ran through his mind. His left eye, not covered by his jet-black hair, glowed a pale blue.

The Dreridians consumed much of the enemy's territory. Now they searched for any planet that assisted in their conquest, finding the enemy hell bent on destroying any trace of their technology in the system. Where most solar systems have a few planets, usually twelve, this one touted nearly thirty.

And so far, the enemy had annihilated nine of more than twenty manufacturing worlds.

"They won't get to destroy this one. We'll wait for them to land on the planet, then launch our attack."

"How sinister, commander."

The navigator sneered with delight.

Before the last battle, every ship received a message from the palace. Lord Pondur gave his blessing to all.

Conquer as you see fit.

Multiple black swirls formed around the planet, catching the Dreridian fleet off guard. In position to attack a vortex on opposite sides, they didn't expect so many at once.

The commander ordered the fleet to change formation. Not enough ships reached the first three vortices. Enemy fighters spewed forth, invading the planet's airspace.

"Follow them!" the commander ordered. "Do not let them damage the infrastructure!" He clenched his fists in frustration. "Defensive maneuvers for the larger vortex near the center."

From how the enemy came, the commander concluded the planet held some importance. On the screen showing images from the surface, powerful shields blocked the assault on major buildings and facilities. The smaller ones got pummeled.

While a third of the fleet moved to intercept the enemy and stop the carnage, the commander's ship headed for what appeared to be the planet's epicenter. Buildings stood taller than anything else on the surface with wide one level connecting ones. A transport hub of at least twenty dock stations sat behind it.

The commander wanted to form a temporary alliance with the planet's leader. So far, his ship had not been shot at or hailed. On approach, he noticed a group of machines lined up at the foot of the main building. Air to space launchers. He recognized those types of weapons no matter the technology. They aimed at the enemy fighters rushing towards it.

To his surprise, the enemy ships in front of the formation were the only ones obliterated as the rest banked out of the way. Half fired down on the launchers, taking a few out. Dreridian forces, finally catching up with the horde, gave chase to stop them.

"This is madness!" The commander gripped the dais railing.

"Transmission from planetside," the comms leader shouted.

"Open the feed."

A garbled audio littered with static interference came through. The translator deciphered the language.

"Despite our appreciation for assistance we know you have an agenda in doing so. Please be aware, should we survive this, the only negotiations will be of equal partnership. If that is not your intent, then we will consider you yet another enemy."

The commander reared back at the bold statement. They were not a race to trifle with.

He contemplated what his next move should be.

False compliance?

His fleet could assist then turn the tables. They would be in no position to argue if the enemy caused too much damage.

Then the unthinkable happened.

Blinding bands of light shot from two vortices opposite each other, raining down on the planet, engulfing a third of its mass in the center. The blast hit, spreading out. With no way of escaping, the commander dropped to his knees for impact and yelled.

"Shields! Full power! Dive!"

The traveling rays of destruction seared the top and left side of the ship as it plunged into the surface, burrowing deep.

We failed!

The emergency lights flickered before going completely out.

News of the Dreridian fleet reported as lost after attempting to stop the enemy destrucion of yet another planet manufacturing its war weapons reached Lord Pondur days after his return from Azrom. Details of the assault displayed on his office holoscreen taunted him as he sat at his desk with a finger on his temple.

Lord Pondur tilted his head and scowled at it. He never knew what the enemy had up their sleeve.

Such a dastardly move.

According to footage from a nearby intact satellite, the enemy tried occupying the planet. What remained of the planet's defenses and Dreridian fighters on the ground formed a resistance.

Was it worth fighting for?

With how the enemy reacted, his mind gave a resounding yes. But, looking at it objectively, he would lose too much. Unless he sent another fleet to combat them. No other Dreridian force was close enough.

It would have to be Yaos or Azrom.

Which also opened a chance for that fleet to pull the rug from under him and take control of the planet themselves.

He raised his head and let his arm drop onto the desk. Tapping the commlink, he waited for it to connect.

"Greetings, Lord Pondur," the general answered. "How may I serve you today?"

"Come to my office."

He disconnected the feed before he could hear his reply.

Within minutes, the general arrived with a worrisome expression.

"I'll be blunt." Lord Pondur stood, straightening his burgundy waist coat. His glare pierced the general. "I want you," he flicked a finger at the holoscreen then planted his hands, fingertips raised, on the desk, "to get those creatures off that planet and chase them to hell if necessary."

The general's face relaxed, as if relieved.

"Of course, your grace. Gladly. Hostages?"

"Absolutely not," Lord Pondur replied tersely.

"So, annihilation if probable."

"That is what I want."

"It shall be done."

The general bowed his head, then backed out of the room.

Lord Pondur stared at the bottom of the screen where a ticker-tape continued its announcement of the lost fleet. He knew better than anyone that it wasn't lost. If anything, those soldiers would find a way out and fight to the death.

Just hold on until the calvary arrives.

The enemy would eventually get bored when it becomes clear they won't wipe out the planet with so much alliance interference.

At least I don't have to worry about Lassa throwing their hand in the mix.

Home

Silence engulfed the conference room while Chardon and his cabinet members stared at the holoscreen floating above the table. Lassa, their original home world, rotated slowly as smaller screens showing the surface popped up beneath it. Everyone felt a sense of awe combined with trepidation.

They contemplated the next course of action.

Jaron glanced over at Volma, the head of engineering. Her brow furrowed. She rested her chin on two raised fingers, then tapped her lower lip. Jaron nodded.

"We need to send out a scouting unit," Volma finally said. "See what the surface is really like. These images are not accurate."

"From what I witnessed, Lassa is still healing." Talas crossed his arms. "But I do think it can sustain a small amount of inhabitants."

"I'll put together a team to collect data on emerging resources." Ganna's tone sounded dejected. Wounded. Chardon held his tongue. "I've already reestablished the gate so only we can access Lassa."

"That's reassuring," Chardon said. "I don't want the Dreridians or anyone else attempting to land there."

Modas fidgeted on the giant cushion in the corner of the room. His feelings were on the fence regarding their home world. So much pain tied to it made him leery of the planet's intentions. Though it stemmed more from the being who embodied it.

Sensing the mood shift, Jaron tilted her head in amusement. The Lassa side of her peeked out. Their arrogance and disdain for New Lassa showing. In an instant, it disappeared, and Jaron looked down with guilt.

Chardon looked around the room at his people.

He noticed the way their energies seemed in flux, not sure what level it needed to be at. Should they show excitement, be hopeful? Or remain cautious and not move until they had all the data?

This is when he desired Halfar's input. He understood him having to stay on Azrom to advise Romnus. As the planet bombs' creator, he'd always be held accountable for any incidents that arose.

"Lt. Treshur is sending more info on lingering aftereffects we may encounter. I'm not sure he should join the scout mission."

Chardon saw Ganna's face twitch when he mentioned Azrom's science officer. *What is that about?* His gaze moved to Kelin. The man smirked. *He knows something!*

"What is the timeline?" Volma asked. "I think we should take at least an entire year for observation." Her expression changed to sorrow. "If Lassa is indeed healthy enough to take on inhabitants…" her voice trailed off.

That was the question.

Chardon heard the rumors spreading about relocating back home. The last two centuries on New Lassa saw it being modified to accommodate their race. Halfar, out of guilt for being the one who destroyed their home, used his resources to assist.

"So who's going?" Mara, Jaron's daughter, asked. Her voice hiked up with glee. "I want to see what it looks like now."

"Is that you volunteering?" Volma replied, her brow raised.

"Hmm." Mara glanced off to the side.

"Sending a group that represents each of us would be ideal." Talas added. "How will Lassa react to energy users, warriors, and manbeasts back in her folds?"

"Are you saying she may reject us?" Kelin said incredulously.

"Possibly." Chardon eyed Jaron. "She may still be angry."

"That's not what I felt," Talas answered.

"She didn't have any animosity towards you to begin with," Chardon quipped.

"I could plead me case." Jaron smiled.

"Absolutely not!" Chardon and Volma shouted in unison.

Jaron reared back from the verbal assault. The other members glared at her.

"The last thing we need is conflict between the two of you. We'll let Lassa decide if she'll let you return." Modas spoke angrily.

As much as he loved Jaron, Chardon knew he felt a sting of betrayal. Trinon kept silent in the corner across from his father. He also didn't like the idea of his mother going to Lassa. Born on New Lassa, he didn't have the same attachment.

"And, that's why I won't go to Lassa with my team," Ganna said.

The sadness in her voice made Chardon cringe. This subject caused more tension and strife over the past few years since Lassa's rediscover.

But we have to go!

"Volma will head the first research team. Trinon." Chardon turned to him. "You will escort Ganna's second team. Kelin, you'll be lead on the mission." He met Talas' gaze. "I need you here."

"I understand." Talas uncrossed his arms and stretched them across the table. He pulled them back into his lap. "I shouldn't be the only one communicating with Lassa."

"I'll leave it up to you," Chardon addressed Kelin, "on who you want to take."

"Would you like me to update the council on our decision?" Volma asked. "I know you invited me here because of my status on Lassa before the fall."

Chardon frowned. Of course they needed to be informed. He just didn't trust most of them due to the incident with his parents and the manbeasts.

"There's no need to go over any logistics. Simply tell them we're sending a scout team. If they want any more than that, send them to me."

"As you wish, leader." Volma bowed her head.

"I think that's all for now." Chardon uncrossed his legs and stood. "I'm headed back to my chamber if anyone needs me later."

Modas rose and followed him out, leaving the others to finish their drinks before exiting as well. Jaron's gaze fell on Ganna as the two neared the door.

Both had sins to atone for.

Kelin and Talas walked together into the muted sunlight grown brighter over the decades. They shielded their eyes until their vision adjusted. Field workers paid them no mind while children too young to do tasks, ran around screeching in delight.

"Do you already have a list of people in mind?" Talas asked.

"Somewhat. I think Chardon's judgement is off, again."

"Why do you say that?"

"Because I'm also the reason Lassa endured such a fate."

"True." Talas stopped. His head hung low. "That said. I would rather you go than Jaron or Modas."

Kelin's hands balled into fists at his side.

"That she even suggested going! The audacity! Even Ganna knew better."

"They need to merge." Talas glanced at him. "I've integrated my current self with my original. Jaron has not. She's letting the Lassa side dominate at will."

"Modas has kept his distance, not helping the situation."

"At least we both know Trinon is reliable."

"I think I'll take Mara on her offer." Kelin snickered.

"She could bring down the tension. May I make a suggestion?" Talas watched Kelin's fists release then place both hands on his hips. "Take my second in command and his lieutenant."

"That's actually a good idea." Kelin stared at the sky.

"What is that supposed to mean?"

Kelin's gaze shifted to him. "Really? That upsets you?"

"Whatever." Talas resumed walking, leaving Kelin to catch up.

"Don't pout." Kelin leaned closer and whispered, "It makes me want you, and I have too much work to do."

"Aren't you the one who said there's always time for mating?" Talas gave him a side stare.

"Don't tempt me," Kelin warned. "I don't have that kind of restraint right now."

Out of the darkness of space, the shadowy outlines of eight large ships materialized within Lassa territory. Two science convoys, two scouts, and four battle cruisers. Lassa shone bright with gradient shades of orange, yellow, and pink.

Kelin stood on the captain's dais of the first ship's bridge. He stared in awe at the planet. The time passed seemed long yet it reality short. His crew kept busy with their tasks. They would launch the scout units first. He watched the two ships ease towards Lassa in opposite directions and disappear into its stratosphere.

The silence of space overtook the sounds of consoles beeping. He barely heard the shifting of bodies adjusting in their seats, of the soft padding of fingers tapping the workstation panels. A calm before the actual work began.

"Status?" Kelin ordered.

A crewmember turned his head around to answer him.

"All systems are ready. Lassa shows no signs of hostility."

"Good. Prepare for landing once the scout ships start relaying their initial data."

The battle cruisers maneuvered away from the planet to face the void as a line of defense. A Dreridian observation ship sat farther out, close to the moon. Weapon signatures alerted the Lassians to consider it a threat.

"Keep an eye on the Dreridians. I don't trust them." Kelin ran a finger back and forth across the bottom of his lower lip. "Why are they still here?"

"The first science ship is hailing us," the comms tech said.

"Send it through."

Trinon's face and chest came on the main holoscreen. His usual jolly smile absent as he stared at him.

"I know you want to wait for the scouts, but I feel we should go now. No need to waste time out here. Our battle ships can handle any disruptions."

"I'm just as anxious." Kelin pursed his lips. "We must be patient."

The way Trinon's expression changed akin to disdain made Kelin nervous. A little frightened by it.

He didn't like it when the manbeast didn't appear happy. As if reading his concern, Trinon's face lit up.

"Well, I guess there's no sense arguing about it then." His eyes squinted shut as he smiled widely. "Ha-ha! See you on the surface."

The feed went dark, leaving a heightened state of anxiety. Kelin already nervous about being wrapped in Lassa's essence once again.

Would she forgive me?

Ten hours went by before the scouts sent an all clear to the remaining ships. The two science ships approached the planet. As they neared the first layer, a shimmer of light engulfed them. They traveled through a multicolored vortex of white and yellow with speckles of green.

Magnificent! Kelin cried out inwardly.

This would be the first time a Lassian ship entered the planet's atmosphere from space to land on the surface. The gates allowed them to bypass all of that. Seeing the transition take place, Kelin didn't want to arrive any other way in the future.

He noticed the consoles on the bridge flickering, their screens nothing but static. Every gauge went haywire, yet the ship stayed on course.

Lassa is guiding us in!

The ships burst from the clouds and slowed down, cruising over a vast swath of land. Kelin sucked in air through gritted teeth as he took in the scene.

Lassa was indeed still healing.

Lush forest sprawled below beside a hostile terrain with pools of primordial ooze. The ocean resembled a hodge podge of crystal-clear sections with dark churning waves scattered out. Red fiery patches marred sections of sunlight. Multiple seasons took place across the surface.

Menacing and beautiful all at once. A pale peach glow emitted from the center of the planet. Lassa's presence reached out and touched everyone's mind.

No words were spoken, yet they understood.

Welcome home, my children.

Trinon's body buzzed as if walking through an electrical field the moment he set foot on Lassa's surface. The swampy ground sucked his feet down, covering the tops of his boots. He breathed in the air, noticing the scent of new life coming from the forest ahead. The bottom of the ship's ramp had already sunk, disappearing in the muck. Above, the sun barely shed any light.

He turned to his brother, Jakar, and found the towering man-beast rooted in place. His eyes stared off into the horizon with a blended expression of awe and sadness. Ah! This is his home. Trinon felt Lassa's pull at his core. He couldn't imagine experiencing the horror of being torn apart along with your world.

"Are you okay?" Trinon asked gently, not to startle him.

Jakar ignored him for a moment, then turned his gaze to him.

"I remember this place." He averted his eyes and scanned the area. "This forest, this land." He closed his eyes. "We thrived here, despite the hardship." Opening his eyes, he inhaled deep, letting his chest expand, then relaxed as he let it out. "Come. Let's see what condition she's in."

Everyone referred to Lassa as female. The entity had no form, yet it seemed to agree with that assessment. Lassa identified as such. Then I will honor that. Trinon smirked as a gentle caress ran through his body. A bit touchy feely too.

The rest of the group exited the ship to follow him and Jakar into the dense forest struggling to expand its hold in the swamp. They kept close, not sure if any wildlife had come into being over the centuries.

"Is the terrain the same?"

Trinon swept a low-hanging branch out of his way.

"Not exactly. Some parts are brand new." Jakar glanced down. "The ground was solid. Tree roots covered the floor."

"Yeah. These trees are too young for that."

From the rear of the group, Mara came rushing up to them, breathless with excitement. Her eyes gleamed as she looked every which way, taking in the scenery.

"Can you believe it?" Mara exclaimed, slapping a hand on Jakar's shoulder. "Our home! She's not dead and gone."

"I read the report." Trinon said. "Halfar sent a neutralizer to stop the devastation. It came too late."

"It shouldn't have happened in the first place," an energy user behind them spat.

"All because Chardon couldn't keep their legs closed," another added in disgust.

Trinon turned to grab hold of the man. Mara beat him to it. She had his neck in a vice grip, lifting him off the ground. Her eyes glowed with blue energy.

"If those vile words spill from your lips again, I will end you." She glanced towards the rest of the group. "That goes for anyone."

Jakar placed a hand on her forearm, feeling the muscles bulge as she kept hold of the man. She glared at him. He let out a sigh as he pushed down. Mara's expression changed to resignation, and she loosened her grip. The man fell back with both feet on the ground and his butt deep in the mud.

The sky darkened above them. Oh! Trinon saw the same look of trepidation on Jakar's face. Lassa did not like the situation. Hurt feelings permeated the air.

"Enough." Trinon addressed the group. "There's no need to hash out old wounds and past wrongs. We are here to see the rebirth of our home world. Look up." He pointed to the sky. "Is this how you want Lassa to see you?"

They all went still.

Many refused to look, instead hanging their heads in shame. The mood shifted. Dull sunlight returned, parting the dark clouds.

"The research teams must be elated about now," Mara said, breaking the silence.

"Oh, I bet." Trinon could see a few scout ships heading in different directions. "Ganna won't know what to do with all the data she'll get."

The small scout ship landed on the outskirts of a hostile area. Four phenomena occurred simultaneously on the surface. Volma observed them from the window while the ramp extended for the team to exit.

A stream of crystal-clear water ran along the edges of thin volcanic rivers. Brushes of blues, greens, and yellows littered the floor on the other side while what looked like a lightning storm hovered above.

On the horizon, the scattered pieces of the planet fanned out into the stars. Volma chose this area to see what effect such damage had on Lassa. Chaos. Which didn't surprise her. In fact, she felt deeply enamored at how the planet went about reforming itself instead of trying to make something new.

"You've done well." Volma smiled. A wave of pride emanating from her core washed over her. She chuckled. "You always did like praise."

Ganna's chief assistant stepped out of the ship alongside her, and they both stood staring at the plain. She set down her metal case and shielded her eyes with one hand.

"I know we said we'd assess the damage and plan to repair it. But this may be beyond ours and Lassa's capabilities."

"Giving up so soon? We haven't even started yet." Volma went to the edge of the stream. "Well, let's start with getting samples of everything. I want to know if we can build any habitats. Small ones for now."

The assistant's gaze swung over to her, wide with surprise.

"You plan to bring people here?"

"Of course. A research team, field workers, and builders."

"But we don't know if…"

A menacing aura filled the area. Everyone looked around, searching for the cause.

"Are you implying that Lassa would harm us?"

Volma glanced back at her.

"No!" The assistant blanched in horror. "Of course not!

The ominous sensation dissipated.

"You probably shouldn't offend her after just getting here. Those dark clouds we passed earlier must have been from another group acting up."

"She's a tad moody, isn't she?"

The assistant nervously looked at the sky.

"Can you blame her? She's been through a lot."

Tension permeated the area the moment Kelin set foot in it. He recognized the location despite its haphazard formation. The temple and commons once stood in that very spot centuries ago. His chest tightened. Tendrils of anger caressed his soul, tugging at his core. He gripped the front of his jacket, taking a large hold of fabric in his fists.

Please! He squeezed his eyes shut. Forgive me. I know. Tears dripped onto the dirt below. There's nothing I can do to atone for my sins.

The rest of his entourage stayed clear of him, seeing his body hunched over in pain. They scanned their surroundings, then realized what was happening. Not one offer of pity from them.

He expected none.

Kelin fell to his knees, his forehead touching the ground. Lassa would make him suffer. The invisible tendrils burrowed into him like tiny drills. He clenched his teeth to stop any screams. Refusing to cry out, he endured every attack.

Sensing his resolve, Lassa eased the assault, lingering on the surface of his skin. Sadness. Kelin heaved a deep breath as drool oozed from his lips. The tendrils became soft, almost feathery. They soothed the pain they inflicted only seconds ago.

He stayed down until Lassa's essence left him. Still reeling from the side effects, he rose to his feet and looked out at the horizon.

"You deserve worse than that," one warrior blurted.

Kelin looked over his shoulder at him.

"I know that better than anyone here. What's your point?"

Some turned away, embarrassed.

Stating the obvious did nothing for no one. He gathered his composure and proceeded down the hill's slope towards the center.

Not only was Lassa recreating the area, but small creatures also lurked near the once core field. Tiny strands of light stuck out from the mushy soil.

So, you really do want us to return.

A glitch in the air made him and his entourage look up. In the clouds, they saw an image of a Dreridian ship moving towards the gate. Kelin grimaced.

"What do they think they're doing?" Talas' second yelled.

"Looks like they want to join us," Kelin replied.

"Well, that's not happening." An energy user scoffed.

Feeling Lassa go from playful to irate made him chuckle. So different from the being sharing her essence. Kelin frowned. Jaron needed to figure out a solution soon. Or Lassa would take it all back.

"Let's spread out in groups of four and survey the area," Kelin ordered. "We'll meet back here at sunset."

When everyone dispersed, leaving him with Talas' second commander and two others, he turned to them.

"Make sure to tread carefully. We don't want to poke her. She seems a bit…"

"Sensitive?" The energy user offered.

"On guard?" The warrior added.

"Yeah, something like that."

He tilted his head as Lassa psychically flicked him in jest.

A smaller craft emerged from the Dreridian ship on the outskirts of Lassa. It maneuvered towards the side of the planet away from any prying eyes that may linger in the vicinity. For all the captain knew, the Lassians could have a checkpoint. That's why he avoided the center.

Lord Graggor sent a message to test the perimeter. To attempt to land on the planet and join in the expedition that arrived there. Which puzzled the captain.

Were they invited?

The Lassians didn't seem too keen on them joining the show. He knew the ships detected their presence as they cruised across their line of sight before entering the strange vortex at Lassa's center.

The closer his ship got to Lassa's space, the more its shimmery vortex seemed to expand around as if tracking it. Lord Graggor had warned him the planet was sentient.

You don't like uninvited guests, do you?

"Drop us to cruising speed and stay on this trajectory," he ordered the navigator.

"Switching engines to propulsion. Quarter speed."

The captain rose from his seat on the bridge's dais and crossed his arms. He watched the vortex become a sea of colored static in the main viewscreen. An electric buzz coursed through his body as the helm touched it. All the systems on the ship flickered, then went dark the moment it entered.

For what felt like hours, the ship sailed in a spectacle of vibrant yellows and blues. When it reached the end, the ship's systems came back online. The captain gaped at the scene. His navigator stared at his console, glancing up at the viewscreen multiple times in confusion.

They sat at an angle across from the center vortex of the planet, close to where the main ship remained.

We're back where we started!

The captain rubbed his chin.

"It seems," he eyed the navigator, "Lassa doesn't like us."

"How? Why? What kind of vortex spits you back out like that?" The man cried.

"Because there's a gate attached to it."

Well played.

To his astonishment, the planet's color tinted green for an instant. A playful display, as if it knew it had tricked them. The captain's eyes narrowed. He didn't like being toyed with. Swirls of dark blue emerged, covering the center vortex.

Access denied

Conquerors Delight

A small fleet of ten Azrom armada ships burst from the vortex deep within Boretkz territory. They slowed to cruising speed as the last one exited before the hole snapped shut. The system consisted of twenty planets ranging in size with five moons.

Dreridians occupied three in its center. Azrom had purposely arrived on the outer rim to avoid them.

The lead ship's commander stood on the bridge's raised dais with his arms crossed. He stared at the five planets sprawled before him. Flexing his biceps caused the coat's sleeves to expand. It lay open, exposing the black battle suit beneath. His dark green eyes narrowed.

"Scan all five," he ordered the surveillance tech. "I want to know what we're dealing with. How much energy we have to exert for this."

"As you command." The technician focused on his console.

When the Dreridian's objective to dominate the enemy system became clear, Empress Farin advised Azrom's fleet to grab one or two planets for themselves. It had been a long time since they conquered a world.

His mother, Lady Haldris, recommended he take the mission. He knew an incentive benefiting their house lay somewhere in that request. Not that he minded. Azrom needed new trade.

"Three of the planets are heavily armed. The other two show barely any inhabitants. No trace of infrastructure."

"Hmm." The Commander lifted one hand to rub the bottom of his chin. "Which one has the most weapons?"

"The mid-sized one to our left."

He averted his gaze to the foamy green and pink orb.

The tiny dark speckles making up satellites surrounded it.

We'll take that one. And one of those smaller planets. We can use them as a base of operations."

"Of course, sir." The tech nodded to his comms tech. "Open the channel."

"Ready the fleet to advance," he commanded. "The four rear ships will take control of the small planet on the right." He then addressed the communications tech. "Send a hail to our target. Let them know we don't wish to destroy the planet. Surrender would be greatly appreciated."

"Yes, sir!"

The commander watched him send the message, and they all waited for a reply.

"Commander," the surveillance tech called out. "There is a vortex opening on the opposite edge of the system."

"Signature?"

"Razznian."

The commander chuckled.

So those reptiles had the same idea.

It made sense they would look toward the edge. They didn't like being stuck in the middle of anything. He wondered if they too would attempt to avoid violence this time. A smile crept on his face. Once the Dreridians realized what they were doing, he imagined the ire on Lord Pondur's craggy one.

Take that, you greedy warmonger.

"Planet's weapon signatures are active. Land space missiles aimed at our ships." The technician frowned. "They're capable of piercing our hulls."

"Incoming message," the communications tech yelled.

The translator finished processing the language and played it.

"Your kind prey on others for your own agendas. Dreridians crawl over us looking for opportunity. We are finally free of that race's tyranny only to have them and others like you coming to take over. The answer is no. Any move to occupy our planet will result in a defensive attack."

The commander sighed.

He agreed wholeheartedly. Unfortunately, that wasn't how things would go. He knew one barrage of fire from their armada ships would decimate entire regions on the planet. That's not what Azrom wants.

"Position our ships in an arc. Target the satellites."

While the four rear ships broke away and headed for the smaller planet, the rest maneuvered around the target. As the commander predicted, the moment his ship's weapons went hot, ready to take out the satellites, a bombardment of firepower shot from the planet. They penetrated two ship's shields, causing holes on the bridge and underbelly.

One show of force as a warning.

The commander nodded his approval.

"Open the channel." The tech tapped an icon on his console. "I commend you on showing your conviction. Before you ready your weapons for a second round, I suggest you scan our weapons and the position of our ships and decide if you want us to return in kind."

He dropped his arms and laid them over the dais' railing.

"Planet satellites are scanning us."

The surveillance tech snorted.

"As a sign of mercy, I will demonstrate a quarter of our might." The communications tech cut the feed. "Ships one, three, and five set cannons at thirty percent. Avoid hitting any major facilities."

No need for acknowledgement. His commanders knew their roles. He watched the weapon bays of the three ships glow blinding hot blue then unleash onto the planet. Pity aroused in him. Bursts of explosions littered the surface. There would be massive repair costs.

When it ended, he saw the channel waiting to be opened. He nodded to the tech.

"Stop. You've killed enough."

The commander gripped the rail in frustration. Queen Farin wanted Azrom to change how they conquered. He wanted to avoid bloodshed per her instructions. This was not the way.

I've already failed.

"I assure you, that was never our intention. We only wanted to make a contract with your planet for trade purposes. Why?" The commander seethed. "Why did you fire without negotiating first?"

"Negotiations?" The feed paused. "You demanded surrender. Not once did you convey room for talks."

The bridge went silent. They were right.

His wording caused the misconception. Words Azrom always used when taking over a planet. Instead of surrender, he needed to suggest a meeting. And then, if talks failed, proceed to conquer.

"My apologies." The commander lifted his head, loosening his grip. "We will compensate for the damage. With the situation now too far gone, we need to meet and discuss plans going forward."

"If that is what will stop you from destroying our home."

"You have my word." The commander placed both hands around his neck and massaged the back with his fingers. He waited for the feed to end and tilted his head to look at the ceiling. "What a travesty."

"Coordinates being sent." The communications tech turned his head towards him. "Do you want to send a report to the generals and the royal council?"

The commander winced.

"Let's hold off until after the talks."

He didn't want to see or hear the berating he would get from not only his mother, but the Empress herself.

I made a mistake.

On the opposite side of the enemy territory outskirts, Sars watched the debacle of Azrom taking control of the medium planet ahead. That race never had any tact, he mused. They always attack first, ask questions later. They mocked the Razznian spy network, not seeing its worth. Yet, their new queen saw it differently.

As an asset.

Sars ladmired his bridge crew and smiled with pride, exposing his fangs and split tongue. For this mission, he gathered his trusted soldiers, now promoted but still wanting to stay at his side. Even the young lieutenant, Prac, volunteered to come along.

I've become popular.

He smirked. Much to the general's chagrin.

Still some trust issues there.

"Set scanners for that second tiny planet on the edge."

Sars pointed to the yellow orb in the corner of the main viewport. "Try establishing communication," he said to his soldier.

"Oh! Are we showing Azrom how it's supposed to be done?" His second in command asked, letting his tongue slither out. "Rub it in their faces?"

"That's not my intention." Sars tapped a finger under his chin. "But not a bad idea."

"Any sign of the enemy swinging back around?" Beldur asked the scout leader.

"Nothing showing up. I think they may have fled for good."

"No." Prac came onto the bridge. "They're going to launch an attack on every alliance planet."

"They seem a tad bitter," Dolan, his navigator, laughed.

"Hmm. They do seem to hold a grudge." Sars added.

Something about the planet seemed familiar.

From the earlier scanners, he noticed regions with hot spots and realized they were ideal for refineries. The planet could be a satellite for mining Razznian ore to distribute on that side of the system. Cut down transport costs.

"Contact established." The soldier's eyelids became slits. "They sent a visual. Bringing it on-screen."

As the horrific image of the surface blazed across the width of the bridge, a voice came through.

"You can see we are not in any position to defend ourselves. What is it you want from us? The Boretkz have destroyed everything."

Sars' already thin lips pulled inward. So that's what the enemy call themselves. They finally had a name for the cur of five systems' existence. Seeing how much damage the enemy inflicted proved his point.

That tiny planet indeed had been used as a refinery.

He could see the yellowish smoke that coated the atmosphere coming from ruined machines.

"We have not come here for conquest." Sars nodded to the communications officer to broadcast his face. "Our race is known for mining ore. Your facilities looked promising."

"And now we are nothing. We no longer have the capacity to help you or our contracts."

"Don't be so sure." Sars straightened his posture. "I will make an appeal to our emperor to repair and resume operations. That would mean you must give up control and become a regency of the Razznian empire."

A long silence followed. He understood their misgivings.

To relinquish your home to outsiders was no easy decision. But, they had no choice at this junction. The feed returned without the images. A small creature with a round head and giant lidless eyes shining bright green replaced it. In contrast, were long arms that reached mid-thigh.

Sars' observation of the tiny race made it clear their physique's advantage. They could produce ten times more than any ordinary sized being.

"Will that include working without compensation?" The race's leader asked.

"Absolutely not. The only way for your kind to thrive is through revenue. It would do us no good to see you fall into debt."

Even Razznian miners were paid a living wage.

We're not that monstrous!

"Then we implore you to plead our case with your emperor. We would be forever in your debt." His head bowed forward and Sars nearly panicked that it would teeter over. When it stopped halfway and came back up, he sighed in relief. "For now, we must finish our recovery efforts."

"To show a sign of good faith, I'm sending a team to assist you. Please accept this token of compassion."

"We thank you. The only landing area still stable is on a plain in the north region. You will see it clearly as it has been wiped bare. We await their arrival."

The feed ended and Sars waved to the communications officer to sweep the surface with scanners. On screen they could all see the area in question. A large swath of land razed. Its surface the color of newly exposed flesh. A gaping wound left to heal on its own.

Sars almost felt bad for letting any ship land on it. As if it would be painful to the planet. His shoulders slumped.

The enemy made it harder for other empires to take over their system. And that was the point. To ruin it all so no one could reap the rewards they enjoyed.

We'll see about that.

☼ ☼ ☼

Being promoted meant having access to the docks closer to the palace. Sars looked out onto Razzna's surface in the tail end of recovery itself from the planet bomb's effects. All five trade federations cited Azrom for the incident. The Dreridians seethed for years, having to cover half the costs until they were reimbursed.

While the ship docked, he saw General Frit coming out the lift with his entourage of minions. Among them, the head of commerce. Good. That's who I need to hear this. The crew headed for the ramp as it extended. Joyous chatter erupted as they exited the ship. Home. Sars made a mental note to check on his offspring after the meeting.

"Commander Sars," General Frit came to stop a few feet from him. "I received your report. Good work finding such a gem in enemy territory."

"I aim to please the empire."

"Emperor Kraznan is eager to hear more."

"I would like to hear the details," the head of commerce said.

General Frit did an about face. Sars and his group followed him to the lift.

"I won't lie. I'm a bit envious."

No doubt.

Sars grinned.

Getting a step closer to the general made him hopeful.

The lift went through its zig zag maneuver through the palace until it reached the throne room. Its doors opened to the usual sight of scholars and state leaders moving about, keeping busy in the eyes of the emperor.

Lord Kraznan sat on his throne with two servants fanning him with giant leathery leaves. His massive tail swished across the floor beneath him.

"Ahh, Commander Sars. Welcome home."

"Greetings to you, my lord."

Sars and his men dropped to one knee and bowed their heads.

"Enough of that." Lord Kraznan waved a hand, gesturing for them to rise. "I hear you bring great news."

They stood and Sars stepped forward.

"I found a small planet perfect for refining our ore. They have agreed to fall under your rule and accept minimal compensation.

The head of commerce opened his tablet to scroll through his report. He tsked at the images.

"The enemy really doesn't leave much to chance, do they? The damage is severe."

"Is it salvageable?" The mining administrator asked.

"Of course. It will take more effort than normal."

The head of architecture leaned forward to speak.

"I propose we rebuild in stages. Get one region up and running, then use any funds generated for the next, and so on."

"A perfect remedy." The head of commerce turned to the emperor. "Do you agree, my lordship?"

"Yes. I like it." Lord Kraznan addressed Sars. "You will be the ambassador for them until I appoint a Regent."

"My lord?" General Z blurted in awe.

"We don't really need that planet for ourselves. I plan to give it to someone who can benefit from its location."

"Since we'd only ship ore there for processing, the finished product will ship to planets within the nearest trade organization. Which we do not have rights for yet." The head of commerce tapped his tablet's screen. "I've sent the requests already and should receive a reply by end of the next moon cycle."

"The Dreridians got ahead of us because they're a federation certified empire." Lord Kraznan's red eyes glowered. "What is the timeline for reconstruction?"

"If we start now," the head of architecture replied, "less than three years."

Gasps of surprise followed by elation filled the room.

"Commander Sars." General Frit glanced over. "Take some time off. Enjoy your family. You leave next moon for your new mission."

Sars and his men bowed their heads.

"I am grateful for the reprieve. Thank you."

"I expect more great things from you, Commander," Lord Kraznan bellowed.

"Of course, emperor."

Sars lifted his head and headed for the lift, his men in tow. Time for recreation and some downtime. He had a feeling his next mission would last longer than he liked.

☼ ☼ ☼

Sunset on the Dreridian home world brought dark hues of orange, blue, and purple. Civilians strolled the boardwalks offering evening entertainment while the factories continued their work. Commerce never slept.

From his office desk, Lord Pondur stared through the windows overlooking the industrial district. He sat in reverie, keeping himself calm before he opened the report waiting on the holoscreen across the room. He knew what it would say.

They're not even hiding it well! He chided the alliance.

Taking a deep breath, he averted his gaze from the soothing scenes of trade to the holoscreen and tapped the read icon on his virtual keypad.

The screen lit up with multiple pages cascaded diagonally. He scrolled through them until he found the summary. That should have popped up first. Already frustrated from working day, he cursed the officer in charge. His tea, now lukewarm in the cup beside him, didn't look enticing. Not wanting it to go to waste, he drained the delicate thing of its contents.

Now!

He speed read the summary.

How audacious of them!

Of course, he expected such a move from the other alliance leaders. A new territory ripe for the taking? Their pledges went out the window on that front. I can't blame them. Lord Pondur wanted to monopolize Dreridian stakes ahead of the others. It seemed Azrom and Razzna smelled it in the air.

His only consolation was Lassa not throwing their hat into the fray. And he understood why.

Lassians were not conquerors despite having the capability.

He went over the number of planets in the enemy's quadrant already under Dreridian rule compared to the ones snatched up by the others. Should I save one or two for Lassa? They were caught up in the enemy's first wave of destruction over a millennium ago. Spoils of the fight would be a nice gesture. Because Chardon would not think of taking revenge in that way.

His office door slid open for his general to enter. The officer had an air of authority with squared broad shoulders and straight posture, wearing the imperial uniform.

"Greetings, Lord Pondur." He gave a short bow of his head. "To what do I have the honor of assisting you with this evening?"

Lord Pondur pointed to the holoscreen. The general eased into one of the chairs with his back to the windows. His eyes roamed the summary and the pages behind it.

"They move fast. Do you want to deter them?"

"Slightly." Lord Pondur rested his head on two raised fingers. "Don't want to jeopardize our little coalition."

"I only see a problem regarding Azrom. They're being greedy."

"Yes. Definitely curtail their efforts. I have a feeling Queen Farin doesn't want too much scrutiny. She's trying her hand at it and will see the redundancy soon enough."

"Ahh. Her first taste at conquering a world."

Both snorted in amusement.

"I need this to be," Lord Pondur sighed, "handled delicately."

"If I may speak frankly."

"Proceed," Lord Pondur gestured with a wave of his hand.

"We've already procured the major trade planets in the region. The rest are merely satellite centers. I know our empire seeks dominion."

"Yet you feel we are stretched thin after so many millennia?"

"My apologies, your grace. I'm only looking at it from a military perspective."

"No, no." Lord Pondur waved it away. "You are correct." He ran a finger beneath his lower lip. "Hmm."

"I can have blockades set up in the uncharted areas ahead of the alliance forces. That way, as they patrol the systems, our presence will be known."

"Not very delicate."

"By no means hostile, either."

Lord Pondur thought for a bit. Would Azrom and Razzna see it as aggression? He knew the other races weren't a threat. A handful of planets added to their reigns meant nothing in Dreridian eyes. Insignificant. At the same time, he loved the idea of getting under Azrom's skin.

"I like it. Do it."

"As you command, your grace."

The general stood, using a talon to scratch an inch in a crag on his face. He gave another quick bow and exited the room.

Within minutes, Lord Graggor arrived and sat across from him at the desk. He slammed a bottle, bulbous at the base, and came to a skinny spout, onto the surface.

"I bring you a rare spirit from the neutral zone."

"Oh? Are we celebrating?"

"Of course." Lord Graggor lumbered over to the shelf of glassware and picked out two snifters. He came back and set them to the side while he opened the bottle. "Production has resumed on the enemy's home world. They do mostly assembly of goods, but it's a start."

He poured the glasses halfway and handed Lord Pondur one. They breathed in the liquor's aroma, closing their eyes.

"What interesting notes."

Lord Pondur took it away from his nose for a second, then sniffed it again. "Pungent, yet savory."

"Did I mention it is quite strong?"

"Good. I need that right now."

They took a sip and winced at the burn coursing down their throats.

Lord Graggor coughed.

"Definitely a sipping drink."

Lord Pondur felt his eyes widen more than they'd ever, causing his beady eyes to water.

He set the glass down and removed the handkerchief from his jacket to dab them.

"I'll have to take it slow. Sleep will be good tonight."

"I concur." Lord Graggor took another sip, rearing back at the sting. "I saw the general's proposal you greenlit."

"Is there any information you can't obtain within seconds?"

"I like to stay on top of events. Your assessment of Queen Farin may be dead on."

"She's young. I remember my first conquest."

Lord Graggor coughed in awe.

"Your grace, that was a messy affair."

"I still succeeded," he shrugged.

"True." Lord Graggor leaned back. "Are you still thinking of gifting Lassa with an enemy territory?"

"It's on my mind. The question is if Chardon will accept it."

"Speaking of Lassa. You read the reconnaissance report?"

"Hmm. Fascinating. The planet itself is sentient and not friendly to strangers."

"You can't really blame it after being invaded and stripped of their resources."

"I need negotiations to start so you can get access to the surface. The more data on that race, the better I can plan my next move."

He absentmindedly grabbed his glass and took a big sip, instantly regretting it. He clutched the front of his jacket and squeezed his eyes shut to ease the pain.

When it finished going down, he exhaled loudly.

"Lord Graggor," he gasped.

"Yes, your grace?"

"Next time, let's save the hard stuff for our leisure times."

"Of course, your grace. My apologies."

Lord Pondur recovered his austere demeanor and let his head fall back over the chair. Being a reigning monarch drained him some days. Yet, he wouldn't trade it for anything else. With competition on the rise, he felt a yearning to do more. What he really needed was a protégé. Someone he could mold into a leadership role.

Would you be interested? Lord Chardon?

CHAPTER TWO

Planet Wrangling

Sars' ship entered Nasfir airspace followed by two escort vessels. Their size less than a quarter of his. Babysitters courtesy of General Frit. Even as an ambassador, personally appointed by Emperor Kraznan, Sars felt the reptile had it out for him.

Trust me a little.

His men and he boarded the convoy ship accompanied by a magistrate, an accountant, and the head of commerce. He kept close watch on the salamander exuding an air of joy from traveling.

Most appointees never left Razzna unless deemed absolutely necessary. The fact that his race loved jetting around the galaxy raised many questions among others. Sars suppressed a grin. He would have to rein in the head of commerce's jubilance.

"Oh look." The head of commerce pointed to the palace as their ship approached. "Not very big is it?" He crossed his arms. "I guess they're more modest than us."

The palace didn't tower over everything else. It simply stood apart by its architecture. Where the other surrounding buildings were the same sized grey stone structures, the palace had a more gothic style. Its steepled roof had scalloped edges. The arched windows covered its face instead of rectangular ones.

Unimpressive.

Sars remembered Earth having similar buildings. They called them castles or manors in the older European regions of the planet. Many attached to forts. Encompassed by deadly moats.

Servants gathered at the entrance while soldiers scrambled in place to create a pathway to the platform landing that rose above a flight of steep stone stairs. Sars grimaced at those.

The planet's race had bipedal reptiles with some still sporting tails. None derived from snakes, only lizard types.

The convoy ship passed over the palace to land at the Southern ship docks behind it. Activity seemed low without any trade ships. Workers took their time locking down theirs, doing double checks since they had the time. Four delegates greeted his entourage at the end of the ramp as they exited the ship.

"Welcome to planet Nasfir," the first one bowed their head to Sars. "Our emperor is delighted to have you."

"Thank you." Sars gestured a hand towards his group. "I have brought two palace magistrates and Razzna's head of commerce." His gaze landed on him.

"I look forward to speaking with Emperor Xanic."

The head of commerce smiled.

"Please, this way."

The four turned around so Sars and his group could follow. They rode a lift down to the surface level where a transport waited. A sleek dark metal vehicle with bay windows for passengers to view the scenery. Plush purple velvet benches lined the inside.

"Well, this is quite decadent," a magistrates uttered in awe.

"Our species likes our creature comforts," the other added.

The transport lifted off when they settled in and sped towards the palace. They marveled at the lush terrain, in stark contrast with Razzna. After an hour, Sars spotted the line up at the entrance.

They've stood there all this time?

None seemed uncomfortable in the muted sun partially blocked by the buildings. Their cloaks and robes fluttered gently. Sars felt common. Like he didn't' reach their level of discipline. He glanced over and saw the rest of his party straightening themselves anyway they could.

The transport stopped at the start of the pathway and let them out. As they walked down, Sars noticed the silence and how still the welcoming line kept. A stark difference in obedience between Nasfir and Razzna. He couldn't put his finger on it.

Emperor Kraznan ruled with an iron fist and rewarded those who benefitted the empire.

Razznians had a level of fear towards their ruler. This feeling. An unadulterated one permeated the air. It intensified when the palace doors opened to the royal heirs flanking Emperor Xanic.

Sars had only seen images of the monarch. The closer he got, he realized his throat had tensed. Anxiety gripped him, causing his steps to slow.

Emperor Xanic's massive body bulged with muscles. His tail resembled that of a salamander only thicker and deadlier. A mane of dark brown hair flowed to his waist. His eyes made Sars pause. Green irises with vertically slitted pupils full of menace and power.

He had never felt anything like that from Emperor Kraznan. Some Razznian scholars cited Xanic's people as inferior to theirs. A splinter from the original. Sars begged to differ. That appeared to be a miscalculation by his observation.

A female and a younger male stood on each side of Emperor Xanic. Ahh! His empresses and their sons. All four exuded authority, yet an underlying fear lingered. When Sars and his party reached the platform to stand before them, they shrank inward.

Emperor Xanic towered over them by nearly a foot. The two empresses not much shorter with their sons equal to them. All had dark manes, the one son's cropped short above the shoulders.

"I hope you had a safe journey," Emperor Xanic greeted them. "The enemy still lurks the stars."

Sars had trouble swallowing, as if his mouth had dried up. He finally generated enough saliva and gave a forty-five-degree bow.

"It was uneventful, thanks to the alternative coordinates, so yes. We're appreciated them. The enemy can be sneaky."

"Let us relax. Then you'll me about this unexpected visit."

The royal family turned away. Sars noticed one empress had a tail, as did her son. They swished slowly beneath their gold and red brocaded robes across the platform. The other and her son did not. Wearing blue and gold to differentiate from their counterpart. Even from behind, they stood majestically.

A brush of wind hit Sars' backside as half of the soldiers broke ranks and flowed into a formation ahead of the emperor.

The same happened with servants.

He saw the rest turn and move up behind. An entire horde moving as one in a tight line down the great hall must have been a sight to see, Sars mused.

The head of commerce leaned towards him.

"I take it back." He eyed the fifty-foot ceiling. "Grandiose indeed."

Giant pillars thirty feet apart formed a row on both sides.

The only sound came from the soft thud of the soldiers' boots and the shuffling of servants' feet. Sars and his men could feel the unspoken rule of silence during the procession.

They came to a set of double doors that reached the ceiling. It took four soldiers to push it open. A throne room sprawled ahead of them. Sars' eyes calculated its measurement as identical to Emperor Kraznan's. Except it appeared three times its size due to the amount of natural light streaming in from the twenty-foot windows on three sides. Three of which sat behind the thrones on the raised dais.

Too bright!

Compared to Razzna's with its dark, cave like aesthetic, it felt austere yet inviting. Sheer flowy curtains drifted side to side from air coming through the open shutters. Regal.

Emperor Xanic and his empresses walked up the steps to their thrones. While they sat, their sons remained standing on each side of the dais. Servants handed out chalices of drink to them, then Sars's party. They carried a long table to the center and set it down so they could set their drinks on it.

"To the continuation of our species."

Emperor Xanic raised his chalice.

They raised theirs, repeating the toast. After everyone took a swallow, the servants at the throne took the chalices away from the royal family.

"Now." Emperor Xanic's gaze bore down on Sars' entourage. "Why has Kraznan sent you here?"

The way he said his name without the honorific made them flinch. As a relative, it was natural for him to do so.

Sars snapped out of his awe.

"As you know, we're traveling the enemy's territory to salvage planets damage by their wave of destruction."

"Yes. Razzna, Azrom, and a few other alliance races are out expanding their reach."

"There's one I assumed ambassadorship over. A small refinery planet. Its location is not ideal for our contracts. Emperor Kraznan would like to gift it to you."

"Is that so?" Emperor Xanic leaned forward to rest his chin on his fist. "A gift you say? And how does that benefit me? Taking over regency for a ruined world."

"It's not ruined. Razzna is funding their recovery."

"But it's not producing our goods. It's mining Razznian ore."

"Correct. You would get the revenue from contracts on this end of the system."

He saw a few heads of state halt their tasks and turned to him, then glanced up at Emperor Xanic. Tension filled the room. *Did I say something wrong?* He looked to the head of commerce. The reptile seemed disturbed by the reaction as well.

"Before you declare any flaws," the head of commerce raised his arms out as a gesture of peace, "please listen to the details."

"Continue." Emperor Xanic leaned further, his elbow dug into his thigh.

"Since we would only be transporting the raw ore to the planet, there would be no other business for us. The planet also needs funds to operate. Razzna only wants fifteen percent. The planet will receive thirty."

"Leaving fifty five percent," Emperor Xanic dropped his arm and sat back. "Am I to assume that is my share?"

"Correct, your eminence. That is part of the gift. Commander Sars will relinquish his ambassador title. You will now have a stake in Razznian ore."

"Hmm." Emperor Xanic's eyes narrowed.

A statesman near the bottom stepped out to the center.

"What is the catch? There is more to it than that, isn't there?"

"Not a catch. Only an adjustment after a certain period."

The magistrate nervously cleared his throat.

"It's still beneficial to you."

"Speak." Emperor Xanic's voice pierced through the room.

Sars found himself stiffen instantly.

"After fifty years, the split would go up to forty-five percent," the head of commerce replied.

"You'd still get forty percent revenue," the magistrate added.

The statesman looked to Emperor Xanic and nodded.

"So Razzna has decided to give us a piece of their monopoly." Emperor Xanic smirked. "How generous."

The other magistrate removed a tablet from under his robes. He brought up the document notarized by Emperor Kraznan.

"Will you accept this gift from our empire's lord and emperor?"

The statesman took the tablet from him and handed it up to the servant stationed in the middle of the steps. They then gave it to Emperor Xanic who scrutinized the document thoroughly before gesturing to another servant on the end. The servant rushed over, holding out a small slender metal block.

"I will accept." Emperor Xanic took the block, then tapped the acknowledgement icon on the screen. "I thank Razzna."

The servant retrieved the block as the tablet got passed back down to the magistrate.

"Transfer of power and ownership of planet Ektos is now complete." He returned the tablet to its hiding place.

Sars and his entourage gave Emperor Xanic a deep bow.

A scaly faced man in the background clapped his hands twice. Servants carrying platters of food flooded the room. More tables arrived, connecting to the first. After mere minutes, a large banquet had emerged. The royal family rose from their thrones to join Sars and his party.

The atmosphere became relaxed, though still a bit staunch. Sars tried to give a genuine smile as the food came around. A sudden thought hit him.

Emperor Xanic's planet was itself under Lassian regency. How would that work? The deed done, he mentally washed his hands of it.

I need a neutral zone.

Chardon lay in bed staring at the ceiling, reluctant to get up for the upcoming meeting. He covered his face with both hands and loudly exhaled. The stale breath drifted up his nostrils, its stench making him frown. His arms fell limp to his sides.

How should I handle all of this?

The hover lights in the ceiling's corners glowed dimly, casting shadows along the walls. He wasn't ready to have them any brighter for now. Thoughts of each planet under Lassa's regency swam in his mind. They had yet to conduct any real negotiations on how he would govern them. Merely an assessment of the worlds and what they offered in terms of trade.

His hands ran across the empty space beside him where Halfar once slept. No. I won't tap him for guidance yet. Everyone assumed he would do that instead of figuring it out for himself.

They still don't see me as a trustworthy leader!

Clenching his fists, he squeezed his eyes for a moment before letting out another deep breath. The Lassa issue was another wrinkle to deal with. Planet and being wise. First things first.

Chardon rose from the pillows and sat upright. The thin sleep robe pulled against his shoulders, forcing the neckline to rise. He focused on the time display above the door frame until his vision adjusted enough to see it. Twenty minutes until the meeting.

With a heavy sigh, he swung his legs over the edge of the bed and set his feet on the plush rug beneath. Unlike Halfar, who preferred an icy surface, Chardon needed warmth and comfort. Especially now. He glanced longingly at the giant basin set further in the room. No time for that. Sending a pulse of energy into the air, he brought the hover lights to a medium glow. Enough light to see clearly.

At the washing station, he pushed the robe from his shoulders and let it fall to the floor. Naked, he cleansed himself in silence, feeling a sense of loneliness. Halfar would usually do it for him. His hand halted running the wet cloth across his abdomen. He hadn't missed Halfar this much in a long time.

Focus!

Finished washing, he went to the wall on the other side.

A panel appeared when he pushed on it, opening to reveal shelves with neatly folded robes inside. He eyed the white and blue ensemble for official gatherings. Not wanting to deal with the ceremonial garb, he chose a plain sand colored one with a sleeveless cream cassock. Slipping brown leather sandals on his feet, he headed out of his chamber, leaving the hover lights on.

He walked down the hall towards the exit, contemplating how to get permission from the neutral zone. They were none too happy the last time his people held a meeting. A sting of rage pricked him. He pushed it out of his mind.

New beginnings, he chided himself.

Sunlight hit assaulted him square in the face, making him gasp in horror. He raised one hand to shield his eyes while the other gripped the front of his robes. The orb had gained a little more brightness over the years. He hadn't prepared for it.

I've turned into a vampire!

He smirked at the notion of the mythical Earth creatures.

Sounds of movement and children frolicking pounded his ears. New Lassa bustled with life. He dropped his hand, enduring the daylight. Council members already entered the temple up ahead. Their faces scrunched in frustration and ire at being awake so early.

Morning meal wasn't for another two hours. Chardon felt an inkling of sympathy, himself not wanting to be up.

Ganna spotted him and stopped at the doorway to wait for him. And there's another problem I have to deal with at some point. Chardon hung his head, letting a yawn escape, then met her gaze as he approached.

"You're not looking too rested, leader."

Ganna gave a crooked smile.

"You don't look too swift either," he countered.

"Well, there's so much to do these days and not enough hours."

They walked side by side into the temple. Servants came out of the conference room empty-handed. Good. Drinks were already on the table then.

Ganna moved to the side to let him in first and followed.

The council sat on cushions around the table pouring refreshments from the carafes lining the middle. Volma passed the one in her hand to him as he sat at the end. The liquid's pale green color let him know it was a fruit tea with energy herbs. They would all need it.

"I thank you all for coming at such short notice." He poured a glass and set it before him. "I know it's early, and you had more pressing matters."

"You're the one who ordered this daybreak meeting," the head of agriculture scoffed. "How come you're the most put out by it?"

"It's not like I wanted to." Chardon's eyes narrowed. "This is a necessary evil."

I want to go back to bed!

"So," Und sighed. "What are we discussing so urgently?"

"The planets under our regency."

Chardon took a sip and noticed the room go silent.

Volma's lips pressed thin. She nodded before taking a drink.

"Yes." She set her glass down. "Those need to be addressed.

"I want an official decree and meet in the neutral zone."

"Aren't we banned from the last time?" A council member asked with a raised brow.

"I surely hope not," another said.

"Then the first step is to negotiate the meeting place before sending out invites," Volma added. "With a guarantee from us not to repeat the former."

"We haven't finished their assessments yet," the first council member said.

"Our relentless fiends had a hand in that," Ganna interjected. "And we still aren't in the clear. They're making more messes across the five systems."

"Which is also why I want to get this all done." Chardon looked around the room at his council. These are the people keeping their race together. "We need to know how many of our allies are willing to assist us."

"If they deem themselves allies at all," another member said.

"Have you consulted this matter with Halfar?"

The man sneered. His back went rigid as the other members glared at him.

"Halfar may be knowledgeable," Chardon began, "but he is not the leader of our race." He tilted his head down as he stared at the man. "I am."

"Of course. My apologies, leader." The man lowered his head.

"Now, let's get this started so we don't miss morning meal with our families."

Und snorted, the corner of his mouth going askew.

"Then we need a plan of logistics to offer the neutral zone."

The discussion geared towards the details and Chardon listened intently. At one point, he caught Ganna's attention.

She nodded her approval.

☼ ☼ ☼

The neutral zone's monarch, Chancellor Eydine, stared at Chardon in the holoscreen. Her demeanor, so calm, so serene, somehow screamed with mistrust. A hint of hostility glimmered in her eyes. The ethereal, pale green glow surrounding her blocked out the backdrop of her chamber.

This won't be easy.

"Lord Chardon. It has been a long time since you graced me with your presence." Her lidless eyes blinked. "To what do I owe such a meeting?"

"I have a favor to ask." Chardon cleared his throat.

"Surely not to hold some clandestine event on my home-world? I'm certain you've learned your lesson."

"Please be assured," Chardon offered, "that was an incident not of my doing. This new venture is to bring my regency planets together as a united front. I guarantee…"

"You cannot guarantee nothing." Her glow shifted to a hint of orange. "I didn't take you as being naïve."

Chardon's eyes narrowed, glowing in his reflection on the screen. The monarch's demeanor turned defensive.

"I am not that, nor taking this lightly. For this galaxy to thrive, it needs the cooperation of every soul."

His head tilted down, making his stare menacing. "Or have you forgotten there is an enemy who cares not about your neutrality?"

"Careful, energy being."

The monarch pulsed out dark blue hues.

"Are you not one as well?"

The two stared each other down for what seemed like minutes. Finally, the monarch leaned back, blinking. Her colors reverted to a sheer peach.

"Fine. I will grant you this request. There must be safeguards in place. If another incident occurs, I shall use my full authority to annihilate all parties involved."

"That's over the top, even for you," Chardon snapped.

"Take it or find another neutral zone. Though I doubt they would be friendly."

"Why?" The monarch reared back at his venomous tone. "Why would you go so far over a trivial matter?" Chardon gritted his teeth and took a deep breath. "I have never treated your kind with malice."

A sadness washed over the monarch, followed by what Chardon could only describe as shame.

The two had their differences on regencies and show of force. Both their races had suffered in the beginning. Chardon felt Lassa's evolution would have geared towards technology like theirs if left alone. Instead, they became a race of fighters.

"My apologies, Lord Chardon. Halfar's deeds shadow yours. It's my misjudgment to assume you're alike in mind."

"He is no longer Supreme Ruler."

"Yet, he still maneuvers as one."

Chardon unclenched his fists, realizing he had done so.

"No. You're not basing it solely on him." He raised his chin in defiance. "Sestis."

The way the monarch's colors fluctuated before stabilizing proved him right.

"She was a nasty creature." The monarch tilted her head. "Are you certain her core is destroyed?"

"Absolutely."

The monarch let out a heavy sigh.

"When do you wish to schedule this meeting of rulers?"

"Soon. I need a united coalition to combat the enemy attacks."

Soldiers marched across the screen behind the monarch.

She glanced over her shoulder, then focused on him.

"We're preparing." Her colors shrugged? "As a precaution."

"And who hasn't learned their lesson?"

She smirked.

Or rather, that's how he interpreted the twitch of her mouth.

"Send me the details. I'll ensure you have the best conference."

"Thank you. I am forever grateful."

"Yes. You should be. And make sure your people behave."

The holoscreen winked out and Chardon slumped in relief.

Ganna entered the room, sliding into the seat beside him.

"It sounds like we are a go."

"Now, to get all the logistics in order and contact each leader."

"Don't forget to pick your delegates."

Chardon sighed as he sat straight.

Who did he want to accompany him? Volma was not due back for another year. He felt constantly utilizing Trinon was unfair. Jaron? With the whole Lassa mess? No. What did the meeting need? Innovative minds, with the common sense to not go off the deep end if things go awry. Ganna eyed him with suspicion.

But I do need her!

"I'd like your take on it, since you'll be one of said delegates."

Her eyes went wide.

"Ahh. I am honored." She gave a sheepish grin. "In that case, I have a list of people who may prove beneficial. We'll have to bring a few back from Lassa, of course."

Chardon nodded.

"I anticipated that."

"Barbon is more level-headed than Modas. Talas needs to be there, whether he wants to or not." She tapped her lower lip with a finger. "Maybe one or two cabinet members."

"I'll leave it to you then." Chardon stood. "I'm tired."

"It angered you to be compared to Halfar and Sestis."

He turned to her, astonished.

"You were listening the whole time?"

Ganna sat back in her seat, crossing her arms.

"She had no right to say that. Even I know better. At the same time," she locked eyes with him, "she wasn't wrong in making such an assessment."

"It's no secret I let Halfar advise me on occasion. He's the only one I know who has ruled an entire race with…"

"Fear and blood?" Ganna offered.

Chardon frowned at her.

"Order and strength."

"Oh, Chardon. Come now. He's a tyrant. It runs in his soul."

"Farin is his child. Do you still say that?"

Ganna uncrossed her arms and leaned forward.

"Without a doubt. You may want to take a closer look at your preceious offspring now Azrom's Queen."

Chardon started to protest then clamped his mouth shut. Excess saliva pooled within. While he moved to bring together his regent planets, his child held the reins on one of the most powerful races in the galaxy. It would be asinine to assume she hadn't changed to become a competent ruler.

"She's not like her father," Chardon finally said.

"No." Ganna rose from her seat. "She's far more ruthless."

They left the room. Chardon fell into a deep silence.

Is she? I hope not.

A Necessary Discussion

Even with only her father and Romnus present in the lounge room, Farin still felt outnumbered, insecure. Which she knew she had no reason to be. Yet one thing nagged her. The royal advisors secretly voiced a lack of confidence in her rule. Romnus sat slumped with a hand over his eyes. His drink only missing a few sips.

Still wearing the fur collared robe that blended with his hair, he resembled a massive beast filling every inch of the chair.

Well, he is, in a way. Her lips pressed into a tiny smile.

Her father sat next to him, all lean muscle in contrast. His erect posture as he brought the glass with swishing green liquid to his lips to take a decent swig conveyed a picture of royalty despite his true nature.

Another monster of Azrom.

The dark room, coated in blackness with only hover lights in the corners giving a soft ambience, added to her anxiety. She gathered the folds of her black robes and wrapped them around her legs. Romnus and her father also wore black. They all blended with the room like shadows.

She gripped her glass and tossed half its content down her throat. Relishing the burn. It never got easier to consume spirits.

"I would like to discuss a delicate matter," Farin blurted.

Halfar's brow raised as he set down his glass. Romnus didn't move. Instead, he let out a loud sigh while dropping his hand.

"And what does it entail?" Her father seemed dubious.

"As personal advisor to the Supreme Ruler, I thought you had already discussed this issue." Farin eyed Romnus. "But his behavior the past few moons tells me otherwise."

Both men stiffened as if insulted.

If that's how you feel. Farin shrugged inwardly.

Everyone could see Romnus falling into the complacency of a tyrant. Similar to her father during the height of his reign. No one wanted to move forward. They admonished the commander who followed her instructions, albeit after the fact. She defended him and refused to condemn her decision.

"Careful." Halfar's eyes narrowed. "I do this for the sake of Azrom and as a courtesy to family."

"I know this. Azrom appreciates your guidance." She turned her gaze to Romnus. "This is also for our people."

"What is it?" Romnus' gruff tone flared anger within her.

"This has bothered me for a long time. We have many planets under Azrom rule, yet we haven't tapped them for the battles with the enemy."

"What do you mean?" Halfar tilted his head. "They're fighting as well."

"Not all of them." Farin clenched her fists, then released them. "And many do so under duress."

"Because they were conquered," Romnus spat. "They have no choice but to comply with our demands."

Her father stared at her, confused.

"What do you mean by this? Which planets are not contributing to the fight? I have gone through every battalion and did not see any discrepancies."

"I know you have. But the numbers don't add up."

Romnus leaned forward.

"Are you saying, we're being lied to? Fed false numbers?"

"Something to that effect."

"That is unacceptable!" Romnus gritted his teeth. "How dare they when we spared their lives."

"Should I finish the job if that's the case," Halfar quipped.

"No!"

Farin slammed her fist on the table, shaking the carafe of liquor. Romnus and her father reared back in their seats, awestruck.

"That's part of the problem. Azrom conquered, leaving each

world in ruins with no help in recovery and demanded they fight under our umbrella."

"As they should, instead of being ungrateful," Romnus replied.

"The fact they weren't annihilated is testament to my restraint." Her father took another swig from his glass. "Why are you upset?"

Farin glanced at them back and forth. Her stomach felt queasy as her abs tightened. They're not listening! More accurately, they didn't care. The hover lights in the corners of the room flickered, causing the shadows to shift along the table.

"Are we not, as regents, responsible for their wellbeing?"

Her voice came barely above a whisper.

"What would we know of their way of life?" Romnus asked.

"My point exactly! We should have asked."

"Why would we after a conquest?" Halfar smirked.

"Would it not be in our best interest to know what strengths and weaknesses benefit Azrom?"

"All only need to obey our decrees," Romnus answered angrily.

"Is that the advice you gave my mother when Lassa acquired regency over those planets Sestis took?"

Her father locked eyes with her. The glint in his eyes swirled with indignation.

"I would if I thought your mother listened to me."

"So, you don't care if a rebellion erupts over our neglect?"

Halfar's eyes grew wide.

"If any of them rebel, we will wipe them from the cosmos."

Farin shot up from her seat, her hands clenched tight. Romnus and her father glanced at her, unsure expressions on their faces.

"And that is why Azrom is no longer held in high regard. I won't let our standing be tainted by your outdated views!"

"Don't you dare!" Halfar rose, furious. "Azrom reigns supreme!"

Romnus reached out and grabbed her wrists.

"Stop this. You're being naïve."

Farin wretched her arm from his grip, shocking him. Her father backed away, sensing the rage emitting from her.

"If neither of you are compelled to strengthen Azrom, I will do so on my own."

She left the room, and her half-downed glass of liquor. No time for drinking. Her mind needed to be clear for a remedy.

Farin retained her Perma grin while Lord Kel dismissed his attendants from his court chamber. She had arrived unannounced, having snuck through the palace side entrance. Taking out the two sentries alerted their counterparts further in of an intruder.

Sloppy.

It had been a while since she used her stealth.

After months of going through data, crunching numbers, and getting advice from higher scholars, she found a solution. The next obstacle would be luring the other houses to her side.

Lord Kel knew the moment she entered his palace signaled her discussion was only meant for him. He scrutinized her attire. A black bodysuit under a hooded black cloak secured at the waist. She pushed the hood off and let out a sigh while waiting for him to finish whispering orders to the last soldier for his palace guards to stand down. When the two royals were finally alone, Lord Kel glanced over his shoulder at her.

"Lady Farin," he drawled out her former title before smirking, then turned away. "What brings Azrom's queen to my palace in the early hours of dawn?"

Farin circled the plush chairs facing each other in the center of the room. She picked one, glancing around to take in the aesthetics.

Austere. Like Lord Kel. Intimidating. It conveyed Azrom might with minimal effort.

"I want to show Azrom our rule has meaning. That we're committed to change and the five systems opinions of us."

"Oh?" Lord Kel strolled along the wall of bookcases, tapping a finger on each shelf. "Is Romnus on board with this change?"

Farin's brow furrowed, a glow in her eyes pulsed.

"I'm not sure." She raised her head higher. "But there needs to be movement in the right direction."

Lord Kel turned towards her. "Romnus never wanted to rule. He's a mere a child. As is your father."

Yes. Compared to Lord Kel and Lady Hadris, her father and Romnus were underlings. Products of their own fathers who ruled with iron fists, engulfing Azrom in countless wars.

And the people resented them for it.

His gaze bore into her.

"You, in comparison, are an infant."

Farin's mouth down-turned.

"I hear what the masses call me."

"The infant queen," Lord Kel spat. "It shows a lack of respect for your reign." He paused halfway to the chairs. "What is it you wish to accomplish?"

Farin tried to hide her excitement mixed with apprehension.

"Azrom has conquered many worlds, correct?"

"That is true."

"Yet we did so without negotiated a plan for those planets."

Lord Kel's eyes widened in disgust as he scoffed.

"Why would we? Our might is our word. We take what we want." His expression soured. He glanced down, conflicted. "The enemy thinks the same way."

"Exactly! Azrom needs to change." She leaned forward. "We have all these worlds as potential allies. If one would ask, they would rather side with the enemy than remain under Azrom rule."

Lord Kel slid into the chair across from her.

"Then what do you propose we do?"

"I want to talk with those planets." She smiled. "In secret."

Lord Kel leaned back, staring at her for a moment. He ran his finger along the top of his chin.

"Nothing you do can ever be a secret, Queen Farin."

"That's where you come in."

"How so?" His eyes lit up with intrigue.

"Your house heads the compliance force for those planets. I want to go with one of the units on a special diplomatic mission."

"And how do you plan to pull this secret outing off?"

"I will go as one of your appointed soldiers from your inner circle. I need two royal scholars to accompany me."

"All inner guards under my supervision are male."

"I know."

She watched the solution hit him.

"Have you run this past our Supreme Ruler?"

Farin tilted her head. A twinge of fury make her eyes glow.

"I was unaware I needed my mate's permission to represent Azrom when I am Queen."

Lord Kel let his arm drop.

He burst out laughing, causing Farin to flinch as she reared back in her seat. He abruptly stopped, narrowing his eyes.

"You seem to rule more than Romnus. Which is no surprise. The blood of tyrants runs through your veins." He gave her a side glance. "Although not prone to go insane."

"Will you help me?"

Lord Kel grinned.

"Hmm. Sneak the queen off the planet incognito under Romnus' nose? I would gladly comply." He made a flourish with one hand. "My Queen."

"That seems too easy an answer."

His willingness made her uncertain. The other houses created an elaborate coup decades ago to murder her and Romnus. Now they all went about as if nothing happened. She couldn't pinpoint Lord Kel's agenda.

He stood and walked to his desk. Turning, he leaned against its edge.

"I'm interested to see how you sway the planet leaders to fight for Azrom of their own accord."

"And if I succeed?"

Farin rose from her seat to face him.

"Then you should have Romnus step back and name you Supreme Ruler."

Farin's insides tensed at the thought. Her goal never entailed stripping Romnus of his role. Lord Kel folded his arms while he stared unwaveringly at her. If that's what needs to be done.

She locked eyes with him.

"I agree."

"Good. I will have you join a unit that wouldn't blink an eye at your status. You can only have two mid-tier scholars. I won't risk the lives of my elites."

"That's fair. I appreciate your participation in Azrom's future."

Lord Kel glared at her, placing his hands on the desk.

"Don't thank me so quickly. If you don't succeed, I will be the first to denounce you."

Farin smiled. She understood the risks.

"I wouldn't have it any other way, Lord Kel."

Delaying the inevitable ended when Chardon saw Ganna's eyes flicker a different color than usual and Jaron attack a child in the fields for disobedience. Tackling either issue made his head hurt. Which order he chose didn't matter. He contemplated on the path of least resistance. Or at least, less demand for his patience.

He rocked back in the chair of his private office, hands clasped behind his head. The globe lights hovering above moved closer to him, casting shadows on the desk. His robe sleeves slid down to his elbows, bringing awareness to his lightly bronzed skin.

Chardon stared at his toned arms. He volunteered in the fields often to gauge how his people felt about their lives and his leadership. Lately, the consensus included fixing the two issues at hand. Jaron had become a menace whenever Lassa to take over.

And Ganna.

Well, that messy situation needed to be handled delicately.

He let out a loud sigh and sat straight, slapping his arms on the desk, stretching them across. A pair of legs in the doorway startled him to push back into his chair. His eyes glowed electric blue as he seethed.

"Why'd you not say anything? You scared the shit outta' me!"

Talas smirked, his body leaning against the frame as if he were in a photoshoot.

"Such harsh Earth language." He grinned. "I was admiring your struggle."

"My?" Chardon frowned.

"I always know what you're thinking, leader."

"Shut up. I'm not that transparent."

Chardon rose, fixing his sleeves.

"If you say so."

Talas pushed off the frame.

"I come bearing a remedy on one of your dilemmas."

"Why do I feel whatever you suggest I won't like?"

"Hear me out."

Chardon rested his hands on the desk to hold his weight. He envied how much talent for strategy Talas wielded. It frustrated him having to rely on him and Jaron for complex decisions. Then again, that was the whole point of leaders having a cabinet of experts.

They couldn't do it all alone.

I certainly can't.

Talas stopped in front of him on the other side of the desk.

"We need to find a vessel for this Lassa." He locked eyes with Chardon. "They are no longer a key part of our home. What lies within Jaron has its own core and personality nurtured through their life experiences."

"That's true. There's no way to integrate with Lassa itself."

"Lassa doesn't want..." Talas struggled to find the right term. "Them, it, her." He waved away the rest. "You know what I mean."

Chardon winced at the brutality of it. The being known as Lassa had evolved to the point of separating themselves from the planet's core instead of continuing as an extension of its will.

"And where would we find this new vessel?" Chardon slid his hands off the desk. "And do we demand they call themselves something else?"

"Absolutely!" Talas exclaimed, his fury visible. "I refuse to call them that after my connection with our homeworld." He stopped, took a deep breath, and exhaled slowly. "As for a vessel."

Chardon's eyes widened, realizing what Talas would suggest.

"I don't think we've done that in over a millennium!"

"That doesn't mean we don't know how. She does."

"Who is another problem I must deal with."

"Two birds, one stone?" Talas shrugged.

"Ugh!" Chardon placed a hand on his stomach.

"You feel that way but this has given you a decision."

"Yeah, I know. Still." Chardon winced as he bent over. "It makes me sick."

"If Halfar were here, I'd joke about you being knocked up."

Chardon stood straight, dropping his arms.

"Really? That's a nasty Earth saying too."

A golden glow pulsed in his eyes.

"Oh stop being so dramatic."

"Who?" The audacity coming from Talas almost made him laugh. In truth, he felt a bit insulted. "You're not serious?"

"Huh?" Talas turned away. "I may exaggerate on occasion but you're a walking ball of emotion. Quick to act on whatever mood comes out."

"What made me nauseous…"

"I know why." Talas walked off. "She does the same to me."

☼ ☼ ☼

Medical workers rushed around the bay handling patients in their stations. Only a few dozen laid in recovery pods. From the digital readouts on the ends of them, most were minor injuries. Nothing dire. Chardon felt relieved.

He headed towards the second wing, where they treated more serious conditions. Those patients came from the battlefields.

As part of the alliance forces, New Lassa couldn't get out of reporting for front line duty. Lord Pondur made it a condition from the start when he delegated Talas and Jaron to assist. The enemy so far showed no signs of backing down.

He reached the end of the wing and stood at a door with no keypad or console to open it. Instead, he had to wait for the person on the other side. After a minute, it receded into the wall and shifted to the side.

"Hurry in," Ganna called out. "I'm in the process of something."

Chardon went into the secret lab. The door sealed behind him.

He glanced over at the cryochamber sitting far back on his right. Where Ganna experimented on Talas. Stopping himself from being reminded, Chardon approached Ganna from behind.

Multiple holoscreens overlapped each other above her as she tapped icons with lightning speed on the virtual console on her desk. An enormous 5D image of what looked like a corrupted core spin in slow motion on a white platform in the center of the room.

"What in all of Lassa are you developing now?" He dreaded the answer the moment he asked. "I hope it's not detrimental to us."

"Of course not!" Ganna snapped without looking up. "If anything, it can very well solve one of our major problems." This time, she turned her head to look over her shoulder at him. "That issue," she emphasized the first word.

"What a coincidence." Chardon stood beside her. "I came to ask about an intriguing proposal."

"I won't be pleased, will I?" Ganna paused the calculations on the screen directly before her and rose to face him. "You must want something in return."

"Always." Chardon glared. "I still don't trust you. Not fully."

"Understandable." She crossed her arms. "What is it?"

"You're already doing it. Though I don't know why you started."

"Ahh. Well, I counted the cores without vessels. It saddened me to think of how many are lost to us."

Chardon nearly choked on rage and disbelief.

"Don't you dare pretend to care about those lost souls!"

"What? I'm being sincere!" Ganna retorted.

"You only want to know if you can create new vessels!"

"Everything I do is for the love of Lassa and our race!"

"You only care about science!"

Ganna's expression turned to pure rage. She grabbed the front of Chardon's robe and pulled him to her.

"And that nasty personality is part of why we don't respect you," she sneered, speaking slowly. "You're a shitty leader."

Chardon's eyes glowed bright yellow. His aura shimmered.

"Take your hands off me," he said quietly.

Ganna shoved him away from her and stepped back.

That's when he noticed the tears smeared on her face.

I hurt her feelings? Nonsense! Then his words hit him. Oh. He raised a hand, palm out, to her.

She stepped further away from him.

"I–I'm sorry. Ganna." He reached out to her. "Please. I don't know why I said those things. They just came out."

"You meant every word."

Chardon grabbed her face, forcing her to look at him.

"We need to fix our relationship. I know that. You don't make it any easier."

Ganna glanced to the side before her hands pushed him off.

"Neither do you."

"Is there any progress?" Chardon walked to the nearest chair by the platform and plopped in it. "A timeline would be great."

"In a hurry?" Ganna went back to her station.

"Aren't you?"

"It's true, Jaron has been insufferable since Lassa awakened."

"Now you're being nice?"

"Hmph. So." She stared intently. "What do you want in return?"

Chardon calmed himself before replying.

"I want you to remove your father's core from yours."

Ganna sat still for a long time. Chardon couldn't tell what she was thinking. Her face appeared blank, as if her core had been ripped out. Then her eyes turned steely.

"No."

"It's not a request." Ganna again stared blankly at him. "For this process to be completed successfully, we need him in entirety. Not a fragment you keep hidden and tap into when you get stuck."

"I am fully capable of…"

"No, you're not."

"How could you…" Ganna leaned forward, ready to launch from her chair.

Chardon pointed to the image on the platform, then to the holoscreens.

"The proof is right there. You don't know how to decipher it all." He watched her expression crumble. "I wouldn't ask if I didn't think it necessary."

"It's all I have," Ganna whispered. The sadness poured from her. "This." She placed a hand on her solar plexus. "Is all that I have left of him."

"But you're wrong." Chardon watched her head snap up in surprise. "Once it's placed in a vessel, the core will heal over time."

Her eyes widened.

More tears streamed down Ganna's face as she clutched the front of her robe. He didn't try to console her. Instead, he watched her cry. It fascinated and terrified him all at once. Seeing her like that confirmed his suspicions.

It also made him aware how right she had been.

I really am a shitty leader.

Resurrections

That old familiar rage welled up inside Ganna. Her father's core rebelled, frustrated with her failures and being kept locked away. She only tapped into him when the need seemed dire. No apology could atone for her sins.

Ganna lied to Chardon when he asked if there were any vessels compatible with her father's. She had buried his fragments retrieved from the battlefield. Unlike Mandra, his core was intact. He could be regenerated.

She never found the courage to do so out of selfishness. With him gone, she rose in status. Her greatest accomplishments came when she used his knowledge instead of working it out on her own.

She felt like a fraud.

His damaged vessel lay in the regeneration cryochamber. Skin stretched from the armless right shoulder reached over to connect with the right side of his face. The other half gone. Leaving a wide gap between the remains of the neck and clavicle. She assembled the rest in a fashion that, when fused, would resemble a body.

His core pulsed in her hands.

No one assisted her in the extraction. She had locked herself inside her lab and endured the excruciating pain alone. No one heard her screams.

None cared. She imagined her enemies relishing in her pain.

My enemies. Were they?

They did threaten to wring her neck at every turn.

Her weakened body started to slump. No! She corrected her posture, then with hands shaking with fatigue, slowly lowered the core into the fragments.

Tendrils of veins, skin, and tissue inched towards it, wrapping around as they made contact.

"I'm sorry," she whispered. "I know I shouldn't have done it."

She wiped the tears stinging her eyes, thankful no one would see her in such a state. Weakness.

A trait many loved to take advantage of.

The thought of her father coming back terrified her.

Would he be angrier for being trapped? Would he forgive her?

Ganna slid to the floor and stretched out. She was too tired to make it to the other cryochamber. When her eyes closed, she went into the worse sleep of her life.

Banging jolted Ganna from her awful slumber. She abruptly sat up in a panic, hitting her head under the cryochamber.

"Lassa's light!" She held the top of her head as she used one hand to pull herself up. "I'm coming." The soundproof lab made her words unheard and meaningless.

She pressed her palm against her temple and headed for the door's keypad. It slid open right as Chardon raised a fist to strike. Talas stood next to him, looking disinterested as usual.

"What is the meaning of this?" Ganna asked. "All that racket, for what?"

Chardon stared at her. His expression went pale. Talas finally looked over at her and stepped back.

"What have you done?" Chardon gasped. Then he grabbed her by the shoulders and shoved her into the lab. Talas followed, making sure the door sealed.

"Why are you angry?" Ganna shouted. "Unhand me!"

Talas glanced over at the cryochamber. His eyes narrowed.

"Did you do this without assistance?"

His venomous tone puzzled her.

She wrenched herself from Chardon's grasp.

"Of course I did! Why would I let anyone help me?" Chardon stepped towards her. She backed away. "Don't touch me!"

"The procedure itself requires…" Chardon glared at her. "Why did you do this without letting us know?"

"Why? So you could laugh it up at my expense? Give you a good show to tell everyone afterwards?"

The way Chardon and Talas' eyes widened in horror made her almost regret her words.

I'm not wrong!

Talas was on her before Chardon's hands reached her. He got so close, their lips nearly touched.

"Don't you ever assume something so disgusting," he seethed. "We may not trust you at times and yes, we've joked about killing you. But that's all they have ever been."

"Liar," Ganna breathed. "All of you only want to see me hurt."

Her body faltered. Talas went to catch her, but she reared from him, falling into the wall behind her. She struggled to get on her feet and ended up on her side. Turning over, she caught her reflection in the glass panel separating her workstation from the platform.

Ganna squeezed her eyes shut, not wanting to see anymore.

Her hair had turned completely white, the curls loosened. Pale shiny skin glowed as if the life-force within had diminished.

Which it had.

Talas tried to pry her off the floor. She weakly fought, slamming her fist on the floor whenever he got his under her.

"Enough!" Chardon bent down to help Talas get her up. "Stop being difficult!"

They dragged her out of the lab and into the main medical bay area. The technicians watched in awe at her. Chardon went to a group standing by the edge of the critical ward.

"I need you to put her down once we get her into a chamber and make sure she's sedated for the next few days."

"Yes, leader."

Ganna fought back tears as she cried out.

"You can't do this to me! I need to monitor my projects! I need to see…"

The way the technician's gaze bore into her let Ganna know she would not be treated kindly. As if knowing her thoughts, Chardon addressed them.

"If I hear about anyone mistreating or not giving her proper care, I will rain vengeance down on whoever it is."

That startled Ganna, which allowed Talas to sling her over his shoulder like a sack. He delivered her into the nearest chamber by leaning over to let her fall. Her body landed with a soft thud. The technicians acted quickly, activating it as they stripped off her robes. Too weak to fight anymore, she let the sedative put her to sleep.

This time, she dreamed of nothing.

Talas stood in the doorway of Ganna's secret lab. Chardon made sure no one had access to the area and deactivated the seal. He watched the blurred movement inside the frosted over cryochamber.

Mercan.

When Chardon told him what he asked of Ganna, that wasn't part of the plan he had in mind. He had no idea she kept his core hidden inside her, tapping his knowledge.

How insidious!

He never liked the man. For good reason.

Chardon came to stand beside him. Talas glared at him.

"I know."

Chardon leaned against the other side of the doorway.

"Do you? That's not the deal, Chardon."

"It'll work out. Things are different now. He'll have to adjust like we did."

"Where do you think Ganna got her personality?"

Chardon grimaced, wiping his face with one hand.

"Well, it's done now. We have to wait and see."

"If he goes off the rails, I'll end him myself," Talas replied vehemently.

They both focused on the regeneration chamber. Ganna would be back on her feet in a few days. And Mercan would rise again in under a few months.

Wait and see, indeed. Chardon felt a sense of dread.

And rightly so.

Chardon grimaced thinking about Ganna's change. She had let herself age to convey wisdom, pulling from her father. Now she had reverted to her youthful features. It dawned on him that her core's original state stalled when she assimilated Mercan's into her.

Seeing a young Ganna didn't sit well with him. Her demeanor even appeared childlike. Shaking his head, he turned around to leave. Talas blocked his way, arms crossed.

"I feel the same. It's unnerving." He dropped his arms and went towards the door ahead of Chardon. "She's almost doable."

Chardon went pale. They all joked about Ganna not having a mate. None of them thought anyone would ever want her.

"Come. We have work to do." Talas waved him along.

Ganna's body needed to rest for longer, to the detriment of New Lassa, throwing it into chaos. They found out how much they relied on her.

☼ ☼ ☼

Six weeks passed. Mercan's cryochamber beeped, signaling its cycle complete. Frost on the inside turned to tiny dew drops along the glass while chilled exhaust shot from vents underneath. A soft white glow emitted from the edges. Its shield popped open and receded into a slot at the foot of the chamber. Overhead lights flickered to life, bringing a harsh brightness.

Mercan lay fully regenerated, squeezing his eyes shut until they adjusted. He stared at the ceiling while he wiggled his fingers and toes, tensed his muscles, and moved his jaw. Everything seemed to work as intended. Satisfied, he slowly rose to a sitting position.

Scanning the lab, he caught sight of the workstations. Hmm? The left side of the chamber slid down to allow him to swing his legs out. He stood stark naked, unperturbed by the cold air hitting him. After a quick walk around, he found the bin with fresh robes.

Dressed, he went to the nearest station and began tapping on icons. It didn't take long for him to crack Ganna's security codes. They resembled his own.

Stupid child.

He went through multiple files until he found one labeled new awakened protocol. Opening it up, he settled into the chair and brought himself up to speed on the events since he supposedly died. And when he was done, he left from the hidden door that led to the outside. Time to explore.

Chardon stopped dead in his tracks as he entered Ganna's lab to find the cryochamber empty. Talas and Hon came up behind him and did the same.

"When did he awaken?" Chardon cried out in a panic.

"More importantly, where did he go?" Talas went past him to the active workstation. "It seems he got the update."

"Then I know exactly what he's doing, cause I did the same," Hon said. "I wanted to 'see' everything in those files. To decide whether I believed it or not."

"We can't have him running around just…" Talas sighed.

"I did," Hon snorted.

"And you shouldn't have been allowed either!" Talas snapped.

Chardon looked around the lab.

"How did he get out? None of the medical workers or technicians saw anyone come from this direction."

"Oh." Hon smirked. He pointed to the solid wall on the far end of the lab. "There's a secret door that goes out into the fields."

Chardon's eyes went wide, then narrowed angrily.

"She always has some other thing up her sleeve."

"You're surprised?" Talas and Hon replied.

He rolled his eyes sideways.

"Not particularly."

"You should go find him." Hon turned back to the lab doors. "He could be up to anything at this point."

"Where are you going?" Chardon snapped. "You're supposed to help us find some clues for Jaron."

Hon shook his head.

"That ship has sailed now that Mercan is awake. I have more important things to attend."

"You just want to stalk Mota and laze around all day."

Talas pursed his lips.

"You are correct." Hon waved at them and left.

"So." Talas stood akimbo, with a defeated expression. "How do you want to handle him? That arrogant piece of shit will look down on all of us."

"I have no choice."

Chardon scratched the side of his head.

"If he tries to buck my authority, I'll have to show him reason."

They left the way they came, not knowing how to activate the hidden door, and Hon not divulging the trick. Chardon felt a new sense of dread. With Ganna still under, the planet lacked a sense of productivity. He never knew how much that woman coordinated daily. The logistics alone made him feel faint.

Ganna proved worthier than expected.

And Chardon hated that.

Mercan watched the fieldworkers toil under a sun not bright enough. Sunset had begun, casting orange and purple on the thin clouds. Strands of his jet-black hair with a wide streak of white on one side billowed gently in the slight evening breeze. He took a few slow breaths, tasting the air.

New Lassa.

The tragedy of it all angered him. Chardon. A descendant of that thing calling itself Lassa. He had long written them off, the planet none too happy with their decisions as the centuries went on.

And now there are a million new wrinkles to deal with. An old enemy resurfacing. Lassa doing a bait and switch with vessels and cores assisted by his daughter.

"So much potential, yet you squander it. For what? And who?"

He shielded his eyes from the sun lowering into his line of sight. Tension moved through him. He turned around to see a group of people scanning the area.

Ahh! They're searching for me.

Not ready to greet Lassa's new leadership faction, he returned to the lab.

Once inside, he stared at the main door with amusement. Grinning, he reprogrammed, then sealed it.

With the lab all to himself, he brought up the 5D hologram of the core matrix. The soft white glow made the front of his hair an electric blue.

One thing, he agreed.

Getting Lassa out of Jaron was top priority.

Something nagged at Chardon as the search yielded no results. The way Mercan avoided being caught for nearly an entire day meant he had indeed mapped out the planet in its entirety. He read in the records how intelligent, and borderline diabolical, the man could be.

He's back at the lab!

Chardon hustled back, tapping Talas on the shoulder as he passed him. Talas broke off his conversation with a searcher and followed. They reached the lab door and stared at it. Chardon tried the access code he had created. It denied him.

"I warned you." Talas shook his head, placing a hand on his sword's hilt.

"Don't you dare," Chardon chided him, glancing at his hand.

"Only if he provokes me."

"Not even then!" Chardon pressed the commlink icon. "Unseal this door."

Nothing happened for what seemed like a minute.

When it finally slid open, they found Mercan leaning on Ganna's workstation, gripping the edge underhanded.

Mercan turned his head sideways towards them.

"You must be Chardon. Lassa's incompetent leader." Rainbow shimmers enveloped Chardon. "Not too composed either."

"How about not antagonizing people when you first meet them?" Talas' hand never left the hilt. "Or do you need to be shown manners?"

"Laxis." Mercan frowned. "I see you haven't changed much. Despite spawning with an energy user."

"Being a father didn't make you better Lassian," Talas retorted.

"No." Mercan rose from the desk. "It did give me insight on rearing other beings. That failure of a daughter perplexes me."

The shimmers pulsed. Chardon closed his eyes to calm down. They subsided.

"Ganna is far from a failure." Chardon clenched his fists at his thighs. "She's an important asset to our race. She designs the new technologies in our battles and provides spiritual guidance."

Mercan gave them a dubious stare.

Talas' lips turned inward.

"Spiritual guidance?" He stared at Chardon. "From whom and by what reasoning?"

Chardon struggled to answer.

"There was need. Ganna filled it. A self-appointment."

Mercan appeared horrified.

"As much as I deem myself of higher standard than most, I have never claimed to be some vassal of enlightenment."

Talas let out a forced laugh. He released his hilt and bent over to let out the rest. Chardon exhaled through his nose, his lips tight. Hearing it out loud made him realize how deranged it sounded.

"Where is she?" Mercan stepped forward. "Lead the way."

They snaked through the medical bay and stopped at Ganna's cryochamber. Even with heavy frost on the inside, they could see her hair had returned to their silver curls.

"At least she looks like herself again," Talas said. "I'm not sure I could take her looking the way she did before."

"I almost felt sorry for her," Chardon blurted, then regretted it. "I do, regardless."

"Oh? Please, the details," Mercan asked.

"Her hair turned white and nearly straight," Talas replied.

"So she brought herself to the brink of death." Mercan stared up. "Interesting. Such a selfless act." His eyes narrowed. "She must have felt guilty."

The way his demeanor shifted to something almost evil made Chardon move away from him. Talas gave him a side eye glance. That's when he understood. Mercan could prove dangerous.

"Can you wake her? There's no signs of distress, yet she sleeps."

Mercan stared at the cryochamber, leaning over to peer inside.

"Yes, daughter. Why are you sleeping when we have so much work to do? I won't let you skirt from this." He stood and turned to Chardon. "When she wakes up, let's have a chat, shall we?"

Talas glared at him.

Chardon could only imagine what questions the creator of manbeasts wanted to ask him.

News of Mercan's return spread quickly. Many mixed feelings, formed from those already accustomed to Ganna's lead. Tension ran high in the manbeasts' villages. Jaron paced atop a hill wearing her cabinet robes, letting the hems sweep the ground. Modas stayed near the bottom.

Jaron needed to clear her head before the emergency meeting Chardon called. She knew what its agenda entailed. The thought of seeing Mercan again made the Lassa part of her seethe. So much history of bad blood between them made it nearly impossible to reconcile their differences.

Lassa's hateful thoughts swirling inside her were toxic. Jaron stopped pacing and stared at the horizon. She got her fill before Lassa, straining to take over, broke through. Modas felt the shift and leaped up to confront them.

"Why are you coming out now?" Modas demanded.

"Because I have things to say," Jaron turned, smiling sweetly.

Modas stepped back, one forearm covering his mouth.

"No one wants to hear your sorry excuses."

Jaron's eyes glowed white hot in a flash as she walked past him.

"I have every right to voice my concerns."

Their merging proved incomplete, leaving the dual personalities to battle for dominance. On the surface, it appeared to have worked. Jaron's part of the core constantly rebelled.

They reached the common center's entrance with Modas close behind. He usually accompanied Chardon. As Jaron's mate, he watched over her more. A blessing granted with caution.

Hmph! That silly creature.

The conference room felt stuffy. Every cabinet member sat drinking their morning ade while engaging in small talk. They stopped to stare at Jaron as she entered. Modas went to the cushion farther back in the corner. Jaron and Mercan locked eyes. An empty cushion lay directly across from him. She wondered if Chardon did it on purpose.

As she settled into position, Mercan raised his glass and sipped slowly, not breaking his gaze. She saw his contempt and smirked, closing her eyes out of spite.

"Now that we're all here," Chardon began. "Let's get started." He extended a hand towards Mercan. "One of our originators has been restored. If you did not know, Mercan is Ganna's father and the creator of our manbeasts."

Soft hisses erupted. Some members glared her way.

Ahh. They think we're all broken beings.

Ganna sat still. Taking a good look at her, Jaron concluded the rumors to be true. Her rude awakening left her angry and weakened. No longer the top dog. Jaron stifled a snicker. You deserve that! It stirred in her other half. Pity? That's right. Everyone tried to get along and understand Ganna the past few decades. Seeing her shrink in defeat made them uncomfortable.

Mercan placed a data fob on the table. A hologram of New Lassa appeared in the center. Multiple screens popped up around it.

"I've gone through all the archives spanning the last millennium since my demise. Our race's advancements are slow." He glanced around the room. "I am disappointed and disgusted, to say the least."

The atmosphere in the room turned hostile. Mercan couldn't care less. He raised a hand towards Chardon.

"Why was any of this allowed? You call yourselves a cabinet, yet none of you took measures to rein your supposed leader in from destruction."

"How dare you blame this on us?" One member slammed their fist on the table. "We voiced our concerns. In the end, it was our leader's decision."

Nods all around.

Jaron also felt they could have done more to stop Chardon. Are they in denial? She caught Mercan's eye.

"All you've done is repeat a horrendous cycle that began with the embodiment of Lassa." He pointed to Jaron. "You should have found a way to stop this. Instead, you spawned inferior descendants to carry on your agenda."

"Such big words from a scientist with no moral compass and lacks something."

"Oh? I see the divide in species is still intact." Mercan glanced back at Modas. "I'm disturbed by the manbeasts' evolution. How could you let them devolve to the point of revolution? Did you not think to modify them? It doesn't matter that they can reproduce to sustain their numbers."

"You don't get to judge us!" Jaron spat. "We managed to thrive all this time without your input. You're simply jealous that your daughter may have surpassed you."

"I beg to differ." Mercan's eyes glowed bright orange, causing some to gasp while others leaned away in fear. "I'm not the only one judging our race. This farce at trying not to be a superpower has gone on too long." He turned to Chardon. "Are we set to dominate the galaxy or tuck in our tails and hide? Yet again."

The room fell silent. Jaron clenched her fists. She saw Ganna slumped on her cushion like a child after being chastised. I don't like this! Everyone appeared tense, not saying anything to counter Mercan's claims.

"This." Mercan used the virtual keys to zoom in on the vortices for Lassa and New Lassa. "What purpose does this serve? We are capable of defending ourselves, so why create something like this to deter others from entering our space?"

"Why should we allow potential enemies access?" Talas asked. "You say those pose no reason. You're wrong."

"Tell me. Does only Lassian vessels gain access?"

"Yes," Ganna finally spoke. "Non Lassian vessels must travel to a checkpoint that then designates it temporarily as ours."

"That's unnecessary and tedious."

"It's the remedy I came up with to keep our people safe!"

Ganna gritted her teeth.

"Calm down, child. I merely…"

"I am not a child!" Ganna rose from her cushion.

"Sit down." Mercan glared at her. "We are not finished."

The way he commanded the room gave Jaron chills. She had always thought of Mercan as a tool to be used. It irked her when he did things outside of her purview. Now she understood how much she underestimated him. Staring at the data displayed in the center, it became clear. He had indeed gotten up to speed.

The meeting lasted five hours, with two mini breaks in between. Evening meal was only three hours away by the time they adjourned. Mercan watched Jaron pretending not to pay attention as the room cleared. Chardon, Talas, Modas, Ganna, her, and himself remained.

"Now that we're alone." Mercan templed his fingers in his lap. "Let's discuss the other rotten dilemma in our midst."

Jaron's head snapped up, her face scrunched in anger.

"Maybe not word it as such?" Chardon admonished him.

"Oh, it feels accurate to me," Talas replied.

Modas seemed unsure how to react. Mercan could tell he wanted to defend his mate's honor, yet knew he was right.

"You want her back, don't you?" He asked Modas.

Jaron tilted her head.

"He already has his mate." She placed a hand on her bosom, "in me."

"Number one, that vessel isn't yours." Talas restrained himself from yelling. "Second, Jaron is not you, and vice versa." His gaze deepened. "Get out of her body."

"But you forget." Jaron shrugged, raising her hands at her sides. "I no longer have a vessel." Her eyes narrowed. "And I won't be put in some random one to make you all feel better."

"Oh, that won't be necessary. Will it, daughter?"

Ganna pursed her lips.

"Hon inherited your traits and essence. We only need to copy it and create a new vessel identical to your old one."

Mercan saw Jaron's face turn pale.

Her eyes widened in disbelief. No, horror. They won't let that body go. He noticed early on Lassa's obsession with Mandra. To know she was gone forever broke them.

"This is not up for debate." Mercan stood. "You will relinquish Mandra's vessel to Jaron and get yours back."

"Never." Jaron seethed. Electricity flowed through the room as blue light crackled around her. "You'll have to take me first."

"Stop this madness!" Chardon cried out.

"My beloved, make her stop!" Modas pleaded.

Mercan moved forward as she unleashed a ball of energy nearly a foot in diameter.

"Alright. If that's what you want." Mercan brought up a shield that blocked the energy, forcing it to concave around. It hit the far wall, blasting it completely out. He got within inches of her, catching the injection gun Ganna tossed to him. "I guess we'll have to force you out."

He struck the side of her neck and pushed the button that administered the drug. Jaron faltered, her body swaying awkwardly, as if it didn't know which way to go. Her eyes rolled up in their sockets as foamy drool oozed from her mouth. Mercan used a finger to nudge her to the side. She fell to the floor with a thud.

"That was a bit much though," Talas said as he went over to check her vitals. Ganna knelt on the other side of her and did the same. "You could have just hit her."

"Really?" Mercan glanced over his shoulder at Modas. "You think so?"

Talas grimaced. "Maybe not."

"She's down. We can start the procedure when you're ready." Ganna stood.

"Can we force them to change their name too?" Talas asked.

"It's not a matter of them wanting to at this point," Chardon answered as he inspected the gaping hole where the wall used to be. Outside he saw people in a panic, wondering what happened. "No one wants to call them by our planet's beloved name."

Hon watched in fascination at the vessel molding into its final form. Similar to his features, yet truer to the original Lassa. As a descendant of them, Hon disliked the being after their memories flooded in. He agreed with the others. Put them somewhere else besides his mother's body.

"Is it too jarring for you?" Ganna asked, shuffling over to the second workstation. Her father had taken over the main one. "Almost like looking in a mirror when its complete."

"There's enough difference to tell us apart."

"Indeed."

Ganna sat silently going over data.

Hon got uncomfortable seeing her deflated demeanor.

"Are you alright?" He frowned. "Not that I care about your wellbeing."

Ganna looked up from her screen.

"Why wouldn't I be? My father's returned. We're all rejoicing."

"Who is?" Hon tilted his head to the side. "I'm not."

"The greatest mind of our race is back in the fold. How could anyone not be happy about that?"

"Answer your own question." Hon stared at Jaron lying in a chamber beside the nearly complete vessel. "A genius he may be, but his ethics are trash." He glanced over at her. "That's surely where you get it from."

"The vessel's vital signs are stable. You're free to leave. We won't need anymore specimens from you."

"Good. The less I have to contribute to this, the better."

Hon left the lab, running into Mercan as he rounded the corner into the main bay. The two stopped less than a foot from each other, neither wanting to be the first to budge and go around.

"Are you finished giving your essence for the greater good?" Mercan had a playful smile, yet his eyes showed malice. "The vessel is doing well?"

"Spectacular." Hon replied viciously. "You'll be pleased."

"You know, you should watch your temperament. It reads of Lassa's level of arrogance. Their genetic makeup seems strong."

"I'm not Lassa." Hon's eyes narrowed.

"No." Mercan tilted his chin up while staring at him. "You're most certainly not."

Not wanting to spend another second in Mercan's presence, Hon pivoted to the left and stepped around him.

Mercan entered the lab in a rush, bringing an air of excitement. Which fell flat on Ganna who simply turned to address him.

"You're back." She deadpanned. "The vessel," she paused at hearing the beep of the cryochamber.

"Ahh! It's ready. Perfect timing." Mercan went to stand over the two chambers. "Let's get Lassa extracted. Jaron's under far enough, correct?"

"She'll feel some of it but won't awaken in the middle of it."

Mercan glanced at her. The usually vibrant and unapologetic scientist stood motionless, like a statue. Her eyes glazed over.

I've taken her thunder.

Pity. He expected better from her. She should have demanded respect from him. The thought hit him like a brick. That's not right. If anything, he could've acknowledged her accomplishments.

I'm not getting the father of the century award.

"Come. Let's tackle this together."

He watched Ganna move towards him, not looking at him. As she reached his side, he grabbed her face in his hands, forcing her to do so. She stared at him, frightened by the assault.

"You are my child. I would never do you harm. Be proud of your talents like I am."

Her eyes widened with tears welling in the corners. She simply nodded, and he released her.

They sealed the doors and brought down the extractor to hover over Jaron's body. The lights flickered off, leaving only the hazy blue glow of the extractor's beams. Mercan picked up a claw like tool from the instrument table behind him.

"Let's give it a head start."

With no attempt at gentleness, he rammed it down into Jaron's abdomen. The claws spread her flesh open and held the edges of skin in place to expose the pulsing beneath. The extractor lowered onto it and began its work.

Ganna monitored both vessels for any anomalies. Mercan grinned as the core colors shift angrily.

Lassa fought to the bitter end.

95

Bonds

The trip to Azrom always made Ganna nervous.

Her treatment from the previous visits let her know how much they despised her. They had every right to feel that way. She didn't do herself any favors over the years.

Hearing about the joint venture's upcoming meeting, Mercan bowed out of representing New Lassa. He felt Ganna should finish what she started. She bristled at him taking ownership of something that was hers to begin with.

Azrom's royal advisors balked at not being able to meet Lassa's genius. *I'm no longer an asset to them then?* Ganna leaned her head against the port window. She had never felt so lonely and useless in her life.

Azrom workers ran towards the ship as it docked. Ganna walked down the ramp as it lowered. No need to waste time. Lt. Treshur and a handful of royal soldiers waited below. Her stomach churned with anxiety whenever she saw him. She couldn't put her finger on the cause.

"Welcome back to Azrom, Ganna of Lassa." He gave a quick bow. "We are glad to receive you on this glorious day."

"Thank you for your hospitality." Her lips, straining to smile, delivered a tight one.

Lt. Treshur's expression darkened. He took in her appearance. Nothing got past him. *Did he approve? Or had it diminished his possible admiration for her?*

"Please, this way." He gestured for her to walk with him. "I understand your father has been going through your works for improvement."

"Yes. Everyone gets to see my incompetence."

He stopped, turning to her.

"That's far from true. You're no such thing. Is that what he implied?"

Ganna halted a few steps ahead of him. She couldn't bear to raise her head. Instead, she slumped forward, then straightened. Taking a deep breath, she replied.

"I appreciate the sentiment. Truly, I do."

She turned with a tiny smile.

Again, it barely registered, making Lt. Treshur frown at her.

The two resumed their walk to the science bay.

"We've made progress on the second half of the project."

"That's good to hear."

Loud voices greeted them inside. Technicians argued over data and pointed fingers at each other. One in the center of the fray morphed part way. Lt. Treshur appeared before him in a flash and knocked him back ten feet.

"Enough! I will not tolerate such behavior." He addressed the technician in front of him. "What is the meaning of this?"

Another piped up before the first could answer.

"Someone did the wrong testing on one of the specimens. It's now corrupted."

Lt. Treshur pinched his nose. Ganna sighed heavily.

"We can create a new one and go from there. I'd see to…"

"We don't need your inferior input to fix our dilemma," a technician spat.

Ganna reared back, stunned at the venom in his voice. She moved away from them. They still held bitterness towards her for the incident that, in their eyes, jumpstarted the enemy's agenda.

"That I also will not tolerate." Lt. Treshur whirled on him. "You will not disrespect our guest. Is that understood?" The group dispersed; their faces still flushed with anger. He placed a hand on her bicep. "My apologies. Please don't take what they said to heart."

"No offense taken," she lied.

It hurt. Which never bothered her before.

She no longer had her father's stern masculine side to tap into. That was how she thought of gaining respect. By acting as he did. She should've known better when it didn't work.

Wrapped in her reverie as she worked on the data displayed on a holoscreen before her, she didn't notice two assistants snickering off to the left. Lt. Treshur conversed with a group of technicians handling schematics for a new joint weapons system on the other side of the lab. The minor tweaks in the data looked significant.

Does Azrom ever do anything with subtlety?

"Oh," the assistant on the right cried out, "no!"

"Be careful!" The other yelled in fake despair.

Ganna turned to see what they were up to and a shelf holding canisters of liquid tilting towards her. Not knowing what they all contained, she stared in horror. There was no time to dodge it. Using her energy inside the lab would be disastrous.

She caught their disgusting grins as it crashed into her.

Shouting. Lots of it. And close by.

Ganna made out Lt. Treshur's voice. Her body felt damp, not soaked, in certain places. Those dirty monsters! It made her regret calling the manbeasts out of name. Azrom minions were far worse. Feeling woozy, she fell back unconscious.

Cool air blew on her face, making her eyelids twitch. Silence engulfed her, the exception being a gentle hum coming from above. She recognized the sound of central air. Ganna opened her eyes while raising her head from the pillow to sit up. She swung her legs over then stood to survey the room.

The hover lights in the ceiling corners gave a soft blush of peach, warming the aesthetic of what she could only describe as austere. Besides the overly large bed with muted cream coverings, it housed a workstation area, a lounge chaise by the paneless window, and a shelf of bottled liqueurs. She eyed them.

I could use a drink.

A panel slid open on the back wall, letting out faint puffs of steam. Ganna glanced over. Lt. Treshur came out drying his hair with a cream-colored towel.

His natural scent overpowering the cleansers, reached her nose.

"You're awake. Good." He let the towel fall around his neck. "I couldn't trust the medical team after that, so I brought you here to recuperate."

He moved towards the center of the room. Something inside Ganna broke. Before she could stop herself, she flashed into him, knocking him onto the bed. When he tried to get up, she straddled him, catching both his wrists and pinning them beside him.

"Ganna," he said calmly. "I need you to let me go."

Her eyes stung, focusing on his nakedness like an animal in heat. She saw her own eyes glow bright blue in his. He seemed to understand, opening his hands flat, signaling submission. Ganna released him. She gathered the hems of her robes and pulled them off, tossing them on the floor.

Using both hands, she ripped her undergarments to shreds, not caring where the pieces landed.

"I want you."

She leaned over letting her curls brush his forehead.

"I know." His gaze locked hers as she forced herself onto him.

She rode him hard with desperation. As if she would never have such joy again. And he let her. The ecstasy she felt filled her whole body. For the first time in her life, she experienced satisfaction. Her head fell back as she cried out, her back arched while her fingers gripped his chest.

Breathing hard, she gulped down a mouthful of saliva, closing her eyes. She felt his hand grab the back of head and pull her down.

"We're not done yet." His mouth touched the tip of her ear. He flipped her over so he now lay above her. "You don't get to be the only one having fun."

Ganna's eyes widened. His expression let her know he would not be gentle. Just as she hadn't been.

Oh no!

The way he thrust into her with such savagery almost made her pass out. She realized her mating attempt showed her inexperience. He was well seasoned in the art. Ganna felt a different euphoria crash into her. Its intensity shocked her.

His member seemed to swell, causing pain, yet she didn't want him to stop.

A spasm shook her.

Her arms wrapped under his to grip his shoulders.

Lt. Treshur planted his hands beside her on the bed for a final thrust to release his seed. His guttural growl echoed in the room. Ganna gasped, taking in a sharp inhale before screaming. Her nails dug deep into his flesh until all her strength left her.

Her hands slid away and flopped onto the bed. Her body felt like a puddle of ooze. She couldn't focus. More than exhaustion, she seemed to fade into nothingness. What is this? Her thoughts waned. Only darkness filled her vision.

Ganna woke in a panic.

She sat up and looked around. Lt. Treshur lay sound asleep beside her. Puncture marks on the tops of his shoulders made her wince in shame. She gathered the sheet over her to cover her breasts.

What have I done?

Scanning the room, she located her robes laying haphazard on the floor. Strips of cloth scattered about she recognized as her undergarments. She ran a hand over her face.

Oh Lassa's light!

Careful not to jar Lt. Treshur, she crawled to the edge of the bed and slid to the floor. She reached for her robes and quickly donned them. Standing, she turned to give him one last look.

I can't come back here.

A sense of loathing for her own weakness consumed her. Yet another thing I managed to ruin. She fought back tears, pressing her palms into her eyes. With haste, she left his chamber and headed straight for the palace's gateway to request a return. The project would have to be completed without her.

That angered and saddened her.

I really wanted to see it through.

Trinon realized instantly, seeing the look on Ponnae's face.

She won't take no for an answer.

Her pursuit of his affections never ceased. It didn't bother him. He simply didn't understand why she wanted him. A flawed beast still mourning his first love. Harboring deep guilt for her death despite everyone telling him the fault lied elsewhere.

I do care deeply for you. Trinon couldn't muster saying it out loud. Don't leave!

Pushing her away would result in just that. He clenched his fists, letting his talons push into his palms without drawing blood.

"Say something," she pleaded.

He took in all of her. Fair skin, blonde hair, bright grey eyes, and only a few inches shorter than him. A beautiful being, even with the scars covering her body beneath the layers of robes.

That!

Remembering what those Azrom soldiers did to her made him seethe. Anyone else who endured such atrocities would refuse to be touched ever again. Yet she stood before him wanting to be his mate.

"Am I really the one you want?" Trinon held his head down, not looking at her.

"Why do you ask that?" Her hands reached up and cupped his face, tilting it so he was forced to stare into her eyes. "I have never left your side. Or thought of being with anyone else."

"I'm sorry," he whispered.

"Sahmena. It's about her, isn't it?"

Ponnae slid her hands down.

"I need to think." Trinon raised a hand to her face. She stepped back. Panic hit him. "Please. I only…"

"I understand." Ponnae turned to leave.

The sadness exuding from her made him tense with fear. He took a step to go after her, but his feet refused to go any further. There he stood with his arm reached out while watching her leave.

This isn't what I wanted!

"If you don't go after her right now," his younger sister shouted behind him. He whipped around to see the anger in her voice matched her expression. "I swear, I'll toss your body from here to the hilltops."

"It's complicated," Trinon began.

"It's not!" She snapped, pointing to Ponnae. "Go!"

Her command scared him into action. He sprinted after Ponnae, reaching her before she turned the corner around the commons.

"Wait!" He grabbed her arm, turning her to face him. She stared at him in awe. "That's not what I wanted. I didn't want you to leave."

"You said you needed to think." She looked at the ground. "I was giving you time."

Trinon shook his head. He released her arm.

"I don't want to end up being a bad mate or parent because of my baggage." He glanced at her cautiously. "And yours."

Ponnae frowned.

"It's true that sometimes I flinch at being touched. I still occasionally have nightmares. But you have never harmed me." She got closer to him. "In fact, you've been very patient and tender with me." Her hand stroked his cheek. "What more do you want from me?"

Trinon caught her hand and stared at her.

"What? From you? Nothing. It's what you want from me."

"To be who you always have been. Be you."

"Is that all?" He asked incredulously.

"Yes."

Ponnae pulled his head down to her level and planted a kiss on his lips. He wrapped his arms around her hips and lifted her until her feet fangled.

"Eww!" A young manbeast gagged.

"Yuck!" The other next to him cried out.

Trinon gave them a side glance, not disengaging from Ponnae. She giggled, breaking their connection.

"Why are you doing that outside?" The first boy complained.

"Yeah," the other one said. "No one wants to see that stuff."

"Go play," Trinon chided them.

They made disgusting faces as they walked past them towards the fields.

"See?" Ponnae laughed. "You handled them just fine."

Don't regret this," Trinon replied softly.

Ponnae grinned before kissing him again. He squeezed her tightly, finally admitting to himself that he didn't want to ever let her go.

"Oh no!" Trinon pulled away, setting her down. Ponnae squinted at him. "I forgot to check on my mother. It's my turn in the rotation."

"Oh!" Ponnae placed the tips of her fingers to her lips. "You better go then." She dropped her hand and placed it on his chest. "Is she doing well?"

"Hmm." Trinon took a slow, deep breath. "I think, she's angry."

"Well, that's a given."

"But, I also think she's sad. Being reincarnated in the vessel of a manbeast is a loss she can't comprehend."

"That's Lassa's fault," Ponnae snapped. "The cruelty of it, knowing Mandra and Laxis were mated."

Her fury on behalf of his mother proved her love for him. Trinon clasped his hand in hers. She looked away, embarrassed by her outburst.

"Come with me." She looked shocked. "Since you'll be part of my family now."

He watched her blush. Yes. This is how it should be.

His mother would approve.

As they walked together, he remembered how they met in his role as Farin's personal bodyguard. The Azrom queen no longer needed him. He grinned, letting out a quick snort before his thoughts turned sour. Farin may be a ruler, but in his eyes, still a precocious child.

Are you really doing okay, Farin?

Twelve teenagers stood in the war chancellor's office. Massive dark furniture blotted out the natural light, making the space feel ominous. He sat in a rigid high-back chair three times his size behind an impressive desk covered in holoscreens.

He scanned the teenagers, assessing their worth. The queen's first child with the disgraced Lord Chastan among them. Tall and blond like his father, he appeared regal. Those eyes. Not the murky green of his grandfather, a lighter shade, yet they conveyed the same level of authority.

His lips curved mischievously like his mother's.

And he opted to join the training bouts for imperial soldiers.

The other candidates sneaked angry glances his way.

They would learn soon enough their status didn't matter in his domain. Azrom encouraged combat service for everyone. None of them would receive mercy.

"How many of you have held a weapon? Do not speak. Raise your hand."

Only four of the candidates answered. He tsked, disappointed.

What were your parents doing all this time!

Of course the royal brat raised his hand. Between his parents and the royal entourage, they exposed him to every form of combat from the time he could stumble along on his own.

"Lower your hands. I see some of you will have a hard time adjusting. Mock trials begin next moon phase. My suggestion is that you get used to being hurt. None of you will emerge unscathed."

He saw a handful show fear. Their demeanors stiffened as sweat shined on their foreheads. The four with experience didn't flinch.

"I'll send assignments a few days beforehand. You're dismissed."

They turned as one and went single file out of his office.

Well, at least they have that much discipline.

It struck him as he leaned back in his chair. Did Queen Farin know her son had enlisted? Recommendation usually came ahead of the royal candidates. He only had two, and neither were for him.

Farin paced the empty chamber her eldest son occupied. She came to escort him for morning meal since he had not shown up at their usual meeting place. Finding him gone, she contemplated where he could have gone so early. His younger siblings were no help. She interrogated them until they started crying.

Now she felt ashamed and frustrated.

Movement caught the corner of her eye. She turned to see him walk in. He stopped for a moment, surprised. Unsure if he should continue.

"Where have you been? Morning meal has begun."

He hung his head, letting out a loud sigh. Running his fingers through his shoulder length shaggy hair, he raised his head, locking eyes with her.

"I was at the recruitment meeting."

Farin felt her eyes bulge. The strain brought stinging tears. She regained her senses and calmed down before speaking.

"Why would you attend such a thing? Did someone convince you to go?"

"No. I wanted to."

"Why? You don't have to do any of that. There's plenty of time to decide. In another ten years…"

He didn't let her finish.

"I don't want to wait until I'm too old to learn and not eligible."

Farin wiggled her fingers to avoid balling them into fists.

"I would never let that happen. You're still too young. Enjoy your youth. See the world. Have leisure time."

"Like Chafar?" He retorted, then winced at his words.

Sadness crept in as Farin stared at him. That hurt. Her brother only had love for him. To judge Chafar so harshly floored her.

"I'm sorry," he whispered. "I didn't mean that." He stood defiant. "Still, I want to serve to see how far I can go. If I'm no good, I can switch to a palace position."

"You won't reconsider?" He shook his head. "I can force you to withdraw. Advise the war chancellor to remove you from the list." His horrified stare made her feel worse. "I won't do that."

She gathered him in her arms. They were the same height.

When did that happen?

"Come." She patted him on the back, then released him. "We must hurry before your brothers eat everything."

"I am hungry." He touched his belly. "I forgot."

Farin walked behind him as they left. She made a mental note to reprimand the war chancellor for scheduling a meeting during morning meals. Especially today! Chafar had come to visit. Thinking about his ways, and how her son perceived him, she had to find time to discuss it with him.

After eating, Farin did her daily stroll through the palace halls for the masses to greet her. She made an agreement with her son to not speak of his decision. Romnus would chastise them both. Too much drama for the early hours of the day. Royal house members bowed, giving salutations as she passed.

When she reached the empty corridor on the other side, she took a deep breath.

"Tired?" Chastan emerged from the shadows.

"More unsure." Farin clasped her hands above her head and yawned. "So much to do and no one having my back."

"What am I again?"

"You know what I mean." She gave him a nasty side glance as she lowered her arms. "Between the council and Romnus, I'm not getting any headway."

"Well, that's to be…"

"And our son deciding on his own to attend combat trials."

"You can't really be surprised."

Farin turned to face him. His beauty held a sinister appeal. It scared her.

"I don't want him to fight."

"He won't have a choice in our current state. Would you rather he not know how to defend himself? Be one of those royals who cower, waiting to be saved?"

She stepped back at his verbal onslaught.

"That's not what I meant," she said softly. "I only want."

Farin stood lost for words.

Chastan struggled with his emotions.

"Do you think he'll make it through the trials?"

This time Chastan's mouth twitched until a smile grew.

"Not in the least. I do feel sorry for his opponents, though."

"Huh? That makes no sense!"

"No?" Chastan tilted his head to the side, an evil grin on his face. "Our child has learned from the best. He fights dirty. He may not win the fight, but he'll make sure they understand his ferocity."

That made Farin blanch. Yes, over the years, her son received lessons from Batis, Kur, and herself. Knowing how ruthless Chastan could be, it was probably inherent in him to go too far.

"I have to go."

"Meeting with Chafar?"

"Yes. I really need to speak with him."

"He's not like me." Chastan merged back into the shadows. "At least he's more selective about who he mates with."

"Oh? Was I really only a notch in your groin?" His anger felt like hot tendrils stabbing her soul. "Clearly I jest. Stop being so sensitive."

"I didn't find it amusing."

"I'm sorry." She glanced back. "Still going to protect me?"

He didn't reply. Good. No need to state the obvious.

Now. Time to give Chafar a taste of sisterly advice.

Chafar's quarters resembled a harem. A multitude of colored sheer fabrics filled the small space. Cushions lay everywhere. The lowered bed blended in with the decor. Farin couldn't tell where it began and ended. All in complete contrast to her brother's nearly nonexistent personality.

She scanned the room and found lumps under the covers. One stirred, coming out of the layers of sheets. Chafar poked his head up and looked around before his gaze landed on her. He gave a heavy sigh and sat with his back to her.

"Get up," he ordered, "and leave."

The other two lumps squirmed from beneath. A slender male and a shorter, buxom female. Upon seeing Farin, they retrieved their clothing from the floor and rushed out, not bothering to don them. She struggled to keep her composure, fighting back a guffaw.

"The same to you, brother. We need to have a conversation."

"What for?" Chafar reached over and grabbed his shirt draped across the side table, also buried under fabric. "I want to sleep."

"How could you have dragged two people into your chamber right after morning meal and gone back to sleep within two hours?"

"I'm talented?" He half answered, shrugging.

He stepped off the bed onto the plush flooring. Picking up his pants, he pulled them on, then turned to face her.

"Ick!" Farin shielded her eyes in jest.

"You came here." Chafar searched for his boots.

"How can you find anything in here?" Farin moved out of his way as he got closer to the entrance. His boots lay not far from it. "And this!" She waved a hand before her across the room.

"What?" Chafar put on his boots while standing.

"None of this suits you."

He glanced at her. "How do you know?"

That struck her. Did she really not know anything about her own sibling? Thinking on it, she had two younger ones she hardly saw. Chafar straightened to his full height, an inch and a half taller than her. He crossed his arms. His usual stance. Always defiant.

"Seriously, brother. You're a poor impression on the youth."

"That makes no sense."

Farin pursed her lips. He's going to make this difficult.

"Namely, my children."

"Is that so?" Chafar dropped his arms. "I never claimed to be a role model for anyone. Least of all your spawn."

"Don't." Farin placed a hand on his chest and pushed.

Chafar caught her wrist, stopping the motion. He squeezed until she wrenched her hand away. He watched her rub the red mark left.

"I didn't mean to do that. I'm sorry," he said, softly.

"Whatever," she replied in a blase earth tone.

Here lies the problem, she told herself. Their relationship had always been strained. On the verge of fighting, yet never going through with it.

"You resent me." Farin lowered her head, stepping back. The tears spilled from her eyes despite her squeezing them shut to stop the flow. "Don't you?"

"Yes, I do." Chafar didn't hesitate.

Farin covered her face with both hands as she backed away. "Right."

She had one foot over the threshold when Chafar grabbed her, pulling her back in. He pried her hands from her face and forced her to look at him. His expression jarred her. She had never seen him so distraught.

"That doesn't mean I don't care about you."

In her vulnerable state, she bawled like a child.

Chafar, startled, held her close to his body, stifling her cries. He glanced outside, hoping her guards wouldn't come thinking he had harmed her. It happened more than once. She didn't blame him.

"Why do you care what I do?" Chafar loosened his hold enough for her to lift her face from his chest. "I don't bother anyone."

"Because I worry about you." She pushed off. "Everyone is now settling down, finding a mate. Yet you haven't even tried to connect with others." Her eyes narrowed. "Except like this."

"I have needs."

"Take me seriously!" Farin pouted.

Chafar tilted his head.

"I always do."

"Then…"

"Am I to pick someone at random without feeling?"

"That's not what…"

"Did it ever occur to you I'm picky and haven't found my mate?"

Farin's mouth went crooked as she looked away.

"You are definitely that."

Which made sense. Chafar never did anything he didn't like. His pickiness encompassed everything, including food.

"I merely suggest easing up a bit on your sexual prowess."

Chafar sputtered, letting out a snort as he raised a finger under his lower lip. Okay. That sounded bad. Farin admitted to herself. Seeing him laugh. That warmed her soul. He immediately remedied that by returning to his stoic demeanor.

"I'm not a bad influence." He turned from her. "If anything, I'm a deterrent. Does any of your children strive to emulate me?"

"Well, no."

"Then we're good."

Chafar tossed fabrics off a section in the corner and came up with his jacket, sash, and sword. While he got himself together, she shook her head.

"How can you find anything?"

"Organized chaos?" He said in that questioning way of his.

"Stop it! You're just messy."

"Are we still having some sort of talk?"

Farin lifted her chin haughtily.

"Absolutely. Come. We're having a midday garden tea party."

Chafar halted at the door after she stepped into the walkway.

"I'm not some royal lady in waiting."

"Bring yourself on!"

Farin gestured angrily with her hand for him to follow. She saw two of her guards snicker. They must sound amusing to outsiders. She had to admit her brother brought that out of her.

☼ ☼ ☼

Warmth sprinkled with icy cold needles woke the being known as Lassa from her torment. Phantom pains from their core being pried open and yanked out with minimal anesthesia wracked them. They opened their eyes to a wall of shimmering lights surrounding them. Back in their ethereal form, it now had a featureless bipedal shape of energy.

Sorrow. Pity. Fury.

They came in succession like a wave, crashing into their soul. That was Lassa communicating her disappointment. A conversation long overdue. The two beings conversed without words. Both of their colors shifting based on their emotions.

It became clear Lassa demanded they not use her name.

The time had come to sever their ties.

And what should I be called then!

In this separate plane, they couldn't shed tears of frustration. Lassa's shifting colors warned them she didn't appreciate their tone. Yet, their feelings were still conveyed.

They couldn't atone for all the damage caused by their bad judgement and possessiveness. Giving the excuse that they did their best fell on deaf ears. On reflection, instead of doing as they pleased, they should have listened to Lassa's pleas for help.

And now their descendants found a way to nearly destroy her in their absence.

I'm such a fool!

They curled up in a fetal position, wallowing in their despair.

More warmth enveloped them, removing more cold regions.

A part of me. Not me.

Lassa's mind invaded theirs.

Anassa.

Lassa gave them a new name. Despite their rage, they accepted. Even liked it.

Anassa. They repeated it in their mind.

Lassa gently nudged them towards the void behind them. The reunion had ended.

Anassa drifted away until they felt the pull of reality bringing them back.

Anassa gasped for air as their eyes flew open. They hit the top of the chamber with both fists, intent on breaking out. A figure stood over it. Mercan. He grimaced at them and hit the release button. The top receded and Anassa sprung forward, their hair brushing against their thighs.

So much. It spread around them, the length surpassed their waist. They looked down. To their surprise male genitalia drew into the folds between their legs.

Huh. Anassa didn't question it. They knew for a fact the new vessel had both. But for now, they would make a go at being male for a while.

"That was uncalled for," Mercan chastised him. "I saw your vital signs. I was coming to let you out."

Anassa leaped forward and got his hands around Mercan's neck. They tumbled to the floor. He straddled the scientist, pressing down, squeezing. Which didn't do much considering his weakened body.

Mercan overtook him instantly. Anassa went flying backwards, his naked buttocks landing on the cold, tiled floor.

"Really? It's not like we tried to kill you." Mercan swiped the sides of his robes as if they were soiled. "Stop being dramatic and put a robe on." He turned and went over to his workstation. "By the way, we need to find a name for you. Any suggestions?"

"My name is Anassa." He stood and walked over to the bin of clean robes. "Lassa gave it to me."

Mercan swiveled around in his seat in awe.

"Is that so? So you spoke."

Anassa fastened the sash around his waist to keep the robe closed. He pulled his hair in a ponytail and wrapped it into a bun atop his head.

"We came to a mutual agreement."

Mercan crossed his arms.

"Lassa forgave all your sins? I find that hard to believe."

"I didn't say that."

Anassa went to the reflective wall to use it as a mirror.

Fair skin, pink medium shaped lips, and dirty blonde hair. Caramel-colored eyes stared back. Just as I used to be. A smile crept on his face. A beautiful being as always. He felt Mercan's animosity and glanced back at him.

"What are you angry about now? Was ripping me apart as the sedatives wore off not enough entertainment for you?"

"Honestly. No. You need to suffer far more than that."

"Hmph!" Anassa faced him. "Did you forget? I may not have Lassa's name but I still have some of her energy."

"With that weak vessel?" Mercan smirked. "You'll need to train it for a few years, at least before you think about challenging me."

Anassa frowned. True. He raised his right hand to his chest and opened it. A bright yellow orb, two inches in diameter, formed in his palm. That was all he could muster. He didn't tell Mercan that but the man was more observant than he liked.

"That's all you got?" Mercan let out a hearty laugh.

Feeling disrespected, Anassa walked past him.

Mercan grabbed his arm.

"Where do you think you're going?"

"I'm leaving." Anassa glared at him.

"Not until I do a full range of tests and clear you."

"This is why our people would rather have Ganna now."

Mercan's eyes turned hateful, causing Anassa to step back.

"After all my daughter did for you and our race, you all treated her like a pariah. You deserve every ounce of my rage for that."

Anassa went pale.

Ganna took on all of his misdeeds after the fall. With only Mercan's notes and memories to guide her, Ganna was the one who did the best she could.

Shame filled Anassa.

"Sit down." Mercan pointed to the triage station in the corner. He attached the monitoring diodes to him once seated. "Don't more until I'm done."

Anassa obeyed, not asking why he didn't use the body scanner, fearing backlash. Then it struck him.

Where was Jaron?

CHAPTER THREE

Safeguards

Chardon arrived on the Dreridian home world bitter and angry. His transport settled down onto the locking platform of the imperial docks designated for world leaders. He leaned against the bulkhead, staring out the viewport at the industrial landscape sprawling below. Old memories flooded his mind despite having visited multiple times.

His off-white robes, almost a light shade of gray felt heavy as he rose. The hems dragged behind on the floor as if trying to pull him down. He didn't want to be there. Lord Pondur's invitation read more like a summons than a request. And he had to come alone.

No cabinet members or entourage.

He reached the top of the ramp as it extended down and made his way towards the small group of soldiers standing with Lord Graggor at the bottom. That craggy face showed no joy or friendly amusement like usual. This time, he had a serious demeanor.

"Lord Chardon. Welcome back." Lord Graggor eyed the two manbeasts flanking him. "I see you followed instructions. Very good."

Without saying another word, he turned around, signaling Chardon to fall in step with him and be escorted to Lord Pondur's meeting room. They walked in silence. The tense mood made Chardon want to flee. To go back home.

At the room's entrance, two sentries scrutinized them before forcing them to halt. They raised pole weapons to block them.

"Lord Pondur request only Lord Chardon enter. All of you must remain in the anteroom." The first guard nodded to the next door twenty yards down. "Refreshments have been made available while you wait." He met Lord Graggor's gaze. "That includes you as well, Lord Graggor."

"Very well, then." Lord Graggor gave Chardon a small bow. "Enjoy your meeting."

Chardon stood frozen, trying to stop his eyes from widening in shock. Alone? With Lord Pondur? In close quarters?

The guards waited until the others entered the next room before lowering their weapons.

"You may proceed." They stood aside to allow him passage.

The door slid open on his approach, and he walked in on Lord Pondur standing at the panoramic window wall with his hands clasped behind his back. He seemed serene, almost regal, wearing a deep rust red suit with pellums on the jacket. His small, stony horns resembled antennae the way their shadows elongated on the glass.

Lord Pondur turned sideways and raised an arm, gesturing to the table in the center.

"Greetings, Lord Chardon. Please have a seat."

Chardon eased into the one dead center on his side of the room. Lord Pondur joined him by sitting directly opposite. No servants came to accommodate them. To his surprise, Lord Pondur lifted the blue crystal carafe of berry juice and poured two glasses. No hard spirits for this meeting. Chardon's lips pursed. Makes sense.

He figured they both needed clear heads.

"So what are you demanding?" Chardon asked before sipping. Sweet.

"Demand?" Lord Pondur held the bottom of his glass with one hand and the other wrapped around its circumference. He rose it delicately to his lips and tilted it ever so slightly to allow a tiny sip. Chardon grimaced at the show of etiquette. "What a strange choice of words."

"That's how your invitation came across."

"Is that so?" He set his glass down. "My apologies. I asked you here for one reason."

"Really?" Chardon took another sip and winced.

"Would you like that diluted? It can be overpowering."

Chardon slid the glass towards the center as Lord Pondur reached for the clear carafe of water and half-filled a fresh glass. Chardon poured half the juice into it and tasted the results.

Perfect.

"I wanted to give you insight on the best tactics to rule your newly acquired territories. And tell you an irrefutable truth."

"And that would be?"

Lord Pondur's condescending delivery made him hostile.

"None in your circle will assist in flourishing your reign."

"Hmm?" Chardon felt his body heat rise.

"Azrom has no desire to see you become a ruler. If anything, they will thwart you at every turn while encouraging you."

Chardon tensed.

That nagging in the back of his mind returned.

Lord Pondur seemed to notice.

"You shouldn't be surprised. Razzna also wants nothing more than for you to go back as an unknown race with no weight in trade."

"I don't understand." Chardon balled his fists, resting them on the table. "Why deter my people from prosperity?" He raised his head to meet Lord Pondur's gaze, flinching at the menace in his eyes.

"Because your race is dangerous."

A short, simple answer that sent chills down Chardon's spine. He knew what it meant. Everyone in the five systems were afraid of Lassians. But why?

"My race is not a threat. How did you come to such a conclusion?"

"I beg to differ. Your kind is terrifying." Lord Pondur took hold of his glass and again did his slow sipping routine. "Where others seek to limit you, I've decided to show you how to dominate."

Alarms went off in Chardon's head. His hands relaxed as he leaned back. The way Lord Pondur lowered his eyes, refusing to look at him, proved his suspicion.

"What's the catch? What do you want in return?"

"Simple." Lord Pondur set his glass aside. "You don't go after any Dreridian holdings or occupied planets."

"Oh?" Chardon tilted his head back to the side, waiting for him to look up.

Lord Pondur finally met his gaze again and smirked.

"You seem amused. I see. It never crossed your mind." His beady eyes narrowed. "Good. I'm glad we've nipped that in the bud first."

"I haven't agreed," Chardon countered.

Even saying it, he knew his argument was moot. Lord Pondur had thrown down the gauntlet before he began the game.

"I want a partnership where we negotiate on equal ground. If your kind never realizes your strengths, that's to our benefit."

"Because the moment we do, you think we'll try to conquer the galaxy."

"Something to that effect," Lord Pondur shrugged.

"We only learned all of that to defend ourselves. Wanted no part of any of it." Chardon gritted his teeth. "We just wanted to be left alone."

"Is that regret?" Lord Pondur's expression softened. Well, as much as those stony crags on his face could. "Are you going to hide from the universe? Close yourselves off again? Avoid the inevitable?"

"I know!" Chardon slapped the table. His hands stung. "We can't do that."

He took a few deep breaths, then let out a long sigh. Folding one arm below his chest, resting the elbow of the other on its wrist, he let his fingers graze his lips.

"You will show me how the Dreridians came to power?" His eyes bore into Lord Pondur's. "Are you sure about that? Considering how dangerous we are? Your words, not mine."

"Haven't you ever heard the term, keep your enemies close?"

"Yes. Then you deem us as such?"

Lord Pondur's expression darkened, albeit playfully.

"Not yet."

The two never severed their connection as they both took sips of their drink in silence. After some time passed, they began their discussion, mapping out a plan of action for Chardon.

Night fell on the industrial district.

Hover lights flickered on inside the conference room while Chardon and Lord Pondur wrapped up their meeting. The food platter sat mostly empty. A few pieces of fruit and dried meat left.

They had switched to spirits midway.

The drained bottle mocked them.

"Suffice it to say," Lord Pondur leaned back, crossing his legs. "You should keep the details of our meeting from alliance ears."

"That's a given."

"So," Lord Pondur got serious again. "Do we have a deal?"

Chardon snorted, raising his glass with a thin layer of liquor. He finished it.

"I don't have a choice. The last thing I want is war with you."

"A proper decision." Lord Pondur raised his glass, also bearing a mere sip at its bottom. "To a new collaboration."

He tossed back the contents.

They set their empty glasses on the table and rose. Lord Pondur tapped a sensor on the edge of the table.

"Your manbeasts will be here shortly to join you."

"Lord Graggor didn't seem happy about being left out."

"He'll live." Lord Pondur waved off the idea. "Lord Graggor has more important issues to take care of."

The door slid open. Lord Graggor stood behind the manbeasts. His expression blank, as if forced.

"Have a safe journey back to New Lassa, Lord Chardon." Lord Pondur gestured with one hand for him to leave. "We shall meet again soon."

"Thank you for your hospitality and wisdom."

Chardon gave him a quick head bow and left the room. As he turned to follow Lord Graggor and his guards, he caught sight of his eyes. Anger? Confusion? No. He was none too happy at all.

Lassians.

When did the Dreridians assess us as a menace?

Chardon contemplated that even when he strapped into his seat back on his transport.

What frightens them so much?

The intercepted message from Lord Pondur to Chardon mocked Halfar. Each letter glared with bright overlay on the holo-screen floating above him, illuminating his private chamber in the palace. He stood, arms crossed, while he let the words sink in.

Anger flooded his mind.

Talks were in play between the empires on how to handle the Lassians. He didn't want Chardon to become a ruler of worlds. *My beloved, you don't have the right fortitude.* They all understood that. Nevertheless, Lord Pondur jumped over their heads to snatch him as a protégé. Which they all knew to be merely a front.

You greedy, selfish demon!

Halfar tapped the virtual icon at the bottom of the message and watched it blink out. He let both hands drop before gripping the desk's edge underhanded. Leaning forward, with his weight bearing down, he stared at the wall, contemplating his next move.

Chardon would be livid if he found out about his spies keeping tabs on him. He exhaled slowly, then turned his head to look over his shoulder at Romnus. His cousin tried to sneak in behind him. An impossible feat, considering his size.

"Well?" He addressed him.

Romnus leaned against the wall beside the entrance. His black robe with the fur neckline blended in the dark shadows. Only his eyes glowed.

"Why so soon? What reason would the Dreridians have to pull the Lassians in now?"

"My thoughts exactly." Halfar turned around to face him. "It's almost like desperation. What does he know that we don't?"

"Have you talked with Chardon lately? I know you haven't been back to New Lassa in a while."

"I'm not sure my mate would tell me anything, even if I asked."

Romnus rubbed the bottom of his chin, glancing at the ceiling.

"Maybe you should woo them more."

Halfar smirked. "Surely you jest."

"Ahh." Romnus crossed his arms. "You have a point. That was never your forte."

"I don't like this." Halfar leaned against the desk.

"No. Neither do I." Romnus locked eyes with him. "I'm not trying to be cruel, but I don't want your mate to succeed and become an equal of our empire."

"I agree." The hover globes spread to the corners of the room, giving more light. "My goal is to get them back to being a peaceful race that has no need for instruments of war. Keep their gateway closed to everyone."

They stayed silent for a long time, both frowning at the thought. Closing off New Lassa disrupted trade. With the original planet in recovery, they needed more time to reestablish its routes, let alone contracts. Something still nagged Halfar. The Dreridians were all about commerce, the flow of trade. It was almost as if...

"The Dreridians fear the Lassians," Romnus blurted out.

Halfar's eyes widened.

True, the mock battles revealed a deadly side to them. Surprising, but not enough in his eyes to warrant such haste to bring them into the fold. Then the reason struck him. He stared at Romnus, their gaze not severed. Romnus gave a nod.

"We have yet to see the full might of the Lassians." He tilted his head. "Did we not establish that Chardon's powers were on the level of a planet bomb?"

A sickness hit the pit of Halfar's stomach.

By pulling Chardon under his wing, Lord Pondur could learn more about the Lassian race and find a weakness to exploit. Of course, Azrom and the Razznians had the same idea. Rein in their power without giving them the notion they were being oppressed.

"What shall we do, cousin?"

Romnus' sinister grin made Halfar flinch.

"I think it's time I have a serious conversation with Chardon."

"And what will you do if they decide to become a superpower on par with us? Will you abandon your newfound home and family?"

Halfar ran his fingers through his hair, pushing it back from his face, and clasped them behind his head.

"I don't know. I'm conflicted on that."

"As much as Farin frustrates me, I would never leave her side. Even if she surpasses me and makes me bend to my knees."

Halfar stared at him in shock.

"You would give her your title? Let her reign?"

Romnus' eyes glowed brighter.

"I would."

Because Romnus never wanted to be ruler to begin with. Halfar remembered how reluctant he was. But handing over Azrom to his child seemed wrong. Out of the question. Thinking of Farin as Supreme Ruler and Chardon raising Lassa to a new level made his body hot with dread.

"You need to rethink that. As your royal advisor, I'm against it."

"That may be, but I stand by that decision." Romnus pushed off the wall. "You need to ask yourself if you really ever loved Chardon if you can't even do that."

Halfar's face flushed.

"We agreed Lassa shouldn't evolve further! Are you reneging on our deal?"

"Of course not. I'll bring all of Azrom's might to squash down Lassa's ambitions."

"Then what are you saying?"

"I have Azrom's reputation at stake. Farin may agree. We do respect each other despite our disagreements." He walked into the hallway. "Whose side are you on?"

Halfar stood rooted in place as if he had been slapped. In stunned silence, he let his arms drop to his sides. A sudden rage filled him. Lord Pondur knew this would trigger one of three outcomes. His goal to divide and conquer in plain sight.

Chardon was a chess piece.

He left his chamber, determined to sway Chardon towards the opposite direction. If anyone tutored him on how to rule, it would be him. Not the Dreridians. Romnus' words echoed in his mind.

How dare he question my devotion to my mate!

I destroyed a world for Chardon.

This time, guilt didn't deter him. Instead, he felt righteous.

Farin lounged at the foot of the bed inside her and Romnus' chamber. She listened intently without interruption, hanging on his every word. Cringing when he relayed the final conversation between him and her father.

That's a bit harsh!

On the other hand, she knew he wasn't wrong in his assessment. The way her parents interacted with each other always bothered her. More a convenience of lust than love. Territorial. Possessive.

"Was I wrong to assert our position?" Romnus concluded.

She looked up at him. He sat in the plush chair catty corner from her wearing a thin robe loosely cinched at the waist with his chest exposed. Her legs clenched together on instinct, causing her own flimsy robe to allow a peek at them.

"Hmm?"

Romnus glared at her, trying not to stare at her thighs.

She grinned.

"Were you listening," he leaned back, "or just ogling my body?"

"Hmm." Farin relaxed one arm along the curve of her hip. "Both." She bent her other arm to rest her head in her palm. "I agree with you. New Lassa would be a great threat if they should gain power. I love them. And that's why I say this."

"Do you also fear them because of your mother's talent?"

"No." Farin rose, straightening her arm. "It's Because of what other talents may lie in the Lassian race."

Romus seemed puzzled.

"But there are only energy users, manbeasts, and warriors."

"My beautiful love." Farin beckoned him to her. He moved in and let her cradle his head in her bosom. "No one has ever run a full spectrum of the Lassian make up." She felt him stiffen. "What do you think our scientists would find?"

She let him raise his head. "Or Lord Graggor?" His horrified expression let her know he understood the danger.

Farin's brow knitted. She felt conflicted.

What if I had mine analyzed in secret?

Last time she visited New Lassa, everyone seemed preoccupied. Her mother went around in a state of exhaustion.

She's not cut out for ruling multiple planets.

Yet, she had no choice. Giving up such gifts was off the table. Despite that, her powers buzzed right below the surface. A walking bomb waiting to be triggered.

Laxis posed a deadly threat as well. He kept his skills at a neutral level, holding back his true might. And the manbeasts. Engineered using Lassian DNA spliced with a creature of unmatched resilience.

It would be ideal to take some burden off her mother's plate. Go back to living peacefully. Only engaging other races for trade.

Yet she dabbled at the thought of her and her mother ruling worlds. Snatching power from the empires who already had long reigns. From her observation, the current leaders made things worse over the centuries.

It all stemmed from complacency and arrogance.

Especially the Dreridians.

Their self-proclaimed dominance irked her when she knew Azrom was far superior. Lassians posed a greater threat.

She smiled deviously. Her father won't persuade her mother to back down. He refused to allow her to be on his level. Farin understood that about him. In his eyes, her mother needed only to keep watch over her regency planets and spawn for him.

A new sense of resolve consumed Farin. She stroked Romnus' hair, noticing his even breathing as he fell asleep.

We can do it! Mother and I.

Time for a new bloodline to conquer the galaxy.

In the Folza complex conference room, a knot formed in Chardon's stomach. He clutched the front of his robes while the ships from the regent planets' delegates dock at the station.

One by one, their ramps opened to let the representatives exit.

He saw trepidation in Adan's demeanor.

Rightly so. That Chancellor Eydine allowed his people to live, let alone leave the planet, should keep him in line.

Chancellor Eydine stood beside him, her ethereal form pulsing a pale shade of peach. Her lidless eyes blinked in amusement at his discomfort. As if reading his mind, she gave a playful smile.

"I do hope they behave this time." Her form seemed to flutter.

"My cabinet sent them an agreement addressing the situation."

"Yet, you seem nervous." She floated towards the sliding doors. "You should have more control over your regencies, Lord Chardon."

Alone, he placed his hands on the wall window and rested his forehead on it. The doors slid open. He turned his head, thinking it Chancellor Eydine. His cabinet members arrived, taking stock of the layout before choosing seats at the twenty-foot table.

Talas went over to him while Volma set her data fob down. The holoscreens activated, showing all the planets under Lassian regency.

"Strange, isn't it?" Talas said, crossing his arms. "To think we're rulers of worlds."

"It shouldn't have come to this. We barely take care of ourselves."

"True. And the ones we got are ticking time bombs."

Chardon raised his head and let his arms slip down to his sides. T'Halgar exuded caution and pride. Xanic ruled his race with an iron fist. Lombis always seemed shady. A constant scheme stirred in his mind. And then they had Adan and his culprits from Randal II. He sighed, pinching the bridge of his nose before walking to the table.

Modas, Ganna, Jaron, and the head of commerce kept to one side near the head of the table where Chardon would sit. Volma and Talas sat across from them.

"Are we ready?" He asked. No answers. Their expressions, showed they had doubts. "When they arrive, let's go over the agreement once more," he addressed Jaron.

"Yes. No surprises allowed this time."

Jaron still looked exhausted.

Her dark hair sported more red strands, signaling the aging process. According to Mercan, it will reverse over time, removing the markers. This was her first outing since awakening. She had yet to face Anassa. Chardon made sure they didn't meet for now. Too much anger and drama.

"Just, try to be cordial when you do it," Chardon pleaded.

Jaron's lips thinned, her mouth twisted as if debating his order. Everyone tensed. She caught the mood and rolled her eyes. "Fine. I'll be - nice."

Two hours later, Folzan guards escorted the delegates into the conference room. They filed in, mesmerized by the view. Each sat down slowly, not averting their eyes. Jaron cleared her throat to get their attention.

"Apologies." Lombis bowed his head. "We heard fascinating things about Folza. To be here is a treat."

"Well, some of you need better manners." Jaron scrolled through Volma's documents and found the agreement. "Please go over the terms again before we start."

The delegates turned sour expressions Adan's way. He sat indignant, not sure why they warranted such a response. Which enraged Jaron more. Instead of chastising them, she kept silent.

It was a losing battle.

"Yes," Xanic said. "Try not to get us all killed."

"Now that we've established that, let's begin." Volma hid the agreement from view and brought forward the regency map. "As you know, we are a coalition in this war against the Boretkz."

"Such dastardly creatures," Colgar seethed.

"Not very appealing either," Lombis added.

"Our newly commissioned ships helped," Chardon's head of commerce stated.

Adan beamed with pride. The master mechanic deserved the praise. Chardon wished he didn't throw it in everyone's faces every chance he got. He saw Adan open his mouth to elaborate.

"Let's not stroke any egos today." Chardon shut him down. Adan eyed him with a dirty glare. "I have gathered us here so we can get to know each other better."

"That is the same reason the Dreridians claimed when they sent their invitation." Lombis said. His assistant stared at him in awe. "Oh. I wasn't supposed to say, was I." He scanned the room. "Surely you all received one as well."

Chardon bristled at the news. Not that it surprised him the Dreridians were plotting something. That Lombis blurted it out as if he didn't' intend to angered him. Modas' eyes narrowed.

"I'm sure they preferred it stay secret." Ganna shook her head.

"As our regent, I felt you should know about outside forces contacting us without your knowledge." He bowed his head again. "I only wish to keep the peace."

Colgar wasn't buying it. His gaze pierced the statesman, causing him to shrink in his seat. Xanic also gave him a dubious stare.

Again. Shady.

Chardon reiterated it in his mind. He couldn't put his finger on Lombis' agenda. The spineless act reeked of falsehood.

Unexpected Outcomes

Ganna confined herself to her newly reinforced secret lab not long after returning from Azrom. Finding her lab insufficient for his needs, her father had a new lab commissioned on the other side of the medical bays. Which worked fine. She wanted him to be more distant. As much as she loved him, her fear of him exceeded it.

The reports she gathered from the other scientists' notes were sent remotely. She didn't want to interact with anyone. The shame of not doing her duty and throwing herself at Lt. Treshur was too great. The one task assigned to her went unfulfilled.

I'm a failure. Still.

Her accomplishments came about by a glimmer of her core. The struggle to maintain Lassians' safety with advanced technology depleted her every time. Taking on the Azrom project taxed her.

Then her body revolted.

It grew heavy, along with an irrational sense of self preservation. Everyone became an enemy she needed to protect herself from.

After months of hiding, her father had enough, breaking through her lab. Chardon entered behind him, and they both halted near her station. Her father glowered at her protruding belly. Chardon's eyes showed disbelief.

Ganna shrunk inwardly at their scrutiny.

"What nonsense is this?" Her father approached. "We have no time for your selfishness. You didn't feel the need to procreate all these centuries. Why now when we have so much at stake?"

"I didn't do this on purpose!"

Ganna scooted away on her stool.

"Stop." Chardon's expression softened. "Don't be angry at her."

He walked past her father to stand before her.

"You know you need to tell Lt. Treshur about this."

"What for?" Ganna lowered her head, glancing sideways. "I'm sure he wouldn't want such a connection with me."

"That's a moot point, considering he impregnated you of his own will," her father snapped. "He doesn't get to back out now." He reached over and grabbed her wrist. "Hiding won't solve any-thing. Get up. We have a meeting."

Ganna tried to pull away, hitting the wall. There was nowhere else to go.

"I can join remote…"

"I won't tell you again."

Chardon's brow furrowed at Mercan's tone. He tried to change the mood.

"This is not the kind of meeting that you can simply remote in for. Please. Come."

Terror gripped Ganna. She didn't want anyone else to know her condition. Thinking of how Jaron, Modas, or Talas would readily mock her. Their cruel words hitting like physical attacks.

Her father seemed to see the conflict in her demeanor.

"Do you think I would tolerate mistreatment of you?"

Ganna looked up in shock.

"The same goes for me," Chardon added. "You have just as many flaws as I do. I've thought often that you should have mated long ago. This was overdue."

"Hmph." Her father released her. "Your timing is ill desired."

They waited for her to rise from her stool. It took longer than normal, her having to grip the edge of her workstation for leverage. So heavy! She got to her feet and waited before taking a step.

I feel woozy.

She found herself in her father's arms. Startled, she attempted to push him off. He held fast to her.

"Take it slow. Your body wasn't meant to handle this despite what Chardon says. It's my fault for altering your core when you were young."

He turned around, not letting go. "Stay close until you feel like walking on your own."

Chardon followed them out and made sure the lab sealed shut.

The way Jaron's eyes narrowed at first sight of Ganna jarred her. It replicated among the others in the room.

More intensely with Talas.

"Are you serious?" Jaron cried.

"Not another word." Mercan stared her down. "Much could be said about you, but we restrain ourselves, don't we?"

Jaron glared at him.

Talas averted his gaze, choosing to remain silent.

Yes. That Earth saying heard from Chardon about stones and glass houses came to mind. Careful, he chided silently.

He knew his silly child monitored her condition poorly. After the meeting, he would drag her into his lab for a full panel. Her pregnancy on the first try worried him.

During the meeting, he noticed Ganna's attention waning off and on. She struggled to stay focused. Her youthful features a sign of regression. That's why. Removing his core reverted her to the age its inception. She was physically back to being a little over two centuries old.

Some attendees tried to sneak glances at her, doing a double take as they, too, saw the difference. None of them had bothered to really look at her in any depth before. It angered him.

The meeting adjourned, with everyone filing out in haste. Volma stopped next to Ganna, towering over her.

"My sincere congratulations. I wish you a healthy birth."

Ganna glanced at her, confused by the kind words.

When only the two were left, he helped her off the cushion.

"Now. Let's get some full tests to see how you and your spawn are faring."

"I already did," Ganna protested. "There's no need."

"Exactly. You're not the best judge of your condition." He nudged her along. "This is not up for debate."

Inside his lab, he steered her towards the examination table until she got within inches of it. He gave her a stern look.

She reluctantly pulled herself onto it and laid down.

He activated the body scan, then zoomed in on her belly. At first, the image puzzled him, not sure what he saw. Rotating the 3D image, he reared back. Two cores pulsed side by side, surrounded by a thick membrane. The tiny creatures moved about, sleeping. Their sharp talons already forming.

Ahh. Azromnians were hard-shelled beasts.

He'd almost forgotten about that.

Of all the races in the galaxy, his daughter chose one from that planet. He had seen recorded meetings with the man. A pompous ass who happened to be knowledgeable in the sciences. One of the planet bombs' architects. Creating destruction is much easier than something that benefits others. Mercan snorted.

Ganna lay fast asleep. Her eyes closed seconds after lying down.

Mercan hit the call icon on the bottom of his workstation's holoscreen. Within minutes, two medical assistants entered.

"Put her in a recovery chamber. Set it for eight days. I don't want her moving about until I finish my analysis."

"Of course, Lord Mercan," the first assistant replied.

They gently lifted Ganna off the platform and onto a nearby hover stretcher. The scanner blinked off. Knowing Ganna would not contact Lt. Treshur on her own, he went to his screen and mocked up a message for him.

Be mad at me all you want. This is for your own good.

Technicians roamed the work center outside the planet bombs' holding chamber. The far wall overlooked the deadly weapons suspended in their own space time. Arcs of electricity cascading around each one stayed within its housing.

An illusion. The planet bombs were far away from Azrom. The images shown were only for monitoring.

A lab worker entered the room, weaving through the crowded area. They came to a stop near Lt. Treshur chastising a technician. With one finger pointing at a holoscreen, his raised voice fell away, drowned out by the other sounds. He loomed over his prey. Only the technician got the full brunt of his ire.

"Excuse me, sir!" The lab worker yelled at the top of his lungs.

Lt. Treshur looked up, frowning.

He turned his head towards him. The technician took advantage of the reprieve and fled his workstation. Annoyed, Lt. Treshur stood to his full height.

"What is it?"

"You have a private message. It's been sent to your quarters."

Lt. Treshur's brow rose.

"Oh? Who is it from?"

The lab worker fidgeted.

"The message is waiting for you. It appears to be urgent."

"So, important that you're not allowed to tell me even that?"

"My apologies, sir."

The lab worker bowed curtly and hurried out.

Lt. Treshur took a deep breath, then headed out. Before he reached the door, he commanded the room.

"Make sure to check the integrity of the barriers!"

He stepped into the hallway. Silence engulfed him the moment the chamber door sealed from behind. It always amazed him how loud it was inside. No one noticed the high decibels until they came out. A few soldiers strolled the area, supposedly on duty to guard the chamber. They stood alert as he passed them.

Walking into his room, he saw the blue commlink light on the desk flashing. He tapped the receive icon. The origination displayed New Lassa's marker. He didn't recognize the sender. A new cabinet member, perhaps? To have communication access meant they were of importance. He hit the open command on the virtual keypad that appeared on the desk.

"Greetings, Lt. Treshur. This message is to inform you of the consequences derived from your recent mating with Ganna of Lassa. She is due to spawn in a few moon cycles. Should you wish to discuss the issue, my suggestion is to make haste to New Lassa."

Treshur stared with indifference at the wall, letting the audio sink in. A range of emotions, from intrigue to anger, flooded him.

She wasn't going to tell me. He that knew right off the bat remembering how she fled his chamber on her last visit.

This wouldn't be his first child. He had three, each from different females he randomly mated with out of boredom.

His children despised him. The last time any of them saw him may have been a few years ago. He tried to make it a point to visit them at least once a year to stay relevant.

Sometimes he missed the meetings.

Thinking about it, he hung his head in defeat. Placing both hands on the desk to support his weight, he leaned over. Too late to play the doting father. But now. Here lay a chance to do it right. He could visit once a year, maybe more if he chose, to raise them. Teach them.

Then he thought of Ganna. Her young appearance stunned him. What happened to cause such a drastic regression? She was not old by any means. Her aged features derived from being high-strung, overworked. And it all disappeared in less than a year? Which explained her fertility after only one session of mating.

Treshur let out a loud sigh and raised his head. He closed the message and turned around, sitting on the edge of the desk. His shoulders slumped.

You stupid woman. I don't have time for this.

Gathering his resolve, he pushed off to leave, heading towards the throne room to request a ship. With the enemy forces beaten back for the time being, he had time to kill.

Should I tell them? He pondered it on the way. How would they take the news? Ganna wasn't on anyone's friend list on Azrom. If anything, the hatred for her hadn't lessened.

Best to leave it be.

Treshur eased his transport through New Lassa's gateway and came out above a newly built space dock. Seeing how many ships filled the bays drew awe. He never imagined the Lassians had progressed that far in trade. A busy hub lay before him.

Tracking beams guided his ship to an empty hangar where grappling arms clamped it down.

He opened the ramp, smelling the fresh air. Cleaner than Azrom's. Checking with the ship coordinator, he proceeded to the lift that took him to surface level.

Even though he knew where he was headed, it still amazed him that he had no escorts.

They trust too much!

At the medical bay, he sought for Ganna. A tall, intimidating man with jet black hair and menacing eyes approached him.

"Lt. Treshur, I presume."

He recognized the voice from the message.

"Yes. And you are?"

The man ignored the question, walking past him into the fields beyond the entrance.

"Follow me."

Peeved at the man's disregard for him, he obeyed. They went around the building to a small housing settlement. That's new. So much change in a short time. He eyed the man ahead of him. The air of authority bordered on supremacy.

Who are you?

The man entered the door of a unit separate from the others. Inside, Lt. Treshur stood a few feet from the center, his head turned slightly to one side as he stared emotionless at its occupant.

Items strewn haphazardly around the room belied the minimal furniture. Ganna, well into her pregnancy, froze in horror at him.

"Why is he here?" She screamed. Her face contorted at the man. "How could you?" Tears streamed down her face. "Why would you do this?"

"As you can see," the man waved an arm. "my daughter is being difficult. From your expression," his eyes narrowed, "I can imagine why. What purpose did you have allowing this?"

Daughter?

Treshur fought the urge to gasp. Ganna having any family ties never dawned on him. The idea was implied whenever discussions about her arose. Were there siblings? A mother as well?

"My purpose?" He saw Ganna shrink away, moving further across the side of the bed, her knees hitting the bottom. Why is she on the floor? "Should I have one?"

"I am Mercan. My child is trying to escape to her lab when I explicitly forbade it in her condition."

That surprised Treshur.

For him to have enough leverage to deny Ganna her reason for living, made him a threat.

"Pregnancy, in most cases, does not stop one from research."

"When an unknown spawn is at play, two of them, that factors in high risk."

"Two?" Ahh. Twins. Now that's interesting. "Hmm. Again, I don't see the issue."

Mercan went over and grabbed Ganna under her arms. He hauled her back onto the bed. She obediently rolled onto her side like a berated child. Her father unceremoniously tossed the sheets over her.

"I ask you again." Mercan turned to him. "I will not repeat it. What are your intentions with my child?"

The hostile way he spoke, let Treshur know he faced an enemy. Calling Ganna his child as if she had never aged or accomplished anything. Something about his demeanor made him think he'd lose in a fight.

"I was thinking yearly visits. Teach them Azrom ways and such."

"I asked you regarding my daughter, yet you immediately talk of plans for your spawn tells me plenty."

Did I make a mistake? He watched Mercan walk to the picture window on the other side of the bed.

"There is no need for you to insert yourself in their lives. I wanted to at least meet the uncaring monster who desecrated her."

"I take great offense to that." Treshur's eyes turned steely grey. They narrowed as his head tilted forward. "You don't know enough about me to make that judgement."

"Oh?" Mercan's smirk oozed malice. "Are you in love with her?"

Treshur's head snapped up. The suggestion erased his anger.

"I wouldn't say that."

The moment he spoke it, he saw Ganna's demeanor crumble. He knew she had feelings for him and let her do as she pleased. "It's one sided for now. There's no timeline for when or if that changes."

"Stay away from her."

"That defeats the purpose of getting to know her enough to love her."

Mercan had his neck in a vise grip, pinning him to the wall by the door. Treshur stamped down his fear as they locked eyes. The wrath of a father. He had seen something similar with Rass.

"You're not listening to me," Mercan said calmly.

"Please, father!" Ganna raised her head above the pillow. "Don't harm him."

He glanced over at her with disdain.

Treshur used his fingers to get some space between Mercan's hand and his neck. The man's grip tightened.

"I won't leave her be," Treshur gasped. "It's not your decision."

He fell to the floor as Mercan released him. Without looking at him, Mercan walked back to stand by the bed.

"That is true." He stared at Ganna. "Only she can decide what she wants. I still disapprove." Mercan met his gaze. "I can already tell you're an awful parent. I should know since I'm one as well."

He stroked Ganna's head.

"That may be true for now," Treshur replied. "But this is our chance to start over."

"I should have put more safeguards in place." Mercan smiled. "I never meant for her to spawn. Or find a mate, for that matter. Her entire existence was to cater to science."

Treshur blanched. What madness is he spouting? All the pieces came together as the revelation hit him. Father? No. Mercan was a scientist who created things out of curiosity or necessity. Ganna didn't come from love. Her parents were probably the same as them. A one-sided affection from her mother.

Mercan glared at him.

"It's exactly as you think. Her mother adored me. That is why I see the outcome of this union. I won't let her suffer such a fate."

"And you're not listening." Treshur got to his feet. "This is a new chapter I'm willing to try. You would deny my offspring that chance?"

Mercan glanced away, his lips pursed.

"Do as you please." He left Ganna's side and came to stand next to him. "Be aware, if you hurt her in any way, I will end you."

As Mercan exited the room, Treshur found he held his breath. Exhaling slowly, he calmed the anxiety that gripped him.

Mercan's presence brought about an irrational fear. No. He deemed it justified. Something omniscient and terrifying oozed from his core. Treshur realized how little he knew of the Lassians.

Talas conjured a similar feeling within him. By inserting their cores into new vessels, Treshur nor the other races knew how old they were.

Treshur walked over to Ganna. For all he knew, she could be well over a thousand years old. Yet, at the moment, she resembled a young maiden of a few hundred years. Her face buried in the pillow, he could hear her muffled cries.

I don't like seeing her this way!

His image of her being the unyielding, arrogant, and unethical scientist shattered before him. Reduced to a sniveling child.

I must get her back on her feet!

He refused to let her wallow in self-deprecation. For the sake of their spawns, he needed her to be strong willed again. Slowly, he laid his hand on her head.

"Let's take our time."

News of Ganna's condition spread quickly following Treshur's arrival. And she refused to emerge from her chamber to give anyone a glimpse of her pregnant body. Chardon understood her stance. He made sure all low end medical issues got averted to her assistants and major procedures to Mercan.

Treshur watched over her, shaken by the prolong silence. She barely spoke and only when asked a question. He leaned over her as she rested laying on her left side on the bed.

The weight of his arms pressing on the mattress made a dip. "Stop ignoring me. We need to settle this."

Ganna glanced at him.

"What's there to settle? You'll return to Azrom while I remain."

"I will come often to assist in the raising of our children."

"To teach them Azrom ways?"

"Among other things."

Ganna rose her head off the pillow and rested on her forearm.

"My father had me working in his labs before I could walk."

"Is that what you want for our spawn?"

Mercan was not a loving father. He only saw his offspring as a tool to advance his agenda. Ganna's face contorted, proving his theory. She struggled with an answer.

"I aim to let them grow on their own until their teen years, when curiosity emerges."

"You mean just let them run amuck with no structure?"

Her horrified tone amused him.

"Yes. After observing their environment and the people around them, they'll start delving into things. Find out their likes and dislikes."

Ganna's demeanor deflated.

She'd never been given such an option. Treshur could see her wondering what that would've been like. He also thought of how different Ganna may have turned out.

"Fine. I'll try it." She lowered back down. "But if my father…"

"You tell him no." Treshur glared at her. "He does not dictate how we raise our children. Firmly state your position."

Ganna's eyes widened.

"I'll stay after the birth. We need to name them soon."

"A name." Ganna suddenly fell silent. A sad expression spread. "That's important."

"Indeed. Their names will steer their destiny."

Construction workers completed their tasks Ganna barked in their direction. She worked them like dogs to finish the newly designed ground to space cannon. The sun sat at its peak, bearing down on them. Instead of the usual robes and loose fit tunics, they wore sleeveless ones that stayed open midway down the front. Sweat ran down from their necks to their abdomens.

Ganna pointed to an area at the base of the cannon, yelling at a group of workers to give it attention. Strapped to the front of her swaddled in light grey linen lay her newborn sons. They resembled worms with only their eyes and nose visible. She would let no one catch a glimpse of the them.

All her moving about didn't wake either from their slumber.

Treshur watched her with concern. He had stayed for the birthin the delivery chamber. His first time doing so. The moment the surgeon cut open the membrane, exposing both babies to the world, Ganna screamed at everyone in the room to get away. That she would not let anyone murder her child.

Chardon stood rooted at the entrance, horrified by the notion. Mercan immediately grabbed a sedative gun and administered it to end her irrational outbursts. From the time she awakened, neither child never left her side. Even Treshur had to ask permission to hold his own sons.

She trusted no one.

His time to return neared, and he dreaded telling the emperor and his council about the situation. Because now he needed to make regular visits. As he walked across the fields taking in the fresh air, glancing over to check on Ganna, he heard commentary about her from nearby workers.

Further ahead, Jaron and Talas stood side by side, eyeing her.

"She has them wrapped up like a chrysalis." Jaron frowned.

"You'd think there was a hit on her." Talas smirked.

"Well," Jaron gave a side glance. "That is probably accurate."

"Even so." Talas crossed his arms. "She can't keep sheltering them this way forever."

"She's either going to be the worse mother in history or smother them to death."

"Isn't that the same thing?" Talas squinted.

They noticed Treshur and nodded to him. He changed course and headed their way, stopping a few feet from them.

"The gossip and whispers are not helpful," he said.

"No. You're right." Jaron shrugged. "But, you must understand, we haven't forgiven her yet. It'll take some time."

"I do, in fact. Her sins extend far beyond New Lassa. Azrom is not in the forgiving mood either." Treshur crossed an arm and rested the elbow of the other on his forearm. "That said, it would be best if our children were nurtured in an accepting environment."

Talas and Jaron looked shocked, then angry.

"We'd never punish children for her mistakes," Talas snapped.

"What kind of race do you take us for?"

Jaron clenched her fists.

"I'm only speaking on my observations thus far."

Did they not see how they treat each other? He noticed the decline in behavior long ago. Much of it stemmed from Ganna's attempts to advance their race. To make them part of the galaxy as equals. No good deed went unpunished. He knew all too well after the creation of the planet bombs.

"From what Ganna has told me, you were a peaceful race, not interested in the surrounding worlds. A collective. You should return to that."

"I agree." Chardon's voice carried towards them. He also kept watch on Ganna, wearing a sad expression. "We won't slide further. I won't let us. You can leave with confidence."

Treshur looked over the three, and realized Jaron and Chardon gave off the same vibe as Mercan, except only at a quarter of the intensity. Is it because they're descendants? Not originals? The first time he met Ganna, she seemed to suppress her true essence.

Now he knew why.

Which brought up another dilemma for him. Should he relay the information he attained to the council? Doing so could lead to misunderstandings. And if Dreridians managed a spy or two on Azrom, they may use it for nefarious purposes.

"I will take you at your word, Lord Chardon."

He resumed his walk through the fields, taking in the changes of New Lassa. It was turning into a proper home for them. He circled back to the construction site and came up behind Ganna.

She whirled around, ready to unleash a tirade, thinking him a worker, and halted. With her mouth left gaped open, she stared in confusion. Pursing her lips, she relaxed.

"I thought you left for Azrom." She looked away, struggling to keep her composure.

"You would have me leave without saying goodbye to you and our sons?" He tilted his head, not sure how to take her statement. "Are you now going to act as if there is no bond between us?"

"That's not…" Ganna's jaw clenched. She took a deep breath. "I suspected you wanted to get back sooner than later. Them not being your first offspring."

Treshur let out a loud sigh, startling her.

"Ganna. Your low expectations and paranoia are frightening at times." Her eyes widened. He stepped closer to her and bent down, kissing the small patch of his sons' exposed foreheads. He saw her body stiffen. "Until we meet again, little ones." He raised his head and locked eyes with her. "I will treat you well as long as you do the same." He brushed a curl from her face with the tips of his fingers.

Ganna fought back tears, not wanting the workers to see her weakness. Treshur shook his head at her. Cupping her face in his hands, he kissed her lips softly.

She stepped back, uncertain how to react.

"Don't overdo it." Treshur backed away before turning to leave. "Our sons need you clear-headed and well rested."

He didn't bother to look back. Knowing Ganna, she was straightening herself out and pulling the swaddle cloth back in place to cover their sons completely. One thing he had to admit.

He never favored one child over the other. But these two.

What beautiful creatures.

He had no qualms about having them covered up like that. When people saw them, they would stand in awe.

At the docks, he boarded his ship and waited for permission

to enter the gate that led back to Azrom. So many thoughts ran through his mind. The trip gave him time to arrange them.

On Azrom, Treshur made his way down the palace corridor to the meeting room. A page ran towards him with the request as he walked down his ship's ramp. He tsked at having an audience with the council right after landing. Rounding the corner of the entrance, he saw Rass, Batis, and Kur in attendance.

"Congratulations on your return," Kur yelled. "I didn't think you were coming back after being gone so long."

Treshur winced at his verbal assault.

"Yes, why would you be on New Lassa for so long? I assumed the project Ganna worked on with us was exclusive."

"I went for the birth of my new spawn."

"You mated with a Lassian?" Batis snorted. "Well, that's quite unexpected. Who could…" His' eyes widened as he stared at him.

"There's only one Lassian who craves your attention," Kur laughed nervously. He tried not to show his disdain.

"Yes, that is true." Treshur didn't elaborate.

No need.

Rass glanced over at him with subdued horror.

"You didn't. How could you? With her?"

Rass' tone dripped with ire.

"Do not speak ill of my spawn's mother," he warned them.

"How does that even work?" Batis mouth down-turned.

"That's surprising." Romnus entered the room with Biandra and Halfar. "I never thought you would cave to her advances."

Halfar covered his mouth as if ill.

His hatred of Ganna ran deep.

"More like she demanded my attention and took the initiative."

"And so?" Romnus' gaze met his. "Any images of this child?"

"They are twins. And unfortunately, no." They stood confused. "She refused to let anyone see them, let alone take an image. She keeps them wrapped up to avoid the public eye."

"You've not seen your own spawns?" Rass exploded.

"Of course, I have," Treshur spat. "Don't be ridiculous!" He calmed down. "Ganna has an extreme paranoia that someone may try to harm them. And her, for that matter."

"She's not wrong." Halfar's face scrunched in anger. "Many wished for her death."

"Well." Kur sighed. "This calls for celebratory drinks and meal."

"Please." Treshur raised a hand. "No need for that. It would cause strife with my other offspring."

"I think they're old enough to understand."

Romnus let out a huff.

"Does this mean she is stepping away from our joint project?" Halfar asked angrily.

Treshur fought back his own rage at his tone.

"No. She is still on board. After the last incident, I feel the need to request a separate lab area."

"That won't be necessary." Rass leaned against the beam in the room. "I have reprimanded the others for their behavior. It won't happen again."

"Now that we are all here, let's get this meeting started," Romnus announced.

Treshur stared Halfar down.

The two connected. Halfar gave a facial warning. What little knowledge each had about the Lassians origin they would keep secret.

Delayed Consequences

Imperial guards burst through the fourth house rebel leader's chamber. They dragged him out while more guards did the same with occupants of the traitor wing. Loud cursing and screammsechoed in the halls. The residents turned their heads as the guards paraded them through the main corridor.

Brutal sunlight from the wall windows illuminated the traitors' walk of shame. The leader kept his eyes ahead, occasionally glancing at the floor when higher status residents glared at him. Nothing to be done about his fate now. At the entrance, Elendar argued with General Kur. The imperial guard behind him shoved his hand into the middle of his back. An attempt to make him stumble.

He refused to budge.

"I won't allow this!" Elendar yelled.

General Kur turned his gaze on the leader.

"You obviously couldn't keep him in line. Nor his influence that created this rebel group. You agreed to the execution order."

"I did no such thing!" Elendar swayed before correcting his posture. "Granted, they deserve punishment. Not death."

Elendar turned to his brother.

"See what you've done, Lanen. I can't protect you when you do reckless things!"

Lanen stopped a few feet from him.

"I didn't think you cared," he replied softly.

Elendar's eyes widened, making him feel guilty.

"Load them in the transport!" General Kur ordered. "Our Supreme Ruler and Queen demands an audience before the rites."

"Don't do this!"

Elendar went to follow him as he turned to leave.

Dalfir grabbed his arm and pulled him back.

"Let me go!"

"It's alright." Lanen said as he passed. "I'll try to save the others."

General Kur laughed.

"For what your little rebellion has done," he glanced back at Lanen. "I hope you all suffer." He caught Elendar's horrified face. "You're not allowed to watch. We have some sense of mercy."

Lanen entered the transport and sat in a space further down on the bench. The ride to the main palace turned silent. He thought about the optics of executing so many royal relatives.

Would they really kill us all? He caught sight of holoscreens surrounding the outskirts where people would gather to watch the proceedings. A small crowd already formed inside the gates.

More curses, along with hisses, greeted the traitors. The guards pushed them on, not protecting them from thrown objects and fist blows. Lanen marched forward, undeterred.

The throne room felt eerily gloomy. He expected a festival to appease the masses. Royal advisors, heads of states, and imperial guards lined the sides. Their hostility permeated the room. Queen Farin and Supreme Ruler Romnus sat above, staring down at them like vermin.

"So these are the traitors who brought harm to Azrom." Queen Farin leaned forward. She rested her chin on her raised hand, the elbow on her knee. "Are you prepared to die for your sins?"

Pleas of mercy and forgiveness erupted. Romnus' eyes glowed.

"Enough! You dare beg for mercy after what you've done?"

Lanen stepped closer to the throne's base. He knelt on one knee.

"Queen Farin. Supreme Ruler Romnus. I know our misjudgment and acts of betrayal warrant punishment. The rules cite death, yet the order is at your discretion. As the leader, I'm responsible for convincing them to go astray."

Queen Farin raised her head.

"Oh? You wish to sacrifice yourself in exchange for their lives?"

Sounds of dissent filled the room. Royal members squirmed in anger. He could hear the same coming from the masses outside.

A page emerged from the side entrance and hurried up the steps. They whispered to them, then backed away.

"It seems Lord Elendar is quite upset. He has vowed to avenge all of you should your demise become eminent."

Gasps sounded. Lanen pursed his lips, exhaling sharply through his nose. That won't do. He thought of his mate, who abandoned him centuries ago. The offspring who probably despised him.

I have nothing to keep me here.

He looked up and found Queen Farin staring at him. A frown formed on her face as they locked eyes. Like she saw his soul.

"I know." Queen Farin gripped her throne's armrests. "I'll grant your wish. You take the punishment for all of them. In exchange, I let them live."

"No!" A group of his relatives cried out.

"Lord Lanen, you can't!"

"We won't let you do this!"

"Please! We will take our fate as they see fit."

Lanen hung head for a second, listening to their pleas. I won't budge. This is my decision.

"Bring in the Grulog tamer," Farin ordered. "The big one."

Her sinister smile made everyone in the room flinch. She sat back against her throne, never severing her gaze with Lanen.

Imperial guards parted the group of traitors to make a pathway for two men in full length waterproof black garb. Each carried the giant whips used to tame Grulogs. The ten-foot beasts that roamed the barren hillsides.

Two guards strung Lanen up, tethering his arms to the rings embedded high in the pillars on each side of the room. He didn't fight, letting his head hang forward.

"What do you say, my love?" She turned to Romnus. "Will fifty lashes be entertaining enough?" His face tensed, visibly disturbed by the suggestion. Queen Farin focused back on Lanen. "Let's see how many strikes it takes to end your life."

Lanen made one vow to himself.

I will not scream.

The first tamer positioned himself to the right of him.

He lassoed the whip to gain momentum. The first blow tore into his clothes and reached flesh. The razor like thorns ripped them open as they snaked around his body before leaving.

I must endure until I no longer feel pain!

At first, the masses cheered, seeing justice be done. It turned to disgust and fear when after the fifteenth strike, Farin ordered, with eyes gleaming with bloodlust, "This is no fun." She turned to the other tamer waiting to switch if needed. "You. Join in the fray."

The tamer, shocked by the request, hesitated.

"As you wish, my Queen."

He stood on the other side and struck in succession.

Blood pooled under Lanen. His vision blurred, making it a hazy blot. The pain subsided. His body went limp.

A hushed silence enveloped him.

Did the room go quiet, or am I on death's door?

"Yes! That's better." Queen Farin smiled widely, her expression one of evil. "Tear him apart. Make sure his house relishes in this sacrifice for their sake."

Lanen closed his eyes. No reason to cling to life any longer.

Farin felt the mood shift immediately. From the reactions, she knew she resembled a monster. Worse than her father when he lost his mind. Romnus stared at her in horror. The traitors wept loudly, while Lord Lanen's blood sprayed onto them. The gruesome sight made her insides clench. It was far more than she wanted to display. She wanted to make a point about executing their own.

This went too far.

Fifty lashes turned to eighty-five by adding the other tamer. She watched Lanen's body sway in the air with each strike.

He no longer moved.

No! That's not what I wanted!

With the last strike, they released the tethers. Lanen's body fell into the puddle of his own blood, splattering it to create a pattern.

Farin rose from her throne and walked down the steps.

"Is that to your satisfaction?" She addressed the audience inside the room and those outside watching on the holoscreen.

"We're you entertained?" She kept the façade of enjoying the bloodshed as she scanned the traitors' faces. "It seems I must agree to the terms. You are all free to shame your house once more."

Whispers began.

Among them, she heard the term she expected.

Monster.

Other members muttered, "such evil," under their breaths.

Farin walked over to Lanen and knelt beside him. She could tell he had a spark of life left. Leaning down, she whispered in his ear.

"You say you want to protect them? If you value such things, you will fight to live. Is this what you want Azrom to be?" His fingers twitched. "If not, then open your eyes," she demanded. "Show me your resolve. Don't you dare die!"

She stood, gesturing to the medical team waiting in the wings.

"Take him to the dungeon. If he still lives by morning, treat him. Then send him back to his home." She glared at him. "If they choose to welcome him back." They opened the portable stretcher and rolled him onto it until he was again face down. Most of the wounds covered his back. "Tell no one. Understood?"

The two medics nodded.

As far as the witnesses knew, Lord Lanen had met death in the throne room. Farin turned back to go up the stairs. The way Romnus and their entourage looked at her, stopped her in her tracks. She forced a smile and went back to her throne.

"How messy," she huffed. "I guess we should move to the conference chamber until this is cleaned up."

Romnus didn't speak. Biandra turned her head away from her.

"How could you?" The words were barely audible.

Farin realized instantly how this looked in her eyes. Her father had done the same to Biandra decades ago. She seethed inside for not removing her from the room beforehand.

I'm sorry!

Batis gave her a look of disappointment. General Kur tsked in disgust while General Rass stared in awe. Even he, a lover of bloodshed and carnage, felt the scene over the top.

☼ ☼ ☼

Dungeon guards hardly ever cared about their charges. Prisoners were meant to suffer. Even Batis, a superior officer who had been stripped of his rank, received the proper level of torment for his crimes against the then princess Farin. At times, the guards craved it.

This time was different.

Knowing the harm caused by the fourth house, they had agreed with the execution. Since the traitors' return, the sentiment waned. Enough killing of their own. A few factions still held resentment until the day of reckoning. Seeing Queen Farin's viciousness stunned the masses. That Romnus stood by and let that happen to one of his bloodline angered many.

What could he have done, though?

The first guard weaved through the dimly lit corridor that led to the farthest cell. At that moment, no one would dare defy her. His eyes adjusted to the gloom and focused on the figure lying in a heap against the wall. The energy beams across the entrance buzzed softly.

"Lord Lanen." He called out to him. No movement. "Lord Lanen." He stirred, raising his head to peer at the guard. "We've come to check your wounds and brought food." He deactivated the beams. The other two guards behind him went inside. "Please make sure to eat."

Dungeon guards trained for emergency medical care eliminated the royal physicians getting their hands dirty. To come down into the filth. The first guard frowned. It insulted him and his men. They kept the place fairly clean despite its aesthetics.

Not supposed to have the comforts of home.

He observed Lord Lanen's slow moves, letting the other guards check him before accepting the warm broth and bread. He still couldn't handle meat. Him being alive proved nothing short of a miracle. It took nearly half a year for him to recover. Each day in the beginning, a touch and go. Later in the day, they would transport him home.

Thank the gods!

To lose a potential royal house head would devastate them.

Queen Farin.

Now they all knew the Infant Queen to be a monster.

Far worse than her tyrant father. That moniker would be retired.

She was no longer viewed as a child.

The first guard accompanied the transport team to personally escort Lord Lanen to the fourth house. He needed to see it through, not trusting them to be careful with him. At the palace entrance, the head maid greeted them, directing them to the side doors to prevent the rest of the house from seeing Lord Lanen's arrival.

He had never been in the fourth palace. The sprawling halls of tan, gold, and sandstone awed him. So different from the main palace's stark white with hints of green and blue. The group went through three long hallways before ending at the opposite wing where the traitors' housing lay.

A royal guard stepped from the center of the entourage and helped his men guide the hover stretcher into the far chamber. He halted at the door and turned to bow his head.

"Thank you for bringing him home. Lord Elendar is most grateful."

Once the stretcher cleared the door out of sight, the dungeon guard breathed a sigh of relief. His duty now complete, he left with the others back to the main palace.

☼ ☼ ☼

Sensing a presence in his chamber, Lanen raised his head off his pillow and peered into the darkness. A better bed allowing comfort replaced his old one. And it worked. He didn't want to get up.

His vision landed on the woman standing at the foot of the bed. Though her face remained blurry, he could feel her apprehensiveness.

"I didn't mean to wake you."

Her remorseful tone made him tense.

"It's fine. What brings you so far into the palace?"

"Am I not allowed to check on my mate?"

"You haven't referred to me as such in centuries." Her guilt thickened. He tried to push it away. I don't want it! "No need to worry. I'm staying clear of the main halls."

"That's not…" Her hands clenched. "I'm worried. And so are our children."

He doubted that.

His children hated him. Their reasoning still a mystery.

"If it's okay with you, can we visit when you're feeling better?"

"I have never stopped you or them from seeing me." He laid back down. "Do as you please."

She lingered.

"Welcome home, Lanen," she whispered, leaving the room.

Her visit left him feeling like he had wronged her somehow. Again. Curling into a fetal position under the covers, Lanen cleared his mind. The first person to see him and he couldn't muster enough energy to tell her to leave.

For weeks he kept to himself, not leaving his chamber. He also refused well-wishers, not allowing his comrades to show pity. The one person he couldn't avoid was Elendar. After a month and a half, he showed up, visibly angry.

"What are you doing?" Elendar entered his chamber in a whirlwind of energy. Far more than necessary. "I need you to get yourself together and help me."

"Do what, exactly?"

Lanen sat in the high-back chair next to his bed. The ornate carved armrests gleamed from being recently polished. He wore a loose long-sleeved tunic and leggings. His hair lay undone across his shoulders, the rest hitting the middle of his back.

Elendar breathed sharply. His royal garbs made him look more intimidating. Well, not to him. He often found Elendar insufferable. He didn't want the head title or status, so he relinquished it to him.

That was part of why his mate felt upset about it. She could have been the lady of the fourth royal house.

"We have much to repair in this house. Since you're the cause of our strife, you will help rebuild it."

"That's fair." Lanen slouched, letting his arms hang over and his legs spread wide. "I have no intention of you taking it on alone."

Elendar's expression changed. He stared at him.

"Are you still not moving well?"

Lanen raised his brow in surprise.

"I could ask you say the same." He noticed the way Elendar held his posture. Compensating for a wound close to his hip. "Should either of us attempt such a feat?"

Elendar frowned.

"It's not like we don't have assistance."

"Those lazy advisors and lords who haven't done their duties the past two centuries? I hope you're joking."

A touchy subject that needed addressing, Lanen tried to feel optimistic. An awkward silence fell between them. To break it, he changed the subject to an even more depressing topic.

I can't help myself, can I?

"My mate came to see me."

Elendar's gaze widened.

"What could she want?"

"A truce?"

"She's the one who started the battle."

"I should try to fix it. For my spawns' sake and mine."

"Hmm." Elendar tilted his head. "I guess that would be best. I started fixing my relationship with mine."

"We need to. This house won't stand if we can't keep our family together."

"I'm not forgiving our illustrious queen for what she did!"

"Apparently, no one is with her."

"It was monstrous!"

"I know her reason."

"What?

"It's a secret between us."

Elendar didn't like that. Not knowing anything behind the scenes always made him squirm. Lanen chuckled at his confused expression. How childish! He didn't elaborate.

"Fine. Have you talked with your son yet?"

His son had opted to become a philanderer and run a small commodities venture. It disappointed him, knowing his son could do better. His daughter was no better. Living off her status instead of doing anything of value.

Then again, he never wanted them to go on the same path as him. The battle scars were too harsh a reminder.

"He wants to speak with me. I just don't know how to approach."

"Demand his presence. He's not doing anything productive."

☼ ☼ ☼

Lord Kel tense in frustration watching his youngest child walk down the palace corridor, only to be accosted by three royal guards. Those soft features did nothing to identify the child as his, nor his mother's. Dark blonde hair bordering on light brown touched the area below their shoulder blades. Not quite straight or wavy. Pale skin and pink full lips accented the exotic features of their face. An understated beauty from their lack of presentation.

They did it to avoid attention.

The guards pushed and taunted. Grabbing their hair. Touching them inappropriately. Not letting them get away until they got bored. His child took it in stride, not showing fear. Another day in the palace.

Lord Kel kept their lineage a secret. Two of his eldest and a handful of advisors knew. He regretted the hardship and abuse they suffered at the hands of his own family.

It shouldn't have happened.

I've failed you.

They came within a few feet of him and bowed their head like any royal member would. Except they didn't have to do that. Lord Kel seethed. Don't do that! When it seemed they would continue past him, he held an arm out to stop them.

"Did I offend you, Lord Kel?"

Soft spoken, they held their head down.

"Do not leave my presence without stating your day."

"My apologies, your grace."

Lord Kel clenched his teeth. Why is this so hard?

"How does your work fare? Are you having any difficulties?"

"Everything is well. My duties are limited to the library."

"As a mid-level scholar, you need to broaden your knowledge."

"Of course. I'll look into what tasks the elders want me for"

The awkward air felt stifling. Lord Kel lowered his arm.

"Good. You may proceed."

When they were hallway down the hall, Lord Kel realized his clenched fists. He loosened his fingers, letting blood flow normally.

"That went better than expected," his personal assistant said.

"I didn't want it to be this way."

"Then you should have announced their existence long ago. You made a deal with Lanen to keep them safe."

"And I failed."

Their child had been beaten, raped, imprisoned, and falsely accused of wrongdoings. Yet he refused to bring them under his protection. Nothing he could say or do remedied those incidents. Instead, he brought swift vengeance on those who harmed them. Many not understanding why they were being persecuted.

His eldest sons found his actions disgusting.

Why go through that for a spawn you won't recognize?

A valid argument he had no answer for. Nomin constantly berated him for it. The only person allowed to talk to him that way. He learned long ago he needed someone to keep him in line.

Be a confidante.

The child's mate died in battle, leaving them to raise three spawns alone in a hostile environment. The place they called home. He arranged a sprawling chamber on a separate wing of the palace for them. Their mate requested it after their union, isolating them from the rest of the royal members.

They have no allies to turn to.

"What are you thinking, my lord?"

Nomin expressed concern.

"Would Lanen forgive me?"

"No. I'm sorry to say that ship has sailed."

"I want to speak with him once he's out of recovery."

"Elendar would demand a reason. He would forbid your entry

if you weren't of royal blood. Are you going to reveal the truth to get access to Lanen?"

"If I must." Lord Kel felt his chest tighten.

"Not your greatest idea."

His sins were many and cruel. All done out of selfish needs. Because he could, he did. Destroying lives along the way.

First Elendar, then Lanen.

Thinking since he had already infiltrated that house, there was no reason to look elsewhere for prey. His eldest children no longer respected him.

"Send the request." Lord Kel resumed walking.

"As you wish, my lord."

The three soldiers were still laughing when Lord Kel closed in on them. They barely had time to turn and bow before he nodded to his guards. With quick speed, the guards cut them down. Nothing lethal. Blood sprayed from the cuts across their chests as they fell back onto the floor.

No words were spoken. The guards sheathed their swords and fell back into formation behind Lod Kel. He glared at the heap of soldiers as he stepped away. Up ahead, he addressed the sentry at another corridor entrance.

"Send a medical team to that hallway." He nodded his head back towards where he came. "Make sure they recuperate in the dungeons for a few days."

"Yes, your grace. I will dispatch them right away."

Knowing that wasn't the sentry's duty, Lord Kel marveled at his haste to get a replacement at the entrance. The soldier head down to the soldiers while tapping his earpiece to call for a medic.

"At least you know they still fear you," Nomin quipped.

Lord Kel frowned. He never set out to run his house that way. Where did it all go wrong?

Not one hover light glowed in the gloomy chamber. Elendar barely made out the forms of the furniture. On the bed, he noticed the lump moving under the covers. The plush carpet muted his footsteps as he approached the side of it. Lanen's head lay exposed. His body appeared curled on its side in a fetal position. Pain still etched his face. Elendar tapped down his rage.

"Lord Kel has requested an audience with you. I have stated the condition that I be present in case he has any nefarious ideas."

Lanen opened his eyes. A sadness fell over him.

He wiggled his arms out and rose on his side.

"What could he want? He's done enough to this house."

"His message's tone seemed quite agitated."

"Is that so?" Lanen slouched.

"You need to get up and dressed. Do you need a chambermaid?"

"No." Lanen let out a sharp sigh, sitting up. "I can handle this much." He swung his legs over and planted his feet on the floor. "I've survived worse than clothing."

Elendar tried not to stare at the faint lines where the tamer whip tore Lanen's flesh. The wounds were too deep to erase. One could only see them if they got close enough.

"I'll wait for you in the main hall."

He left his brother to be alone for a while. It would take him longer than usual to get ready. No rush. If Lord Kel really wanted an audience, he would wait for as long as it took. Dalfir met him by the entrance. His scrunched facial expression meant a lecture for Elendar about strolling the palace halls alone.

They entered the main hall where all four of his children also stood in attendance. The two with Dalfir and the other two by Lord Kel. The stark difference in features allowed one to recognize who fathered which.

Elendar stared at Lord Kel's spawn. The taller, muscular one had short cropped dark blond hair while his leaner brother had long, jet black hair past his waist. Like replicas of Romnus and their father in reverse.

A court servant came to the door.

"Lord Kel of the third royal house has arrived."

They turned sideways and gestured with one arm for them to enter. "Proceed."

Lord Kel flowed into the hall as if he ruled it. His expression changed when he saw Elendar's ire. The way his offspring glared at him didn't help the mood.

"Greetings Lord Elendar. I come bearing no ill will."

"That remains to be seen" Elendar retorted.

"I assure you." He addressed his sons. "I see you're doing well in your duties."

"It's the least we can do," the dark-haired one replied.

Lord Kel scanned the room.

"Is Lord Lanen not joining us?"

"He'll arrive shortly. His movements are limited these days." Elendar said.

Within minutes, Lanen entered with his slumped posture and defeated demeanor, making everyone uncomfortable. He locked eyes with Lord Kel. Elendar couldn't put his finger on what transpired between them. But saw the seriousness of it.

"Lord Kel." Lanen moved further into the hall, not straying too far from the entrance. "I heard you requested to speak with me. What could you want now?

Lord Kel tensed. Nomin glanced away.

"When you left my palace long ago, I didn't think of what to do with the child you spawned for me."

"You forced me to leave them with you after you were done with me."

Elendar did a sharp intake, curbing his urge to attack Lord Kel. That monster even dared to take my brother? What madness.

"What's this?" Elendar bristled. "Humiliating and destroying me wasn't enough?"

"I'll admit, I was angry that you wouldn't bend to my will. So, yes. I chose to try my hand at decimating your house further. Knowing his mate and children had abandoned him, he seemed an easy target."

"And this visit regards this child?"

Dalfir held in his fury as well.

"Our child has been through hardships. I'm certain you had spies check on them."

"You promised me you would care for them as long as I told no one and returned home." Lanen's eyes glinted.

"I know. I broke that promise. But you must know that it wasn't by design."

"It was," Lanen seethed, yet he remained calm. "By keeping him a secret. Not acknowledging him as part of your household. You are the reason for their torture."

"Wait!" Lord Kel's muscular son turned to him. "You denied them their status? To what end? Why subject your own child to…"

He stopped, his eyes wide.

"Rumors of a scholar the palace members abuse for fun has been going around. Don't tell me…"

"Things got out of hand. I would never want harm to come to them." Lord Kel exclaimed. "I punished anyone who did so."

"That doesn't wipe the slate clean." Elendar leaned forward, clenching his fists. "The damage was already done."

Lanen stood silent. Everyone did the same, waiting for him to respond. His face went slack, void of emotion.

"Release them." He looked up at Lord Kel. "It's obvious you can't care for them. We will provide a safe haven here."

"I can't do that." Lord Kel's eyes narrowed. "They are a mid-tier scholar in my house. I can't let them go."

"That's not a valid argument," Dalfir stated.

Elendar fumed inside. He didn't know what the remedy for the situation entailed. As much as he despised what Lord Kel had done, he saw his side of it regarding the child's scholar status.

"You will do this." Lanen's tone dripped with venom.

"You must understand…"

"Then allow them leave to come here." Elendar calmed himself and let his arms relax. "They will reside here for one year. If they choose to remain, you will not interfere."

Lord Kel struggled with the proposal. Lanen closed his eyes for a moment.

"Their scholar duties can be temporarily transfered here. This way, they can familiarize themselves with our libraries."

"That sounds doable," Lord Kel's assistant, Nomin, answered. "Nothing is lost in this transaction. Please consider it."

"I will ask them." Lord Kel glanced over at Lanen.

"No." Lanen's stare burned into him.

"No?" Lord Kel looked confused. "Why?"

"I will ask them myself."

"You haven't set foot in my palace since." Lord Kel protested.

"Then I suggest you grant him access," Elendar said. "You owe them both."

Internal Conflicts

At the sound of his study chamber doors opening, Lord Kel turned from his desk to address the subjects he summoned earlier. Two of his elite personal soldiers and two midlevel scholars stood before him. Their heads bowed slightly in greeting.

"We are here as requested, my lord," the soldier farthest left announced.

"Yes." Lord Kel's gaze roamed the ensemble while crossing his arms. "I have a special mission for you."

The four relaxed their stance and focused their attention on him. He took a few steps back to lean against his desk.

"As you may know, Azrom has regency over many worlds. Most by conquest. Since the war with our new enemy, only a handful have contributed to the cause."

"Treasonous!" The other soldier hissed, then tsked in disgust.

"Hmm. Is it?" The scholar on the right gave him a side glance.

Their counterpart leaned forward to better see the soldier.

"Would you volunteer assistance to the ones who invaded and took control of your planet if it were not implicit you do so?"

Lord Kel tilted his head at seeing the soldier's aura smolder.

"I have appointed a representative from my inner circle to head this venture."

He saw them frown, dubious of who he referred to. Every elite in his service knew he had an even more secret detail unseen. Bringing one out into the open would be unprecedented. Lord Kel motioned to the sentry outside the door.

"Lead him in."

They turned to watch a soldier round the corner and entered.

The clack of his black knee-high boots echoed with each step. His approach seemed to move in slow motion as they stared in awe.

Gun metal armor with the house crest surrounded by swirls etched into its surface covered the waist and chest. A midnight blue body suit lay beneath. The matching cloak secured on the shoulder clasps flowed behind him as if being lifted by an invisible wind.

They glimpsed the jet-black hair in a fish bone tail braid that swayed across his lower back. Well-toned arm muscles bulged at the sleeves. His demeanor and presence struck fear in them as he passed. Though his face appeared serene, emotionless, his gait and piercing grey eyes told them he had slaughtered many.

Lord Kel looked on, amused by their reaction.

They're not wrong. He is indeed deadly.

The soldier stopped between the group and bowed. When his head rose, his eyes locked with Lord Kel's.

"Reporting as you command, my lord."

Lord Kel couldn't hold it in any longer. He unleashed a hearty laugh, throwing his head back, then immediately composed himself.

"To think even my elite has someone who makes them cower."

They broke out of their stupor, regaining their dutiful posture.

"I present to you, Commander Avaris. He will lead this mission with my full confidence."

"What exactly is our mission?" The first soldier asked.

"Commander Avaris will relay the details once you are enroute." Lord Kel's eyes narrowed. "Your only priority is to ensure his safety at all costs. Even if it means your death."

Their horror-stricken expressions instantly turned to anger. The second soldier and scholar opened their mouths, ready to protest. Before they could respond, he glowered at them.

"Yes. He is that important to me. Do not question my decree."

Lord Kel moved off his desk and sat in the overlarge cushioned chair behind it.

"I look forward to your reports," he addressed commander Avaris. "Dismissed." He waved a hand at them. "And safe journey."

Still miffed, the four exited the chamber, flanking Commander Avaris in the center.

Farin kept silent as he walked with his protectors. He hadn't been in male form for a long time. To reestablish his bearings, he practiced in secret. Still a bit awkward. Hence the fierce expression when he entered the chamber. Sensing their fear, he silently apologized.

Reaching the dock doors, it opened to a transport waiting to take them to the underground shipyard. They climbed in and got into comfortable positions. It took off into the tunnel at high speed, plastering them to the backs of their seats. Farin gritted his teeth to stop his mouth from flapping open.

The transport slowed to a crawl, stopping at the hangar. Twenty-foot-tall solid metal doors slid open with a loud shush. Air concaved inward around their frames. Beyond lay thousands of ships, as far as the eye could see. The rest were out of view. Farin had only been down there once. The sight of so many magnificent ships made his chest tighten with pride.

A crew finished the last checks for the convoy ship on the right. Without saying a word, Farin marched up the ramp. His entourage followed. He wanted to get started right away.

There was no time to waste.

☼ ☼ ☼

For ten days, Romnus scoured the palace in search of his queen. His bedchamber remained cold and empty without her. A tightness in his chest warned him of the reason. Farin voiced concerns about how Azrom dealt with the conquered planets. Halfar agreed with his and the council's decisions. Over time, she distanced herself from them, not attending the royal meetings.

As a last resort, he sought out Chastan. He would know Farin's whereabouts. It was his duty. If he won't answer, maybe Chardon could shed light on Farin's thinking.

He strolled silently to the deepest part of the palace where the corridors narrowed, then opened to shadowy halls. Party areas long forgotten and unused for over a century. Light layers of sandy dirt covered the floors. How did that get in from outside?

His footsteps made swish sounds with each step.

Chastan emerged from the ceiling, piercing the dark with his blond hair and fair complexion. He wore all black. His cloak swayed as he crawled the wall in an upside-down position. Flipping upright when he reached a few feet from the ground.

"I know why you're here." Chastan stepped closer, leaving a four-foot space between them. "She's quite angry."

"I get that. She didn't need to vanish."

"You, her father, the council. Every single one of you ignored her ideas. Treated her like a child."

Romnus growled, baring his teeth.

"We did no such thing! I didn't…"

He stopped, realizing the lie he uttered.

Chastan tilted his head at him.

"She needs time to rethink her role in this empire."

"What?" Romnus' tensed, afraid of what Chastan may say.

"She has left Azrom and will return in two years. She asks that you do not try to find her."

"No! that's too long!" Romnus moved forward. He felt Chastan's murderous intent. "She can't just leave her throne."

"According to who?" Chastan gave him a pitiful stare. "That is part of why she no longer wishes to be present."

Romnus hung his head. He never intended to push her away. Halfar and the council had more experience. The incident with the fourth house traitors scared him. He didn't want her to turn into a tyrant thirsting for power.

"She cannot be gone that long. I stand by my decree."

"And how will you do that?" Chastan's aura shifted further. Romnus wondered if he really wanted to fight. "Will you announce her absence?"

Romnus stood dumbstruck. Of course not! If anyone found out she had left the palace, let alone Azrom, the chaos would consume the empire.

"What would you have me do?" Romnus snapped.

"That's what she relayed to me. She has decided to leave on a journey of leisure to see the other worlds in the system. As queen, she should familiarize herself with them while enjoying her youth."

A sputter erupted from Romnus' lips as the corners twitched. The explanation sounded ludicrous. Then again, the courts would breathe a sigh of relief. They didn't need to worry about her antics.

"Send her a message. She must return by the end of one year."

"You know she won't do as you say. She'll come back when she feels like it."

Romnus clenched his fists. He knew that better than anyone. He turned away and walked back from where he came.

"Just do it. I will figure out the rest."

Darkness enveloped Chastan as he returned to the shadows. Romnus felt his presence disappear.

Farin has left me!

The thought hurt him to his core.

Please. Return to me.

The first guardian eyed Commander Avaris dubiously, not sure if his hunch was correct. Something about the way their charge moved screamed importance far beyond Lord Kel. He watched him go behind the bridge crew, double checking instruments and data. As if learning instead of dictating. His counterpart and the two scholars seemed to not notice or genuinely weren't paying attention.

He waited until the man sat in the captain's seat on the raised dais in the center of the bridge.

"So, tell me, Commander Avaris." He leaned over the bar set behind him. "This mission. Do you really think you can persuade these leaders to pledge allegiance to Azrom?"

"Nothing gained from doing nothing."

"True. But many of them are presumably hostile."

"That's why you're here." Avaris glanced over his shoulder. "To make sure we come out of this alive if it comes to that."

His counterpart scoffed.

"We should just bombard their planets. Force them to comply."

"Which accomplishes what?" Avaris glared at him. "The goal is to strengthen our hold, not demolish it."

The first scholar nodded.

"What was that saying Lord Halfar said once? You can trap more bees with honey."

"Such a ridiculous notion," the other guardian spat. "Earth terms make no sense."

"Let's see how the first talks go before we write this mission off." Avaris settled back in the seat. "It'll tell us how to move forward with the others."

"That's assuming it goes well," the other scholar said.

"Either way, it's a gauge we can work with." Avaris' stare was glued to the darkness of space. "Prepare to open the vortex," he instructed the navigator.

The first guardian noticed the way he crossed his legs. As if sitting on a throne.

Who are you, really?

Exiting the vortex, their ship switched engines and headed for the surface. The world's leader had granted permission beforehand. It coasted towards the open dock ahead atop a massive structure with spikes protruding from its corners. Grappling arms reached out on approach, took hold and wrenched it down onto the clamps.

"A bit aggressive," the first scholar stated.

The motion rocked the ship, causing everyone on the bridge to hold on so they didn't get tossed.

"I feel they're not welcoming us," the second guardian added.

"Then they shouldn't have agreed to this meeting."

Farin stood when the ship stopped rocking from the arms rough treatment. He made his way to the ramp as it lowered. Four angry aliens waited below.

Here goes nothing!

The conference room had a slight chill to it.

Much like the reception the leader and his soldiers gave Farin and his people. They all sat around a square table that took up a third of the area. Farin barely got his ass in the cushioned curve seating when the leader slammed his fist down.

"Have you come here to subjugate us further? Was destroying most of our livelihood not enough?"

Still leaned forward with both hands on the table, Farin looked over at him with steely eyes. The leader flinched, visibly shaken. His soldiers shrunk back in their seats.

"Did you not want to negotiate new terms? Was I mistaken in thinking you wanted a peaceful resolution?" Farin moved to rise.

"Wait." The leader held up his hand in defeat. "My apologies. I am just unsure of your motives."

"Then you should ask first," the first scholar replied.

"Better yet," the second continued, "wait for our representative to speak before casting judgement."

Farin finished sitting. He drummed his fingers on the table then let them slid into his lap. He locked eyes with the leader.

"I've come to ask for a partnership. As you know, our new enemy doesn't discriminate who they attack."

"You want our compliance?" The leader blinked.

"In exchange, we will rebuild your infrastructure and establish a new trade hub."

The soldiers seemed to perk up. Ahh. Farin realized they had to be his military advisors. He heard they pulled double duty as heads of the monarch.

"That sounds too easy. What do you really want?"

"No deception. This benefits both parties."

The incredulous stares were almost comical. Even his guardians and the scholars looked shocked by the terms.

Good. This is a decent start.

After so many delays and the need to return home multiple times, Chardon resumed his meeting with the regent leaders. Ganna opted out of attendance, leaving Volma and Jaron to help him. Once again, Folza allowed them entry, since nothing happened previously.

"I require that you tell me what you need," Chardon implored the regent planet's representatives.

They went silent, contemplating the request.

Adan already voiced satisfaction with his planet's deal with New Lassa. Contracts from other worlds flowed in at a steady pace. Twenty percent of the revenue went to purchasing materials and upgrading tools.

The other leaders took part in the alliance and hadn't thought to ask for anything else. Chardon knew they had needs. The Dreridians wouldn't have given them to Sestis otherwise. Planets in the decline after being ravished by them or Azrom.

How dirty. He hated the way the alliance races operated. Not even the Razznians went that far. Well, unless it was Azrom. They really despised each other before joining forces.

Colgar rubbed his chin, staring at the wall.

"It may sound trivial, but we could use more vendor contacts for building supplies."

"That's not trivial at all. Your planet already suffered from the battle with Yaos. And now you have massive damage from the Boretkz. Rebuilding your infrastructure is the first goal."

Volma took notes on her tablet, not looking up. She would have more questions later. Jaron simply nodded in agreement. As usual, Modas remained silent in the far corner of the room.

Emperor Xanic frowned, his tail swishing across the floor. Chardon received a report from the Razznians about appointing a regent planet in enemy territory. Did they really need my help now? He glanced around the table. Compared to the others, Xanic's planet appeared the most stable.

"I will wait and see how trade goes with our new acquisition." Xanic's tail stopped moving. "If a supplemental business seems necessary, I'll accept your assistance."

"Fair enough." He turned to the ambassador. "Anything from your ruler?"

That planet had a thriving underworld of dark trade. Their revenue relied on illegal contracts. Yet, on the surface, everything appeared legitimate. The population had no idea how corrupt their leadership was.

Until it all collapsed. Now they struggled to make ends meet with the heavy sanctions the Dreridians placed on them.

"Like our counterparts on Andal, we too would benefit from an injection of new business. Our lifestyles suffered from Dreridian restraints. It would be nice to bring back our celebrations."

Lombis smiled pitifully.

Which pissed Chardon off. There's always one. Where Colgar was humble and Adan and Xanic straight forward, this guy screamed untrustworthy on all levels. The ruler had yet to accept Chardon's invitations. Always sending the ambassador.

Jaron looked over at him. Their eyes met.

He may not be relaying your message to the ruler.

Jaron sent telepathically.

Chardon stopped himself from rearing his head up in surprise.

The thought had occurred to him, but he decided that would be ludicrous. Why hide the fact their regent wanted to help?

Then what is his agenda? Chardon snapped. *It makes no sense!*

Volma's eyes narrowed. She thinks so too. He glanced back at the ambassador.

"I want to keep the sanctions in place for now. We will get a handful of orders to see how it goes." Chardon saw his face twitch, the smile falling as his eyes stormed. "I've looked into your world's finances and I'm not sure you won't slide back into your old ways."

"Of course, I understand." Lombis bowed his head. "I was under the impression you were giving us a chance to redeem ourselves with this proposal."

This time, even Colgar, Adan, and Xanic stared incredulously at him. Volma averted her focus from the tablet and glared at him.

"Second chances are earned. We have yet to hear a strategy from your ruler or his cabinet. You've given us no information on the matter, thus far."

"Have I not?" He mocked surprise. "Is that so? Well." His attention returned to her. "I will get that to you post haste."

"Let's break for now." Chardon rose. "I need fresh air."

As everyone exited the room, Jaron held him back.

"Don't push it." He turned to Volma. "Same for you. We don't want him suspicious."

The three walked into the corridor.

Four guards immediately attached themselves to their party. They left the complex on the ground level and walked along the paved atrium. The sun, still high in the sky, lit up the colorful, crystal-like flowers. Their translucency made the area feel ethereal.

A messenger ran up to them from behind. The first guard stopped him, asking the reason for his presence, then let him pass.

"An urgent message for you, Lord Chardon."

Chardon presented his wristband for the messenger to tap it with his. The blue light indicating a receive notification flashed.

"Thank you."

The messenger ran back. Chardon resumed his walk.

"Not going to read it?" Jaron looked at him, confused. "He did say it was urgent."

Chardon chuckled.

"Unless we're under attack, it could only be Ganna or Halfar."

"The two neediest beings in existence," Volma snorted.

At the outskirts of the city, the guards ordered them to circle back the way they came. Chardon didn't ask permission to venture out past the main hub. He felt Chancellor Eydine would deny it.

Inside the conference room, Chardon went to the other side of the room to read the message before the others arrived. He tapped the link on his wristband. A small hologram popped up.

I have gone on an expedition to bring Azrom back to its former glory. My hope is that you also elevate Lassa and we rule both worlds with an iron fist.

My silly daughter has finally flipped her lid. Chardon chuckled, then went stoic. He recalled his meetings with Lord Pondur. That he now had regency over multiple planets.

Why not? Why shouldn't I strive to be a supreme ruler like Halfar? An emperor of his race like Xanic or Kraznan?

Something stirred within him. A sense of new power.

I'm tired of being seen as weak and incompetent.

He ended the message. Walking to the table, he caught Jaron's gaze. Whatever look he had startled her because she flinched. Chardon took a deep breath to calm himself. Right as the others flooded in, he put on a wide smile.

☼ ☼ ☼

"What do you mean, she's gone?"

Halfar asked Romnus, his fury visible.

Instead of keeping Farin's absence completely hidden, he opted to at least tell her father. Months had already passed, and no one questioned her absence. A telling sign of how the palace perceived her. It angered him.

He invited Halfar for a midday drink in the lounge chamber. White mist floated from the carafe of green liqueur in the center of the table. Both their glasses sat half empty. Romnus leaned back.

"She needs time to reassess her role and live a little," he replied with a straight face. "Or have you forgotten her age?"

Halfar's eyes narrowed.

"What did you do this time?"

Romnus frowned. Despite it being partly his fault, he didn't like being called out.

"You mean, what did we all do?"

"What are you talking about?"

"The rumors. The moniker our people attached to her. What did we expect her to feel after all that? She felt mistreated. Like a child."

"Which she is," Halfar retorted. His expression softened. "The Infant Queen." He smirked. Then his mood fell. Hearing it come from his own lips felt wrong. "I would be angry too."

"She says she wants to take two years away from Azrom."

Halfar slammed his fist on the table.

"Absolutely not! Tell her no!"

"As I've stated, she's already gone. I ordered Chastan to relay a message giving her one year."

"And her reply?"

"There hasn't been one."

"This is your doing." Halfar reached for his drink and took a sip. "You've been slipping on how you reign and she's lost confidence in you. I'm trying my best to guide you on the right course."

"I hope you're joking. Cousin." Romnus glared at him. "I wouldn't be Supreme Ruler if you had lived up to your status."

Halfar halted his drink midway to his lips and glanced over the rim at him. His forest green eyes glinted as if sparks lit up in them.

Neither spoke for a long stretch, not severing eye contact. Finally, Halfar took a deep breath, sipped his drink, and set down the glass.

"Fine. We're both in the wrong."

"Truer words have never been spoken." Batis leaned against the door frame, his arms crossed while a devious smile spread. "Glad to see you found out."

"How do you know about this?" Romnus demanded.

Batis pushed off the frame and sat next to Halfar. He grabbed a glass and poured himself a drink.

"The day she stopped coming to meetings. I had a feeling she had something up her sleeve. She seemed," he paused. "Agitated. Determined."

"You should have told me!" Romnus cried out.

"Why would you keep that from us?" Halfar yelled.

Batis took a sip and stared at them with disinterest.

"Why didn't you already know how she felt?"

His words slapped Romnus with painful reality. Halfar sat stunned into silence. He wasn't wrong. Their neglect led to this.

"So she's out gallivanting the system." Batis swirled his glass, watching the liquid move with its motion. "Do you really think she's on a vacation?"

"What else would she be doing?" Romnus asked, confused.

Batis looked at him. His expression dead serious.

"Usurping your reign." Batis looked disappointed. "What do you think she's been doing this whole time?" Romnus gave a blank stare. "If you ever want to find her, you need only search the archives."

Romnus had done so on numerous occasions. Farin stood out in the great hall. Not many scholars visited the place.

Which was a problem on its own.

Batis continued, addressing Halfar.

"Your child probably knows more about Azrom and its might than you." He pointed his pinky finger at Romnus. "And especially you." After taking another sip, he said, "I'd be prepared to step down in the next decade or so, if I were you."

Romnus thought about how diligently she studied the old records. How she perused battle plans when there would be no reason for her to engage in such things off-world.

I've made a mistake!

Halfar seemed deep in thought as well. Instead of an expression of understanding, his brow furrowed with severe ridges. He prided himself on being the most knowledgeable. Even the council didn't research the archives as they should. For the second time in his life, he feared for Farin's against her own father.

Batis caught the same sentiment.

He downed his drink and stood.

"Our pretty little queen is more formidable than you think. If you keep underestimating her, she will eat you alive. As the one who trained her in combat, she is a force to be reckoned. Tread carefully."

When he left the room, Romnus filled his glass and took a gulp. In truth, he had forgotten. Farin would no longer be the carefree, helpless child of before.

Come back to me! He pleaded once more.

They needed to talk it out. Protecting his queen took priority.

CHAPTER FOUR

Trade Secrets

"So Azrom looks to negotiate under the pretense of deception."

The ruler of the regent planet turned sideways to speak as he walked ahead of Farin and his entourage. His swagger commanded an air of superiority that even had him in awe. When he turned to face forward, continuing to escort them, Farin wracked her brain on why it seemed so sinister yet also familiar.

His dark blond wavy hair brushing the bottom of his shoulder blades. The maroon leather waist coat and leggings with black boots. Full of arrogance.

Talas! He reminds me of Talas.

Except Farin had never seen the Lassian warrior with so much confidence. Then again, he hadn't visited or paid much attention in quite a while.

"Whatever do you mean?" Farin felt uneasy.

His entourage went on alert.

Out of the seven worlds they visited so far, only two ended up hostile. Those he cracked down on resorting to violence. This one, he wasn't sure about.

Their greeting, though cordial, came off cold. Indifferent. They showed a lack of respect for any representatives of Azrom. After being taken to the planet's ruler, he saw it intensify.

"And you want to continue with this game." His exasperated tone flared Farin's anger. "You may call yourself whatever you choose. I know who you are."

The first guardian got closer to Farin, startling him. He regained his composure before the ruler could sense it.

"What is he implying?" the first scholar asked, puzzled.

They arrived at a conference room that at first appeared empty. Within seconds, Farin noticed the air move. Dark cloaked soldiers surrounded them.

"Your oppression nearly crippled my people." The ruler turned around to face them. "We survived by going behind your backs and setting up new routes."

"Which is a violation of the decree," the second scholar piped up. "That alone is justification for this inspection."

"You don't seem to understand." The ruler raised his arms. "We will no longer abide by your rules."

Farin whirled around and pushed the first scholar towards the doors. The loud clank of a sword striking the floor echoed from where he once stood. With him out of the way, Farin pivoted in time to unsheathe his sword and block the ruler's strike.

"Thank you for such a grand opportunity to rid Azrom of its monarch." The ruler leaned close, whispering it in his ear. "Romnus will have no choice but to retaliate."

Farin jumped back to make some distance. The ruler refused to play fair. He charged forward while two other soldiers uncloaked themselves to join in. Farin ducked under, blocking one with his sword, then punched his razor-sharp talons into the other. He ripped his claws out and used that hand to lift himself up into a handstand. His legs bent around and kicked the ruler entering his space.

"I knew it was you." The guardian took out two more soldiers while his counterpart defended the scholars who backed out into the corridor. "This was a dangerous venture, my Queen."

"What?" The second guardian yelled.

"Are you certain?" The first scholar asked incredulously.

"Commander Avaris is our Queen!"

The second guardian yelled, fighting off multiple assailants.

"Indeed." The first guardian replied, backing up further to force Farin and the others down the hall.

Farin's shocked gaze fell on him. He landed back on his feet and ran behind him.

"How?" Farin skewered an enemy soldier and kicked him out

of the way. "The whole point was to be incognito."

"You can't really fool anyone when you fight like that. No one else moves like you."

Well, damn!

Farin agreed. The one thing he couldn't hide or change.

"Let's get out of here!"

"We can't get to our ship without a fight." The second guardian eyed the horde of enemy soldiers coming up behind them.

"Fight?" Farin turned to the first guardian. "Initiate plan two."

He tapped the commlink on his wrist. White noise erupted.

The ruler came into the corridor grinning maniacally.

"Were you trying to contact your ship? I blocked all signals. My forces are heading up to destroy your little fleet." He smirked. "You should've known better."

Farin raised his chin, staring downward at him.

"Stop this now or be annihilated." His eyes glowed. "I won't give you a second chance."

The ruler seemed to hesitate, not sure if he was bluffing. Farin expanded his telepathy, reaching the mind of the weapons technician.

Rain fire on the capital.

He could feel the shock and pain of his intrusion, then resolve.

Within minutes, the building shook as Azrom fire pummeled the area. The ruler grabbed hold of the door frame as the quake forced him to slide backwards. He stared up in terror at the hairline cracks in the ceiling. Farin's entourage looked confused as well.

"What's happening?" The ruler yelled into his wrist link.

"Azrom is attacking!" A voice came through.

The ruler glared at Farin.

"You brought this on yourself," Farin admonished him. "Do you still want to defy our rule? I can arrange seizure of everything you hold dear. Strip you of your title." He tapped his sword against one shoulder. "I may still do that." His eyes narrowed. "You've pissed me off."

The term, there's always one, stuck in Chardon's head. Ambassador Lombis' words and behavior sent multiple red flags. Adan pulled him aside while leaving to whisper in his ear to move with caution. The other representatives clearly didn't trust him either.

Great!

With the last meeting over, his entourage thanked Chancellor Eydine before heading to their ship. Volma kept absentmindedly reaching for her tablet, eager to start crunching the data. Jaron had a scowl, knowing she had to report her opinions to Talas. Chardon would take of relaying the information to Ganna and Mercan.

Inside the enormous transport hub, he took in its configuration for the first time. New Lassa, though a third of its size and not as grand, had similarities. Expansion was on the table. The planet had plenty of room without encroaching on the population.

"What is your next action, leader?"

Volma whipped out her tablet.

Jaron leaned back in her seat, crossing her arms.

"I think a visit to Suma Andal is in order." She glanced at Chardon. "They've cut themselves off from Colgar's rule."

"Yes, I have a feeling the one he appointed to run Suma is long gone. Exiled, imprisoned, or dead."

"But what do they gain from this?" Volma frowned, her gaze glued to the screen. "Lombis must know we won't release funds to rebuild without speaking to Colgar's proxy on Suma."

"He's gotten away with it so far," Chardon replied.

"Prepare for first jump sequence," the ship's AI announced.

Volma stowed her tablet in the pocket under her seat. Jaron relaxed as hers reclined, allowing the tiny tendrils that administered the sedative to emerge from its sides. They slithered into her flesh.

Chardon tried not to tense up. He still hated space travel. Every one of the tiny tubes pricked him, making him wince.

Thank Lassa, the drug worked fast.

When he woke from the first leg of their journey, Chardon tapped the commlink for the bridge. He had decided on a new plan while sleeping. The situation garnered an immediate remedy.

"Change our destination to Suma Andal."

Jaron and Volma, stirring out of their slumber, immediately bolted upright.

"Contact Trinon and Talas. They'll meet us there. Tell them to bring a small fleet. Just in case."

"In case what?" Jaron exclaimed. "The last thing we need is a civil war."

"Then they better behave," Chardon snapped.

"We'll arrive a few days behind the Ambassador. Our fleet should be there within two days after us." Volma rubbed her eyes with the bottom of her palms. "Plenty of time to observe and do a quick reconnaissance.'

Jaron sighed, letting her head drop forward.

"I guess combat mode will be in effect once we get there."

Chardon smirked at her.

"When are you not in combat mode? Even when mating, you fight like a beast."

Jaron's eyes flared bright blue, her lips curled back to bare teeth.

"You don't know that," she seethed. "How dare you say that?"

Volma clamped a hand over her mouth to muffle her laughter. Jaron angrily turned to her as a warning. It only made her eyes squeeze shut in amusement.

"Both of you! Crude and lacking compassion." Jaron closed her eyes and took a deep breath. "I won't forgive you," she glanced over at Chardon, "cousin!"

This time, Chardon sputtered before breaking into a laugh. It changed the mood. Now that they were more at ease, the situation at hand could be dealt with rationally.

"New course mapped. Please prepare for jump sequence."

Despite only having two hours between jumps, they obeyed. Chardon loosened himself up. Once they come out and reach Suma Andal, he had to be ready.

Suma Andal.

A pristine ball of translucent white, pale green, and pink. Beautiful.

Chardon stared in amazement. He didn't expect such scenery. Ahead of him lay a checkpoint. He ordered the ship not to cross it until the fleet arrived. No need to announce their presence yet. Although Jaron advised they probably already knew.

Volma sent a small drone undetectable by most systems due to its size. Its powerful lens belied that. They received clear images of the surface. Which contrasted with the outer aesthetics.

The palace stood majestic against its immediate surroundings. On the outskirts proved a different story. Colorful banners and flags littered poverty-stricken towns. An attempt to show everything was in order. Each area had deep divides in the caste systems. The Earth saying, the haves and have nots, entered Chardon's mind. The footage did not surprise the others. Jaron simply pursed her lips in disdain.

From both sides of the ship, vortices opened for the Lassian fleet and a convoy vessel. The checkpoint lights flashed.

Well, no need to hide now.

"Incoming hail, Lord Chardon." The communications tech tapped his console to bring it up. "It's under an invader code."

"Should we…" Volma began.

"Open the channel," Chardon ordered. "I don't have time for these theatrics."

Invader code? The disrespect seeped into him. He was done playing games.

"Please approach the checkpoint for inspection or be categorized as an invader."

The male voice of what could only be the operator demanded.

"This is your regent, Lord Chardon of Lassa. If you choose to deny my ships' entry," Chardon paused for effect, "then I will assume you want to be annihilated."

Silence permeated the air.

Neither side spoke for nearly two minutes.

"My apologies, Lord Chardon. We had no notice of your visit."

"Because this is an impromptu call."

"Of course. Per our protocol, will you indulge us and proceed to the checkpoint?"

"Gladly. Standby."

The feed ended, leaving a bad feeling on the bridge. Another feed popped up.

"That's telling." Talas' face filled the main screen. "Just so you know, there are ships from other planets sitting in hidden hubs."

Volma frowned. She zoomed in on a few images.

"Is that what those are?" She leaned forward, then straightened her back. "I had no idea."

"Does this mean we've caught them engaging in underground business?" Trinon asked from behind Talas.

Chardon turned to Modas standing quietly near the doors.

"It may come to a fight. Don't kill him, even if he deserves it."

"Understood."

The fleet remained outside the checkpoint while the two convoy ships descended on Suma Andal. Weapon systems trained on them sat inactive as a show of acceptance, but Chardon knew they would power up in an instant if needed.

Six guards and four royal court members greeted them as they exited the ships in the palace dock. The tense atmosphere proved they were up to no good. Some of them shifted their eyes back and forth, checking the surroundings.

Out of the corner of his right eye, Chardon saw dock workers block the view of obvious merchants while covering up a shipment with heavy tarp.

Hmm? Well, look at that.

The court members engaged in insignificant small talk along the way. Talas noticed the route veered away from the center, where the proxy ruler's throne room lay. Instead, they entered a spacious chamber resembling a situation room. Ambassador Lombis awaited them behind an eight-foot-long desk set in front of two floor to ceiling windows.

The capitol loomed below. A juggernaut of trade activity.

"Lord Chardon!"

Lombis spread his arms wide.

"Why didn't you tell me? We could have come together instead of wasting your ship's energy cells."

"I decided on the way home that I should take a look at your world while out and about. Is this not a good time?"

"Oh. It's quite fine." Lombis moved from behind the desk and stopped a few feet from him. He gestured to the seating area. Plush high-back chairs and loveseats arranged in a semi-circle filled the left side of the room. The surrounding shelves held various artifacts and old tomes.

Talas and Jaron made a face, signaling Chardon to decline.

"Actually, I came to speak with the proxy ruler. Colgar voiced some concerns. Why were we not given audience when I specifically requested it upon arrival?"

Chardon saw Lombis' expression darken. Others in attendance grew tense while trying not to draw attention. Tiny blue sparks flicked along Volma's fingers.

"To be honest," Lombis answered in a defeated tone, "Our leader has been in poor health these days. He stays confined in his chamber and has handed the dealings of the planet to me."

Lombis held a hand to his chest and sighed heavily, bowing his head. Modas gave him a dead stare, amazed at the performance. A bold-faced lie.

"That's all well and good." Chardon's eyes narrowed. "I still need to speak with the ruler of this planet. You may have the reins, but you remain only a representative."

This time, Lombis' tone came out sternly.

"I insist our leader not be disturbed for trivial matters I can handle in his steed."

"Trivial matters?" Jaron drew out her words. "Is that how you see the business between a ruler and its regent?"

"Let's not take things out of context," Lombis blustered.

The guards went on alert, grazing their fingers across their swords' hilts as the court members eased towards the entrance.

"I'm merely voicing why we're unable to comply."

"Talas." Chardon only needed to say his name to give an order.

Lombis turned to him, confused.

In a flash, Talas pivoted towards the doors and shot down the corridor leading to the throne room.

Trinon followed, matching his speed. Caught off guard, the soldiers dashed in pursuit. Chardon's glare dared Lombis to move. The man smiled, shrugging, then sat in one of the plush chairs.

"I'm not sure what it is you hope to find, Lord Chardon. But, please, be my guest."

A message came across Chardon's wristband.

Throne is empty. Only scholars roaming the premises.

"Volma. Do you have the data on the proxy ruler?"

"I do." Volma pulled out her tablet and brought up a bio-scan. "I'll overlay the map of the palace over it."

Lombis became uneasy. He looked around at the remaining guards. Eight in total, they were no match for Chardon's entourage.

"Locating the proxy now."

"Go." Chardon tilted his head to her. Jaron followed as her protection. When he turned his attention back to Lombis, the man had moved. "What do you think you're doing?"

Lombis had reached a secret passage on the other side of the seating area. His hands gripped the sides, ready to disappear into its dark hole. A wall of flesh that was Modas blocked his escape. Twice his size, Modas towered over him like a menace.

"There's only the two!" One of the guards yelled.

They converged on Chardon, thinking Modas preoccupied was enough to hinder his assist. They were wrong. Being outnumbered meant nothing. Chardon built a ball of energy and unleashed it on the first four. Their bodies flew back, smoke drifting off them from singed skin and fabric.

Modas grabbed hold of Lombis' neck and tossed him back into the chamber. He landed near the large desk, hitting his head on the edge. For a moment, his vision turned to white noise. It cleared in time to watch Modas pummel two of his guards to the floor like the beast he was.

His massive fists rained down on them in succession, never missing. Blood flew with each strike. The brutality of it made the two left standing to retreat further into the room.

They quickly realized they had nowhere else to go.

Another message came.

Found him.

Followed by Talas.

Enroute.

"Grab him!" Chardon ordered Modas.

"Understood."

It only took two steps for Modas to reach Lombis. He picked him up by the back of his collar and proceeded to drag him backwards out the door behind Chardon. The two guards hesitated to move, then gave up, slumping against the wall.

"Unhand me! This is unacceptable!" Lombis screamed the whole way. No matter what he did to try dislodging himself from Modas grip, it failed. "I am the one in charge of Suma. You cannot disrespect me this way!"

They reached the personal chamber of the proxy ruler where Volma and Jaron already waited inside. The smell of burnt flesh wafted in the air. Five guards lay smoldering on the floor. Two by the doors, two more on each side of the giant bed, and a higher ranked royal guard's body slumped embedded in the far wall.

Talas and Trinon came up behind Chardon as Modas tossed Lombis into the room. On his hands and knees, he turned his head to gaze with hatred at them.

Lying unconscious on the bed, the proxy ruler resembled a twig under a sea of blankets. His body had withered to almost nothing. Volma switched her tablet to medical diagnostics and scanned him.

"Poison and starvation." She frowned. "Not enough to kill him, though." She nodded to a tablet by the bed. "They still needed his official seal."

"Where's the rest of his cabinet?" Chardon asked Lombis, his glowing blue eyes burrowing into him. "Speak!"

Lombis grinned with a defiant expression. Trinon grabbed his neck and lifted him off the floor. His feet dangled as his eyes bulged from struggling to breathe. Terror filled him. Trinon smiled.

"Your regent asked you a question. Please respond."

"Ack! Awr…yes." Drool ran out the corners of Lombis' mouth. He took hold of Trinon's wrists, trying to pry them loose.

"I will," he gasped.

Trinon let go. Lombis fell in a heap, rubbing his neck, coughing. With hot fury in his eyes, he glared at Trinon. Only to flinch back at his in return. Far more sinister than he could ever muster.

"They perform their duties in a separate wing of the dungeon." Lombis stood, brushing off his robes. "If you had left well enough alone, we could have disguised the profits with legal contracts." He tilted his head in jest. "Now you risk sanctions if you expose us. I thought you'd be better than this." He smirked. "Lord Regent."

Before Chardon could move, Talas stepped forward and hit Lombis in the abdomen with both hands. A burst of air shot out to concave around him. He went flying into the far wall. His body mirrored the still unconscious guard on the other side.

Talas picked up a guard by the front of his uniform.

"Get your men and show us to the cabinet members."

The guard barely opened eyes, seething at his captor until Talas released him. He crawled to his feet and went to rouse his men. They angrily escorted Talas and Trinon out into the corridor.

Chardon calmed himself.

The rage he felt hearing Lombis' words wanted to spill out. That wouldn't solve anything. Modas scanned the room before focusing on him.

"They were betting on you going along with their routine once you found out."

"They thought it'd be further down the line in their mind," Volma added.

"Maybe in the past, with your lack of instincts," Jaron said. "But now." She shook her head. "They can't pull the wool over your eyes this time."

"Is that one of those weird Earth sayings?" Volma asked.

"Yep." Jaron picked up the tablet on the nightstand. "Well, it looks like the coffers are doing fine. And look at that." Jaron turned the tablet around for them to see. "A brand new shipment of illegal goods has been approved."

Chardon grimaced, his mind working on how to fix the mess on Suma. Sanctions?

He wondered if the trade federation saw it that way. Would the Dreridians take their side or his?

"As regent of Suma Andal, you must take responsibility for their actions." Lord Pondur stared at Chardon and his cabinet from the split holoscreen hovering above the conference table. On the other, a proxy from the trade commission waited patiently. "That being said, I believe we can recommend adequate restrictions."

Ganna sniffed, rubbing her upper lip.

"We do appreciate that, but what we're looking for is a way to maximize trade despite this setback."

"Yes," Volma added. "We don't want to be in a bind with our existing contracts."

The proxy raised his head and locked eyes with Chardon.

"Are you creating a foundation for your own commerce?"

"Not just New Lassa." Chardon narrowed his eyes. "Our home world along with the other regent planets."

Lord Pondur seemed uneasy. Jaron's lips pursed at his reaction and nodded to Chardon. The proxy looked confused.

"We were under the assumption that you would work under Dreridian tutelage."

"I've been giving Lord Chardon guidance in my spare time." Lord Pondur straightened his waistcoat. "He's still inexperienced in his role as ruler."

"Yet he;s established a knowledgeable cabinet of advisors."

Jaron leaned back, straightening her posture.

"Our goal has always been to elevate our leader. We appreciate your observation." She turned to Lord Pondur. "We also thank you for spending time to show our leader the ins and outs of trade from your perspective."

Volma cleared her throat, getting everyone's attention.

"My position in the cabinet as head of engineering also entails working with infrastructure and agriculture. Expansion is key."

"You want to branch outside of Dreridian territory?"

The corner of the proxy's mouth rose in amusement.

"How interesting." They addressed Lord Pondur. "To set this in motion, you would need the approval of the five systems' council. Can that be done so late in the reports cycle?"

He definitely looks miffed about it! Chardon smirked at Lord Pondur's sour expression. Ha!

"Oh, of course." Lord Pondur laughed nervously. "That can be arranged within the year. He glanced at Chardon. "Would that suffice?"

Chardon tilted his head in confusion.

"Why must we go through such a process?" He asked the proxy. "Are we not already part of the five-systems trade network?"

"Not quite." The proxy linked his fingers on the console. "The contracts created by your mate, Sestis, were provisional. Very little trade happened. Some regent planets she never established for revenue."

"Yes, I recognized that part." Chardon still didn't understand. "But we couldn't do business without registering with the guild, correct?"

"Hmm. About that." The proxy gave Lord Pondur a sinister stare. "If the Dreridians allowed you a deeper look, you would find third party agreements. All structured under their registration."

Ganna hissed, her nostrils flaring. Lord Pondur shrugged, not the least bit offended.

"It's all strictly business." He addressed Chardon. "You understand, don't you Lord Chardon?"

"Of course." Chardon hid his disdain for the Dreridian. "Let's have an in-depth discussion later about this."

"I will send the documentation to apply for registry." The proxy smiled. "I look forward to the trade council and hear what the Lassian race has to offer the five systems."

When their feed ended, leaving Lord Pondur still connected, Ganna addressed him.

"You're a devious little creature. I'm looking forward to a deep dive of our contracts."

"I'm sure you'll find it fascinating," he replied.

"You think we'll find it daunting," Volma stated.

"And stay under your umbrella." She added with a frown, knowing that's what he thought.

"We may surprise you."

"Which is fine." Lord Pondur leaned forward. "Whether you get your own registry or remain safe in our hands, I'm curious to see how you navigate the world of commerce."

He tapped his console, ending the feed.

The holoscreen disappeared.

Jaron templed her hands and rested her chin upon them.

"What say you, leader?" She turned her head towards Chardon. "You already know my answer."

"And ours," Volma added, nodding at Ganna.

Chardon chuckled then threw his head back in laughter. His shoulders shook, rising up and down. After wiping his eyes, he stared out across the room.

"We will apply for our own registration and cancel the ones with the Dreridians."

"Excellent." Volma rose from her cushion. "I will get started on gathering the necessary information to complete it."

Ganna stood. "I'll be working on proposals to present." She headed for the door, then looked over her shoulder at Chardon. "I'm assuming I'll not be there."

"Huh?" Chardon and Jaron exclaimed.

"You're not getting out of this," Jaron retorted.

"Oh. Well, then. I better make a good impression."

Jaron watched her leave before getting up. Chardon used his hands as leverage to push himself off the floor. They didn't head for the door. Both contemplated what their actions would mean in the grand scheme.

Lassians were coming into the realm, ready for conquest.

Now deemed a race on the verge of becoming a superpower, the Lassians had no choice but to attend the galactic delegation meeting taking place on Folza. A conference hall similar to the one on the Dreridian home world awaited them.

The wall windows gave unobstructed views of the city hub, with the transport communication tower looming above it.

Folza guards guided their party to the clear cubes assigned to them. Chardon, Mercan, Modas, and Anassa were together. Jaron, Talas, Kelin, and Ganna occupied the other next to them. The din of voices rose as the other delegates stared at Mercan.

Mercan was a mystery. His presence alone made one feel weak and helpless. As if standing in the shadow of a god. Anassa gave off the same vibe. And rightly so. Chardon realized too late exposing them to the galaxy may be a mistake. Mercan glanced over at him and smiled.

Oh. This is what the two of them wanted.

An uneasiness consumed him. Seeing Talas, Mercan, Anassa, and Ganna together in one room never felt this ominous before. It dawned on him that they constantly minimized their aura.

On this day, they did not.

Across from their cubes sat Azrom's delegates. Romnus and Halfar stared at them in stunned silence. Farin's lips pressed thin with anxiety. Kur, Rass, and Treshur tried to keep their authoritative composure. The Dreridians, catty corner to their right, appeared to react the same. Lords Pondur and Graggor gazed at the Lassians with apprehension.

Once everyone was seated and the doors sealed, the translator modules lit up.

Chancellor Eydine did a brief greeting, then turned the meeting over to her head of state. Each faction had presented reports on their economy, social standings, and proposals. The combined data floated on holoscreens before each cube.

Mercan stared deadpan at it, unimpressed.

In fact, his eyes glinted with slight ire.

"Let's shed light on the issue at hand," the Folza head of state suddenly announced. "The Lassian race made tremendous gains in a short period of time. Rivaling the five systems' trade leaders." They raised a hand, gesturing towards them. "Please, explain how you were able to gather such intel and implement them."

All eyes focused on the Lassians.

"I will tell you a secret," Mercan began. His eyes glowed for a few seconds. He used his right hand, palm up, to wave it across the two cubes. "In the beginning, we were merely energy. Simple lifeforms self-contained on a peaceful planet called Lassa. No need to interact with other worlds. No need to leave our own. For millenniums we existed floating around untouched."

Lord Graggor wrung his hands, already knowing that much about the Lassians' past. Chardon noticed Halfar fidget in his seat. He feared the outcome of the reveal.

"Out of nowhere, a hostile race rained down. Invading our home," Talas continued. "We watched and endured as they ravaged it. Depleting our resources."

"Lassa didn't know what to do. Unleashing her fury would devastate her surface. Kill everything in its wake," Anassa added.

"So we waited until they grew bored. Taken all they could from us. And left." Mercan scanned the now silent hall. Every delegate sat rooted in awe. "That is when we collectively decided to evolve."

Chancellor Eydine bowed her head in acknowledgement. She understood their sentiment. As a similar race of light energy, they, too, were forced to change.

"For the first time, we floated out into space. I became a scout, traveling further than the others to learn of the worlds not just in our solar system, but beyond." Talas templed his hand and rested his chin atop them. "The things I saw, terrified me. Yet, I knew they were important to retain."

"As I became the embodiment of Lassa, my task would entail assigning roles to the eldest of us." Anassa tilted her head to one side. "One would comb through all the information collected and suggest a new form based on it."

Gasps erupted.

Lord Pondur's ashen expression spread throughout the hall.

"Did they say they were the embodiment of their planet?" A delegate asked in shock. "What does that mean?"

Romnus glanced to his right, down the row at the Razznians. Lord Kraznan had reared back in his seat. The implication sounded terrifying. And he knew it was exactly what they were all thinking.

"I came to the conclusion that we needed physical bodies to defend our planet." Mercan laid his hands flat before him. "But we didn't want to lose our core energy. With the knowledge I attained, I created the current core exchange system."

Talas took over from there.

"What I learned became the catalyst for an armed force to combat invaders. I taught the masses everything I could decipher as useful techniques. Together with Mercan, his daughter Ganna, and Lassa, we achieved our goal." He looked around the hall. "You want to know how we got such mass amounts of intel. We never stopped collecting data." His eyes narrowed as he tilted his head down. "Everything we learned came from all of you."

Shouts of outrage and concern filled the hall. Finally, a delegate broke through.

"Wait! We were informed this invasion took place a little over a thousand years ago. But you've stated existing many millennia before that. How old are you?"

A hush once again fell in the hall.

"Hmm." Mercan rubbed the bottom of his chin. He turned to Anassa. "What say you? I haven't really calculated that."

Anassa thought for a moment, staring at the domed ceiling.

"I believe Lassa shared her consciousness and power with me nearly four thousand years ago. Though we were already beings on that world. I can't say."

Looks of horror. Fear. It cascaded across the delegates like a wave. Treshur went pale as he stared at Ganna with new insight. He had an idea of her age. She would be the youngest among the elders at over a thousand years old.

"What did you say?" Lord Pondur contained his terror to glare at the Lassians.

Mercan matched his angry expression.

"That you are an inferior species who should know their place, Lord Pondur." His gaze landed on the Azromnians then the Razznians. "The same goes for all of you."

"We have studied your kind for so long," Talas interjected. "Yet, we left you alone to continue your reigns of conquest."

"We've seen enough." Anassa's body seemed to shimmer. Chardon sat back in his seat not sure what they intended to do. "Our new goal is to take what is owed us. To become leaders of this galaxy."

That did it.

Chardon watched chaos erupt as delegates spewed insults at them. Chastising them for their arrogance and vowing to defend their territories. Ganna merrily perused data on the tablet she whipped from her robes.

Talas locked eyes with Kur. His mouth curved into a smile as the Azrom general crossed his arms. Both men communicated the same sentiment.

Come. Try me.

Reassessment

A dark mood blanketed Lord Pondur's chamber, blending with the absence of light. Only the blinking signals from factories outside illuminated the walls. Hidden in the shadows that masked his features at his desk, he sat holding a fluted glass that dangled between his fingers. His arm hung limp over the armrest while an empty gaze focused on the far wall.

He didn't bother greeting Lord Graggor when he entered. Both remained stunned by the revelations at the conference. Lord Graggor went to the liquor shelf and poured himself a glass of hard spirits. He sat in the chair across from Lord Pondur and took a sip.

"It's worse than we feared."

Lord Pondur's eyes shifted towards him.

"Is that all you have to say? This is not worse." His beady eyes narrowed. "It's terrifying. Those beings." He couldn't find the right words to finish his thought.

"Beyond ancient. Nearly omniscient. Yet, they feign ignorance."

"You're mistaken." He saw Lord Graggor's expression change to dubious. "Not ignorance. Avoiding certain elements so that they don't know. To gain a thing means owning up to it."

"They always said they never wanted to be a superpower."

"And now they've changed their minds."

Lord Graggor adjusted himself in the seat.

"I beg to differ. Did you see the look on Lord Chardon's face when that creature Anassa spoke?"

A beam of misty light passed across the window walls, exposing the furnishings in the room. All the metal glowed like jewels for that brief moment before darkness engulfed it again.

"And Lord Chardon did nothing to contradict them. I saw something in his eyes. A new kind of curiosity. He was wondering if Lassians could pull it off."

"That would be a devastating blow to our empire."

Lord Graggor's eyes bulged.

"And our trade network." Lord Pondur leaned forward to set his glass on the desk. He slumped back and let out a sigh. Lord Graggor took another sip of his drink.

"You regret teaching him your knowledge of galactic trade?"

Lord Pondur grew angrier. So stupid!

Yes, he felt that way. He taught a fledging ruler how to conquer.

"Now that you know more, what's your assessment of Ganna?"

Lord Graggor went deep in thought, sipping his drink.

He finally set it down.

"That despite her age, she's still a child compared to Mercan. His tutelage before his demise helped her immensely."

"This Mercan." Lord Pondur's frown deepened, "disturbs me."

"I fear he and Anassa would seek revenge on Azrom."

"We cannot allow that!" Lord Pondur slammed a fist on his desk, shaking his drink. The liquor swirled violently before settling. "Their trade is finally back on track after their little planet rebellion when Romnus took over."

"We did lose a lot of revenue," Lord Graggor added, nodding. Then his beady eyes squinted. "Do you suppose Queen Farin would side with her mother's race?"

Lord Pondur's craggy brow rose. He sat up straight in his chair, adjusted his waistcoat. He'd forgotten about the young halfling on Azrom's throne.

"Hmm. That is the question, isn't it? I doubt she'd jeopardize Azrom's trade for a piece of vengeance." He leaned over and lifted his glass. Before taking a sip, he asked, "What do your spies say?"

"Ahh!" Lord Graggor exclaimed, gleefully. "That is what I came to tell you." He tossed back the rest of his drink. Resting his arms on the desk, he leaned forward. "There's an Azromnian envoy visiting their regent planets. Some good will inspection to gauge their loyalty."

"That should have been done long ago," Lord Pondur snorted.

"But it wasn't. Halfar nor Romnus cared much about them."

"True. They were only ever interested in the conquest. Never the governing of those planets. Why now?"

Lord Graggor seemedready to bounce out of his seat with joy. He feared for the chair if that happened.

"This envoy is being led by an unknown commander. Even the others in the entourage are dubious of their standing. They claim to be part of Lord Kel's inner circle of imperial guards."

"I still don't see the connection."

Lord Pondur gave him a side eye stare.

"The description of this commander." Lord Graggor's eyes widened as far as they could. "It matches Farin in male form."

Lord Pondur halted his sipping, looking over the rim of his glass at him. He slowly lowered it to the desk.

"Is that true? Can it be confirmed?"

"My spy obtained battle footage from one of the planets." Lord Graggor smirked. "It seems they're struggling with negotiations." He waved that away. "Their movements, along with the one arm morphing, sealed the deal."

"So." Lord Pondur nodded. "The queen has made her move."

"I believe she will take the throne from Romnus. She's been brushing up on Azrom's history the past decades."

"She would rival her father."

"Except she won't be a tyrant." Lord Graggor wagged a finger.

"No. She's much smarter than that." Lord Pondur drained his glass. "That's also what worries me."

Queen Farin was something new in the five systems.

Not obsessed like the rest of the higher powers with conquests and trade. Necessary, but not the end goal. She would advance Azrom without bloodshed.

And bring their fragile alliance to its knees.

Azrom might ruled a few major parts of the five systems.

A feared race known for conquests that left much to be desired. Every Supreme Ruler over the last two millennia labeled a tyrant. Romnus felt a heavy boulder in his chest when he heard the Lassians revealed their true selves. He grew uneasy knowing these beings had lived for millenniums.

Before Azrom learned to fight on its own.

Halfar sat silent across from him in the back chamber hidden behind the throne platform. Batis lounged on the end of the sofa, dangling one leg over the edge. A half empty glass of liquor held in one hand as his arm rested on his knee.

The low light of the hover lamps cast the chamber in a gloom that matched Romnus' expression. Farin opted to return to their own when they arrived. He could tell she found them insufferable, not forgiving the way they treated her.

Treshur warned him before they landed to not engage. Something about the way she avoided looking at any of them. Fear gripped him.

Halfar finally met his gaze.

"I don't want Chardon becoming some super being. That Anassa thing is dangerous. I never trusted Ganna from the start."

"And her father. Did you know of him?" Romnus asked.

"I didn't," Halfar spat vehemently. "Why would they keep such a secret?"

"Hmm?" Treshur tilted his head in amusement. "Surely you know the answer. I already deduced that."

"What gives me pause is the fact that Talas is also ancient. Their first scout to peruse the galaxy, collecting information to defend Lassa." Batis' head fell back. His gaze shifted sideways at them. "What do you think he left out in all those reports?"

"What do you mean?" Romnus gave him a warning side glance.

"Do you really think he told them everything he saw? If that were the case." He stopped there, returning to focus on his drink.

For a split second, Romnus frowned in confusion like the others, until it hit them.

Like a slab of concrete cracking them in the teeth, they all flinched, baring teeth as they seethed with realization.

If Talas had done so, Lassa would be the end of everything they knew. Azrom, Razzna, Yaos, even the Dreridians empire would be nothing in their eyes.

Pure dominance.

"So, what do you think Farin is thinking about now?" Batis swirled his glass and made eye contact with Romnus. "I warned you."

Halfar leaned forward, his eyes full of fury.

"We stop that from happening! I won't allow my mate or my daughter to get caught up in their delusions of supremacy!"

Romnus stared at him in awe. What was that about?

Batis and Treshur both looked over at him with a strange horror. For the second time, they all felt they had to shield Farin from her father's wrath.

Another revelation hit him. Sestis. Her actions made Lassa a regent over other worlds. The first steps to becoming a ruling race. He had no idea how many the other empires granted during her campaign spree.

"Has Chardon divulged their number of regency planets?"

Halfar regained his composure, though still not calm.

He rubbed his chin.

"From what I gathered, it appears to be seven or eight."

Treshur and Batis kept silent. No. That didn't sound right. Halfar had to know that. The way Sestis went about, it had to be at least twelve, possibly twenty. Halfar's brow furrowed.

"Is Chardon keeping the other's identity from me?"

Batis burst out laughing, startling them.

"You can't be serious!" He glared at Halfar. "Chardon has no idea how many planets they have. But, I assure you, they will find out soon."

"Most would be low level trade planets." Treshur raised his glass. "Combined, they make a substantial coalition. If Chardon wants to advance Lassian might, the game is already set."

Romnus saw Halfar seething at the thought. He also felt an ominous tug. Would Farin help her mother gain a foothold in the five systems? He remembered the report regarding Chardon's secret meeting with Lord Pondur.

A plan to raise a new leader under his thumb to stir chaos.

Lord Pondur can hardly spit, he's so angry! Romnus snorted. That's what you get for trying to bring down Azrom by elevating an unknown.

Lassians were clearly that. Even now.

In the deep shadows of an empty hall, Farin sat in a foldable chair at a table she had dragged in from an adjacent abandoned chamber. The holoscreen projection from her tablet emitted the only light. Her hair and robes blended with the darkness while her fair face appeared almost alabaster. With arms and legs crossed, she read the message on screen.

My child, I am setting up a new commodity that will benefit both Lassa and Azrom. One of our regency planets' trade wasn't being optimized. Trinon is being sent as the ambassador. I also want to heed your advice on relations. This visit may prove fruitful in that regard.

Farin felt the corners of her mouth tug until a smile formed. She surely looked maniacal. All the more reason to enjoy the outcome. Everyone in power she encountered underestimated her and the Lassians. The conference only perpetuated wariness and deeper hostility. No one trusted Lassians nor her due to age.

Let's prove them wrong, mother.

Especially her father. She felt his wrath creeping in to stop them. He didn't like competition. And definitely not from his own bloodline.

Rain dousing the planet's surface created large puddles that flooded the pathways carved through the citadel below the Lassian ship. From his seat's viewport, Trinon looked down on the dense forests of Planet L'Ang-Usai. Only two seasons occurred.

A humid tropical summer and this one. Torrential rains.

His body tensed the closer the ship got to the palace located deep in the largest forest. He saw hordes of people already gathering in the courtyard at the entrance. Their colorful garbs nearly glowed in the gloom.

Fifty years? Is that how long it's been?

Beside him, Und kept silent with his arms crossed. A scowl spread on his face.

"If you start wallowing in self-pity, I'll crack your skull." He didn't even look at him as he spoke. "We don't have time for that."

"Are you worried about me, brother?" Trinon smiled. "I know they forgave me." His eyes lowered. "Doesn't make it hurt less."

Und dropped his arms and turned to him.

"I didn't say it wouldn't," he snapped. "And you never had anything to be forgiven for in the first place."

"Arriving at the main palace. Please prepare for landing," the ship's AI announced.

Trinon could hear the rest of his entourage strapping back in. Four warriors, two energy users, and two manbeasts comprised the group. Small and non-threatening. As the new ambassador, he wanted to keep the reunion friendly. The visit also had a business agenda. A warrior who assisted Volma and the head of agriculture on New Lassa came along.

The landing platform came into view as the ship lowered amongst the trees. Their tops swayed in the blast of air from the side ducts. When it settled, workers in bright blue and red robes rushed forward to lock the ship onto the mechanical chocks. The ramp opened to Trinon and his group standing at the top.

They walked out, getting sprinkled by the rain. Trees blocked most of the downpour. At the bottom, four guards in bright blue and yellow robes waited for them. One looked familiar.

"Lord Trinon, it is good to see you again," the man said.

Ah! Trinon remembered. He's the emperor's cousin.

"Please, there's no need to address me like that." He held up a hand to stop him. "I'm still the manbeast you know."

The man shook his head.

"No. You are here as an ambassador to our regent, Lord Chardon. We must do things the proper way." The man smiled sheepishly. "That's not to say we won't greet you as family to start."

Und rolled his eyes, looking away in frustration. Trinon returned a crooked smile and let out a small laugh. They embraced, slapping each other on the back before disengaging. The man held him by the shoulders for a moment.

"We've prepared your favorite dishes." He finally took notice of Und. "Are you not satisfied with our greeting?"

Und's eyes widened.

"What?"

Trinon burst out laughing.

"Please forgive my brother, Und. He's sort of a sour person."

"Trinon!" Und warned him.

"I see. Come. Follow me." The man addressed the rest of the group more so than Trinon. "We can chat on the way."

The smooth walkway from the platform gave way to hard packed soil that expanded towards the palace courtyard. Between the leaves and foliage, fruit of every color hung, giving a jovial atmosphere. Trinon breathed in the damp air mixed with their sweetness. His anxiety returned as they arrived at the courtyard.

On the palace steps Emperor Rahmsa and his two daughters, Radine and Hersia waited. Trinon felt his legs grow heavy with each step forward. Although neither had looks like their deceased sister, the resemblance made his chest hurt.

Seeing his struggle, the emperor stepped down to greet him.

"My dear Trinon," the emperor cupped his face in his hands. "Do not fret over the past. I want you to be at ease."

Trinon rose his head to stare at the older man.

The dark brown hair fell to the middle of his back. A long, dense beard touched the top of his abdomen. He appeared regal in a heavy dark blue velvet like robe with gold trim.

Almost akin to the Norse gods on Earth he read about.

"I'm sorry. I know." Trinon straightened his posture when the emperor released him. In that instant, Und came to his side and whacked him on the back of the head. Trinon stumbled forward, catching himself so not to fall. "What are you doing?"

"I warned you." Again, he didn't bother to look at him.

A snort erupted, followed by laughter. Und frowned. Trinon let out a sigh. He would've thought his brother had settled down after finding a mate. How Liula put up with him boggled his mind.

A huge banquet awaited them inside the throne room. The doors remained open to allow a view of the rain and forest beyond. It felt like a party out of medieval times. Or something like what he thought it would entail. Servants passed around oversized steins of brew while others plopped down platters of meat at each table.

Trinon sat in the center, flanked by the sisters. The emperor was to his right and Und on his left. The princesses catered to his needs, never letting his drink go dry or his plate empty.

Und glanced over at him.

I know!

He had to conduct business in the morning. Telling them he had a mate may anger them. That's not how he wanted to start the day. For now, he would endure their affections.

☼ ☼ ☼

Trinon woke up naked in a massive canopy bed drenched in sheer pastel fabrics. A princess lay on each side of him. Shit! He'd drank too much. Indulging their whims for days on end.

Muted sunlight filled the room. The gray sky refused to allow more than that. He ran his hands down his face and breathed deep.

On the left, Radine ran a hand across his thigh and went for his crotch. He smacked her hand and moved it back over to her.

"Stop that. We have business to attend today."

She opened her eyes and pouted, shrinking under the covers until they covered her nose. He reached to his right and smacked Hersia on the hip.

"Up. We can't keep your father waiting."

She too, stirred, pouting.

A servant came in, bowed to them, and went to the embedded bath basin on the other side of the room. The sisters perked up.

"Oh! Are we bathing together?" Radine asked.

The servant bent over the basin, swishing herbs in the running water as it filled, turned to look over his shoulder.

"Your baths are being prepared in your chambers. The emperor has instructed that Lord Trinon have some alone time this morning."

"You heard him." Trinon took hold of Hersia and dragged her to the other side with Radine. Both not happy with the outcome. "Out. And cover yourselves before leaving."

They climbed off the bed and did just that. Instead of donning their robes, they merely held them against their fronts. Trinon fell back against the pillows, spreading his arms wide. He stared at the swirling pastel colors on the ceiling. A room to set a calming mood. He had no doubt about the reason.

Exhaling, he closed his eyes and listened to the water trickle from the spout.

"You bath is ready, Lord Trinon."

"Please stop calling me that. It makes me uncomfortable."

"My apologies. We're just trying not to offend your delegates." Trinon rose onto his elbows.

"They'll be fine. I prefer just being treated the same as always." The servant walked towards him, stopping a few feet from it.

"But you know, Trinon. You came to us as a representative of our regent. We only reacted that way because you dictated it as such."

"And nothing's changed. Chardon's not a dictator. Nor I."

"Of course." The servant bowed. "Please enjoy your bath. I'll send some fresh fruit to hold you until the morning feast is complete."

"Morning…feast?" Trinon cringed. "That's not necessary."

"The emperor's decree."

The servant left, closing the double doors behind him. Which Trinon realized in horror were wide open the entire time.

Those two!

He didn't know whose race were worse exhibitionists.

Them or Azrom.

He went to the basin and eased himself in. The steaming water wrapped around his body as he submerged. Various scents from the herbs wafted in his nostrils. Every muscle relaxed.

This feels right.

Yet doubt lingered. He didn't feel deserving of such royal treatment. He wasn't family. Not anymore.

☼ ☼ ☼

Morning feast was yet another spectacle of exotic meats and produce paired with a nonalcoholic day brew. Light conversation filled the hall. Trinon sat in the center if it all, growing uneasy by the minute. For three days, this went on with no talk of business. The evenings spent strolling the pathways and reminiscing.

When the fourth day arose, everyone moved to the throne room where the emperor took his place flanked by his daughters. Trinon and his entourage remained standing at the foot of the platform staring up at them.

As it should be in his mind. Even if Lassa has regency over them, it was still their planet. The emperor stayed to rule it.

"So, what brings Lassa's representatives to our humble planet?" The emperor asked.

"As you know, we created contracts with other worlds to trade your produce." Trinon clasped his hands together. "Although we made some profit, it is far below what we anticipated."

"Hmm. Well, we're harvesting according to incoming orders." The emperor turned to his head of agriculture. "Explain the issue."

The councilman stepped forward. Tall and muscular, he seemed to embody the spirit of the land.

"We have a lot of excess produce when harvesting. Ripened goods get picked regardless. The orders get filled, but then we have to find creative ways to use the leftovers. Of course, we consume as much as we can ourselves."

"Which brings me to suggest a remedy," Volma's assistant, Koggen, piped up. "I noticed the various fermented fruit brews and condiments. In addition to the current contracts, we want to draw up new ones to trade at premium compensation."

"What does that entail?" Emperor Rahmsa looked dubious.

Trinon understood his concern. The planet had an abundance of produce. Mass harvesting over time would dwindle its resources. Leaving the planet close to barren of its natural goods.

"I assure you, we won't overstress the environment for any unreasonable quantity." Koggen raised his arms as a show of faith. "We want to be your allies, not a regency that simply lords over you."

"I respect your rule and think of you as an extension of my family," Trion interjected. "I'd never allow harm to you if I can avoid it."

"I know that better than anyone," the emperor stated. "We feel the same."

The atmosphere began to feel awkward with Trinon and his entourage standing. Servants brought in a table and chairs from the adjacent hall. Even then, the emperor didn't like how he had to look down on them. When he tried to convince Trinon to allow him to sit with them, he was shut down.

"Now." Koggen set down his tablet after entering a few figures. "Let's start with tackling the excess produce issue. What have you been doing with them?"

"Most of it gets turned into condiments. That seems to be the best remedy. We have a stockpile because of it."

Koggen glanced over at Trinon staring at the ceiling, deep in thought. He looked down at them.

"Is that the same condiments we had at our meals?"

"The same, yes."

He turned to Koggen.

"I think we have a better remedy." He nodded. "What do you think?" He scratched the back of his mane. "Quality over quantity."

"I agree." Koggen scrolled on his tablet and made more entries. "We propose changing the contracts to accommodate only top tier buyers. Make your produce a high-end commodity as opposed to something anyone can get."

"Less volume, more profit," Radine exclaimed.

"That." Koggen pointed at her. Emperor Rahmsa frowned.

"What about our current ones? Would we have to turn away those clients?"

"Not at all," Koggen replied. "We simply renegotiate the terms."

"And the condiments?" Their head of agriculture asked.

"Another high-end product sold in bulk," Trinon answered. "There are so many conferences with attendees who demand top quality consumables."

"Think of it as elevating your market to the next level."
Koggen smiled brightly.

"Then our products are no longer for the common client." The emperor sounded disappointed. "We are a humble people. Not being allowed to help those in need doesn't sit well with me."

Trinon, Und, and Koggen, reared back in horror.

Koggen waved his hands before him.

"No, no! That's not what we're suggesting."

Trinon let out a sigh, placing his hands flat on the table.

"What we mean is the contracts are to be satisfied. Anything outside of that is for your determination."

"Oh," the emperor breathed in relief. "That makes sense. My apologies for assuming you would think that way."

"I would never bring anything against your people's values." Trinon reached and turned his hands palms up at the emperor. "Please trust me."

"I do. Like a son. You know that."

After hours of talks touting ideas of how to proceed with new contracts, they came to an end. With the table and chairs removed, Trinon and his people once again stood before the emperor.

"We must return to New Lassa and report on our meeting," Trinon told them. "I wish we had more time."

"I concur. You mustn't ignore your family ties."

Trinon's knees went weak, causing him to crumble onto the floor. With his head hung low, he placed his hands flat.

"Again, I ask forgiveness for the loss of your daughter. I know I'm not worthy of your affections."

Emperor Rahmsa frowned.

"Have I not told you numerous times it is no fault of yours?"

The harsh tone made Trinon look up.

"Refrain from such groveling. It doesn't suit you. Stand up!"

Trinon obeyed, feeling ashamed of his sudden display.

"I'm sorry. That was not regent behavior."

"If you truly wish to repent." The emperor gave a wide smile. "You can take my daughters as mates."

The two princesses smirked, glancing at each other knowingly.

"My apologies, but I've already taken a mate."

Trinon bowed his head.

"I know." The emperor's gaze bore down on him. "There is nothing barring you from taking more. Have you not already planted your seed during your stay?"

Trinon blanched. Of course, everyone knew of his days being held hostage by the princesses in his chamber.

"That was…" He couldn't muster a response.

"Now we are officially bound as a family. As it should be. This is how you honor my daughter." He came off the throne along with the princesses. He held Trinon's face in his hands. "Will you accept my surviving daughters as your mates?"

"Please, Trinon?" Radine tilted her head playfully.

"You would deny our offspring if we happen to be carrying them?" Hersia cooed.

"Of course, I wouldn't!"

Trinon reared back as the emperor released him.

"Pay them no mind," the emperor waved a hand at them. "You should ignore their teasing."

Yes. He knew better than to indulge them. They always taunted him, laughing at their sister whenever she chastised them for it.

The emperor addressed them.

"Send him off, properly." To Trinon he said, "I'm happy now. She would want this. Come back soon." He eyed his daughters. "I have a feeling you'll be greeted with young ones by then."

The princesses each took hold of an arm and walked with Trinon down the pathway.

Und gave him a side glance as they left.

"And do you plan to explain this to Ponnae? She is due soon."

"Oh! There'll be more siblings." Radine replied joyously.

"You must bring them on your return," Hersia added.

Trinon turned to Und. He could feel judgement from the rest of his entourage.

"Carefully, I guess. I don't think she'd mind, actually." Trinon looked up in thought. "Azrom has no set decrees on mating."

"We can't wait to meet her." Radine smiled with her eyes squeezed shut. Her elation made Trinon flinch. "Send us a hologram message."

Letting out a long sigh, Trinon nodded.

Inside the ship, he watched them wave goodbye. Und settled in his seat and tsked.

"Couldn't imagine you with one mate, let alone three. Ridiculous."

Trinon tilted his head away, giving him a side glance.

"I said the same about you."

Und glared at him.

"I," he emphasized, "will be a great father, unlike you."

His words struck like a harpoon in his chest. Trinon fought back the hurt, averted his gaze. Und grabbed him by the shoulder and forced him back around. He saw the horror in his eyes.

"I didn't mean that. Please. That's not what I think."

Trinon removed his hand.

"I know," he whispered.

The two brothers sat in silence. They fought each other for so long that old habits died hard. Both needed to learn how to speak without malice, whether joking or not.

The convoy ship eased down onto docking clamps, cutting its engines when they locked. Workers went around checking the hull for damage while the ramp extended.

Chardon stood waiting at the bottom with Volma. He took a deep breath to calm himself. Volma eyed him cautiously, not sure why he seemed nervous.

Air circulated outward in the enclosed terminal. The breeze never reached past the center and made him feel ungrounded. Advancements continued to pop up everywhere on New Lassa and he didn't like it. He feared that to be the same fate as Lassa.

Trinon came out with Und and the rest of their entourage. Chardon tried to sus out why they had such awkward expressions. All trained on Trinon.

What has he done now?

When they came within a few feet, Chardon addressed them.

"Welcome home. I know you just arrived, but we need to get your reports beforehand."

"We figured as much." Und glanced back at Koggen with his gaze still glued to the tablet. "He's been ready the whole trip."

They followed Chardon and Volma to the common halls. The cabinet members sat gathered in the room, chatting excitedly about what news they'd deliver. More revenue meant more resources to support relocations to Lassa.

Once Trinon's group settled, the meeting began. The carafe of spiced juice being passed around ended up empty in the center. A servant came in to replace it, then hurried back out. Chardon's chest tightened. Another issue he had to address soon.

"I take the negotiations went well." Volma nodded at Koggen. "Show the data for us."

The warrior placed the tablet on the data platform before her. Holograms of documents and images hovered above, rearranging to sit below the forms. Everyone scrutinized the information, taking their own notes.

"Were there any problems?"

Chardon turned to Trinon and Und.

"Oh, none at all," Und replied. "They literally implied that anything Trinon wanted, they'd gladly give it."

Trinon's lips pursed as his brow furrowed.

Chardon tilted his head.

"Is that so? I know they have a great affinity for you." He smirked. "I didn't think it was to such extent."

"Let's just say it warrants a discussion later." Und gave Trinon a disappointing stare.

"I look forward to hearing the reason." Chardon leaned forward, resting his clasped hands on the table. "Now, what was the outcome?"

Volma copied the data as it displayed during their report.

The other cabinet members grilled Trinon and the technicians on exact wordings, leaving Und out of the discussion like he wanted. Chardon silently chided him for not engaging as he should.

At the end of the meeting, everyone filed out. Trinon and Und walked outside with Chardon to his personal office inside his home. He sat at his desk and waited for the two manbeasts to take a seat in the straight-back chairs opposite him. He had replaced the flimsy made ones long ago after Modas crushed one sitting down.

Damn behemoths.

"So," Chardon leaned back in his chair with his hands linked, resting on his abdomen. "What mischief have you gotten yourself into this time?"

"Why do you assume I had an issue?" Trinon asked defiantly.

"Cuz, I try to stay under the radar at all cost," Und replied matter of fact.

Chardon nodded. Trinon looked down, embarrassed.

"I was basically ambushed the first days of our arrival."

"Ambushed?" Chardon's looked dubious. "By who?"

Und snorted but kept silent.

"The emperor's daughters." Trinon frowned. His gaze lowered. "They seemed to want a more solid connection than trade."

"Oh!" Chardon sensed where it led. "And did you oblige?"

"I didn't have a choice," Trinon cried out, raising his head to him. "Like I said, it was an ambush…"

"To collect your seed for their empire?"

Chardon met his stare and chuckled.

"It was disgraceful," Und chimed in. "He got drunk and spent days rolling around in bed with both of them."

He glanced over. "Did that knowingly, while his mate awaits here on the verge of birthing his first child."

Ponnae. Chardon grimaced.

That ravaged body being pregnant did her no favors. She had remained bedridden the first two months as a precaution.

"And the result?" By their faces, he knew the answer.

"We received word halfway through our return that both daughters are with my spawns."

Trinon looked away shamefully.

"I shouldn't have let my guard down."

Chardon burst out laughing, startling him. Und crossed his arms and used one foot to tilt his chair back. Trinon looked mortified, which only made it more comical. Regaining his composure, Chardon smiled at him.

"How serendipitous! That means we have an advantage now. With ties to theire royal bloodline, our venture gains legitimacy."

"Our share in its trade gives us a monopoly."

Und rocked forward, letting the front legs of the chair slam down on the floor.

"Good job, brother."

Ah! He does know how this all works.

"Yes. This is a good thing. I'm sure Ponnae will understand. Azrom doesn't have the same social structure regarding blood ties."

The messiness within the royal family came to mind. And the consequences stemming from the brothel. Ponnae grew up in that environment.

Trinon sat in the chair he pulled close to the bed watching Ponnae sleep. Large pillows piled behind her head propped her up. With each breath, her belly rose and fell at a slow rhythm. One hand rested flat atop it. He leaned over for a closer look at her parted lips and smooth face.

No nightmares this time.

Her eyes fluttered open.

They stared at each other, neither speaking.

"You look guilty," she finally said.

Trinon frowned, sitting back.

"What'd you do now?" She wiggled herself upright. "Tell me."

"I, well," he clasped his hands and lay them on the edge of the bed. "You know I went to L'Ang-Usai where I lost my first mate." Ponnae waited for him to continue, which made him nervous. "Her father and sisters sort of coerced me into…"

Ponnae cocked her head, giving him a dubious stare.

"Sowing your seed for the sake of their empire?"

Trinion's head came up in shock.

He looked over at her with wide eyes.

To his surprise, Ponnae snorted.

"You…how?"

"It makes perfect sense. They felt like they had lost you before. After getting to know you, I get it."

"Ha." Trinon grinned, embarrassed. "And here I thought you would be disappointed."

"I am." Her expression darkened. Trinon reared back, not sure how she'd respond. "You left them impregnated and now missing the birth of their offspring."

Oh! That's her concern?

"I didn't want to miss yours. You come first."

She let out a loud sigh, rubbing her belly.

"I appreciate that. But you need to make things right with them." She flicked his forehead. "Are they coming to visit or will we go to them?"

"You wish to meet them?" Trinon asked incredulously.

"Their offspring would be this one's siblings. Of course."

Once again, Lord Kel found his solitude interrupted by an uninvited guest. While leaning against the edge of his desk with his back to the door, he glanced over his shoulder. Imperial guards of the first house stood at attention on both sides of the frame to allow Queen Farin entrance.

Dressed in all black, she appeared ready to battle despite the long robes. That never deterred her from delivering deadly blows.

Her pale face showed exhaustion and fury. No doubt an aftereffect of dealing with her father and Romnus.

"Queen Farin," he stood straight, turning sideways to address her. "What devious plans are you roping me into this time?"

"Leave us," she commanded her guards.

"All of you, out."

Lord Kel motioned to his and the scholars working nearby.

Only them and Lord Kel's personal assistant remained.

"You look stressed, your imminence," Lord Kel said, amused.

The way her brow furrowed made him regret his words.

"My apologies. It seems you're here on a serious matter."

Farin scratched the side of her left cheek with a finger and looked away. She dropped her hand and let out a loud sigh.

"I have a business proposal for you."

Lord Kel gestured for her to sit on the plush sofa as he took the opposite side of the other sofa chair across from her. Nomin sat in the chair on the end, distancing himself from the monarchs.

"I did hear of your success negotiating with our regent planets. If all is well, what's the issue now?" Nomin asked in confusion.

"Azrom trade has been stagnant for centuries. The contracts we had with the outer rim were temporary and have expired."

Lord Kel rested his outstretched arm atop the sofa.

"True. We are complacent. What does that have to do with me? I don't handle trade. Merely enforce regulations and uprising."

Nomin leaned forward.

"I think that's what she's getting at, my lord."

"I want to create an alliance with the third and fourth house."

The atmosphere in the room turned dense with the weight of her words. Lord Kel eyed Nomin and kept his own confliction at bay. Each royal house had its agendas and saw the others as rivals.

At worst, enemies. A family that eats itself.

"My queen, that is quite an audacious plan." Lord Kel leaned his head to one side. "And how did you come up with this idea?"

"I heard a rumor you spawned a child with Elendar's brother. That you didn't acknowledge the child as your bloodline, causing great suffering."

Lord Kel saw the rage in her eyes. He knew well how awful his judgement looked. How it felt was much worse. If a remedy arose, he'd use it. How did she hear about it? Lord Kel wondered about spies in his network. No. Farin noticed everything because she observed Azrom as a whole.

That's what made her dangerous.

"That's also true." He grinned. "I'm trying to fix my mistake."

"Then you need to solidify the bridge with the fourth house through him."

"Hmm?"

Nomin perked up in surprise and stared at Farin in awe. At first, Lord Kel couldn't wrap his head around what she implied. It hit him like a battering ram. He also looked at her in disbelief. Not that he hadn't thought the same.

"My queen, are you suggesting what I think you are?"

"Take it as you see fit." Farin placed her hands in her lap, and let her head fall back. "In order to show our people what we can achieve, I must force it into existence."

"And that would be?"

"The fourth house knows more connections than our usual trade. They demonstrated as much with their rebellion. I request your enforcers to accompany every deal to ensure order."

Nomin nodded.

"Yes, that way there's no delay in setting logistics under our guidelines. It would make negotiations much faster."

"Streamlining." Lord Kel leaned forward with both hands on his sides. "I had suggested this over two centuries ago to Halfar's royal council."

"My father feels there's no need for change."

"You want Lord Elendar's brother to facilitate the orders." Nomin rubbed the bottom of his chin. "He does have knowledge of vendors outside our networks."

"He can bring Elendar up to speed." Farin clasped her hands together. "This needs to be…" She struggled to find the words.

"Discreet?" Lod Kel offered. He narrowed his eyes. "A secret?" Farin looked up at him. "I see."

His mouth curved into a sinister grin. Putting the plan to work meant the results were not being seen for a while. Once revenue gained strength, the council would try to find out how and why. By then, Farin's reign would be complete.

"Circumventing the council and your father is dastardly," Nomin stated. "I like it. Lord Kel, I approve this measure."

"Is playing matchmaker for political gain and power your goal?" Lord Kel smiled deviously.

Farin's expression went stoic, her eyes glowering.

"If it brings Azrom to its former might, I'll do that and more."

Lord Kel sat back and brought his arm up again to rest on top of the sofa. Though initially startled, it didn't jar him like it should. A thought came to mind.

"Should I feel sympathy for your brother?" He watched her lips purse. "Does this mean Lassa and New Lassa will be more than just worlds we have ties with?"

"I'm not laying out every step of my plans." Farin retorted.

"Of course not. Nor will I divulge my enforcers' every move when deployed."

"I won't have it any other way. As long as there's a favourable outcome."

Lord Kel stretched his arms out, arching his back. He slapped the edge of the sofa and stood. Nomin rose from the chair.

"Come, Farin. Let's have a meal while you're here. I can't have our queen in the palace and not entertain her."

Nomin's lips went inward for a moment.

"It would look bad on our house, you see."

Farin rolled her head, stretching out the kinks, then got up.

"I guess we should keep up appearances." She glanced at Lord Kel as he came to her side. "You wouldn't dare call me by my name in others' presence."

"Absolutely not. I don't have a death wish."

"Huh?" Farin smirked. "I'm quite sure you could take Romnus if necessary."

"Surely, you jest, my fair cousin."

Her eyes conveyed exasperation.

Lord Kel smiled, dismissing it. Nomin gave him a stern look. Neither found it amusing. Could that assessment be correct? Possibly. He had more battle experience than Romnus. Thinking about the consequences of Farin's plans, he came to a conclusion.

If Romnus didn't move aside and let Farin take the throne, he would do it for her.

Changing Fates

Disgusted glares shot at Lanen from every passerby in the halls of the third royal house made Kel tense with anger. Nomin gave him a warning look. Fury over the rebellion lingered, yet no one wanted the culprits executed.

"How does our child fare in the fourth house?" Kel asked.

His steps slowed, forcing Kel to match them.

"He's keeping busy in the palace archives, learning from scholars there. On the off days he stays in female form around the children. They don't mind either way."

"Of course not," Kel chided. "He's their mother."

"Mmm." Lanen's lips pressed thin as he looked down.

"I want them back," Kel blurted. Lanen to stop. "This is their home. They belong here. I won't let harm come to them ever again."

"Another promise?" He glanced at him. "Why should either of us trust you now?" His fingers relaxed. "You let it happen. I stayed despite what you did to me."

Kel flinched.

Hearing it out loud stung. Even so, he needed to convince him to stay. Not only for the deal, but his own selfish request.

"That also means you." He resumed walking and Lanen fell in step with him. "Our union started off with deceit. I did grow to care for you. Greatly."

"Is that so? You want me and our child to return to such a hostile place?" Lanen scanned the halls. "Where we don't feel safe?"

Kel sensed the tension in the air as they walked. Some royal members and guards met his gaze unabashed, letting their feelings known. That would end.

He refused to allow such blatant disrespect in his palace.

"You will be. And, yes, that's a promise I'll keep. On my honor."

They reached Kel's private chamber. The two sentries grimaced at the sight of Lanen before reluctantly opening the doors. Kel made note of their behavior, nodding to Nomin. When the three stepped into the center of the room, the doors slammed shut.

"Now that we're alone," Kel walked over to the large picture window overlooking the courtyard. "Let's speak freely."

Nomin gestured for Lanen to sit on one of the high-back chairs. He obliged and settled down.

"We have a proposal from Queen Farin." Nomin pulled a tablet from his robe's sleeve. "A joint effort with our house to redirect trade."

Lanen's brow furrowed. His eyes darted to the side.

"What business would the fourth house have regarding trade? And, have you forgotten? I am still considered a rebel. That said, my goal is to help my brother's house thrive. I need to right my wrongs."

"We haven't," Nomin replied. "This benefits the third house."

Kel turned from the window with his arms crossed.

"Elendar doesn't need you on hand. You can atone anywhere. I prefer it be here, with me."

"Have you not run this proposal with Elendar?"

Nomin cleared his throat.

"It is a delicate matter. We would prefer you to persuade him."

"Because he trusts my judgement?" Lanen responded incredulously, his eyes wide.

"In all seriousness, yes," Nomin said. "Your plight doesn't negate your knowledge of the trade routes."

Kel watched him slump in the chair, contemplating those words. They had a valid claim. The plan's downside would bring minimal strife at best.

"If I agree to this, what's your reward?"

"It's not a single thing," Nomin answered. "This is for the sake of Azrom."

Kel walked over and leaned forward, almost touching his forehead with his own. He gripped the armrest as they locked eyes.

"My only reward is having you here by my side," he whispered.

"You want me?" The sad tone made Lanen's chest tighten. He lowered his head, severing their gaze. "How could you? I'm a liability."

"Not to me." Kel stood. "Will you help our queen fulfill her dream of Azrom's new era of might?" He tilted his head to one side and grinned.

"I will hear the details."

Kel gave Nomin the go ahead. He walked back to the window and tuned out the conversation. The only thought on his mind was how to remedy the situation with Lanen and their child's family.

Family.

He had neglected his previous mates per their requests. His other children held no love for him or their youngest sibling. For the first time, he wanted to do right by them. That meant coming clean. He dared anyone not to abide his decision.

☼ ☼ ☼

Guards, scholars, and advisors crammed in the royal chamber conversed loudly about the late summons from Lord Kel. They glanced angrily at Lanen standing on his left. A sign of respected status. He never gave the previous mates who spawned his children such attention.

Kel stood leaning against the edge of his desk with arms crossed. He observed their actions, letting them show their hatred for all to see. His advisors expressed anger and shame towards their colleagues' blatant disrespect.

The outer guard stepped into the doorway.

"Mid-scholar Kanen has arrived as summoned!" They moved to the side, allowing them to enter. His height equaled the guard's at a little over six foot three. Wearing the white robe and blue cassock with silver lining of the fourth house, he walked with trepidation into the chamber. Seeing their long dirty blond hair that matched Lanen's, Kel inwardly flinched at his beauty.

The chamber hushed.

His inner court guards lined the walls while the scholars formed a row before him. His advisors moved to the right side corner.

"Come, my child. There's no reason to fear in my presence."

A scholar hmphed, averting his gaze from Kanen. Realization spread across many faces as they stared at the young scholar.

Kel's glare reached them.

"From this day forward, this house will recognize mid scholar Kanen as my offspring. My royal blood runs through their veins."

Gasps erupted. The first advisor stepped from the group.

"Then why did you have him removed from the palace?"

Kel shot him a furious look.

"Because I feared for their safety. For too long, I allowed others to harm and disrespect them. At the time, it seemed the best remedy."

"That's not the answer, my lord!" The second advisor cried. "If you had only declared him yours, this wouldn't have escalated so far."

"That does not excuse the abuse at the hands of members in this house," the first interjected. He eyed the scholars. "No amount of apology can forgive such behavior."

"I sent them to study with the fourth house scholars to gain knowledge from both." He turned to his child. "Did you enjoy your stay there?" They nodded. "Were their archives at least interesting?"

A few scholars sputtered, before regaining their composure.

"Yes. They had many documents I had not encountered here."

The second advisor lowered his gaze.

"Now that you have returned, your studies can continue with your mentor."

Kel watched his child's face scrunch with anxiety.

"I do not know how that would be."

Silence so thick it could suffocate filled the room. The advisors stared at the scholars. They turned to each other in bewilderment and fear. Kel uncrossed his arms, visibly angry.

"What do you mean?"

Kanen glanced nervously at the high scholars.

"I was assigned one but informed by the head scholar that

they would not be available for my training."

"Then who assisted in your studies?" Another advisor asked.

"Their assistant gave me a list of the required courses. I opted to complete them on my own." He looked away as a handful of scholars seethed. "Was that wrong?"

"You did what needed to be done. Please do not worry," the first advisor replied.

The third advisor turned to the scholars.

"Who is assigned as his mentor?"

The group parted near the center. Each scholars' eyes landed on a lone man in black and gold robes signifying his high ranked status. He blanched, his eyes widening in horror. Kel crossed the room to stand before the group.

"Explain yourself."

"Lord Kel," he stuttered, "please understand. My intention was to indeed mentor this child." He looked away. "My heavy workload prevented me from doing so. I sent another to facilitate his learning."

The second advisor frowned.

"But the reason you were chosen is because your duties were lessened to accommodate him."

The scholar's expression fell. Caught in a lie, he didn't know how to respond. Kel's lips curled.

"So, you deliberately refused to do your duty. Pawning it off on someone else who had no desire to help my child."

"My lord," the scholar cried out, fearing his life. He outstretched his hand. "Please let me…"

Another high scholar stepped from the group to stand before Kel. He placed a hand on his chest and bowed his head.

"Lord Kel, please allow me to stand as mentor for this child." He raised his head. "I will assure to advance his studies."

Left with no way to save face, the other scholars around the previous mentor lowered their furious gazes. The aforementioned assistant hid behind him, hoping to avoid backlash.

Kel turned to his child.

"Would you accept him?"

"I would be grateful to have a true mentor. Thank you."

The high scholar bowed to Kanen then stepped back. Kel scanned the room.

"I summoned you all here expecting some decorum. I see that my reign is lacking."

Words of disagreement flew to appease him. He raised a hand. They went silent.

"I suggest we adjourn for now, my lord," the first advisor said.

"That's ideal." He waved a hand towards the doors. "You are dismissed." He glanced at the guards along the wall. "All of you."

"As you command, my lord."

Everyone except Nomin, Lanen, and Kanen left the chamber. Kel went around his desk and plopped into the chair. He let out a sigh and rested his head back. Lanen went to Kanen.

"I didn't know how bad it was here. You don't have to come back." She glanced over at Kel. "He can't make you stay."

"It's fine," he answered softly. "This is the only home I know. My children were born here. If this makes it better, I'll stay."

Kel lifted his head.

"I won't allow harm to come to you while I breathe."

"I know you tried to avenge me. No one else had the power to do that to those who hurt me."

Kel stared at them in shock. His personal assistant pursed his lips and looked sideways towards the ceiling.

"I've advised you numerous times it would not go unnoticed." He gave the child a sorrowful smile. "I'm also certain many came to the same conclusion regarding your bloodline. Especially your half siblings."

Kel leaned forward and covered his face with one hand.

"This is not how I wanted it to be." He looked over his hand. "Please believe me."

Lanen embraced Kanen while eyeing Kel. He bent his head back down.

Why did family bonds on Azrom always suffer?

Chafar let the wind tousle his long hair as he leaned over the stone wall's ledge overlooking the outskirts of the palace domain. The hilt of his short sword held by a belted holder grazed the stone, causing a tiny screech. He closed his eyes to the sound of family dysfunction.

The argument carried out into the north wing's outer pathway. Midafternoon turned to evening, giving weight to the loud voices. Inside, Treshur stood angrily while his youngest, Thonlan, berated him for having more offspring and insulting Ganna. The personal guard who accompanied him stayed silent near the entrance.

"How could you mate outside our race with that?" Thonlan pointed at Ganna. "You don't know what she really is!"

He went to push her away. Treshur had enough. He blocked his son's blow and stood between the two. Ganna seemed ready to engage in the fight.

"You will not speak to her in that manner. I won't allow it."

"Oh!" Thonlan spat. "So, she's special? You treat my mother and the others like insignificant bugs, but you put her on a pedestal?"

"I've done no such thing!" Treshur clenched his fists. "I've checked on you every year and never abandoned any of you."

"That means nothing," Thonlan seethed. "Fine. Do what you want. I don't care!"

He whirled out of the room, half running. His guard didn't bother to follow.

Chafar watched him barreling down the pathway, unaware of his surroundings. He let his arms resting on the ledge dangle over for a moment while he exhaled slowly. Farin had hinted earlier that a lower member of the royal house fancied mating with him but decided against it after she advised them of his sexual escapades.

That's not very nice, sister.

She pointed him out, smirking like a villain, and left for a council meeting. Chafar followed his every move for two months. Something primal, akin to territorial, stirred in him. The hairs on his skin would bristle whenever he saw him speaking with others.

He knew it was an irrational thought.

This felt different from the previous conquests he bedded.

And now, to find out from this current incident he was one of Treshur's sons, surprised him.

No matter.

Right as the son rushed past him, with not a glance or greeting, Chafar grabbed hold of his bicep. He yanked him into his arms.

"What do you think you're doing!" Thonlan struggled to get free. "Unhand me!"

Chafar pulled him forward and walked towards his chamber. He cursed and yelled the whole way, desperate to be released.

"Do you know who I am? I'll have you executed, Lassian!"

When they reached Chafar's chamber, he brought him close and kissed him. With every opening to speak, Thonlan protested.

"What are you doing? Stop this!" His eyes teared up. "Please. Let me go!"

Sensing his fight subside, Chafar moved slowly to the bed and laid him down gently.

"You can't do this to me," he cried as Chafar stripped off their clothes with ease. "You can't…"

His body shifted to female form right as Chafar parted their legs to center himself between them. He leaned over and sealed their lips as he entered their womb slowly. He felt their body tense beneath him. They tried to gasp in pain and couldn't. Only able to open their mouth wider for Chafar to kiss them deeper.

Tears streamed down the sides of their face. Chafar could tell what they meant. Not pain, shame, or anger. A sadness mixed with gratitude for being wanted. For that reason, he didn't mate like a starving animal. He took his time and made them relent until nightfall.

Chafar watched her endure a terrible sleep. Her lips twitched in response to her jaw almost clenching. Deep lines formed on her brow. He stroked her hair, keeping it out of her face. At times, she would relax, making her expression smooth out. Such a beauty. He never got a good look at a distance. Up close, his territorial instinct heightened.

This one is mine.

His mind immediately forsook all others.

A warm breeze drifted into the room. The pros and cons of the main palace not having any doors on the outer chambers. Outside, the dark sky took on a menacing charcoal hue, signaling a storm. The perfect weather for staying in.

Her eyes flew open as she tried to rise off the bed. Pain struck and she let out a gasp, falling back onto the pillows.

"Do you feel better now?"

"You brute! How dare you do this to me!"

"I was quite gentle. You needed to relax. Release all that pent up rage."

Her expression changed to embarrassment. She averted her eyes to stare at the opposite wall.

"That's none of your concern."

"I felt you shouldn't go around the palace like that."

She turned her head towards him.

"You think I don't know about you?" Her eyes narrowed. "So am I just another one of your conquests to brag about?"

He saw the hurt in her eyes.

"I never brag. And the answer is no." Chafar pulled her close and kissed her while his hand moved across her thigh between her legs. She stiffened, trying to push him away. "I'm not ready to let you go yet."

"S-stop. I h-have a…" her body relented to his teasing. "A curfew. Ahh!"

"Then you should stay so you don't get caught."

Chafar whispered in her ear.

He removed his hand and positioned her beneath him. This time, she didn't resist, yet he still felt her anxiety. It would take a few more mating sessions to crack that barrier. For a moment he got distracted thinking how many then chastised himself for not paying attention. She required full engagement.

For three more days, he refused to let her go. Not that she seemed to mind, despite halfheartedly protesting. After their last bout of mating, Chafar noticed she didn't move. Her entire being appeared to drop. She fell into a deep sleep that no matter what, he couldn't rouse her.

Oh!

Knowing he had kept her far too long, he slid off the bed. Either her incompetent guard or palace enforcers would start scouring the grounds for her. He looked at the pile of clothes on floor. The robes would fit tight on her current body.

Dressing first, he gathered her robes on the bed and went through them, finding the inner slip. With careful movements, he got it on her, then the outer robe. He loosely fastened the sash and nodded at his handy work.

He left off the leggings and boots. No need for those.

Stretching his arms up into the air, he exhaled, letting his abs cave in. He brought her close to him in a princess hold and lifted her. Adjusting the weight, he proceeded out of the chamber into the main pathway. The sun brightened the sky, not yet high enough to cast shadows. A gloomy morning after days of rain.

Royal house members stared as he leisurely walked towards the lower level of the palace where families of those in service to the supreme ruler resided. The dim lighting on the bronze painted walls made the hallways inside feel darker. Like an old medieval scene.

The stares continued.

He felt the two guards' presence following him.

He entered her chamber and gently laid her on the bed. Pulling the covers out from underneath, then over her. The guards stepped into the entryway.

"We have a curfew for those in residence here." The first stood firm, his hand on the hilt of his sword. "The rules must be abided."

"What does it matter now?" Chafar turned to face them. "I have brought them back."

"They didn't ask or was granted permission," the second spat.

"Why is that even necessary?"

"You should know to obey our rules while here, Lassian."

The first sneered.

"Is that so?"

The second one's face scrunched in frustration. He slapped his partner in the chest with the back of his hand.

"Leave it. We don't need the infant queen coming for our heads."

Chafar bit the inside of his mouth. He flexed his fingers, feeling the itch to draw his short sword and slit both their throats.

The first snorted.

"Hmph! Yeah. We'll deal with them later."

"I'd prefer you didn't disturb her. She's incubating."

The way the two guards glanced at her in disgust enraged him. He breathed deep to calm himself.

"Disgusting." The second stepped aside, creating an opening between them. "We'll send a physician later. You need to leave."

The first kept his fingers on his hilt. Chafar gave them a dubious stare before obliging. As much as he wanted to stay and make sure no harm came to her, he knew causing a scene would be worse.

He left, glancing back once.

They eyed him murderously, then walked down the corridor. They had more house members to berate about curfew violations.

A curfew. Why?

He decided to ask Farin about it at evening meal.

On the way out, he caught a glimpse of the three brothers throwing verbal assaults. He heard them insulting their mothers and each other. Is that an inherited behavior stemming from Treshur?

The oldest with dark bone straight hair past his shoulder blades wore a guard uniform. Its insignia told him his schedule was limited to twice a moon cycle. Enough to show his status in the palace.

In the center stood the third born. A mop of curly brown hair framed his face. He had a playboy's air. His pristine robes devoid of dirt let Chafar know of his useless standing. A scholar intern pin graced his inner robe's collar. Which meant he roamed the archives all day without learning a thing.

The second born, stood slightly taller than the other two. His dark blond hair had minimal waves touching the bottom of his ears. He wore a lab coat signaling he worked in the science division like his father. Authority and common sense oozed from him.

His insults nowhere near the level of nastiness as his brothers hit deep. They reared from him with shocked expressions.

Chafar shook his head, feeling the rage inside him ease. Brothers fighting. He smirked. Farin made him furious.

Though nothing compared to the manbeast siblings.

They were all feral.

☼ ☼ ☼

The sounds of yowling shattered Mota and Hon's peace inside the playpen. Two small bodies rolling in lumped together. They crashed into the sides of the stables, knocking over tables until they hit the far wall. Their older siblings came running in behind them as Mota and Hon rose from their stoops.

They watched in horror as the dark haired one grabbed hold of the fairer one's mane. He yanked their head to the side, exposing the neck, and bit down into his shoulder. Blood spurted onto his face. The other screamed, his eyes wide in terror.

For a split second, Mota and Hon stayed rooted in place, not believing their eyes.

"What is wrong with you!" Mota ran over, whacking the him in the back of his head. "Let go!" Startled, the little one released his teeth from his sibling's flesh, leaving deep marks.

"What's all that commotion?"

Jaron came into the area and stopped cold.

The wounded child wailed in agony. She raced to his side and put pressure on the wound. Seeing how bad it was, the dark-haired child bawled. His anguished cries nearly broke Mota's heart. Blood dripped from his mouth, mingling with snot and tears.

"What have you done?" She went over to the little one. His wailing made her pause. "Who taught you something like that!"

She tore a strip from her robes and wrapped it tight around the wound. Turning to Mota, she yelled, "let's go," while lifting the child gently. To the older siblings she ordered, "Hurry to the medical bay and tell them we're coming."

They sprinted off, passing their aunts and uncles.

Jaron gathered the wounded child to her. He went into shock, stiff in her arms. She and Mota hurried to the medical building. Hon reached down and hugged his crying child, taking the hem of his robe to wipe the blood from his face.

"Spit it out," he commanded. Between sniffles and cries, the little one did so. "Don't you ever do that again." Hon controlled his tone to avoid escalating the issue. "Shh. It's alright." He rocked him in his arms.

He saw his own siblings coming in. Why were they all here?

"Where did they learn to fight like that?" Mara asked, entering.

"If I were to guess, not from any of us," Jakar replied.

They waited in silence for Hon to console his little one. The wailing and sniffles ceased as he snuggled into his father's chest.

The two older siblings returned with ashen faces. They stared at their baby brother, finally settling down.

"We saw some Azrom soldiers fight like that once," the first said. "I never thought any of us would copy it."

Und clenched his fists, narrowing his eyes.

"They're always a bad influence when they come here."

"Azrom has a different family structure riddled with strife. It doesn't surprise me."

Mara leaned against a stall's beam.

The other sibling glanced at Und, then hung his head.

"They see you and Trinon fighting all the time, though."

Trinon stopped at the doorframe. Und averted his eyes.

"Yes, that does factor in." Mara glared at her brothers. "Neither of you can be called role models for the little ones."

"You need to figure it out," Hon snapped. He rose, holding his now sleeping child tightly. "This is getting old."

He didn't look at Trinon as he left the playpen area. Und sat down on a stoop in defeat. Jakar turned to Trinon.

"This is what your fighting can result in. Do better."

"Well, now the whole reason for us all coming here is ruined,"

Mara pouted.

"This is obviously not the time to celebrate," Jakar said.

With so many siblings, many of their birthdays overlapped.

"No." Their younger sister glared. "This is the perfect time. Once the little one is cleared for release, we'll try again."

"A celebration of old and new," Una whispered.

"Old?" Mara cried out. "Who?"

☼ ☼ ☼

Mist formed in layers along the tops of the mountain terrain where Und and Trinon lounged on a moss-covered boulder. They stared out at the horizon, waiting for the sun to break over. Its light colored the sky in hues of pastel yellow, pink, and blue. A picturesque setting. The chilly morning air remained still, letting the sounds of nature fill it.

"You know I care about you very much," Und said quietly. Trinon lowered his gaze. "Maybe even to the point of over protective."

"You don't need to be."

"Trinon," Und sighed heavily. "You're reckless and have such convictions."

"Is that why you despise everything I do?"

Und's expression turned ugly.

"The reason I feel disappointment is because you hide behind that stupid mask. Not showing your true self."

Trinon fidgeted against the boulder, suddenly uncomfortable.

"No one wants to see who I truly am. That's not what they want from me."

"For Lassa's light!" Und rose his shoulders off the boulder to look over at him. "That doesn't matter! I would have more respect for you if you just..." He struggled to find the right words. "That happy, smiling thing you do to appease everyone pisses me off."

Trinon's head fell back to rest on the boulder. It did get tiring after a while. But he couldn't change on a dime. He decided long ago to show empathy better suited his needs. To be himself would drive many away.

"You hurt like everyone else."

Und glared at him. "You've lost more than most. As yourself and that core you carry."

"I don't want to…"

"If anyone has a problem with you telling them how you really feel, they can go drown in the ocean!" Und cut him off. He settled back and closed his eyes. "You're my litter brother. We've shared the same womb. Fought each other for dominance." He opened his eyes at Trinon. "How could I not love you more than life?"

Those words washed over Trinon like a typhoon. His arms went limp at his sides as he stared at the brightening sky. A pain spread through his entire chest. He felt angry tears sting his eyes.

"You say that knowing I've felt that way about you always. Who's being disingenuous now?"

"I don't like fighting with you," Und replied. "I just want you to find some sense of joy before it's too late."

The sun's rays beamed across the horizon, disintegrating the colors of dawn. The two manbeasts took deep breaths, cleansing their lungs with fresh air.

☼ ☼ ☼

Thonlan, lay in bed exhausted for no reason. She had done nothing all day, yet her body felt fatigued. Heavy. Her swollen belly didn't protrude enough to hinder movement despite being due in less than two months. Then again, she knew her diet contributed to that. She wasn't hungry most days.

Rumors about her condition spread throughout the palace. Household members threw disgusted looks her way whenever she walked the halls. Even her guard abandoned her, not offering protection as his duty entailed. Especially from her brothers, who taunted and pushed her. They avoided her until recently.

She kept the hover lights dimmed in her chamber, not liking any brightness. The long black sleeping robe didn't stop her shivering even under the covers.

I don't feel well.

Raising her head off the pillow, her hair, now cascading down her back, hung in tangles. Large strands fell against her face.

Her arms shook as she held herself up. Sensing others in the room, fear gripped her. She looked over at the entrance and saw her brothers standing in front of it. Blocking any exit.

"I see you're still lazing around as usual," the oldest spat.

"Well, what do you expect?" The third brother said. "He couldn't even make it through level one combat training."

"You couldn't find any worthwhile skill to justify your title." The second brother shook his head in disappointment. "Just a useless royal who only obeys their mother's whims."

"And none of you don't?" She swung her legs over the edge and placed her feet on the plush carpet. Her angry gaze fell on them. "At least my mother knows what she wants."

The oldest came at her, grabbing the front of her robes. He whirled her around.

"You're talking back all of a sudden?"

The third stepped forward.

"You sully yourself with that Lassian, tainted your Azrom blood and spawning whatever that is." He pointed to her belly. "Does it even have Azrom might?"

"Stop." The second brother moved towards them. "This is not what we came here for. We should leave."

The third brother punched her in the stomach. She felt pain fill her entire body. Before getting halfway to the floor, she came back up and returned the blow, knocking the first back as well, forcing him to release his grip. She didn't have enough strength for a fight, but she had no choice. Her second brother tried to break it up and ended up being assaulted by the other two himself.

They got her on the floor and she saw her third brother's boot come towards her side. She couldn't block it in time and took the full hit. Her entire stomach blazed with fiery pain. Right as she moved to get away from him, her eldest brother grabbed her by the waist, lifted her in the air and threw her across the room. Her body bounced off the wall and landed a few feet from it.

Laying on her side, the agony gripped her. She felt wetness pool beneath her.

"No! No-oh!"

Her right hand clawed the floor, trying to get a hold to pull herself away. Tears blurred her vision. My child! Please! Muffled sounds of arguing surrounded her. She screamed, terrified of what came next. For her unborn spawn. Her consciousness faded.

Chafar walked the corridor to find Thonlan's guard chatting with the brothers' guards. They stood near the entrance of her chamber looking in, laughing, then their eyes bulged. The first guard saw him and immediately moved to stop him.

"You do not have permission to be here!"

The guard's fingers barely touched him.

Chafar sent him flying with one punch to the chest. The other guards tried to detain him as well, and he threw them back with brute force. He entered the chamber.

His eyes scanned the room, zeroing in on his mate bleeding on the floor. The second brother reached out to reason with him. His words fell on deaf ears. Chafar knocked him down with a blow to the head. With lightning speed, he rushed the other two, who also tried to avoid harm. Everything became a blur.

When he realized he had taken the brothers out, Chafar stood in the center of the room with one arm still raised from the up-swing of a punch. He lowered it and went to his mate's side.

"Hey. I need you to stay with me." His hushed tone trembled with despair. "I need you. So fight."

The guards bustled in. Thonlan's cautiously moved towards him while the others berated Chafar.

"Have you gone mad?" The first shouted. "Do you know the consequences for assaulting a royal house member?"

"Being the sibling of the queen won't save you from our wrath, Lassian!" The third guard yelled.

"Shut up!" The second brother got to his feet. He turned to his guard. "Call the physician here at once."

They all finally stopped and saw the blood spreading. The two brothers on the floor lay horror struck by the scene they created.

Chafar picked her up, cradling her in his arms. Her blue blood stained the sleeves of his white tunic.

"No need." His eyes narrowed as he tilted his head. "Move."

Fearing what he might do if they refused, the guards made a path for him. The fury pumping in his veins fueled his steps. House members gave him a wide berth, their eyes landing on the blood dripping onto the marbled floors.

This solidified his decision. She would no longer reside in the lower palace.

Or Azrom.

"I told you not to do it. I said stop." The second brother held the side of his head, wincing. He turned to his guard. "Send a message to the main palace. Alert the royal physician of their arrival."

They stared at the bloodstain in the carpet. It spanned nearly a foot in diameter.

So much blood.

"I didn't mean to…" the first sputtered. "It was a reflex. I…"

"This isn't what I wanted," the third brother cried out.

"There is nothing any of us can say to atone for this." The second brother walked out with his guard. "I pray our young sibling comes out of this alive."

The third brother walked into the hallway and summoned a group of servants.

"We need this chamber cleaned. Change the carpet if you must. No one is to know what happened here. Do you understand?"

He watched their faces turn to shock when they looked inside.

"He asked if you understood," the first brother seethed.

They nodded.

"Good." The third brother signaled his guard to leave with him. "I leave it in your hands."

The first brother took a final scan of the room before following.

"Our father won't like this."

☼ ☼ ☼

Farin's personal chambermaid set a drink tray on the bedside table. When she left, Farin wiggled herself into a comfortable position on the plush chair. Chafar pulled the other chair over to sit across from her with the table between them.

She poured him a glass from the carafe.

"You set me up."

Chafar took a sip while she poured herself one.

Farin grinned, tilting her head to one side.

"You think so?" She smirked at his glare. "I merely warned him about you."

"And then you told me he noticed my presence."

"Doesn't everybody?" Farin's brow rose. "You don't exactly keep yourself hidden."

"They hurt her." Chafar set his drink down. "And our spawn."

This time, Farin bristled.

"There will be consequences for that." She let out a loud sigh. "You shouldn't have dusted their brothers though. That opened a slew of drama in the lower palace."

"And what would you have had me do, then?"

"I mean," Farin shrugged. "If you were going to go all out, you should have killed them." Her eyes seemed to glow. "That's my thinking."

"Now what?" Chafar picked up his drink.

"I'll talk with Treshur. We'll find a solution." She raised her drink. "Congratulations on becoming a well-rounded adult."

"You don't really expect me to toast with you for that."

"Oh, come on." Farin smiled, tilting her glass gently.

Chafar reluctantly clinked his against hers.

"Thank you, sister."

"Hey, I get to be an aunt for the first time. A newborn I can spoil rotten."

"Absolutely not."

Farin laughed, throwing her head back with glee. She wiped her eyes as she finished, becoming serious.

"Yeah. I did. They were a perfect match for you. I knew you would attach yourself to them on sight."

"Stop manipulating people. You could have just told me instead of being sneaky."

"But, there's no fun in that." Farin gave him a stern look. "Do you regret it?"

"No." Chafar's shoulders slumped. "I guess my promiscuous days are over."

"Thank Lassa!" Farin shouted, rolling her eyes.

"I will get you back for your deceit."

"Oh?" Farin's lips curled back. "I look forward to it."

Imperial soldiers came into Chafar's chamber to rouse a sleeping Thonlan. She jumped onto the other side of the bed to get away from them. Then she noticed her missing child. The basinet sat empty. She panicked, screaming as she lunged towards them. Two of the guards easily subdued her, dragging her out into the outside corridor.

She fought the entire way to the throne room. They deposited her before Supreme Ruler Romnus and Queen Farin. Her father stood by the foot of the throne. Off to the side, Chafar waited in the shadows.

Down on her hands and knees, she looked up at them through tears, making everything shimmer.

"As of this day, you are stripped of your status in the lower palace." Her father's words cut deep. Everything she had was tied to that one title her mother clung to. "Your mother has declared to sever her bond with you aas well." Her fingers clawed the floor. Hot tears dripped onto her knuckles. The pain of hearing that sucked what strength she had left. "You are exiled from Azrom and sent to New Lassa with your mate."

Her father came to kneel before her.

"This is what's best for your wellbeing and safety." He lifted her chin with one finger. "I do not wish you to leave. But I want you safe. To be happy without all this."

He stepped away to let Chafar take over.

"Come with me." He held out his hand.

She bent over until her forehead met the cold marble floor.

No one wants me here!

My own mother. My brothers. Even father feels I should leave.

She looked up. Chafar's stare startled her.

He wants me. All of me.

Her hand shook as she placed it in his. He dragged her up and held her in his arms until she relaxed.

Four imperial guards escorted them out to the roof, where the gate to New Lassa sat open, waiting.

A servant came forward with their child wrapped in white cloth. They handed him to her. Queen Farin walked over and caressed the baby's cheek with a finger. She took hold of her shoulders and locked eyes with her.

"Take good care of my nephew." She glanced over at Chafar. "And my brother."

All she could do was nod. Her father took Queen Farin's place. He cupped her face with both hands.

"I will come see you on my next visit. Make sure to bond with your younger siblings."

The gate operator gestured for them to proceed.

She hesitated for a moment. Chafar waited until she moved first. Together, they entered the swirling dark abyss. Time and space warped around them. On the other side, she saw fields of yellow grass under the midday sun. People milled around in various colored robes. The gate console sat directly ahead with the operator nodding to Chafar in greeting.

Chafar wrapped an arm around her shoulders.

"Welcome home."

Home.

The term hit her. She realized she had never considered Azrom her home. It was simply a place where she happened to be born.

A planet she lived on.

More tears streamed down her face.

Could I really call this my home? She hugged her newborn closer to her bosom.

I'll at least try.

CHAPTER FIVE

Merge

The Azrom fighter vessel settled down on New Lassa's landing platform in a field across from the new gate console. Auto clamps locked it down while the ramp extended. Exhaust fumes mingled with the Northern cool breeze.

Treshur wore simple attire, leaving his uniform behind for the visit. A first for him. He always donned it regardless of his tasks except for when lounging in his quarters. Even then, he sometimes dressed in it in case a situation arose. Be prepared for anything.

That was his mantra.

For some reason, his subconscious decided normal clothes were the way to go. Thinking as he walked down the ramp it made a valid point. His visit was personal, not in any official capacity. He could see Ganna's lab attached to the medical bays on the horizon.

He gave a nod to the gate operator then proceeded towards them. Ganna still refused to let anyone watch over the twins. When Mercan forcibly took the infants from her arms one day, Treshur didn't like the way he glared at them. Like they would be a specimen on his experiment list. That's where Ganna got that expression.

Coming also gave him a chance to check on his exiled child. Chafar promised to take care of them and their newborn, now reaching the age of two. He flinched, remembering the royal decree. How distraught his child became with every word uttered. Those tears haunted him.

He may not be the best father to his children, but he never wanted to see any of them hurt. Anyone who harmed them would feel his wrath. Which put him in a bind for the current situation since his other sons were the culprits.

How do I remedy that?

Lost in thought, he reached the lab faster than expected and ran into a medical technician exiting one of the side doors.

"Ahh!" The technician bounced off him, hitting the door as it closed. "My apologies, Lt. Treshur." They gave a curt bow. "Welcome back to New Lassa."

"No. I wasn't paying attention. The fault is mine. Thank you."

"Ganna is away at the moment." The technician frowned.

"What is it?" Treshur's body tensed.

"Oh!" The technician waved a hand in protest. "It's nothing." They hung their head. "I must be going."

Treshur watched her sprint off towards the nearby village. He went around the building to the adjacent one and entered. Assistants worked at their stations not giving him a second look as he passed through the winding walkway to Ganna's inner chamber. The doors slid open. He stopped in his tracks.

Mercan stood at a workstation scrutinizing the 5D hologram of a field creature spliced in layers. From afar he saw how its system connected. And that the gorged veins meant the dissection process killed it. Monster. As a scientist, not even he would do such a thing to gain insight on a specimen.

"Your mate has fled her own lab to avoid my presence." Mercan didn't look over at him for a long time. When he turned his head to do so, he smirked. "Sad, isn't it?"

"You can't blame her." Treshur walked into the lab. He stayed at least two arms length distance away from him. "Your love of science surpasses hers. Frighteningly so."

"Hmm." Mercan's eyes glinted. "You think so?"

Mercan turned away from the hologram to check the readout on the opposite screen. Treshur glanced at the data. He recalled Ganna telling him how they created manbeasts.

Warning signals lit up in his mind.

Was Mercan about to bring into existence another species to rival them?

If so, he wondered how the manbeasts would react.

"I'm going to find Ganna and our twins."

The way Mercan snorted made him pause.

"I'm surprised you haven't examined our spawn with your usual fare of brutality since you find them disgusting."

Mercan turned halfway. His eyes grew brighter with disdain.

"I've no interest in those inferior things. Ganna's flawed genetics proved not dominant."

"What are you saying? I thought all Lassians intrigued you."

"Are you feigning ignorance?" Mercan's expression darkened. "What kind of scientist doesn't recognize the absence of the very thing that makes our race thrive?"

"You speak riddles." Treshur forced his fingers not to clench.

"Have you not realized one glaring fact? Chafar has no core." Mercan's eyes narrowed. Treshur felt his widen in awe. "Neither does Farin. Or those monsters you spawned with my daughter."

Treshur stood speechless. The revelation made his head swim in a sea of thoughts.

"I don't understand," he whispered, looking at the floor.

Mercan glared at him.

"It seems Azrom blood reigns supreme after all." He focused back to the screen. "Ganna should be at the temple with your offspring clinging to her."

Treshur backed out of the lab, not daring to turn his back on the diabolical scientist. He didn't face forward until the doors sealed shut before him. It never occurred to him to do a full examination on his own children. He assumed Ganna had already done that. Now he knew Mercan saw it all in a glance.

On par for an ancient being.

He would talk about it with Ganna. Afterwards, he needed to find Thonlan. They deserved an explanation on why the decree came about. Outside, he raised a hand to shield his eyes from the sun. The temperature rose. Thankful for deciding to wear lighter clothes, he headed for the temple.

With her child swaddled tight and secured on her back, Thonlan took cautious steps into the midday air. The soft wind lifted strands of hair that tickled the sides of her face. She tried to straighten her posture despite the pain. All the adrenaline that rushed through her body during her exile depleted instantly when she arrived.

She remembered the looks of despair as she collapsed. Chafar seemed calm, but she knew better. He remained at her side the forty days she lay unconscious. Thonlan smiled. He did the same when she almost died in childbirth. Her wrecked body required years of recovery. Exile did her no favors, setting her improvements to zero.

She walked around the town until coming to its edge, where the fields sprawled out before her. The wind picked up from behind, sending her hair flying forward to cover her face. When it died off, strands of hair webbed across, forcing her to brush them aside. She spat softly to get it out of her mouth.

The fields' tall grass and vegetation swayed. It had a calm Azrom could never achieve. The workers went about leisurely harvesting with children, laughing and running around, not bothering them. On Azrom, the task operated like a well-oiled machine. No one cracked a smile and got it done before afternoon light.

Intrigued, she waded into the shallow part where the grass hit her knees. She could feel the blades brush against her legs through the robe, soothing them. A worker came up to her. Startled, she reared back, tripping on a small mound. They caught her before she titled away.

"Careful. You don't want to wake that precious child and distress him." The worker patted her arms. She scanned the area around her. "You forgot your basket." Thonlan pursed her lips, not sure how to answer. "No worries. We have extras further in. Come."

She took Thonlan's hand and guided her towards an area where other workers harvested blue and yellow fruits the size of plums. The gradient colors made them appear unreal. As promised, there was a stack of weaved baskets piled in the center of the field.

"Here you go." The worker picked a medium-sized basket.

They handed it to her. "Take your time. There's no rush. It goes by faster than you think." She nudged her son's cheek. "Make sure you don't wake him up. He should enjoy his nap in this nice weather." She glanced sideways. "You should do the same. Enjoy it."

Thonlan carried the basket in front of her as she walked through the patch, observing the other workers. After seeing how they picked the fruits, she found an untouched area. Getting into a deep squat with her feet flat on the ground, she followed their lead. Her son didn't make a sound, not once stirring.

The picking grew sparse at some point, so she stood to find another spot. Instead, the worker who led her waved her arms in the air, whistling. Its high pitch defied logic. Thonlan saw other workers' heads pop up around the field.

"That's all for today. We're done! Your hard work is always much appreciated." She smiled wide, proud of the haul as everyone moved to load their baskets onto a transport waiting nearby. "We'll distribute the excess not being exported next week."

Thonlan thanked the worker after she unloaded her final basket and headed back towards the town. Near her home, waiting on the back side of the building, stood her father. She slowed her steps, not sure if she wanted to approach.

Her body decided for her.

The next step faltered, forcing her to try correcting it without falling. Right as the ground came closer, her father grabbed hold of her shoulders. He eased her to the wooden bench attached to the structure and eased her down.

"You need to be more careful!" He chastised her in a low tone. "Here, give him to me. I came to get acquainted anyway."

Thonlan held onto the bottom of the waddle while her father undid the wrapping that secured him. She let him slip down until the bundle was free. Her father lifted him up by his underarms.

"Ahh. There you are, little one."

Thonlan stared up at him, confused by his joyous demeanor. As if sensing that, he held her son to his chest and let out a loud sigh.

"I had to, my child. It was the only way to keep you safe. I couldn't chance anyone harming you again. Be your brothers, their guards, or some royal imbecile wanting to make a name for themselves."

She grimaced, not sure if that justified being exiled.

"What about my title being stripped?"

"Did it truly bother you?" Her father's expression saddened. "It's only at your mother's behest that they gave it. She insisted."

Thonlan hung her head. True, that status meant everything to her mother. When they didn't pass any of the exams, her mother berated them. Called her worthless, ignorant, and a disgrace to her own status. Thonlan's life revolved around her mother's wishes.

Nothing she did ever benefited herself.

The same held true for her brothers. They only did what their mothers demanded.

Rustled footsteps from behind made her turn around. Chafar came towards her, looking concerned.

"I searched everywhere for you. Where have you been?"

"I helped out harvesting fruit in the fields," she replied.

His face scrunched, his brow deepened in waves.

"You're in no condition to do such tasks."

Her father also made the same face.

"I agree. That was reckless."

Chafar ran a hand across the back of her neck, massaging it.

"That title was a throwaway. It stemmed from your father being employed as a royal scientist and warrior." He leaned over her. "But now, you have an actual tie to the royal bloodline."

Oh!

Thonlan's mouth opened in surprise. She clamped it shut.

My mate is the brother of the queen!

"You didn't need that fake title."

Chafar wrapped his arms around her.

"As for your mother." Her father's shoulders slumped. "She didn't understand the consequences of denouncing your lineage to her and her royal status."

Thonlan's eyes widened at the thought.

"They revoked her status as well," she answered softly.

"As they should have," Chafar chuckled.

"She's been moved out of the lower palace wing. Her friends in the royal circle abandoned her. They didn't bother to see her off."

"That's…" Thonlan lowered her head.

How sad.

All that ambition and deceit to gain superiority wasted. She felt sorry for her.

"Don't pity her," her father said. "She brought this on herself."

Under the waterfall located in the northern forests, Trinon sat on a flat stone, wearing only a loincloth. With legs crossed and his wrists resting on his knees, he allowed the rushing water above to pummel him. Each dousing the weight of a sledgehammer. The sound like rolling thunder.

Small creatures scurried about. One skirting across his thighs. A massive bird soared, calling out with a high-pitched shriek.

He didn't feel or hear a thing. His mind was elsewhere.

Deep in his core, he searched for Mandra. A broken soul bursting with strength he felt too afraid to use. Hon had grown exasperated at him not tapping into his full potential. It arose an unknown fear.

Irrational? Maybe. He focused on the incomplete core and dove inside. To make it work. To become whole. He had to merge with her splintered source.

Mandra grabbed hold like a vise. Despite much of her soul being diminished, she could comprehend her situation. And what Trinon wanted. Her essence dug into him. It resembled sharp talons tearing into an enemy. Nothing loving or gentle about her approach. Which made sense as her memories flooded into him.

A fierce warrior with no time for hesitation, regret, or frivolity. She loved intensely the same way she fought. She seemed to detest his way of living. Chastising him for such weakness as they became one. Trinon finally understood. Being accommodating to others served no purpose. Everyone could see the ruse.

He only fooled himself.

And badly, at that.

Sight, sound, and feeling came back to him in a rush as he opened his eyes. His body revolted from taking it all in. Vomit spewed forth before he could stop it with his hands.

Giving in to the process, he leaned forward and let it flow into the water around him. Every muscle ached. His hearing, improved tenfold, made him wince.

The abilities of an ancient manbeast. The first generation of their kind.

Such power!

With the integration complete, Mandra's part of him taught him how to calm his senses. Control the surge within. A new way of thinking came over him.

Everyone will have to deal with me as I am!

Another thought amused him. Standing, he walked over to the edge of the river where his clothes lay in a neat pile. He dried off with the oversized towel he brought, then dressed. In his long-sleeved bodysuit covered by a dark blue cassock, he flung the towel over his shoulder and headed home.

Ponnae would be napping with their child. He needed to explain things first. After that, he had to visit the next important person in his life.

☼ ☼ ☼

At first, Talas felt he had lost his mind. The presence coming from behind him grew stronger by the second. Not wanting to turn around, he tried to keep his focus on the training platform where two warriors sparred using double wielding sword techniques.

"Feeling nostalgic?"

A hushed, honey tone in his ear made him bristle.

The intimacy, along with such close proximity, indeed felt that way. He knew what they meant, and it didn't pertain to the training arena. A hand reached around his waist and tugged him closer.

"What are you doing?" Talas hissed, containing his agitation.

"I'm just being playful," Trinon replied in the same voice.

"Which is something you have no idea how to do."

Talas turned around to face him.

Trinon snorted, taking a step back, only giving him barely enough personal space.

"How intriguing to see our roles reversed in this new era." Trinon tilted his head back at an angle. "I think I like being such a domineering male. It suits me better."

Talas frowned. He didn't bother to comment. Mandra and he used to share the same height. With her now part of Trinon, she loomed over him with unbridled aggression.

"Here you are, the one capable of spawning now." Trinon grinned. "Did you miss me, Laxis?"

"Like you, I've merged with my original self. Miss you? Are you really asking me that?" Talas spat.

Trinon stepped back. The playfulness fell away. For the first time, Talas saw the real him. He exhaled, slumping his shoulders before straightening his posture.

"About time you showed up. I thank Mandra for making you see the light."

Trinon corrected his posture and laughed. Sinister. Yet, Talas found it refreshing.

"Yes. We had a bit of a struggle at first."

"Well. I'm glad." Talas turned sideways to him. "And so we're clear, you were always manly," he said making quotation marks in the air with his fingers.

Trinon pursed his lips. Then he placed a hand on Talas' cheek and leaned in.

"I could get rid of Kelin and regain my place if you want to join me once more."

Talas slapped his hand away. He wasn't even angry at the dig.

"My place, and my love, is with him and our offspring. Pay attention to your own new family and fix your issues with Und."

"You're no fun." Trinon moved away.

"Is that your idea of amusement?" Talas shook his head. "You really have no grasp of it. You nor Trinon."

"You're right." Trinon's expression went blank. "I thought I'd try it since as Trinon this was such a crucial thing. How did we ever keep this up for so long?"

He clasped his arms behind his head and looked at the sky. Talas smirked at the signature stance of the manbeast whenever he strolled the village. That air of carefree confidence no one else could pull off.

"I think you'll be fine going forward." Talas walked towards the arena. "Try not to scare anyone. They need time to adjust."

He could tell by Trinon's silence it fell on deaf ears.

"Except for Hon." Talas stopped halfway and glanced back. "Scare that arrogant beast into submission."

Trinon's eyes lit up with joy as he stifled a snort. His smile spreading ear to ear. He dropped his arms and pivoted to the right. His long gait took him out of sight within seconds. Talas gave an evil, lopsided grin.

Kelin came out of the supply shed and smiled warily at him.

Oh, he heard all of that.

"You know, Hon is trying his best, too." Kelin held the bundle of training spears close to him, keeping the tips a good height above his head. "None of us can atone for our actions this time around."

Talas nodded.

"Oh, I know. Still," his eyes flashed. "That won't change how I feel about that cretin. Someone needs to teach him a hard lesson."

Kelin looked upwards in defeat and continued to the arena.

"I think you're envious of how he holds himself."

"What did you say?" Talas seethed, stomping after him.

"I mean," Kelin shrugged. "As they say on Earth. He gives zero fucks."

That stopped Talas. The truth smacked him in the face.

Which angered him more.

A blanket of tension covered the gold themed chamber down the corridor from Elendar's. The rich drapes and carpet, with a hint of red in their patterns, gave it extra weight. The previous lord's awful aesthetics remained in various sectors. Elendar didn't feel the need to strip the house of them.

Until now.

He saw Dalfir staring at one of the high-back chairs with similar upholstery. Not disdain or admiration. Disappointment? Footsteps echoed from the hallway.

They both turned to see Lanen enter in male form wearing the third house colors robes over a bodysuit.

"Brother." Elendar crossed his arms. "What is so urgent you wished to meet on the far side away from the council?"

Three chairs sat in an arc. His gaze followed Lanen as he took the chair on the end. Dalfir's brow raised.

"As you know, I had a meeting with Lord Kel."

"Yes," Elendar seethed. "His deeds know no bounds." He glared at Lanen. "You should have told me sooner."

"I trusted him to abide by his words."

Dalfir scoffed. "That was your first mistake."

"What's done is done." Lanen leaned forward. "This is much more dire."

"Is that so?" Elendar dropped his arms. "Speak."

Lanen's clenched fists rested on the chair's curled arms.

"Our queen has a plan to bring Azrom back to its former glory. To achieve this, she needs both our houses to work together."

Elendar balked at the notion. Dalfir frowned.

"Work with that wretch who ruined our lives and that of our children?" He yelled. "Absolutely not!"

"Please, bear with me. This is not about our hurt feelings." Lanen locked eyes with him. "This is for Azrom and healing the strife between the houses."

Elendar bared his teeth, his eyes narrowed to slits.

"We can recover without such things."

His tone hissed with venom.

"Can we?" Dalfir sat on the loveseat facing the chairs. Elendar's rage deflated. "Is that true?"

"Our contracts are a mess. Most of that is my fault." Lanen hung his head. "I fed into the lower merchants' greed instead of what would profit Azrom."

"You did us no favors." Elendar moved to the center chair and propped his foot on it. "Queen Farin has taken more interest in trade lately." He tapped his bottom lip with a finger. "I found it curious." Elendar's furious expression returned. "Still."

"She proposes the third house act as enforcers as we negotiate new deals." Lanen sat back. "We would also set new routes to link with the enemy territories."

"This all sounds feasible." Dalfir templed his hands below his chin. "Which, if all goes well, puts Queen Farin above Romnus as ruler. She'd have done more for our people than him."

"Exactly." Lanen glanced at them.

Elendar gasped, his eyes wide. Then worry crossed his face.

"Are you saying we're to push Romnus from his throne in favor or Queen Farin?"

"In fairness, he never wanted to rule." Lanen grimaced. "She has Lord Kel's full backing if it comes to that." He eyed Elendar. "Does she have yours?"

"I need assurance first." Elendar didn't think himself stubborn on the issue. It was a great risk that could harm not only his house but the others. "Sending our merchant leaders out to solicit deals after that tragedy you caused is a hard sell."

Lanen retrieved a data square from his breast pocket and handed it to Elendar. He set it down on the platform table. A hologram full of information exploded in the air, turning slowly counterclockwise. Dalfir got up for a closer look.

"That's..." he whispered.

"Impressive," Elendar finished. "Such extensive research."

"Our queen left no stone unturned." Lanen stood and walked towards the table. "This was enough to sway Lord Kel and I."

"Ah, I get it." Dalfir smiled. "The snag is with the royal council. They may try to silence the queen if it threatens Romnus' reign."

Elendar whirled around to face them.

"Would they dare?" His raised voice echoed. "True, we have not had a queen in centuries. Hell, a millennium even. That doesn't mean she is incapable of ruling."

"Yet, that is what most of them feel," Dalfir added. "As awful as it sounds, our race does not see Supreme Ruler as a female role."

"How outdated and droll!" Elendar snapped.

"I agree. So." Lanen nodded at the hologram. "Will you assist?"

Elendar stared at the massive amount of information before him. The queen's thoroughness intrigued him.

Working with Lord Kel left a nasty taste in his mouth. He would swallow it for the greater good.

"Lord Kel wants to make amends as well," Lanen blurted. "I'll stay with him for a while to bridge the gap between our houses."

That pulled Elendar from his thoughts.

"What did you say?" His brow furrowed. "There's no reason for that."

"I want to know my child and their children more."

His sad tone made Elendar pause his outgoing criticism. So much time wasted. Even his children spawned with Kel had harsh words for their parents. Nothing could make up for it.

"Fine. I will allow it." He looked at the hologram. "I'll inform the queen our house is on board." Turning to Dalfir, he pointed at the table. "Make a copy and assemble a meeting with only our trusted advisors. The council can wait."

Dalfir went to the other side and opened a thin panel. He took out a similar data tab and set it next to the original. Once the data transfer began, Elendar walked towards the nearest window. Through the partially opened drapes, he watched transport ships sail across the horizon.

Queen Farin. A hybrid of Lassian and Azrom blood. Yet more in tuned with our people than we are. Maybe the time had truly come for Azrom to set aside its patriarchy and let one who embodies both lead them.

☼ ☼ ☼

Reaching the outskirts of the forest, Chardon and Farin came to a clearing alongside a gurgling river. Lassa's sun gave off a hazy glow. The planet's debris from its near destruction spanned the sky. Small creatures scurried across the pathway.

"She's not doing so bad." Farin ducked under a branch as she moved it to the side. "Everyone made it sound like she was dead."

She walked to the bank's edge and looked up. A winged creature landing on her shoulder, pecked it a few times, then flew off. "The dark atmosphere feels soothing. Quiet." She inhaled deep. "I like it."

Farin suggested the meeting place to see what the Lassian homeworld looked like. She could feel a slight tug of familiarity that stemmed from her mother's DNA flowing in every fiber of her being. A welcoming sensation like a hug enveloped her.

"Lassa is resilient." Chardon stood beside her. "That doesn't mean she's not angry."

"As she should be." Farin glanced over. "Plotting revenge?"

"I'm not." Chardon didn't return her stare.

"Well, if you do decide that option, let me know first. I'd really like to avoid having Azrom turned to dust when I'm getting it back on its feet."

"I would never allow that." Chardon clasped his hands in the sleeves of his robe. "As much as our people despise your father for his sins, no race deserves annihilation."

"Hmm?" Farin tilted her head away from her. "Not even our enemy? Those damned Boretkz?"

Chardon frowned. His eyes glowed blue, then subsided.

"Not even them. I want them to suffer."

Farin nodded. "That's fair."

"Are the chess pieces in place, as they say on Earth?" Chardon eased down onto the grass, crossing his legs. "I feel like something's missing."

"I have the third and fourth houses working together." She plopped onto the ground and leaned back, supporting her weight on her elbows. "Chafar has established a secondary royal bond between New Lassa and Azrom."

"Oh? Trinon also has a royal bond with one of our regent planets."

"Yay!" Farin laughed, her head falling back. "He's such a menace. I wondered how long he'd play the victim."

They stared out into the trees on the other side. A soft breeze rustled the tops, making them sway. Silence spread with only the sound of the wind in their ears.

"So, what's missing?"

Chardon sighed, leaning over to pick at the grass.

Farin pondered it for a moment.

"I think we need to establish dominance over the Dreridians somehow. Maybe under Lassa instead of New Lassa." The sky seemed to darken. Farin looked around then up. "Really? Why are you mad about that?" She chastised the planet.

The hazy glow returned. A defiant feeling flowed in the air.

"You must remember," Chardon said. "Lassa wanted to be left alone. She went millenniums without contact from other worlds."

"Doesn't want to get involved? Well, fine." Farin pouted. She lay flat, spreading her arms out. "I think once everything is in place, we'll have to deal with the backlash from Romnus and father."

"I can handle your father." Chardon fingered a small stone before tossing it across the water. He watched it skip a few times then sink halfway. "Romnus won't be an issue. He already sees the writing on the wall."

"True." Farin took a deep breath. "I fear for your safety, is all."

"Where does that come from?" Chardon's eyes squinted.

"I don't know why, but it feels like father would try to take you out if he deems you a threat. Regardless of his love for you."

Chardon's lips thinned at the thought.

"You're probably right." Chardon laid back. Resting his hands on his chest, he let his body relax. "So, we're truly going forward?"

"It only makes sense to advance into conquering worlds after all this." Farin glanced at the debris trail. "We'll keep Lassa and New Lassa separate. How's that?"

Chardon chuckled, sensing relief in the air.

"Just, so…" Farin rolled her eyes. "Stubborn."

"What's next?"

"The trade reports. That will tell us how we're doing and if anything needs to be tweaked."

"That's a given, genius."

Chardon flicked the side of her forehead.

"Ow!" Farin reached up and rubbed the area. "I'm not a child."

"Of course you are. You just happen to rule an empire."

Again, Farin pouted. She rose into a sitting position.

"The last thing is to get Razzna on board."

"Listen to you, being a strategist."

"I have ambitions." Farin smiled proudly.

"Indeed." Chardon placed his hands behind his head.

"We created a window with Nasfir. Does Azrom still want to hold the contract it has with the Dreridians over Razzna's mines?"

"I think renegotiations are in order. The whole thing shouldn't have happened."

"You father has a pattern of overreacting."

A heavy silence fell. They both knew Halfar to be unstable, even irrational at times. And bode ill for everything and everyone around him. The water rippled from aquatic lifeforms moving beneath the surface. Chardon caught sight of one and cringed. Nothing enchanting about its misshapen face and lumpy scales.

Farin eyed it as well.

"That's from evolving in such a strenuous ecosystem."

She pointed at it.

"Would you still eat it?"

"Nuh uh." Farin's face scrunched in disgust. "Not a chance."

"It could be an exotic food for trade?"

"Mother," Farin sighed. "Let's not get crazy. We'd have to send images of that thing. No one in their right mind would buy it."

Chardon laughed loudly. His eyes closed as his head tilted back. The mood finally lightened up. Such heavy content on ruling others always made them tense. They didn't know if all the work going in would pay off. Or if their people embraced the idea of both races combining.

"You know, if you keep sneaking off, the royal cabinet will have a few choice words."

Farin scoffed.

"Their incompetent. I see no reason to listen to them. Even the scholars have abandoned their tasks."

"That's not good."

"Umm." Farin grinned. "Lassa's spiritual advisor has been MIA with her duties as well. Right?"

Chardon's eyes widened.

Ganna had essentially checked out of teaching about Lassa. She had advisors, true enough. They took her lead and also did nothing. Lassa seemed to bristle at that. A gust of wind flattened the grass while pushing them forward.

"Wow." Farin moved the hair spider-webbed across her face so she could see. "Someone is feeling important."

"Yeah." Chardon had to do the same with his hair. "She's a bit moody these days."

Caged

In the gloomy abandoned chamber in the palace's far wing, Farin paced the dark, deep in thought. The hem of her flowing black robes dragging across the dusty floor made soft swishes. A single hover lamp above the charred mantle barely glowed, casting a hazy white that only reached its edge.

The shadows above moved towards her. Chastan landed silently on his feet behind her. She glanced over her shoulder. He stood far away. Half his features concealed.

"You should venture outside the palace once in a while."

"I do whenever you leave." He went silent. "Except for your last mission."

"I feel like you're still punishing yourself."

She felt him move closer.

"Isn't that appropriate?"

Farin frowned.

"That's not what I want." Her hands clenched together. "I was disappointed. What you'd done defied everything I knew about you."

"Because I was afraid."

She turned around to face him. He averted his eyes as he walked a few feet from her. His expression made her chest tighten.

"Of what?"

"My growing love for you. At first, I wanted to see how far you would take it. If your father found out and tried to execute me. Thinking Romnus would save me."

"So. I was simply someone to play with."

Chastan turned to her, locking his gaze.

"Then I realized how much I wanted you. I always did what I

wanted, only caring for myself. Being with you scared me."

"And so you did that to make me hate you."

"I started to hate myself. The only way to break our bond was self-sabotage."

"You regret it?"

"Every day." He lowered his gaze. "Seeing how Romnus also lusted after you, I should have known better. He wasted no time taking my place."

Farin stepped closer to him.

"But I loved you first."

The silence grew heavy. They stared at each other for a long time. She caressed his cheek. He leaned his head into her palm.

"If I hadn't done those things, would you have stayed with me?"

"Hmm. Is that really a question?" She smirked.

Raising his head, he grabbed her waist.

"Don't tempt me. I still want you."

She saw the restraint in his posture. How funny!

He always relented in the end.

"I know."

"The scandal would plague the entire planet."

Rumors flew about the queen having her way with anyone who served themselves up for royal favors. None of it true. Her tryst with the father of her oldest child didn't make the cut for good gossip.

"I doubt that."

They touched foreheads, blending in the dark.

"You need to tread carefully."

"I have you to protect me, don't I?"

Chastan moved from her a bit.

"I would strike Romnus down if necessary."

"I hope it doesn't come to that. He says he loves me."

Farin kissed him lightly on the lips. He let out a sigh.

"Don't. I warned you."

"Maybe I need you more than you think."

He lifted her with ease, planting her on the black stone ledge carved out from the wall.

His lips brushed hers while his hands ran under her robes to rest between her thighs.

"I wanted to always be yours."

"You are." They kissed deeply. When they disengaged, the taste of him lingered. "Don't leave my side."

"Never," Chastan hissed softly, covering her mouth with his.

Farin wrapped her arms under his and around his shoulders as he entered her. The familiar ecstasy filled every fiber of her being. Her love for him differed from Romnus and Batis. Out of the three, Chastan got honest with himself over time. Which only made her cherish him more.

He could be relied on. His loyalty absolute.

And that is what she needed most.

☼ ☼ ☼

Tumultuous clouds hovered over the conference wing of the commons. They matched the intensity inside.

"I despise your very existence," Talas spat out at Anassa. The being gave him a disinterested stare. "That said, you are the only one who agrees with me."

They stood face to face, leaned over a data platform in the smaller room. A hologram of the enemy planet hovering above turned counterclockwise. The hover lights dimmed, removing glare.

Anassa, feeling no desire to be of any sex that day, chose a form absent of their characteristics. Mainly, no genitalia. They liked having such flexibility.

"Revenge won't be as sweet as you think."

Anassa tilted their head.

"You don't care about that." Talas smirked. "You only want to make them feel the same as we did eons ago."

"Hmm." Anassa pushed up a bit, letting their head rise above Talas. "It's what I want, yes. But will they mourn any harm it sustains?"

Their plan to hit the enemy where it hurt they held in secret. They had voiced their opinion during a meeting years before. The council smacked down the notion.

Chardon and Ganna showed interest with their expressions. Sanctions weren't good enough.

"How do you plan to get a combat ship out there?" Anassa slid their arms off the platform and crossed them.

Their hands disappeared in the loose folds of the robe's wide sleeves. "I'm sure the security council will want a valid explanation."

"That's easy. I want to scout potential sectors for New Lassa business purposes."

"Which is true." Anassa smiled. "After the fact."

Talas placed his hands flat on the platform. He averted his gaze to focus on the hologram. Data below the image showed how much the Dreridians took. Despite being the first to arrive there, the trade moguls seemed to have a hard time snatching territory. The enemy refused to be conquered.

"I think the Dreridians are going about it the wrong way."

"Agreed." Anassa removed one hand to tap the zoom icon, then back into their sleeve. They stared at the industrial district. Forty percent of the facilities smoldered. "I have a proposal."

"Oh?" Talas crossed his arms, standing akimbo. "What's in that devious head of yours?"

"Destroy it." Anassa's eyes glowed bright blue. "All of it. Stop production of everything. We can rebuild it as we see fit."

A sinister grin spread on Talas' face. Yes. That sounded better.

"The Dreridians would lose their minds." Talas' smile widened.

"What little momentum they achieved would be gone."

"I'll speak with Chardon about steps after our plan's completion."

They grew silent, lamenting on Chardon's leadership evolution. Sestis wanted to be a tyrant, collecting personal perks. She had no intention of making Lassa a superpower.

Her way induced fear and distrust.

"I have no problem with Chardon becoming an equal to the other leaders."

Anassa's smile went crooked.

"Even Azrom?" They raised a hand towards their lips, allowing an opening of the sleeves. "Though Farin is taking the reins there."

"Taking vengeance on Azrom is not in the cards. No matter

how we spin it, the planet itself is not at fault."

Both their expressions darkened. Anassa glanced over at him.

"Halfar is to blame. But what would be sufficient punishment for his deeds?"

"I say we leave it to Chardon." Talas dropped his arms to his sides. "He's the only one who knows how Halfar works."

"You need me to come with you." It wasn't so much a statement or a question. More of an anticipated outcome. "Our weapons can only do half the damage."

Talas stepped from the platform to pace the side of the room. He came to the back wall where a map of New Lassa hung.

"Will Lassa let you use that power?" He glanced over his shoulder at them. "Or is yours independent of theirs?"

"Do you think Lassa would argue over this?" Anassa countered. "No."

Talas remembered being enveloped in Lassa's essence. The rage she felt when the subject came about. A slow burn like seething.

"Now that we've established our feelings," Anassa tapped the icon to freeze the hologram. "When do we want to execute them?"

"There's a sanctioned Dreridian scout expedition scheduled on the next new moon. I've already requested to join."

"Oh, ho!" Anassa yelled. "The betrayal would be outstanding!"

"They'll get over it." Talas grinned.

"And how do you explain my presence?"

"It gets you off New Lassa and out of the council's hairs."

Anassa frowned. They felt they deserved more respect. As if reading their mind, Talas turned around.

"Respect is earned, Anassa. You've done nothing so far except make everyone more infuriated with you."

They pouted.

"Because none of you are willing to understand me."

Footsteps coming down the corridor made them look towards the door. Anassa cut the data feed and placed the chip in the storage compartment under the platform's edge. Talas exhaled and walked back towards it.

The footsteps halted on the other side of the door. They watched the latch rotate down as it creaked open.

Chardon and Jaron stood in the doorway.

The four locked eyes with each other, not speaking. They all knew why they were meeting in secret these days.

"Whatever you're planning," Chardon said, "leave Azrom out."

"Noted," Talas replied.

"Wouldn't dare," Anassa added.

Talas gave Jaron a nod.

"I hope you make wise decisions for our stake in these matters."

Jaron pursed her lips, her eyes conveying false audacity.

"I know my role in this."

Talas and Anassa passed them as they came into the room. A changing of the guard. When they stepped into the corridor, hearing the conference room door shut, they stared down at daylight haloing the building's entrance.

Over two hours had gone by.

Alliance ships eased into position around the enemy planet. Dreridian check points scanned their vessels as a show of dominance. None of the ship commanders felt amused. Most carried heavy payloads, uncertain if the enemy's capacity to hit them from the surface still existed.

Instructions to refrain from attacking the planet flooded the data feeds. Onboard the Lassian battleship, Talas snorted. He read it and waved it away. The communications officer disconnected from it. Anassa giggled, covering their mouth with their robe sleeve.

"A bit paranoid, aren't they?"

"They have every right to be," an energy user replied.

Excitement and trepidation permeated the bridge. Everyone on the ship knew the plan. Endorsed it unanimously. Hitting the planet won't resolve their notion of vengeance, but it would make them feel slightly better.

"If we knew how to drain their resources like they did to Lassa,

I'd take that." Another bridge crewman said. "Maybe a little more."

"I agree." Talas leaned against the command dais railing. "But that defeats the purpose of snatching it for ourselves. It does no good for trade if the planet can't produce."

He could sense the disappointment followed by understanding.

"We need to get close enough to annihilate that sector without getting caught in the blast."

Anassa pointed to two other alliance ships nearby. "First, we get rid of those meddlers."

To avoid suspicion, they chose two other ships to accompany them. They would break away as they closed in on their target. Talas thought about feigning a malfunction that required them to veer off in the opposite direction.

It could work.

The three alliance ships cruise over a deforestation area. Patches of dried, bare surface among healthy trees resembled scars on flesh. Chatter on the open channels between the ships voiced the lack of love the planet received. Only results mattered in the enemy's eyes.

On the Lassian ship's right, outside the scouting route, lay their target. Talas heard talks from the other captains about negotiating with the Dreridians. Below, enemy troops watched them pass, their weapons ready to shoot them down.

Dreridians may have formed a blockade and occupied certain regions, but they could not defeat them on their own turf. A stalemate commenced.

Which Talas gladly took advantage.

He signaled the navigator with a nod, then the comms officer. The ship dipped and tilted ten degrees to its right.

"To all Alliance captains," the comms officer anounced . "We're experiencing a stabilizer malfunction." The ship rocked from another dip. "Breaking formation to investigate the issue."

"Lassian ship, do not attempt to land," the Dreridian captain ordered. "Any ships doing so the enemy will deem hostile and they will attack."

"Noted. We have no intention of landing."

The comms officer assured them.

The ship turned at a forty-degree angle and drifted towards the sector. When it went more than a few kilometers out of reach, nearly halfway to it, the Dreridian captain came back on the feed.

"Lassian, you are veering too far off course. The area you're heading towards is an important industrial hub. You need to alter your trajectory."

Talas glanced over at Anassa.

Oh, we know.

The Dreridian's goal entailed taking control of the plants and forcing them to churn out products below costs. New construction or revamping the process took time and funding. Neither of which they wanted to do.

More warnings from the Dreridians and other ships, became more frantic the closer they got to the target. A scout ship deployed from a hangar one hundred miles behind them headed their way.

They won't make it in time to stop us.

"This is good." Talas addressed the navigator. "Maintain our position." He turned to the comms officer. "Give the command."

"Open weapon bays one through six. Lock on target and await orders for firing."

Three panels on each side of the ship slid open revealing rounded cannon barrels. They protruded out, then swiveled to lock onto the target. A pale orange glow grew bright until it resembled shimmering white hot lava.

"What are you doing?" The Dreridian captain yelled. "Stand down at once!"

The comms officer looked over his shoulder at Talas.

"The scout ship is equipped with missiles. If one of them hits, it will knock us off course."

"Intercept and destroy them if they launch."

"Enemy is aware," a crew member announced.

Talas saw enemy fighters run towards the weapons stations on the outer perimeter of the sector.

"Life signs?"

"Minimal. It seems the factories are not operational."

"That's what I concluded." Talas nodded. "They wouldn't want to have any product on hand during a hostile occupation."

"Your orders, commander Talas?"

He waved Anassa towards the doors.

"You're up. Go forth and do the worst." To another crew member he said, "Open the hangar. Once Anassa is in the open, fire cannons."

"Incoming missiles from behind," the navigator sighed, unfazed.

"Lassian ship." A new voice rang from the satellite station in the planet's orbit. "Shut down your weapons or be shot down. This is not the agreed course of action. Please respond."

The hangar doors opened. Anassa stood on the edge, peering down at the sprawling sector of factories. One of twenty. Hot air whipped their hair around their face. With arms outstretched, they closed their eyes and tapped into their core.

Lassa. Let me be your vengeance.

Wide bands of searing light whizzed struk the sector. It went up in a fiery ball, a mushroom cloud pluming to the sky. Structures crumbled as explosions from within dismantled the foundation. The now decimated defense stations toppled.

We're not done.

Multicolored static enveloped Anassa, pulsing like a heartbeat. Its light seemed to spray out, then get sucked in as if in a vacuum.

One pulse.

The shimmering lights shot from their body. Anassa planted their feet on the hangar floor, so the force of the blast won't move them. It engulfed the sector in a wave, eating away everything it touched. Anassa stopped the energy flow and felt Lassa's disappointment at such a meager output.

The rear cannon eased out and fired on a missile from the scout ship. Talas glared at the image appearing on the main screen. The Dreridian official who threatened to shoot them down stared back in shocked anger.

"What have you done?" Behind him, crew members scrambled to man consoles. "You've put us in a battle position we weren't prepared for."

"Then that is a failure on your part. We came with no such thought. Enemy territory is just that. Why would we come here and not insert our dominance?"

The official reared back, his eyes wide.

At that moment, the enemy fired on ships in their vicinity. Through the open channels, Talas could hear captains cursing their name as they too activated their weapon bays.

"Retreat from the surface immediately!"

The official ordered every ship.

"Incoming enemy fire," the comms officer yelled.

"Activate shields and close the hangar." Talas watched the sector appear to melt on itself. "Retreat as instructed."

The navigator snorted, suppressing a grin.

Anassa entered the bridge, brushing down their mangled hair.

"She's not satisfied."

Talas laughed.

"I felt that too. Can't blame her."

"The Dreridians mad?"

"Very much so."

"Hmm. Oh well. Our agenda is underway."

The ship turned around and headed for the satellite station, passing the scout ship. Talas and Anassa could see the pilot seething.

The sector may have been one of twenty, but it was also the main hub where the planet's resources converted to power that flowed into the other factories.

A major hit and score for the Lassians, Talas thought. He knew a meeting would come soon to address the outcome.

"Let the negotiations begin," Anassa said.

They gave Talas a mischievous smile.

"I can't wait."

Talas figured Chardon would be livid for a split second. Then Jaron and he had a lot of work to do.

The Dreridian official's scowl made the crags of his face seem fused together. Beady dark gray eyes burned with indignation. Their image flickered several times on the holoscreen until it stabilized.

"Explain the meaning of this, Lassian."

Talas stood on the bridge's command dais, smirking at him. Through the view screen, the devastated sector smoldered days after. Other alliance ships surrounded his as a deterrent. Which he found comical since the deed was already done.

There would be no second round.

"Hmph!" Talas crossed his arms. "I don't see what the problem is. The goal is to take over the operations of this planet. A random bout of retaliation won't negate that agenda."

"Your actions were not sanctioned!" The official slammed a fist down, shaking the image. "Plans were in place for that region."

"Is that so?" Talas shrugged. "I would give my apologies, but," Talas glared at him, "I'm not sorry."

The official reared back from the screen. He glanced behind him, scared for some reason. Talas deduced either Lord Pondur's general or Lord Graggor were listening in. They turned their gaze back towards him.

"We sympathize with your vengeance. This wasn't the time."

"The opportunity arose."

"That sector is now ruined. None of the alliance allocated resources for such a massive restoration."

I know.

Talas glanced over at Anassa hunched over a console trying not to laugh.

"My condolences." Talas dropped his arms giving a forlorn stare. "I assumed a contingency was in place in case we decided to raze the surface."

"Surely you jest!" The official cried. "This planet is a manufacturing hub. Keeping it in check is more valuable than destroying it."

"How about this?" Talas peered behind their head at a smaller holoscreen in the background. "Lassa will take responsibility."

"What do you mean?" This time, the official looked dubious.

Not very trusting, are we?

"Since the area is no longer an asset, we will take it as a trophy."

"What would Lassians do with a worthless sector?"

"I'm sure we'd figure it out in due time."

"It may take decades, no half a century, to repair this much damage!" The official scoffed. "Your race doesn't have the resources for quick recovery."

"All the more reason." Talas tilted his head to one side. "This takes it off the books and eliminates allocation from the alliance."

"Very well." The official appeared defeated. "I'll report this and run your proposal by the trade council." Their brow relaxed, easing his face's crags. "Your kind needs to show more patience."

"Didn't we?" Talas sneered. "Whole millenniums, even."

The official gave a sad nod, turning from the screen before it winked out.

"Patience?" Anassa snapped. "We have that in spades!" They looked over at Talas. "That's the Earth term, right?"

"Yep." Talas stepped back and fell into the command chair. "Now to relay our little mission to Chardon."

"I'm certain Lord Pondur will contact our dear leader." Obviously.

Talas could only imagine the anger Lord Pondur would hold back when discussing the outcome. There was no reason to deny the Lassians' request. Regardless, he noticed the other alliance ships not budging. A precaution in case he decided to hit another region out of spite.

☼ ☼ ☼

A double your fun kind of day.

That's how Chardon saw the message from Talas followed by the urgent meeting request from Lord Pondur via his assistant. An unprecedented yet expected outcome when he figured out Talas and Anassa's plan. Jaron and himself initiated a similar coup, snatching regency over territories neglected by the alliance leaders.

He sat cross-legged on a cushion at the head of the long table in the conference room. His hands clutched a clay tumbler filled halfway with morning brew.

Four seats down on his left sat Jaron, sipping silently from theirs. A holoscreen hovered above the center of the table. Its feed buffering while waiting to establish connection.

They remained calm, prepared for whatever fury the Dreridian leader lashed at them. Jaron let out a snort as she read Talas' message again, running as a ticker tape display on the bottom of the screen.

Right as Chardon sipped his brew, the holoscreen shimmied to reveal Lord Pondur's angry, craggy head. The almost too tight white ascot, nearly glowed in contrast to his dark bronze waistcoat. With one leg crossed over the other, his posture erect, he resembled the aristocrat he was. A tea set lay on a small table beside him.

"Lord Chardon. I must confess your actions perplex me."

Chardon set his drink down and placed his hands in his lap.

"How so? Did you not consider our rage?"

Lord Pondur's eyes narrowed.

"You could've waited. There are other ways to exact vengeance without involving unrelated parties."

"I guess we're merely an unseasoned race who doesn't know any better," Jaron retorted as she set her drink down.

Lord Pondur's expression turned horrified. Those words he had uttered to describe them to another race's leader boomeranged. Chardon glared at him, letting it sink in for a moment.

"You must excuse our lack of knowledge in these matters."

"My apologies." Lord Pondur lowered his gaze. "Of course you would take advantage of the situation." He reached for the teacup, sipping delicately before returning it. "I'm afraid there's no assistance available to help with rebuilding that sector."

"There's no rush." Chardon raised his arms. "We understand."

"I'm certain you have far more important deals to oversee," Jaron added.

A glimmer of hesitation crossed the Dreridian's face. Chardon forced himself not to frown. He could see doubt forming.

"We'll simply funnel what we can into the project until it's brought back up to production." Chardon watched Lord Pondur's thin lips curve. "Then we can use that revenue to reenter trade."

"Yes. That should be the goal." Lord Pondur placed his hands atop his knee. "I will grant your proxy's request. A contract is being drawn as we speak."

"Of course. We'll have more restraint going forward."

Chardon bowed his head as a sign of respect. When he raised his head, Lord Pondur appeared agitated. As if in an internal struggle.

"I'll be rooting for your success." His sour expression matched his eyes. "Let's not do this exercise again."

The feed disconnected.

"He really didn't want to lose that sector." Jaron sipped his drink without looking up. "That had to hurt."

"Talas doesn't know how to half ass anything."

Jaron opened one eye and peeked at him.

"Huh? Did you forget his existence as Sarah?"

Chardon pursed his lips in aggravation.

"I clearly said Talas, not Sarah. The two aren't even comparable."

Jaron set her drink down to the side of her and leaned forward with arms outstretched, clasping both hands.

"I say we wait five or ten years before going in and rebuilding."

"It doesn't matter when we do it," Chardon countered. "They'll realize we have the capability of mass restoration."

"And that we're not sharing." Jaron smiled. "They really don't think much of us except for our battle prowess."

They both exhaled softly. Jaron rested her chin on the table and stared at the opposite wall. Chardon rested his hands on his knees and lowered his head deep in thought.

To become conquerors, the Lassians needed to move ruthlessly. Taking a page from Halfar's reign, they made swift progress. Now to implement the tactics of the trade leaders and bring New Lassa to the forefront.

☼ ☼ ☼

A room full of reptiles.

Chardon felt his skin prickle. The chamber inside the Razznian palace defied logic. Its overwhelming size made one feel exposed. Nowhere to run or hide. No advantage for defense.

His long sleeved, off-white robe with a blue overlay and silver sash made him appear regal. A suggestion from Volma. The hem dragged along, swishing across the lacquered floor.

His delegates followed in similar attire, Jaron's robe colors in reverse, towards the conference table spanning a third of the room. Scholars and soldiers lined the sides twenty feet away. The optical effect added to the room's ridiculous size.

Emperor Kraznan sat at the head of the massive table. His girth appeared to spill over the chair, yet it contained it well. An opening in the back allowed his tail to swing. To his left sat military leaders, including Sars, and who Chardon assumed was his royal council on the right.

Having never been on Razzna, the scenery jarred him.

Jaron stared in awe at the oversized structures. The chamber's space and panoramic windows, she found it ludicrous. Only enough sun to generate warmth came through because mountains on the other side of its location partially blocked it.

"Lord Chardon," Kraznan's voice boomed. It carried across the chamber. "Welcome to Razzna. We have not had a Lassian visitor in quite some time."

Chardon tried not to respond. Jaron glanced over at him. They hadn't brought up Sestis in nearly a decade.

"My apologies for my delayed visit. I should have came long ago as leader of my race." Chardon stopped to give a slight head bow. "Thank you for allowing us into your humble home."

Volma softly snickered.

Chardon gave her a warning stare before lifting his head.

"No need." Kraznan waved his thick hand, spreading out his taloned digits. "I always wanted to meet you. You're nothing like what Sestis described."

A group of scholars led Chardon and his group to their seats at the table, splitting them in two on each side. Jaron and Volma sat opposite Chardon and Modas.

"My council has informed me you have a proposal regarding our mines."

"Yes." Chardon outstretched a hand towards Volma. "My head of state has gone over the conditions of the contract with

Azrom and the Dreridians and found a solution.”

“Solution?” A royal councilman a third down from the others asked. “We were not aware of any issues related to them.”

Volma shook her head.

“No, the contract’s sound. I believe there’s no more need for it.”

The Razznians collectively ahhed, understanding the situation.

“We have met their conditions.” The first royal council member tapped a taloned finger to his lips. “Yet, we’ve not been released. My conclusion was that interest was being applied.”

“Dreridians are being greedy, is all,” Volma answered.

“Azrom also fulfilled their obligation.” Jaron folded her arms. “Though I’m sure you don’t feel that way.”

Kraznan’s eyes darkened.

“I do think they should be punished. But the decision that led to our predicament lies with Halfar.” His gaze landed on Chardon. “The same applies to your home world.”

Halfar’s reign was synonymous with overreactions devastating worlds. Sometimes diabolical. Lassa being the only one he regretted even a tiny bit.

“That said,” Volma continued. “We have the resources to buy out the interest the Dreridians decided to tack on and collect.”

Another council member leaned forward with narrow eyes.

“Would that not put is your debt?”

“You may see it that way,” Chardon replied. “I assure you, it’s not the case. You’ve already accommodated us with a portion of mining revenue for Nasfir.”

“We felt it right to do so after trading them to Lassa.”

“You want nothing in return?” Kraznan seemed dubious.

Chardon didn’t blame him.

Free handouts? He would cry foul too.

“How about this?” Jaron placed her arms on the table, clasping her hands. “You join our trade network instead of the Dreridians’”

Silence fell on the chamber, causing anxiety.

This room is too big!

Modas stiffened, not liking the turn in mood. Everywhere he looked was wide open for attack. Chardon set a hand on his bicep.

Stay calm. There's no threat.

The royal council deliberated with the military leaders in hushed voices. Kraznan burst out in a raucous laugh, scaring everyone. Chardon's nerves sent him in fight-or-flight mode. The council all reared back, startled, while the military officers glanced over at their emperor in terror.

The laugh echoed in the chamber. When he finished, his rounded chest heaving, Kraznan locked eyes with Chardon.

"So you've decided partnering with those creatures doesn't suit you?" He motioned for the closest servant holding a fan. They stepped forward to fan him. "Took you long enough. I could have warned you about them."

"Yet, you didn't." Chardon frowned.

"Some things a leader must find for themselves."

Jaron and Volma shrugged at Chardon. Couldn't argue with that. Being responsible for other races besides his frightened him. For a moment, he thought about trying to give them back. When he realized that option served no one, he chose to elevate his status. Which meant stepping onto the galactic stage in full force.

Like my Farin.

Harsh Decisions

Each royal council member stood in a row along the side of the throne platform, scrolling through documents on their personal holoscreens. Romnus slouched at an angle with an elbow propped up on his throne's armrest laid his head on his fist.

Tension filled the room. His full cabinet waited in attendance for the council to start the meeting. Halfar stood next to him while Biandra sat nearby as usual.

Treshur kept his head down, one finger caressing his chin, as he stared at the floor deep in thought. Both Rass and Kur appeared disinterested. Batis. That smirk told Romnus the outcome wouldn't surprise him.

A council member stepped forward. His holoscreen wavered from the movement. He nodded to the others then spoke.

"Your majesty, the commerce reports are in. There have been unusual fluctuations regarding trade and revenue. We met earlier to go over it and confirm our findings."

Romnus glanced over at Farin's empty throne. She cited having more important tasks to complete. The first fruit Biandra gave him worked its magic to keep him calm. However, it couldn't erase the feeling of dread in the pit of his stomach.

"It appears new contracts and transport routes established by the fourth house resulted in triple numbers."

Halfar's eyes widened. Romnus dropped his arm and sat straight. Treshur raised his head in shock along with the others.

"What did you say?" Halfar took a step forward, ready to come down from the platform. "How is that possible?"

The third councilman in the row came forward.

"From what we gathered, the third and fourth house, in a joint effort, acquired new business. The process so far is smoothing out a few wrinkles."

The fourth councilman nodded.

"I predict it will become streamlined in under two years."

Romnus and the others looked gob smacked. Except Batis. He let out a howling laugh, throwing his head back.

"One planet offers exclusive high-quality goods to a pre-vetted clientele. I believe they're under New Lassa's regency." The second councilman spoke while continuing to scroll. "They cater mostly to special events."

Romnus sensed the question about to leave Halfar's mouth. He grabbed hold of his wrist. Halfar turned to him, eyes dark. He shook his head. Not now. Halfar wrenched away to calm himself.

"Lord Kel and Elendar working together!" Batis sniffed while regaining his composure. "That in itself is unprecedented."

"How did that even happen?" Kur asked, then stopped.

Everyone's gaze fell on the empty throne.

"She's been busy." Treshur crossed his arms. "That said." He looked at Halfar. "We both know what the real issue is."

"You are correct," the fifth council member interjected. "Even with triple the trade and revenue, Azrom has yet to fully recover." He addressed Romnus. "The renovations during your reign nearly depleted our coffers."

"It would take more than this." The first councilman added.

"How is all this being transported?" Halfar asked.

"Oh." The third council member piped up. "The planets we conquered long ago but neglected suddenly agreed to a partnership allowing alternate routes."

That stung.

Romnus saw Halfar seething. Farin was right. They had so many centuries of knowledge in the room, and yet the youngest of them all knew what Azrom needed.

"Who authorized this?" Halfar snapped.

Batis cocked his head.

"Are you really asking that, knowing the answer?"

He shook his head.

"I warned you." His glare bore into them. "Both of you."

"I'm not understanding the anger over this news," the second council member said. "This will benefit Azrom tremendously."

Romnus' sigh echoed in the chamber. Everyone looked at him.

"Have you forgotten our meeting with Queen Farin regarding the matter of fixing our relations with those planets? Or that she proposed new ideas?" Everyone's expressions minus Batis' turned shameful. He seemed amused. "And we shut down her arguments."

"I concur." The first council member raised his head. "That was a failure on our part. It's obvious Queen Farin always had Azrom's best interest in mind."

"We can't work in the dark." Romnus leaned back. "Set up a meeting with Lords Kel and Elendar to see their strategy maps."

"Of course, your majesty." The council members answered in unison while bowing their heads.

This time, Halfar stomped down from the platform before Romnus could stop him. He went up to the second council member and locked eyes with them.

"How many of New Lassa's regent planets are involved?"

The council member had nowhere to step away. Fear covered their face.

"Three of the original five and five newly acquired ones."

"Newly acquired?" Halfar staggered back. "When did they..."

The fourth council member turned to him.

"The Dreridians gifted three of the new regent planets to New Lassa. The other two came from Yaos."

"Now that's surprising, considering how much the ruler of Yaos despised Chardon in the beginning," Rass stated. "It must have been a lucrative deal for him to change course."

Still reeling from the information, Halfar exited the throne room without notice. Romnus frowned. He understood his anger. That didn't absolve him from royal etiquette. Batis gave a knowing stare. Romnus gripped the armrests.

Are you going to be a problem, cousin?

The royal council stiffened, not sure what to do next.

"You are dismissed for now," Romnus ordered. "Send us copies of the reports to go over in the meeting with Lord Kel and Elendar."

"As you wish, your majesty!"

They all bowed again and left in a single file.

Romnus stood.

Biandra stared at him in awe. Batis raised his brow.

"Your majesty?" Treshur inquired, his expression now fearful.

"I need to find my queen." Romnus stepped down and walked through the hall towards the doors. "Do not try to find me for the rest of the day."

It wasn't anger that filled him. Something else. Like betrayal. Or being tossed aside. Either way, he didn't want to feel any of it.

He found her in the library, perusing the third level. Looking up from where he stood in the center of the main floor, he watched silently as she strolled along the curved walkway. She fingered a book at eye level, debating if she wanted it, then left it. When she reached the center, she stopped. Her hands clasped together as she turned her head to look over the railing down at him.

They locked eyes.

"Have you come to chastise me?"

Her playful tone mismatched her expression.

"You're not a child."

Romnus didn't move. Her words stirred fury in him.

"No. I'm not." Farin turned to lean on the railing, her hands gripping the cold, smooth metal. "Are we going to fight like this, or will you come up?"

"We're not fighting." Romnus gritted his teeth.

"But you seem angry."

"Because I am. That doesn't mean I want to fight with you."

Her face softened. She extended her arms out towards him.

"Please come."

Romnus flexed his fists to release the tension, then made his way to the winding staircase with landings at each level. He reached the third and walked across to stop a foot from her.

They faced each other.

"Why are you angry?" She went to reach for him.

He stepped back. The hurt expression on her face angered him more. That's not what he came to do.

"So, you don't want to engage with me then."

"I didn't mean to." Romnus' words stuck in his throat. He closed the distance between them and held her in his arms. She stared at him in confusion. "I wanted you to trust me. To talk to me. Explain what you wanted to do."

"I did." Farin placed her hands on his chest, gently pushing him away. He refused to budge. "None of you wanted to listen."

The hush of the library made him nervous. He knew there was no one else around, yet it felt like they were being watched. Farin cupped his face in her hands.

"I only want what's best for the home I chose. Why is that wrong?"

"It's not. How you went about it is. In my eyes. Do you know how it makes me look?"

"I'm sorry," Farin whispered, kissing him softly on the lips. "That was never my intention. I simply thought you would praise me for taking the initiative."

He covered her hands with his own.

"We should have done it together." He slid her hands from his face. "No matter how remarkable your achievement, I still felt left in the dark. Like I didn't matter."

Farin's eyes widened in shock. She tried to pull away. He kept her there, not letting go of her hands. Tears formed, welling up to spill down her cheeks.

This isn't what I wanted!

He embraced her tightly, burying her face in his chest. For a moment, her arms hung limp. She finally wrapped them around his waist. He listened to her muffled cry, feeling lower than he had in decades.

"I also want the best for Azrom. We are one. I don't want to be separate from you."

She sniffed, releasing his waist. Her forearms rested on his chest as she wiped tears away.

"I didn't read the report." Her voice came out hoarse. "Did it turn out okay?"

Romnus snorted.

"Really? You think it didn't? On what grounds?"

Farin made enough room to look up at him, pouting. Ah! I'd forgotten how childish she could be. How adorable.

"I can't predict how the markets would go! I just set things in motion and hoped for the best outcome."

"Well, it worked out. Everything tripled."

Her expression turned to delight. She smiled widely, with her eyes gleefully closed.

"What are you and your mother scheming?" His serious tone made her step back out of his hold. "Your father's not pleased."

"It's not so much scheming." Farin stared at the floor. "My mother feels the same as I do. New Lassa and Lassa need to elevate themselves in this new era."

"And of course, it makes sense to tie our worlds together." Farin nodded. "That's quite manipulative of you."

"What?" Farin raised her head.

"Did you not coerce our regent planets into helping us? And sending your brother after Treshur's youngest child?"

She glanced away, obviously not sorry. Her lips pursed.

"I only made a few suggestions," she muttered.

Two scholars appeared on the fifth level and cautiously walked to the other side.

So there were others here.

He looked down at Farin until her gaze met his. He nodded at the scholars.

"Oh!" Farin grinned. "I guess, since they're here."

Romnus called out to them.

"You, scholars! Come down here."

They halted in terror, not sure how to hide their reaction.

"As you wish, your majesty," they replied in unison.

While they went to the stairs, bound books in hand, Romnus addressed Farin.

"You may want to visit your mother before your father does."

"I know. I plan to." Her gaze darkened. "I feel a sense of dread."

"Leave soon. I think he's a walking planet bomb right now."

He saw her eyes darken.

Yes, she knew all too well what her father was capable of. Halfar had no qualms about harming her, despite what he's said over the years. He caressed her cheek.

"Tread carefully."

Farin nodded.

The scholars came towards them and bowed their heads.

"Supreme ruler Romnus. Queen Farin. We're at your service."

"First," Romnus said, smiling at her. "Let's get some insight from these two."

Well, the best laid plans are usually fraught with holes. Farin thought to herself while strapped into the seat opposite her father on the transport ship. Her father somehow got wind of her wanting to visit New Lassa and demanded he go along. My plan is ruined. She glanced over at him and flinched at his expression.

He hadn't spoken with her about the report, avoiding the topic whenever someone brought it up. I know why you're angry. Farin saw the way he perused the list of planets under Lassian regency. Commerce tripling without his input irked him, but not as much as seeing her mother taking the path of leadership to dominance.

Farin could tell how much he enjoyed keeping her mother under his thumb. Giving only enough encouragement to feel complacent. Talas, Ganna, and she pushed Chardon out of their shell. Sometimes it angered her, the way he treated her mother.

If he had no qualms about hurting me during my adolescence, that meant mother was in danger.

The ship slowed to a crawl, entering the final gate that opened to New Lassa's surface. It coasted above the fields of tall yellow grass that lay on the outskirts of the ship docks. Engrossed in the information on his tablet, her father never looked up. When the ship eased into an empty bay, his head suddenly snapped up.

That diabolical frown etched on his face.

Per protocol, Farin followed two royal guards down the ramp with her father and his assistant following.

Four more guards made up the rear. Waiting at the bottom stood her mother in male form, Chafar, Modas, and Ganna. They all appeared to tense seeing her father in tow. His expression didn't harbor fuzzy feelings.

"Farin, what brings you here so soon?" Her mother embraced her, squeezing tight while his eyes glanced over at her father. "I'd have prepared a better welcome."

"Hah!" Farin disengaged. "There's no need for that. I come here to get away from the royal treatment."

"Chardon." Her father stepped forward. "It's been a while." He wrapped his arms around him like a python capturing its meal. "I missed you."

An uneasiness permeated the hangar, yet she hugged him back.

"Did you? I was feeling neglected."

He released him and looked over at her brother.

"Chafar."

"Father."

Neither approached the other.

Ganna let out a huff and turned away. Modas glared down at her father with contempt. The two would never get along. With the greetings done, they headed out to ground level and walked along the edges of the field.

The light conversation soured when Halfar moved ahead of Chardon, forcing him to stop. Farin drew a sharp breath. Chafar and Modas went on alert.

"The commerce reports came through. I found it curious."

"Oh?" Chardon batted his lashes. "And why is that?"

"You seem to have more planets under your regency."

"Hmm, yes. I consulted my cabinet. They advised I increase my leadership role as a true ruler."

Halfar grew furious. His hands balled into fists at his side.

"That is not necessary for you," he said through clenched teeth. "Your role as leader of New Lassa is enough to keep you occupied. Others can remotely handle the other regent planets. All you need to do is delegate overseers."

Chardon cocked his head to one side in confusion.

"I'm capable of ruling more than my race, Halfar. Even you taught me a few things."

"That's not why I did!" He retorted. "You're taking control of planets and generating mass amounts of revenue."

"Of course." Chardon stared at him. "Why would I gain a planet and not use its potentials for profit?"

Halfar ran his hands down his face and let them drop. His eyes gleamed with fury.

"You need to sign over regency to a third party and focus on New Lassa and Lassa."

Ganna's eyes widened. Her mouth opened to speak, yet nothing came out. From the corner of her vision, she saw Treshur, Jaron, and Talas approaching. They seemed to have heard him and stopped in their tracks some hundred yards away.

"What are you saying?" Chardon's eyes pulsed with a soft blue glow. "Why would I do something like that?"

"Because that's not your path. Leave he task of conquests to those who should."

"Father!" Farin came to Chardon's side. "That's cruel! And utterly insulting!"

"At best," Talas yelled. "That's rich from a former ruler."

"Get it done by the next year." Halfar stepped closer. "I will make sure to use all my resources to make both your home world and this one flourish."

"Absolutely not!"

"You should do that regardless," Ganna snapped.

To everyone's horror, Halfar grabbed Chardon by the neck, wrenching her forward.

"Why won't you do what I tell you?" He yelled, seething.

The blade of a short sword grazed across his neck, close enough to draw blood. He looked down its length to the person holding it.

"I think not." Chafar's gaze burned into his. "Father."

Halfar released his grip.

As his fingers cleared Chardon's throat, Farin shoved him back.

"What's wrong with you?" She cried out. "You call this love?"

Chafar moved back.

"You've always been overly possessive of mother. I would never let you harm her."

"Dangerously so," Treshur added. "I wondered about your true agenda regarding Chardon as a mate."

"He obviously wanted someone he could control," Talas said.

Halfar lifted his chin with an indignant stare. As if he eyed something foul.

"How dare you question my love for him. I'm only suggesting a more suitable path. Why are you standing in my way?"

"Because you're wrong!" Farin stepped in front of Chardon. "The same way you're treating me for doing the same."

"Yes." Halfar looked at her with disdain. "Instead of guiding Romnus, you decided to usurp his reign and take it for yourself."

Shocked by his admission, Farin stumbled from him. Chardon's eyes lowered a bit as a disappointing smile formed.

"I think you should rest in the far wing of our chamber. Then coordinate with the gate operator to leave."

"No! We need to discuss this." Chardon didn't turn around or stop. He walked further away. "I didn't come here to not see you!" He reached out to him. "Chardon!"

Modas towered over him.

"Then you should have waited to spew that poison until after. Serves you right."

"Lassa's light!" Ganna yelled. "You're not too bright, are you?"

Farin addressed the royal guards and Halfar's assistant.

"Make sure you escort my father to his temporary chamber. I'll check with you all later." She turned to Halfar. "What you've done." Her shoulders slumped. "Makes me sad."

Jaron stayed behind when everyone except two guards and the assistant remained.

"What made you think Chardon would stay in his lane? Were you not paying attention? We have always strived to make Chardon a leader to be reckoned with."

Halfar stared at her in shock as she left the area.

It hit him. The truth of her statement.

Every time they complained about Chardon's leadership, the next words were always for him to do better. To meet their expectations.

Did I just destroy my bond with him?

I messed up. Again.

Forcing himself not to break down in front of the guards and his assistant, he waved a hand, gesturing them to follow him. He knew exactly where he was going. A smaller room with one window and bare furnishings.

As they say on Earth. The doghouse.

Gloomy shadows cascaded across the chamber as light from the lone window waned. The blending colors of sunset gave way to a soft, off-white glow. In the far corner, Halfar lay under a single cover on the pillow laden bed. One arm draped across his face. His clothes were in a heap beside it.

Sleeping naked, as usual.

Chardon stood in the doorway, admiring his mate's vulnerable state. The only time he didn't appear a menace. Halfar's eyes opened beneath his forearm and stared at him. Chardon walked over to the bed and straddled him. The robes bunched around his legs as he leaned forward.

"Have you come to your senses? Can we discuss this reasonably?"

Halfar sighed heavily, letting his arm drop behind his head.

"I don't understand your thinking." He reached out with his other hand and caressed Chardon's cheek. "Why do this?"

"My goal was to become more reliable as a leader." Chardon tilted her head, pressing it deeper into Halfar's palm. "It's hard to rule when your own people don't trust you."

"You don't need to follow Sestis' footsteps. Finish her agenda."

Chardon's head came up.

"That's not what I'm doing. I'd never continue her deceit."

Halfar sat up, embedding his fingers in Chardon's hair beneath his neck.

"I never wanted this for you. Being a ruler can change you."

"Hmph." Chardon lightly gripped Halfar's hips. "It changed you because of your ambition. Your need to show dominance. I'm not the same."

"Please tell me you know how much I love you."

"The only thing that would sever our bond is death."

"No." Halfar leaned close, their noses touched. "Not even that."

Chardon's grip tightened, making Halfar wince.

"Don't ever do that to me again."

"I know. I lost my mind for a moment." Halfar brushed his lips across Chardon's. "It infuriated me to think you would do what she did. And have to deal with those Dreridian horders."

They kissed each other slowly, softly, with no sense of urgency. Chardon sat back.

"You think I can't handle Pondur and his minions?"

He cocked his head.

"That's not the issue."

Chardon shifted to female, knowing Halfar wouldn't notice immediately. Thinking himself the dominant one. Not realizing Chardon being far more needy of pleasure. It unhinged Modas knowing how much she enjoyed sexual depravity by Halfar's hands.

Stripping off her robes, Chardon tossed them to the floor and yanked the cover down to expose Halfar's member. His expression went from shock to amusement. Before he could try to bring her down with him, Chardon grabbed hold of his hair from behind, forcing him immobile.

"Not this time," Chardon whispered. "You submit to me."

She moved her legs up into position and slid down on him. He gasped at the sudden influx of sensations. Her lips sealed his, cutting it off. With fervor, she rode him, and he had no choice but to take the brunt of her ferociousness.

As expected, he wouldn't be denied his moment of control. Halfar grabbed her by the waist and flipped her over, taking one leg above his shoulder to lick under her knee.

"I'll give you what you really want," he breathed.

His thrusts were hard, quick, and deep. Chardon's body arched in ecstasy despite the pain he inflicted. Yes. This was exactly what she wanted. Toxic make up sex.

Entangled in each other's arms, they remained silent, listening to nature from outside through the partially opened window. Evening meal had come and gone. Neither felt hungry. Chardon knew the others would speculate why she wasn't in attendance.

"You've pissed them off."

Chardon nestled her face against his shoulder.

"Undoubtedly."

"I think it best if you stay on Azrom for a while."

"Hmm. True." Halfar kissed the top of her head. "So, a visit to Lassa is out of the question."

Chardon raised her head.

"Why would you even suggest it? Lassa's response would hit a new level of rage."

"You think she'd conjure storms just to chase me off?"

Their gaze met. Halfar turned to focus on the dark ceiling. No need to elaborate on the subject. Lassa viewed him as the enemy.

"Give it time."

"No. What I did can never be forgiven." Halfar rubbed a thumb across her shoulder. "All I can do is try to repair the damage."

"First, you need to reconcile with Farin and Chafar."

Halfar's brow furrowed. No way around that. Seeing the way his children looked at him angered him more. Because it stemmed from his actions.

"I'll pin them down before leaving."

"Good. And visit Chafar's little one while you're at it."

Halfar tensed, realizing he had yet to congratulate his son or be introduced to his offspring. How long ago was that? How old was the little one now?

"I had forgotten."

Chardon smacked his chest, raising her head to glare at him.

"Get it done!"

She eased back down, sliding her hand across his upper chest, then under his armpit. He played with strands of her hair.

"Don't forsake me. I couldn't bear it."

Chardon chuckled.

A laughable sentiment.

The tension in the transport returning to Azrom gave Halfar anxiety. This time Farin avoided looking at him most of the journey. His apology fell on deaf ears. She suggested space to allow her time to think. Chafar refused to discuss the incident entirely, letting him visit his little ones while keeping his distance.

Seeing a second child surprised him. The firstborn already passed the age of five and walking on their own.

Even the royal guards seemed cautious, remaining silent.

To pass the time, Halfar scrolled through more reports on his tablet. The more he read, his thoughts went to rumors circulating on Azrom about Farin possibly upending Romnus' reign. She had the planet's best interest. Moving trade, politics, and society for its betterment. Something he never managed during his reign.

A small fear entered his mind.

Would Azrom embrace such a move?

Knowing Romnus, he would gladly step back. He never wanted to be supreme ruler from the start. This made way for him to exit without compromising his royal status. The ones they all needed to worry about were the royal council. Twice, they'd purged members for attempting coups. The current line up appeared less likely to do the same.

Regardless, he wanted to make sure before his cousin and daughter threw Azrom into chaos.

The ship came out of the vortex. Azrom sat still far away, a small orb. A giant ring floated directly before them.

"Approaching inner gateway to Azrom surface."

Farin finally turned away from the viewpoint and met his gaze.

"I hope you support me in whatever decision I make, father."

"You'll always have my loyalty, Farin." He shut down his tablet and stowed it in the hard slipcase. "My concern is the council."

Farin's eyes narrowed. Her expression conveying uncertainty.

"That's a fair assessment." Her lips pursed as she met his eyes. "I'm still mad at you."

"I know."

"But there's work to do. You even gave your blessing to make me queen."

"And I stand by it." Halfar sighed.

"I didn't think you would take it so seriously."

She bristled at that.

"So, you had no faith in my ability to reign?"

"Honestly," Halfar stared deep into her eyes. "No." He watched her flinch. "I assume Romnus would love and keep you safe. That you wouldn't need to do any of this." His head cocked. "I wanted you to be happy despite the things I've done."

Farin lowered her head in sadness, staring at the floor.

"Azrom is my home now. I want it to be great," she whispered.

"As do I."

The ship shot through the ring to exit on the other side. While it hovered above the docking bay, an operator sat in the floating satellite, tapping on his console. The section below opened to reveal a dark void. Lights flickered on down the pathway as guides for the ship. It eased towards it and entered with precision.

Birth of a Coalition

Romnus knew from Farin's expression that his time to step down had come. The way she entered the royal chamber with Halfar in tow. His cousin seemed emotionally deflated. Whatever happened on New Lassa must have done him in.

The tension between father and child made the room heavy.

When she got within range, he pulled her to him. His arms tightened until her face planted full in his chest.

"I missed you." He breathed into her ear.

"I wasn't gone long," she laughed.

She turned her head and listened to the inner workings of his body. Romnus looked over to spot Halfar ready to turn and run.

"We have much to discuss, cousin. Where do you think you're going?" His eyes narrowed.

Halfar froze in place. He glanced over his shoulder.

"I figured the two of you may need a moment."

Farin disengaged, to Romnus' disappointment. He wanted to hold on longer.

"Really, father." She sighed. "Should I summon the council?"

Romnus and Halfar stiffened.

"How about we take some time to go over the details?" Romnus gestured towards Halfar. "The two of you just arrived home."

"I'd like to relax for a day or two." Halfar's demeanor worsened. "Since I won't be going to New Lassa for a while."

Romnus glanced at Farin, who shook her head. Don't ask. Both men would sit, drink spirits, and converse about it later in the day. Away from prying eyes and loose tongues.

"I guess that's warranted," Farin replied. "We should be well rested in case the council decides to go against us."

"Let's not have another purge," Romnus said in anguish.

"If we must, so be it." Halfar crossed his arms. "One of these generations, a loyal and competent council will rise."

"Well, I'm betting on this one." Farin's lips thinned as she squinted with anxiety. "They also want Azrom to thrive. I'll put my faith in that."

"Faith?" Halfar snorted. Farin flashed a warning stare he brushed off. "Don't be naïve, daughter. Test them thoroughly before giving in to their suggestions."

"Because there will be suggestions and judgement." Treshur walked into the chamber. Romnus bristled at his stealth. Even Halfar appeared uneasy. "I say we convene in three days with documents to persuade them."

He came back with them and stayed in a separate cabin, not wanting to witness the fallout between them if that occurred. Treshur had his own way of dealing with emotional situations. Romnus didn't blame him.

Love made one do unprecedented things.

"There's also the Lassian threat to trade." Treshur blurted.

"What does that mean?" Farin frowned.

Treshur tilted his head back.

"Come now, my queen. There's no way the other factions of the alliance don't see it that way."

Romnus nodded. Especially the Dreridians. They've had an iron grip on trade for nearly a millennium. As if reading his mind, Farin looked up in surprise.

"Taking the Dreridian's place of power would send a direct message to the others."

"Are you prepared for the consequences?" Halfar asked.

"If they chose to oppose us," Farin began, "then they will feel the wrath of Azrom."

"And I assure you, they don't want that," Treshur added.

"Then we have a plan." Romnus took Farin's hand. "Shall we go rest?"

They left the chamber, royal guards following.

Treshur and Halfar went their separate routes. In three days, he would be free of the shackles that bound the Supreme Ruler. He vowed to never let them transfer to Farin. She needed to be free to reign as she pleased.

☼ ☼ ☼

Answers. That's what Treshur needed from Queen Farin. Her moves behind the scenes came together, painting a glorious picture. He wanted to know his place as a cog in the wheel. A feeling nagged him to be cautious. Farin could be quite devious.

At her personal study's entrance, Treshur stopped before the two guards on duty. They stared at him with suspicion. Of course. No one would dare simply show up to request an audience with the queen. There were channels in place for that. He moved to play his card and see how she reacted.

Farin turned from reading her book while pacing. She grinned at him before nodding at her guards to let him in.

"Lt. Treshur. What brings you here unannounced? I don't recall summoning you."

"You did not." Treshur bowed his head. "My apologies for the midday interruption."

Farin snapped her book shut and tossed it on the nearby table.

"So." She spread her arms shoulder width apart with palms up. "What is it?"

Treshur stepped closer, out of earshot of the guards. Seeing this, Farin waved them away. They reluctantly walked out of sight.

"My mating Ganna was of my own accord. I have no regrets about that. What troubles me is how swiftly your brother took my youngest child as his without ever meeting them beforehand."

"Ah." Farin crossed one arm at her abdomen while the other rose to her head, where she leaned into her hand. "Yes. That was indeed my doing."

"For what purpose?"

"Leverage." Farin replied bluntly.

Treshur flinched at the sharp response.

"Against me? I don't understand."

Farin dropped her arm against the other.

Her stare burned into him.

"As a key plane bomb creator that nearly destroyed Lassa, I felt a need to put you on a leash, along with Rass and my father."

"More like vengeance, then?"

"Think of it as a reward and a punishment." Farin swung her arms to her sides. "You are now officially part of the royal bloodline, as opposed to being a mere subject with status. Your movements will be closely monitored, of course."

"I see." Treshur felt rage build within him. "Manipulating my child and your brother is simply folly for you. Their wishes for their own lives meant nothing."

Farin whirled on him, her hand instantly at his throat.

"How dare you say that to me!" Her grip tightened, making him gasp. "I wouldn't have suggested their paring if they weren't compatible. Your son needed my brother more than anyone else. It just happened to fall in line with my agenda."

She shoved him back, releasing his neck. He rubbed the sore spot, feeling the heated areas where her handprint would be visible. A sadness came over Farin.

"You should have been a better father."

The truth of her words hit him. Being a pawn in someone's scheme was par for the course in any empire. That didn't bother him. Making his children vulnerable to it was unacceptable.

"You're correct. I've neglected my duties as a parent." His gaze rose to her. "Still, I would have preferred you came to me instead of forcing the issue."

"There wasn't much time," Farin whispered.

"Now that you have all your pieces in place, what do you want from me?"

Farin's eyes widened.

"Isn't it obvious? Your mind." Farin smirked. "Azrom needs to advance its technology. With Ganna's assistance, both planets can take control of the Dreridian monopoly in that area."

Treshur also went wide eyed at the admission.

"We've talked of surpassing them, but it's almost unattainable."

"Says who?" Farin smiled. "Don't worry so much, lieutenant. I assure you, we'll come out on top. You simply must play the game as instructed."

Treshur took in the young queen. Fierce like her father, thinks like Romnus' father, and the tenacity of her mother. A triple threat. He almost felt a bit sorry for the Dreridians. They would never see something so sinister coming from her.

The royal council looked unsure and apprehensive as they stood beside the throne watching General Kur enter the main entrance. He last did this when he decreed Halfar be removed as ruler. This bodes ill in their eyes.

Romnus sat quietly, unaware. Queen Farin, in contrast, held her posture erect in anticipation. Halfar and the rest of the royal entourage stayed in a close-knit formation around them. General Kur stopped fifty yards from the throne's platform.

"Greetings to our queen, the supreme ruler, and the royal council." Kur bowed. "I, Lord Kur of the second house, have come with a proposal for consideration." He raised his head. "Though it is more of a decree."

The royal council bristled.

Other cabinet members from all five houses crammed the sides of the room, leaving a wide pathway to the throne. They went on alert at his words.

Kur held up a tablet at arm's length as he read from it.

"As head of the magistrate, I have compiled all the necessary ties to invoke this proposal. If any monarch surpasses the current ruler in bettering the welfare of Azrom, they shall claim the title of Supreme Ruler."

"Wait!" the first royal council member stepped forward. "This has not been discussed with us or the cabinet members present."

Uproars in agreement rose from the crowd.

"If proof is presented, the current ruler may accept or contest," Kur continued without missing a beat. "Any interference from outside parties will be deemed an act of treason."

"What madness is this?" The fourth council member spat. "Azrom thrives because of our Supreme Ruler. No one else should take credit."

Uncertainty stirred in the crowd. Everything was for the glory of Azrom. Citing it all stemmed from their ruler's guidance didn't sit well. Especially after Halfar's reign. He frowned at the notion.

"Are you suggesting only our ruler should take credit despite the blood and sweat of others?" Kur stared at the council with contempt. "Does that also apply to you?"

The council seemed to shrink back. They prided themselves on being the voice of the ruler. Not letting Romnus be the one to state their words as his own.

"With the efforts of combining the royal houses and leading the charge for new revenue, Queen Farin has elevated Azrom tenfold. We are on track to regain our former standing in the trade world. And the galaxy."

Murmurs of shock and approval ricocheted.

The council tensed.

"That is all well and good," the first councilman interrupted, "but a queen's place is by her ruler's side. Not in his place."

The room went silent.

Eyes bulged in disbelief at hearing it said out loud. The true feelings of the council and most of Azrom brought shame.

"You only see Queen Farin as a figurehead?" Kur glared at them. "Nothing more?"

"That's not what..." the first councilman started to reply.

"Yes. As it should be!" The third council member held their ground, locking eyes with Farin. "She should give all her efforts and glory to the supreme ruler."

"I disagree." Halfar stepped forward. "I didn't see any of you bow down to me when I threw us into chaos. You and your ilk gladly moved to replace me when the chance arose."

The councilman opened his mouth to respond, then decided against it. Cabinet members in the crowd also held their tongues.

"I decree that Queen Farin be named Supreme Ruler of Azrom." Kur acted as if the conversations before hadn't occurred.

"Lord Romnus will step back to be her guide and confidante."

"This is madness!" the second councilman screamed. "Azrom never needed a queen in all this time!"

"What say you, supreme ruler Romnus?"

Kur lowered the tablet to look at him.

Romnus, slumped to the side of his throne not paying attention, suddenly sat straight to address the room. Before he could speak, the first council member came within range of the steps.

"You must contest this travesty, my lord!"

"Please consider your standing!" The third councilman added.

They all flinched in terror as Romnus' gaze fell on them. His eyes full of malice, they bore into them like hot coals. He averted his stare to land on Kur.

"I accept the terms. I will relinquish my title as Supreme Ruler. It is now yours, my queen." He grabbed hold of her hand and met her eyes. "May your reign bring glory to Azrom."

Loud gasps erupted.

The council glanced around as if searching for something.

"If any should refuse to acknowledge this decree."

Kur glanced over his shoulder at the entrance. Commander Abras walked down the pathway, his hand atop the hilt of his longsword. Visions of the last royal council being sliced in half filled everyone's mind. The current council blanched, stepping back in line to the side of the throne.

"They will be eliminated as enemies of the realm."

Kur continued, eyeing the council.

Commander Abras stopped twenty feet behind Kur on his right. If he had to draw his sword, it would give enough space to clear the tip without striking Kur.

"With full confidence and by decree as magistrate, I give you our Supreme Ruler, Queen Farin."

Farin stood from her throne, still holding Romnus' hand. She placed her other hand on her busom and bowed her head.

"I swear to only serve Azrom. To make its needs my own." She raised her head. "Let us work together as one and see us rise as a mighty race."

At first, the room sat in stunned reverie.

Slowly, the crowd cheered.

Romnus squeezed her hand. She looked over at him, relieved at the outcome. Kur and Halfar glanced at the council members barely containing their rage. They may still become a problem.

Boretkz ships slid to a halt inside the barrier force field that caught them in a net like caged animals. Any that struggled saw parts of their hull ripped apart. A deterrent for the others. The multicolor net shimmered as it spread across the vast darkness of space. Alliance ships surrounded it.

Inside the center Boretkz ship, the leader fumed watching the scene from the bridge. His warriors wreaked havoc on the galaxy for millennia, not encountering much resistance. Now they were being driven into a trap by subpar species who deem themselves mighty. Fearing the Azrom race, who he found to be nothing special.

Then why have we lost?

The whole idea perplexed him. He couldn't find any fault in his implementation. Their weapons far surpassed the Dreridians. Those damned scientists' reverse engineering angered him. That was not in the cards.

Did we really underestimate them?

No. Something put a wrench in the works. They always had the upper hand, ready to annihilate entire worlds for their enjoyment while conquering the rest that trembled in fear. No obstacles in sight.

Except.

Thinking back to the beginning, a revelation came.

Lassians.

Those weak, misshapen life forms of energy that did nothing when his race invaded and stripped most of the planet's resources. What little they had. After decades of scouring the surface, they left with a few ships' worth of useful material.

Yet in a thousand years, they evolved into a powerful foe. On par with the so-called superpowers of the five systems. How?

Their vast knowledge in combat and strategy defied reason.

Then it hit him.

We were the catalyst!

If his race had not invaded their world, they would still be floating around without a care for anything outside their view. Mere beings of no consequence.

Unknown.

The alliance ships moved in, using grappling arms to disable his fleet one by one. The instruments on the bridge consoles went dead. Nowhere to escape. He crossed his giant muscled arms and waited for the hail. With the commlinks down, they would no doubt hijack them and force the feed.

"They're sending a message," the comms officer grunted.

The viewport turned to static then cleared to reveal a humanoid.

"Do not fight. Surrender and we guarantee your lives."

"Maybe we don't want that." The leader glanced around at his crew. "Maybe we die. Self-destruct our ships and take you all with us."

The alliance commander pursed his lips. Ha! They didn't think about that! The man let out a sigh and met his gaze.

"We know you value your people. Let's not jest about their lives. Or yours. There are consequences to your actions. It's time to reap what you sow."

Seeing the looks of relief on his crew's faces, he understood this to be the last stand.

"What? You make us slaves? Take our planet for yourselves like the mongrels you are?"

"We don't deny dividing your planet for trade purposes. But it's still your home. You'll return not as its leader, but a representative for the industrial field."

"I knew it! Slaves!"

"No. You're not listening." The commander snapped. "The details will be stated to you upon return to your world."

The ship rocked from a tractor beam locking on.

They're going to tow us out.

He plopped into the command chair, deep in thought as the jump straps slid out and fastened around him. Until he saw the damage to his home, he couldn't make any plans. Its condition would decide if they surrendered or have an all-out war.

It's mostly intact!

The Boretkz leader stared at the terrain as an alliance ship towed his towards the shipyard. To his left, he caught the mangled remains of a main power facility. His eyes widened as he saw more devastation come into view as they passed.

"Just so we're clear," the alliance commander's voice came over the commlink. "That's not our doing. The Lassians snuck in and attacked out of vengeance. Their words."

The leader's eyes narrowed back. Of course, they would take advantage when his people were vulnerable. Such distasteful actions! It wasn't for conquest or advancement. Just out of hurt feelings.

He noticed many races act on emotion. What a headache to endure. Boretkz were simple. Fighting meant gaining something in return. Same with taking over a planet. If there are no benefits, they skip it.

The planet had minimal damage outside of that. He concluded it as the result of battles on the surface. An unavoidable outcome. The alliance's cordial behavior triggered a warning. He couldn't figure out what they were up to.

Alliance soldiers escorted them to the imperial conference room after docking their ships. Scorch marks lined the hallways. A sign of a fierce fight. The doors opened to a larger assembly of delegates in front of the throne. More alliance soldiers tried to force through the imperial guards to remove the emperor.

The massive creature refused to budge. The Dreridian representative waved the soldiers away.

"Enough. It doesn't matter. Your reign is under our regency. Keep your throne. It meaningless except in the eyes of your people."

The Boretkz leader knelt at the throne platform's base. His warriors followed suit. No one called them out or disrupted the gesture. The emperor rose and glared at him.

"You dare come back defeated! Your pride stripped from you!"

"It is a disgrace, my lord. We will accept any punishment."

"There will be none of that." The alliance representative moved towards them. "This one we want to oversee the industrial sectors." He pointed at the leader. "We can't let all that tenacity go to waste."

The emperor frowned with contempt.

"What of the key hub destroyed by the Lassians?"

The representative's lips went inward as his brow rose.

"They have negotiated with the Dreridians to take control of the region. I'm afraid without excess funds to rebuild, we're unable to assist them. It may take a while to get it back up and running."

The emperor hissed. Having the Lassians control anything on their planet marked defeat. Not wanting to show his disdain, the leader stood and addressed him.

"My lord. I will take over the sectors as they want as punishment for my disgrace. You will no longer need to acknowledge my presence."

"I accept," the emperor spat. "Take those warriors with you. I have no need for them either."

"What a cruel ruler you are." The alliance representative clicked his tongue. "No wonder your race is so unliked in the galaxy."

The leader's mouth down-turned. They didn't understand how an iron fist worked. It made sense for the emperor to toss him and his men away. Incompetence should never be rewarded. This would count as a minor setback. His people had patience. In a few decades, maybe a century, they'll kick them out and regain their home.

All in due time.

☼ ☼ ☼

Delegates from every corner of the five systems attended the intergalactic meeting again hosted on Folza. Chancellor Eydine glanced around at each cube, noting the excitement and anxiety on the occupants' faces.

An emergency summit called by the trade commission to discuss the enemy territory and the recent commerce report began.

She zeroed in on the Lassians. Her body pulsed a soft peach color, indicating intrigue.

Left of center at the front, the Dreridians appeared moody in their cube. Lord Pondur's restless repositioning in his seat revealed his take on the matter. Chancellor Eydine felt a tug of pity for him. It quickly receded when she thought about all the carnage that race caused across the five systems. Twice the amount of Azrom and the Razznians combined.

Servants went to every cube, making sure each delegate had drinks and small snack items to last through the first part of the summit. They also checked the translator module. No one would tolerate misconstrued words. Not at this juncture.

Too much at stake.

As usual, the trade commission sent two representatives from the edge of the outer rim. Their nonsensical forms jarred the eyes. Hard to look at yet fascinating. This time they requested darkened cubes to alleviate the issue.

That didn't stop anyone from seeing the mediator. Two rows of two blinding blue eyes, a toothless mouth, four slitted nostrils, and tentacled fingers.

"Let the summit commence," the mediator announced. His words on delay from his mouth's movements. "We will now go over the reports. Next on the agenda is the partition of the Boretkz planet among the interested parties. After that, restructure of empire status as indicated by revenue."

Murmurs intensified.

Only the top producing empires received first dibs on advanced contracts. Azrom had to negotiate through the Dreridians to get theirs for the outer rim merchants. Going through the reports, it became clear the Lassians had surpassed the other empires in a short span.

"May I ask how the Lassians could have so much productivity, with only five planets under its regency?" A Yaos delegate raised his hand while leaning into the translator. "It makes no sense. The same with Azrom and the Razznians."

The mediator frowned at the interruption, but answered.

"The Lassian empire." Lord Pondur flinched at the use of the term. "Has over twelve planets under its rule." The Yaos delegate's blue skin seemed to ashen. "Razzna has new contracts and routes for their ore. Azrom has also expanded their network." The mediator glared at the others in the chamber. "Any other inquiries?"

When no one else piped up, he continued the report. Trepidation crept in as it went on. The writing on the wall pointed to a shift in power. And the Dreridians didn't like it.

Three hours in, with the reports only a quarter completed, the mediator called the first intermission.

Nearly every cube emptied in haste. Limbs needed stretching and bodily fluids evacuated. Servants replenished the drinks and food items while that happened.

"What do you think?" A delegate asked another in the hallway.

"I think the Lassians may take over as the top empire."

"Fascinating. They were not an empire until a decade or so ago. Such rapid advance is frightening."

"Yes, considering the scale." The other delegate glanced back at the Yaos representatives engaged in a heated argument amongst themselves. "They're being pushed out of the top spot as well."

"The Razznians will take their place." The first delegate said. "I'm glad they got out of that dreadful Dreridian contract."

A loud ding rang through the complex, signaling them to return. The delegates filed back into their cubes.

☼ ☼ ☼

Excitement for the next topic brewed on the second day. Getting in on territory close to the outer rim was a goal they all strived for. The commission restricted it for good reason. Despite the Dreridians invading the Boretktz planet first, they had no rights to it. Hence why they couldn't interfere when other races came to stake claims on sectors.

"The commission has evaluated the applications from each empire requesting ownership of sectors on Boretkz." The deadpan mediator scrolled through the data on his tablet. "After careful consideration, we are granting permission to five empires. Any other race who wants to trade on Boretkz must go through one of these."

A hush fell on the chamber as they all waited for the list. The mediator looked up and saw the stares fall on him. His sigh, let out mist from his noses.

"We delegate ten percent to the Dreridian empire and Azrom. Yaos, seven percent. Jiez five percent. New Lassa, twenty-two percent."

Gasps, followed by fists slamming on the built in shelf tables inside the cubes, spread inside the chamber. Lord Pondur seethed while Lord Graggor tapped his tablet and hunched over.

"What is the meaning of this!" The Yaos leader stood to point a finger at the Lassians. Chardon tilted his head in amusement. Talas sat back and smirked. "How do the Lassians get twice the percentage of land?"

This time the mediator bared the dark void of his mouth, all four blue eyes turning a dark shade nearly black.

"Sit down," he ordered calmly. He waited for the Yaos leader to do so. "If you must know," he sneered, "it is because they have taken responsibility for the destruction of the central hub and promise to bring it back up to production. Since it governs three other hubs, it equates to over twenty percent of that sector." He regained his composure and took a deep breath. "Does that satisfy you?"

Chancellor Eydine chuckled behind the sleeve of her robe. So many hurt egos. As the ruler of a neutral zone, she saw arrogant leaders try to bully her into taking sides. They leave, never daring it again. Seeing how composed the Lassians kept themselves made it all the better.

She predicted the third day of the summit would be chaos. A hunch told her the Dreridians may cause a scene. If not, they might go the retaliation route. Either way, their reign ended when he formed the alliance. A plot to bring the other empires under his umbrella. And it has blown up in their face.

Madness ensued as delegates screamed and pointed fingers. Accusing each other of backstabbing as they vacated the cubes. With the summit now ended, no one seemed to want to attend the feast schedule for the evening. They would eventually show up calmed down.

Chancellor Eydine instructed the servants to hold off bringing out the nonperishables. She advised the cooks to wait until she had a good count before preparing the main courses.

Lord Pondur stood. His gaze landed on the Lassians, Azrom, and Razzna. His beady eyes red with fury. Lord Graggor coaxed him from the cube, also looking over his shoulder at them.

Chardon turned to Anassa and Talas. Jaron and Ganna moved out of the cube.

"What do you think they're so angry about?"

Talas pursed his lips.

"Surely, you jest!" Halfar called from across the chamber as he exited Azrom's cube. "They see you as the enemy now."

"You've usurped their authority," Sars added. The general and the head of Razzna's commerce followed him. They came as proxies for Lord Kraznan. "Plus, you had a hand in getting us from under that contract."

"They need to tread carefully." Talas crossed his arms as he stood. "They've always underestimated our race."

"Well, I think they should get a taste of their own rottenness," Farin laughed. "They treated Azrom like a second-rate conglomerate." Her expression darkened. "I don't like that."

Romnus placed a hand on her back to calm her. She glared at him, then sighed.

"Hearing your title as Supreme Ruler didn't make things easier." Sars scratched the side of his head. "I think the other empires would rather deal with Romnus than you."

"Oh, I know that all too well," Farin replied.

"Now that everything's out in the open," Chardon smiled, "how about we have our own little summit to iron out the details of the true alliance?"

"The one without the Dreridians."

Anassa nodded her head in their direction as they passed the entrance threshold.

"I need air."

RULES OF TRANSITION

The group walked together from the chamber and took the lift down to the market square level. A cool breeze met them as the doors slid open to the outside. They weren't the only delegates taking advantage of the day's last hours. The sun dipped sideways towards the horizon.

"This turned out better than expected."

Talas stared at the sky with a grin.

Flying high above Azrom's main palace, the new alliance flag fluttered in the breeze. Quiet earth tones disrupted by a blood red symbol combining Azrom and Razzna's insignias. Inviting yet fierce. Modest but signifying strength. The masses saw the real thing this time.

Not a hologram.

People bunched inside the stone walls waited impatiently for Farin to address them. Royal guards stationed around the inner perimeter blocked access to the main entrance.

Two giant holoscreens displaying feeds from New Lassa and Razzna spanned the length of the platform. Similar scenery showed on both planets. Their people anxious to witness a new dawn. In the dark of night on Razzna, their ships' red lights peered menacingly at the audience. The midday sun on New Lassa cast a calming shade of pastels across the fields.

Imperial guards got into formation in the hallway adjacent to the vestibule. Tension ran high. Many assumed the alliance would cease after capturing the enemy. With the reports readily available after the summit, it became clear a new power dynamic would arise in the five systems.

After discussing the logistics of their merger, the new alliance nominated Farin as the one to announce it. She refused at first, citing New Lassa's standing. Her parents convinced her otherwise.

Wearing a satin ochre dress with a black overlay and red sash, Farin made her way to the center of the formation.

Her hair hung loose to protect her ears and neck from the bitter cold of winter. No matter how frigid it got, she would endure until the end of her speech. Romnus walked beside her, grabbing her hand as the procession moved out onto the outside platform.

When she reached the edge, Lord Kraznan with his advisors and Chardon with his cabinet members appeared on the holoscreens. The alliance flags flanked them, showing unity between the three races. Romnus released her hand as she stepped forward. The speech was being broadcast on each planet.

"Glory to Azrom!" Farin lifted her hands to her side.

"Victory til death!" The masses' reply rang out.

Farin tried to hide her frustration hearing the old battle cry. Romnus barely hid the grimace forming on his face. *I really need to find a new one. Having Azrom adopt a change after centuries would be no small feat.*

"I've come to tell you officially that Azrom, Razzna, and New Lassa will join to form a new empire. One that rivals the Dreridians."

Yells mixed with approval and confusion spread like a wave. Some seemed dubious. *I get that.* Farin scanned the crowd. So far, she didn't see anyone gearing for a fight. She continued.

"We will no longer need to ask permission to assert our ideals. Or go through others for what we need. Our true might lies in our innovations and ability to rule."

Farin saw determination in her people as the words set in. All the royal house leaders met to go over the reports. Even the lower houses had no reason to disagree.

"We will navigate the winds of change and rise victorious!"

Cheers roared. She peeked over at the holoscreens. Behind the leaders, she could see crowds reacting the same.

"As of this era, we are now registered as the Dominion Empire. Independent of all others."

A short communal gasp disrupted the cheers then resumed. An audacious name that spat in the face of the other empires. Asserting their role as the dominant one. No doubt meetings with the constant pour of spirits were in the works.

Farin kept her fierce stare, not daring to crack a smile.

My face is frozen!

She lowered her hands and clasped them together at her waist. The movement made it feel like her fingers would break.

"I know this may seem daunting. That we are bowing to some lesser status. I assure, we are being elevated."

She unclasped her hands and raised both fists in the air.

"Let us welcome our new role in the galaxy and bring prosperity to our race!"

The cheers turned thunderous. Stomping shook the ground, making the platform vibrate. Dropping her arms, she turned away and walked to the inner chamber. The guards followed, with Romnus back at her side. He took her hand.

"Ow!" She hissed at the stinging pain.

"I did advise you to wear the nanoskin gloves that heated to your body temperature."

Farin frowned as he used both hands to rub hers.

"If I can't endure the cold the same as the masses who waited hours for me, then I can't call myself a supreme ruler."

Her father rolled his eyes.

"There's such a thing as common sense, daughter."

She pouted for a moment, then realized she probably looked like a spoiled child. Resuming her fierce expression, she yanked her hands from Romnus.

"I think it went well." Changing the subject. "There didn't seem to be any uprisings on New Lassa or Razzna."

"Pfft!" Batis covered his mouth with the back of his hand. Farin glared at him. "Really, my queen! That face is so disingenuous."

"I'm trying to be serious!" She snapped.

Her father chuckled and placed a hand on her shoulder.

"Come. I think we could all use a drink to unwind." He closed one eye and peeked at her with the other. "And you look ridiculous right now. What have we done to deserve such an expression?"

Her ego deflated, she resorted to aggravation instead.

The thunderous uproar from outside still carried into the palace. It would take hours for the crowd to disband. More time returning to their homes and posts.

A tightness formed in her stomach.

Now their actual agenda began.

Farin was queen of not just one empire, but one of true might. As Azrom should be.

Full Circle

Decisions had to be made.

The split in loyalty between Lassa and New Lassa grew as their race elevated in the trade industry. A representative for each regency planet, including an overseer for the Boretkz sector, had to be selected. The Lassians divided into two factions. Those who embraced the new power structure, and those who wanted to live peacefully.

Chardon contemplated the best position for himself. He sat on a cushion at the end of the conference table, sipping a hot brew. With his eyes closed, he savored the aromatic steam drifting from his cup. Tuning out his surroundings.

He already restricted Halfar's visits to alleviate strife. It would subside in a decade or so. They would meet outside of Azrom and New Lassa when possible since Chardon had a slew of meetings to attend on other planets. Even their younger children gave him grief over the previous incident.

"Are you really going to ignore us?" Ganna rested her chin on templed fingers. "It won't make your choice any easier."

He slowly opened his eyes to his cabinet members gazing at him expectedly. Jaron's lips thinned as she looked down into her own cup. Volma seemed somewhere else as well, her stare blank.

"My place is on New Lassa. This is where we must establish our reign. And you?" Chardon set his cup to the side of him. "Have you discussed yours with your father?"

Ganna laid her hands flat on the table. She glanced over at her father. Mercan averted his gaze to the ceiling.

Barbon, sitting at the table instead of in the corner like Modas and Trinon, leaned forward.

"There are manbeasts willing to be proxies for the other planets if one from each clan accompanies them."

"That's a given." Volma took hold of her cup. "We want full representation for each one. Especially on the Boretkz site."

The wind rattled the window, caused them to look at the raging storm. A fitting atmosphere for the meeting. The first big weather phenomenon in nearly four years. New Lassa changed rapidly since Halfar sent a planet injection bomb to boost its ecosystem.

"I will go back to our home," Mercan blurted.

Jaron nodded. Everyone knew he had no ties with New Lassa. It made sense for him to leave.

"Then I will stay here," Ganna added. "There's much to do."

Anassa squirmed on their cushion.

"As much as she may hate me, I am willing to endure her wrath. Lassa is also my home. A part of me." They clenched their fists. "I won't be pushed away so easily."

Chardon sighed in defeat. The way Talas and Jaron glared at them for saying such a thing made him nervous. The fight mentality mirrored that of children with adult expertise.

Trinon, sitting with his legs crossed and hands clasped in his lap, finally spoke.

"Ponnae and I would like to move to L'Ang-Usai. Not necessarily permanent but frequent stays."

"That's ideal." Chardon glanced over his shoulder at him. "You have a growing family. I also look forward to seeing their progress."

Trinon's lower part of his mouth puffed out, sending his lower lip inward. He looked like a guilty child.

Volma sipped her cooling brew.

"I will also go home. You only need these two," she gestured to the heads of infrastructure and commerce, "to handle my position."

"I knew." Chardon turned to Talas. "Have you made a decision?"

Talas crossed his arms and leaned back. He looked over at Kelin then Jaron. His fingers drummed his biceps while his brow furrowed.

"To be honest, I feel I should take responsibility for the Boretkz sector." He met Kelin's eyes. "Would you be willing to join me?"

Kelin's eyes went wide in shock.

His expression turned to resolve.

"Of course, I will. Our family could use a change in scenery." He laughed. "Was that a real question?"

"Then all we need is a manbeast to round out of the group." Talas turned to Barbon.

Modas gave him a nod and Barbon rubbed a taloned finger across his bottom lip.

"Hmm. I do have someone in mind." He leaned over more to see Talas. "Would you be opposed to working with Jakar?"

Talas bristled at the thought. Trinon snorted before bursting into laughter. Kelin followed. Jaron frowned.

"Are all of my children going to abandon me?" She angrily tossed a shot of brew down her throat. "I won't celebrate their departure."

"You still have Hon, Mota, Mara and the young ones." Ganna chastised her. "Come now! They're enough to keep you occupied."

"Then it's settled." Chardon took another sip and grimaced at its lukewarm taste. "I will let you all decide on the regent planets. I really need someone of strong conviction to rein in Master Adan."

They glanced at him with the same aggravated expression on his face. Adan proved time and again to be a menace. With his planet getting back on its feet, it still required a prosperous structure. They couldn't do business as usual like before.

So much responsibility!

Chardon tried to ease into his role as the leader of an empire. The title alone filled him with anxiety. Yet he felt a new confidence beneath the surface. His meeting with the Dreridians gave him a boost, seeing the hostility in Lord Pondur's eyes.

All that was left now was to pay his respect to Lassa. Their home deserved that.

She needs closure more than we do.

Chardon scanned the faces in the room. A thousand years in the making.

Lassians had become something new.

Farin swung her legs over the edge of the cliff overlooking Lassa's horizon. The setting sun gave off a purple hue reflecting off the stardust debris. A calm fell on the region. Caravans moved slowly through the valley below. They sought territory to build new homes. She smiled at the lack of urgency, liking how Lassa enveloped them with comfort.

Beside her, Chardon sat with his legs stretched out, dangling his feet over the edge. His propped-up arms supported his upper body. With his head tilted back and eyes closed, Chardon breathed in the fresh air.

"So, what does it feel like to be the leader of an entire empire?" Farin turned her head to the side at him.

"Daunting," Chardon replied without opening his eyes. "I could ask the same to you."

"Hmm." Farin smirked. "I kind of like it. To have such power over those who held it for so long and never figured out how to do it properly makes me feel…" she stared out at the mountains. "Proud, I guess."

Chardon raised his head to look at her.

"To think you are the child of a passive leader and a former supreme ruler. You definitely get your ambition from your father."

Farin frowned.

"He's a narcissistic ass."

"Don't say that about your father!"

"You do," Farin retorted.

"Well, that's…" Chardon exhaled. "I shouldn't either. He does love us."

"I think the word you're looking for is overly possessive. Territorial even."

"True."

They stayed silent, letting Lassa's love wash over them. In three days, they would travel to the trade summit with delegates from the five systems. The Dreridians no longer held a monopoly.

"Will you give them some slack?" Farin asked.

"Will you?" Chardon shot back.

"I mean, they're a greedy little race, I'll give them that."

"Let's just say, I'm still angry about the whole thing."

"Mother, you can't be petty." Farin chided him. "It's unbecoming of a ruler."

"Hmph!"

Chardon lay flat on the grass and watched the sun dip behind the mountains. A dark shadow fell across the region, leaving only the soft glow of the stars. He thought about Farin and Chafar not having cores. Their lifespans much shorter than his own.

A deep sadness made his chest feel like it caved in. To know he would outlive his children brought indescribable despair. He watched the breeze tussle her hair as his vision blurred from tears welling.

Until their last breath of existence, he would see them thrive. To watch Farin rule as queen. For Chafar to find his place in the world and become a warrior of praise. Both their legends living on. Taking a deep breath, he calmed himself. This was not the time to break down in sorrow. Farin needed to see his strength.

Movement from behind made him and Farin avert their gaze towards the trees.

Talas, Jaron, Anassa, Ganna, and Mercan walked into the open, stopping a few feet from the edge. They stared at the dark sky, feeling Lassa's hug.

"We've come back to our home, at last," Mercan sighed. He crossed his arms and breathed deep. "I was certain we'd lost her."

"She's not that easy to destroy," Talas said. "I knew she'd survive."

"Really?" Anassa gave him a dubious side glance. "I didn't."

"Because you're an insufferable makeshift copy with no…" Jaron held up a hand to stop him. He pursed his lips in frustration.

"My apologies. That was uncalled for."

"Yet you said it anyway."

Farin eyed the two and turned to Chardon.

"Do they always act like children?"

They sputtered, ready to protest.

"Pretty much." A feeling of amusement caressed them. "Even Lassa thinks so."

"Well, enough of that." Mercan dropped his arms. "We have a prep meeting before loading up for the summit."

"I guess that means you'll be leaving in the morning?" Chardon asked Farin.

"Huh? Do I have to? As long as I arrive with my delegates, I see no problem."

"Says the Queen of Azrom," Talas smirked.

"You should bow to me, then." Farin smiled mischievously.

"Never, you brat." Talas took her hand and pulled her up.

"Thank you," she said softly. They all turned to her. "I'm glad you let me come here again to meet Lassa." She turned to the sky. "You didn't have to accept me. I'm humbled.'

A gust of wind swept past the cliff, causing everyone's hair to whip in their faces. With that breeze came overwhelming joy. Tears sprung in their eyes.

Chardon faced the stardust debris.

"Thank you for letting me return after all the pain I caused."

Anassa wiped their face, then clenched their fists.

"I'm sorry."

They turned away, not wanting the others to see them.

Mercan clapped his hands with authority.

"Enough! Lassa isn't holding a grudge against us. She knows we did the best we could." He started off towards the trees. "It's our time now to show what Lassa's love and might can do." He glanced back at Chardon. "Are you ready to conquer the galaxy, leader?"

Chardon titled his head, a sinister grin spreading. Not long ago he felt inept, not worthy of leading his people. Always doubting his decisions. And rightly so. Many of his bad judgements changed the fate of more than just his race.

With confidence, he smiled.

"Yes. Let's take our rightful place in the universe." He blew a kiss at the sky. "I will make you proud."

The entourage made their way down to the village level. A streak of shimmering colors lit the sky.

Lassa approved.

End...?

THANK YOU!!

For taking a chance on my hot mess space drama. I hope you enjoyed following my characters' journeydespite where it lead. this was meant to be the last book in the series. But... who knows. I think there may be more to come.

I am always open to suggestions on where to take the story next. If there's a fave character, race, or planet you want to dive deeper in, let me know. There's a cool QR code on the next page and you can always reach me via email or social media.

Happy Reading!!

BOOKS BY MAQUEL A. JACOB

CURVE OF HUMANITY
ORIGINS
SHADOWMEN OBJECTIVE
PURGE SEQUENCE
CRIPPLED EARTH
AFTERMATH
HOMECOMING

POOLS OF DECEPTION
A CURVE STORY

THE CORE SERIES
CORE OF CONFLICTION
SEEDS OF CONVICTION
BONDS OF CONTRITION
WRATH OF ACQUISITION
ACTS OF TRANSGRESSION

WELCOME DESPAIR
A COLLECTION OF SHORTS

THE BLOOD SAGA
BLOOD DOCTRINE
BLOOD DOMINION
BLOOD DESCENSION
BLOOD DEVOTION

ABOUT THE AUTHOR

Hi there. I'm Maquel A. Jacob. My passion for the written word emerged from the age of seven, reading everything I could get my grubby little hands on. Including encyclopedias and thesauruses. At twelve, I got hooked on my first encounter with a Stephen King novel. Each one inspired me to write my own brand of fiction. Combining multiple genres to keep things interesting.

I am a HUGE Anime fan, love a great bottle of wine and rock out to heavy metal music. The Pacific Northwest is where I currently reside, spinning imaginary worlds in my head and daydreaming.

For cool limited-edition Swag, updates, FREE short stories, Newsletters

… and more, become a Patron!

https://www.patreon.com/maquelajacob

Visit:www.majacobauthor.com

Like on Facebook

Follow on Tumblr and Twitter @MaquelAJ1

Join the conversation on Discord

MAJart Works on Instagram

Also find me on Goodreads

Buy Direct at https://www.maquelajacob.com

www.ingramcontent.com/pod-product-compliance
Lightning Source LLC
Chambersburg PA
CBHW061639190726
48289CB00006B/1665